A lightning bolt slashed the ink-black sky.

Earlier, Thistle had blessed the torrential rain. Now, the smuggler cursed it. The shadows of the night blurred, and Thistle shuddered. The premonition descended with the finality of a coffin lid being nailed shut.

Thistle stood at the left hand of a dark-haired man. Swirls of mist curled around their feet and shadowy forms rose up between them, separating Thistle from the stranger. A flash of steel pierced the darkness. The white mist turned bright red, then faded to nothingness.

The smuggler's eyes flew open! Thistle strained to hear, but thunder and wind obliterated other sounds. Lightning flashed, but in the instant it illuminated mountain and glen, Thistle glimpsed the peril.

THE SCOTTISH THISTLE

by

Cindy Vallar

To Karen,
May Rory and Duncan's story
Warm your heart!
Warmest regards,
Cindy Vallar
9-21-2002

NBI
NovelBooks, Inc.
Douglas, Massachusetts

NBI

Published by

NovelBooks, Inc.

P.O. Box 661
Douglas, MA 01516

NovelBooks Inc. publishes books online and in trade paperback. For more information, check our website: www.novelbooksinc.com or email publisher@novelbooksinc.com

Produced in the United States of America.

Cover illustration by Beverly Billings
Edited by Laurie Alice Eakes

ISBN 1-59105-009-X for electronic version
ISBN 1-59105-034-0 for trade paperback

Previously published under the ISBN 1-58697-312-6

Dedication

To my husband, Tom, who allows me to pursue my dreams and introduced me to Rory's waterfall and Duncan's cottage.

Special Thanks

To Joan Maruskin, who read and edited the first draft of *The Scottish Thistle* while teaching seriously emotionally disturbed teenagers and studying for the ministry.

To Robert W. Broomall for his professional guidance and criticisms.

To Sarah Gladden-Thaniel, Margie Tomlin, Michelle Sawyer, Stacy Kreps, Ed Shafer, Tracy Martinez, Bernadette Stankard, Karen Wilson, and Peter Lawrie for their suggestions and support.

To David Roderick Cameron for his suggestions about the cover.

To Beverly Billings, my sister, for making David's description a reality and for designing the maps.

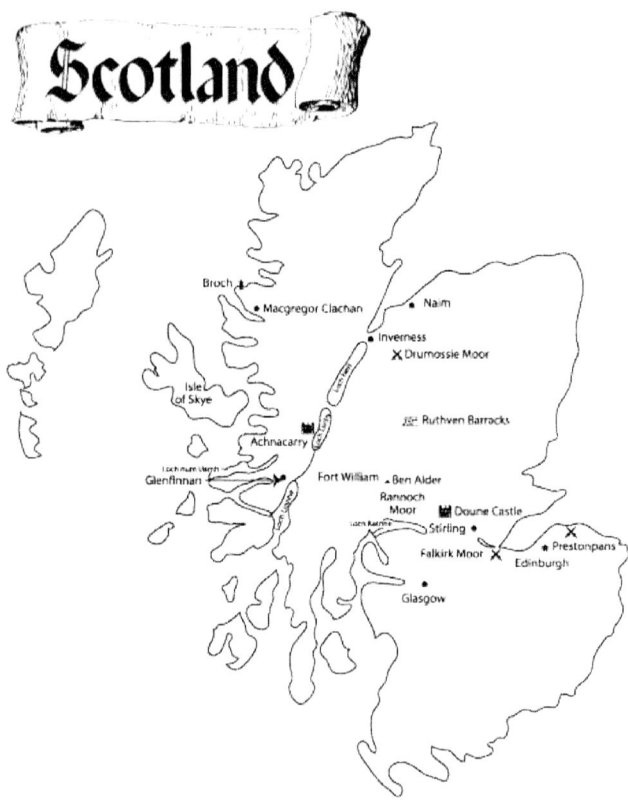

Scotland

Broch

Macgregor Clachan

Nairn

Inverness

✗ Drumossie Moor

Isle
of Skye

Ruthven Barracks

Achnacarry

Loch nan Uamh

Glenfinnan

Fort William

Ben Alder

Rannoch
Moor

Doune Castle

Stirling

Falkirk Moor ✗

✗ Prestonpans

Edinburgh

Glasgow

Cameron Lands

Loch Quoich

Cameron/
MacGregor Clachan

Duncan's Cottage

Loch Lochy

The Wolf Stone

MacOnie
Clachan

Muriaggen

Loch Arkaig

Glenpean's
Cottage

Achnacarry

River Lochy

Loch Eil

Fort William

Maryburgh

Loch Linnhe

▲ Ben Nevis

PART ONE
1744

CHAPTER ONE
THE MESSENGER

Earlier, Thistle had blessed the torrential rain. Now, the smuggler cursed it. A lightning bolt slashed the ink-black sky. The shadows of the night blurred, and Thistle shuddered. The premonition descended with the finality of a coffin lid being nailed shut.

Thistle stood at the left hand of a dark-haired man. Swirls of mist curled around their feet and shadowy forms rose up between them, separating Thistle from the stranger. A flash of steel pierced the darkness. The white mist turned bright red, then faded to nothingness.

The smuggler's eyes flew open! Thistle strained to hear, but thunder and wind obliterated other sounds. Lightning flashed, but in the instant it illuminated mountain and glen, Thistle glimpsed the peril.

A lone rider spurred his mount along the rough Highland track bordered by tall firs. He stiffened, then toppled from his horse. Two caterans emerged from the trees and crept forward. While one searched their unconscious victim, the other rifled his satchel.

As the smuggler's four companions surrounded the caterans, Thistle stepped onto a wind-smoothed boulder. With an arrow nocked taut against the string of the black longbow, Thistle aimed the lethal missile at one cateran's heart and waited.

A flash of white light followed by a jarring thunderclap startled the thief. He raised his head and screamed. His companion dropped his pilfered booty. He fell to his knees and crossed himself. "Please, Thistle, spare us! We meant no harm."

The smuggler's sudden and surreptitious appearance unnerved the caterans. Thistle smelled their fear and snickered beneath the mask. "Are ye saying the man sprawled in the mud is after taking a wee nap during such a fierce storm?"

They cried out, each trying to shout down the other.

"We found him here!"

"He is dead!"

The rider moaned.

"Dead, ye say? Then he comes back to haunt ye." Thistle stepped closer and spoke words laced with menace. "*Truis!* Be gone! If ever I find ye in these glens again, I willna be so forgiving."

The caterans scrambled over each other in their haste to escape. Thistle waited until the darkness swallowed them before jumping from the boulder to kneel beside the stranger. The short wooden hilt of a *sgian* protruded from the man's upper back. Thistle extracted the knife, then bandaged the wound with a piece of black cloth ripped from the smuggler's own shirt.

The stranger moaned. Easing him onto his back, Thistle braced the stranger's head and shoulder against a thigh. The man's eyes fluttered open.

"Can ye ride?" Thistle asked. Time grew short. *If the Watch discovered them, they would all hang.*

The rider nodded. Thistle gave him over to the other smugglers and went to collect the stranger's stallion. When Thistle reached for its reins, the horse flared its nostrils and snorted. Its hooves clattered on stones. Thistle grabbed its halter, stroked its neck, and whispered soothing words in Gaelic. The stallion whinnied, ceased its clawing of the earth, and grew calm. After the others helped the rider remount, Thistle swung up behind him. The two men who took the van wove their way through the rocks and into the woods. Thistle followed while the remaining pair brought up the rear.

Fallen pine needles muffled their footfalls. Firs towered over them, providing some respite from the rain. They climbed the mountain in a zigzag fashion. When they reached the northern edge of the pine canopy, Thistle nudged the stallion onto a rough dirt track along a bluff of jagged cliffs. Immense sea waves crashed against the rocks below, forcing white spume high into the air. The crescendo rivaled the beating of a thousand war drums, while the roiling tempest matched the frenzied turmoil that churned within Thistle.

The Watch, who safeguarded against further rebellion, kept a lookout for outlaws and smugglers, especially those with bounties on their heads. By rescuing the stranger, Thistle compounded the danger faced on their occasional midnight sojourns. Yet, having suffered injustice at the hands of others, the smuggler refused to ignore the stranger who had needed help.

Thistle prodded the stallion toward the ruins of a stone tower, aware that it was foolhardy to remain in the vicinity any longer. When they reached the broch, two men lifted the stranger from the horse and carried him inside.

Thistle turned to the remaining smugglers. "Take the horse to Andrew. He will see to its keeping. Keep a sharp lookout."

They nodded, then hurried on their way. Thistle stooped and entered the narrow passageway of the broch whose ancient builders had constructed the high circular walls of stone without benefit of mortar. Continuing past a tiny guard chamber on the left until reaching a spacious center courtyard, Thistle straightened and looked heavenward. Instead of a sloping thatched roof, the tower opened to a purplish pink sky. The deluge of the past two days had ended; the sun would again shine on the Highlands.

The windowless broch consisted of two tapering concave walls with a staircase between them. Hundreds of years ago the steps had led to wooden galleries, but the timbers had long since rotted away, leaving stairs that led nowhere. The entryway into the staircase was several feet off the ground. After clambering inside, Thistle felt along the outer wall. There was a soft click, then rumbling echoed through the ruin as a stone slab opened.

The small group descended the hidden steps added by smugglers many years after the original inhabitants of the broch had disappeared. Thistle extracted a burning torch from its holder on the wall, and the secret entrance to the stairs closed. They wound their way through a tunnel to an underground chamber where the men propped the stranger against a damp wall.

Thistle doffed a tricorn hat and squatted to examine the man's face in the flickering light. Thistle gasped. *The face in my vision!* The crooked nose indicated that it had been broken more than once. A small scar creased the chin. Dark brown curls fell across a brow bloodied by a ragged gash several inches in length. When Thistle dabbed at the dried blood, the stranger's hand encircled Thistle's wrist and held tight.

"Who?" the stranger whispered.

3

"Who am I?" Thistle asked, transfixed by the man's purple eyes. *The same hue as in the vision.*

The stranger nodded.

"Thistle."

Surprise, then pain, flashed across the man's face. His hand fell to his side.

"Ye must wait a wee longer before I tend to your wounds. Until then, perhaps ye might be after answering a few questions."

The man gave a slight nod.

"'Tis unusual to find a stranger riding alone in these parts. Caterans prey on unsuspecting travelers, especially those daft enough to travel at night. If not daft, then perhaps ye are a spy sent to ferret me out for the excise men."

"I search for a man."

"What man?"

"He calls himself Angus."

"Of what clan? 'Tis a common enough name among Highlanders."

"The nameless clan."

"The outlawed Clan Gregor."

It was a statement, not a question. Thistle despised the necessity of hiding behind a mask, but the law had left little choice. The king had handed down a royal edict against the MacGregors during the previous century, and while other clans had been forgiven for past wrongdoings, Thistle's had not.

"Mayhap I can help, stranger. What business have ye with Angus?"

"I bring a message from Sir Donald Cameron of Lochiel. Angus will understand."

"And have ye a name?"

"Duncan of Clan Cameron."

"How do I ken ye are not a spy come to harm the MacGregors? Can ye prove what ye say?"

The man grimaced. Thistle waited until the pain passed from his face before repeating the question. "Can ye prove what ye say?"

"Rannoch Moor."

Festering memories assaulted Thistle. *Baying hounds. Bloodied swords. Tormented wails. The stench of death.* Thistle's throat constricted. Gasping for air, unable to breathe, Thistle yanked off the dank, woolen mask.

Duncan's eyes widened and he drew a sharp breath. His lips moved, but no words came. His eyes closed and his head sank onto his chest.

Thistle's companions drew near.

"Dead?" Thistle asked.

"No, I think he fainted," one answered, in a voice laced with amusement.

~*~

She pushed open the wooden shutters of the cottage's darkened sleeping room and inhaled the clean air while rays of sunlight warmed her face. She stoked the peat fire burning in the hearth, then turned to face the guest who watched her with skeptical eyes.

"'Twas not a dream?" Duncan asked, his voice raspy.

"No, Mr. Cameron."

"But ye are a lass!"

She laughed and curtseyed.

"And I thank ye for noticing. Who would ever believe Thistle is a woman?" When her guest remained silent, she said, "Mayhap I should not have hastened to unmask myself last night."

"Dinna fash, Mistress Thistle. I owe ye my life, so willna divulge your secret."

"Have I your oath on it?"

"Aye, and my life."

"I require no less, Duncan of Clan Cameron. Betray me or those ye come to see and I willna hesitate to kill ye."

"Should I swear on my dirk?"

His question impressed her. To pledge his bond while swearing on the dagger was a sacred trust that gave her the right to slit his throat if he broke his oath.

"*Mac Dhòmhnuill Dhuibh,* son of Black Donald, chose well. His trust in his courier is not misplaced."

"I am more than a messenger, lass. I am *leine-chreis* to Sir Donald."

His chief's bodyguard? The message was more important than Angus had led her to believe.

"Then ye are welcome here, Duncan Cameron."

"Ye have me at a disadvantage. Ye ken who I am, but who are ye?"

"Rory MacGregor."

At the mention of her name, he arched an eyebrow. She had the distinct impression he recognized the name.

"Have we met before, sir?"

"No, Mistress MacGregor."

"That name is proscribed, so mayhap ye should just call me Rory."

"Then ye must use my Christian name. Are we agreed?"

"Aye, Duncan."

He glanced around the sparse but clean room. "Where am I?"

"Where ye wanted to be."

"Angus lives here?"

Before Rory could answer, a stocky woman appeared carrying a bowl of steaming liquid. She wore a simple white shift beneath a long red and green ankle-length plaid, the top half of which was draped across her shoulder. A snow-white *bréid* hid most of her gray hair. Her scarred right cheek and wrinkled face gave silent testimony to a hard life, but her hazel eyes twinkled with merriment.

"This is Mairi, Angus' wife," Rory said. "Eat every wee drop of her delicious broth. 'Twill help ye regain your strength. My foster mother canna speak, but she understands what ye say. I shall return later to examine your wound." Without giving Duncan time to respond, she turned on her heel and swept from the room.

Outside, she sheltered her eyes and looked for her foster father. Nearby, Angus waited with arms folded across his chest and legs braced apart. Brown and green lines crisscrossed the red belted plaid that stopped short of his knobby knees. He had shaggy white hair and a full beard. His scowl deepened the creases on his forehead and around his eyes.

"Are ye daft, daughter?" he asked, his words sounding more like a growl. "Whatever possessed ye to bring a stranger here? How dare ye allow him to discover your secret!"

She ignored his first question. "I had a vision before the caterans attacked. Do ye ken what I saw, Angus?"

Wariness crept into his gray eyes. "No."

"I stood at Cameron's left hand. Ye ken what that means, dinna ye?"

Instead of answering, Angus countered with his own question. "Since when do ye trust strangers based on the Two Sights?"

"I never trust them for that reason. 'Twas his kenning of ye and the password. Dinna fash. He gave his oath not to reveal my secret."

"And ye believe him? What if Lochiel did not send him? He kens where Thistle lives and who thwarts the excise men and the Watch. If he informs, the persecutions will begin anew, Rory. I am too old to flee again."

She rubbed her forehead to ease the pounding that had started. Her people's fortitude and resilience had helped them survive the many years of savage annihilation by other clans. Although they had found refuge here in the isolated recesses of Mackenzie land, the stranger's intrusion into their lives meant she must calm her foster father's unease. Her position in the clan and her role as Thistle required no less.

"I canna forget what happened fifteen years ago, Angus. Each day I wonder if the killings will start again. I trust Duncan Cameron because he is *leine-chreis* to Lochiel. The bodyguard of the Cameron chief would not swear falsely, would he?"

"No, he would not. Why does he lie in my bed?"

"Ye are the one he came to see. Besides, 'twould be improper for him to stay with me."

"Improper! And what do ye call traipsing around the braes and glens at night dressed in men's trews, Rory?"

She smiled. Her foster father might not approve of her clandestine activities, but he understood her reasons for doing them. People respected and feared Thistle. They thought he protected the MacGregors, even though he assisted any person in need. She surmised that as long as Thistle continued to offer assistance, they would refrain from harrying her clan.

"I willna argue with ye on this, Angus. I have another matter to discuss. The esteem Lochiel has for Duncan implies that the message he brings is of great importance. Might it concern Father's promise?"

Her foster father shifted his weight from one foot to the other. "What promise?"

"Before he died, Father spoke of a secret pact he forged with Lochiel. 'Twas payment for his granting us sanctuary while Father recovered from his wounds. He said ye witnessed the affair and if ever the Cameron chief sent a messenger, I should speak with ye."

"Aye, 'tis true, lass. Did Gregor not tell ye what he promised?"

"He said ye would do the telling."

Angus' face sagged and his shoulders slumped. Had her father not informed his dearest friend that he must shoulder this responsibility? If not, then the pact involved her in some manner. When Angus continued to keep his counsel, she realized no amount of persuasion would make him divulge the secret. Experience had taught her that no one could force him to change his mind once it was set.

"I suppose I should be finding out why the lad has come," he said.

She started to follow him into the cottage, but he stopped her.

"Rory, have ye nocht else to do? I wish to speak with this Cameron alone."

"But…"

"No, Rory!"

She frowned but acceded to his wishes. Whatever his reasons, he preferred that she not hear what Duncan Cameron had to say. She trusted Angus enough to know he would confide in her when he felt the time was right.

CHAPTER TWO
THE PROMISE

Duncan eyed the middle-aged man who entered the sleeping room. He stood with legs spread wide and arms loose. A fighter's stance. His glowering eyes and jutting chin exuded wary hostility. If this was Angus MacGregor, then he had earned the right to distrust strangers.

Once a proud and respected clan, the Gregorach had suffered condemnation by fire and sword. They lost their lands and homes to more powerful clans. They suffered slaughter and mutilation without the right to seek justice or redress. Proscription and persecution had bred suspicion; otherwise the MacGregors would have ceased to survive.

"I understand ye bring a message from Lochiel," the man said.

The growled words and brusque tone warned Duncan that his presence was considered an intrusion. He tried not to take offense.

"My chief commanded me to speak to no other save Angus."

"I am he."

"Gregor of Rannoch promised the hand of his daughter, Rory, in wedlock to a man of Sir Donald's choosing. Their marriage will signify an everlasting bond between the two clans."

Angus' smoke-gray eyes turned steely. He slammed a fist onto the table beside the bed.

Caught off-guard, Duncan flinched. He ignored the burning sensation in his left shoulder and arm, and moved to defend himself.

Startled, the older man stared at the offending fist. He flexed his hand until it unclenched, then he straightened. "Custom requires me to offer ye hospitality, so I apologize for my rudeness. I objected to Gregor's plan, but I could not dissuade him from it. I am bound by my oath to see that his wishes, and those of your chief, are honored. If your claim is true, then Lochiel gave ye proof he sent ye."

"'Tis in my sporran."

Angus opened the deerskin pouch and dumped its contents onto the table. He sorted through the pile until he found a smoky quartz attached to a black leather cord. He held it up and asked, "What is the significance of this heart-shaped pendant?"

"It matches the brooch given to Gregor by his wife on the day they wed."

"Ye are the chosen one?"

"I am."

"What is your standing with Lochiel?"

The question startled Duncan almost as much as learning that Sir Donald had selected a wife for him. *Ye have lived your twenty-seventh year, Duncan. 'Tis long past time ye were wed.* No amount of arguing on his part had dissuaded his chief, and his oath of allegiance prevented him from refusing. Marriage, even to a MacGregor, was preferable to death.

"When my father was my age," Duncan said, "he saved Sir Donald's life. They shared a close friendship, and I grew up in his household."

"What did ye learn from Lochiel?"

"The importance of respect, honor, and loyalty to clan and chief. Every member of the clan is a member of my family, and 'tis important for us to support one another in good times and bad."

"Why did ye not refuse to marry our Rory?"

"For the same reason ye did not refuse Gregor. I swore to serve Sir Donald without questioning his motives. My refusal would dishonor my chief, my clan, and myself."

Angus folded his arms across his chest and looked straight at him. "What ken ye of the MacGregors?"

"People say ye are a renegade clan that robs others and commits bloody murder. Your feuding brought the wrath of the sixth James upon your heads. 'Tis why the Gregorach are proscribed. Many believe ye are also in league with the devil, so they fear and distrust ye."

Duncan numbered some of his kinsmen among the last. Should the superstitious ones learn that Rory was a MacGregor, they would ridicule and taunt her. He already dreaded subjecting her to such torment.

"Do ye believe all ye hear, Duncan Cameron?"

"'Tis my experience that the tales folk tell are often based on fact, but in the retelling they embellish what they ken."

Angus cocked his head to one side. Duncan felt his response had both surprised and satisfied the older man.

"My foster daughter has suffered much in the twenty-two years she has lived. Her father never confided his plans to her, and I dinna ken how she will react when she learns of them. Ye will say nocht. 'Tis myself who will do the telling. Do ye abide by my wishes?"

The request was a reasonable one. Whatever Rory's reasons for the masquerade, she succeeded where few men dared to venture. Thistle's escapades were legendary. To smuggle contraband under the noses of the excise men and to elude capture by the Watch required canniness and courage. Those were rare qualities, especially in a woman. Intrigued, Duncan decided to accede to Angus' wishes.

"I do."

"Ye do what, Duncan?" Rory asked, entering the room. She deposited a wooden tray laden with herbs, water, and linens on the table. She wiped her hands on the apron that covered her ankle-length plaid, then with one scoop of her palm, brushed his belongings into his sporran.

"How long were ye standing there, lass?" Angus demanded.

Indignation spread across her face. "Dinna be taking such a tone with me, Angus MacGregor. The nerve of ye insinuating that I eavesdropped!"

"And dinna raise your voice to me, Rory MacGregor. I can still bend ye over my knee and thrash your backside."

She stood a head taller than her foster father, but Angus possessed the strength to carry out his threat. An absurd image of the punishment being inflicted flashed in Duncan's mind, and he could not contain his laughter. Rory looked from him to Angus and back to him. She began to laugh too.

Angus threw up his hands in disgust. "I have work that needs doing. Remember your promise, Cameron!"

Duncan nodded, and Angus departed.

Rory wiped a tear from the corner of her eye. "How do ye feel, Duncan?"

"If I dinna laugh too much, I can manage the pain."

A dazzling smile lit her face and her sapphire blue eyes sparkled. Unexpected warmth rushed through him. She sat on the edge of the bed; the pleasure vanished. He became keenly aware of her closeness. When she reached for him, he shrank back. He and Rory might be destined to marry, but until he took her to wife, he was loath to do anything that would shame either Sir Donald or the Cameron name.

"I willna bite, Duncan. 'Tis the cut on your brow I must examine. When ye fell last night, ye cracked open your head."

"Canna someone else tend my wounds?"

She frowned for several long seconds, then a mischievous twinkle shone in her eyes. "There is one old woman who delights in tending handsome young men. More than one has come from her hovel looking worse than when he entered. Shall I have Mairi fetch her?"

Rory started for the door without waiting for his response. Drops of perspiration trickled down the back of his neck. He imagined what the woman might do to him, and thought it safer to take his chances with Rory.

"Wait!"

"Ye willna object to my touch?"

Duncan swallowed, then shook his head.

She returned to his side and removed the dressing above his right eye. She turned his face toward the fire. "I dinna think 'tis serious, but should ye feel dizzy or sick or your head pains ye, speak of it."

He nodded. She poured an oily red liquid onto a small piece of linen, then swabbed his forehead.

"What is that?"

"'Tis made from Saint John's Wort. My uncle has told me stories of how knights fighting the holy wars in Jerusalem used it to heal their battle wounds."

"Do ye mean Angus?"

"I was speaking of Iain, my mother's older brother." She replaced the cloth on the tray. "I dinna want to frighten ye, Duncan, but if I am to change the dressing on your other wound, ye must remove your shirt."

Who had undressed him? Since first hearing the name Rory MacGregor, he had faced one quandary after another. The idea of having her look upon his naked flesh appealed to him, but they were not yet husband and wife.

"How long do ye think 'twill take to decide who will tend ye? Me or the old woman."

Again, he saw a glint of mischief in her eyes. He wondered if the old woman existed at all. Perhaps he should call her bluff. He threw off the blanket and swung his legs over the side of the bed, but she blocked him.

"While I am sure ye have nocht that I have not seen before, we should declare a truce to the teasing, Duncan."

"If ye think it best." He hoped the smile he gave her was just a bit wicked.

"I do. Last night I cut off your shirt because of the wound to your shoulder. The one ye wear now buttons. Uncle Iain brought it for Angus, but he prefers laces."

The more Duncan struggled, the less the buttons cooperated. He grew exasperated, and in frustration yanked on the material. That action resulted in fiery pain. He swallowed his pride and sought help. "Rory?"

Without a word, she unbuttoned his shirt and helped him remove it. "Shift down a wee bit so I can get behind ye to work."

He pushed with his right hand and dug the balls of his feet into the heather mattress. He inched forward.

"'Tis far enough." She knelt behind him and unwound the bandage, reaching one arm around his chest and the other over his left shoulder.

Her nearness made him warmer, and the feel of her encircling arms caressed him like the silky softness of rabbit's fur. He held himself still and bit his lower lip, hoping the pain would distract him. Not until she removed her hands did he dare to breathe.

She chuckled. "Duncan, if I make ye uncomfortable, Mairi can look after ye. Her touch may not be as gentle, but she has tended the wounds of Angus and her sons. I just thought ye would prefer someone who can converse with ye."

"Can I speak my mind without incurring your ire?"

"Aye."

"'Tis unseemly for an unwed woman to tend a stranger."

"I tend to many tasks in the *clachan.* No physician ever visits us, so 'tis my duty to care for the sick and the wounded. Ye have the look of a warrior to ye, so I am thinking ye ken about honor and trust."

"I do."

"My people trust me, and I would do nocht to shame them."

"What of me? MacGregors distrust strangers."

"Aye, they do. Since ye protect Lochiel, who once gave us sanctuary, and he sent ye to meet with Angus, they dinna object to me seeing to your wounds. They trust me, and ken I will protect them. Even if it means killing ye."

"Ye have nocht to fear from me, Rory. I gave ye my word. I willna go back on it."

"Good. Now, can I continue with my work?"

He nodded. "Will I have the use of my arm soon?"

"I believe so. The heavy layers of your cape and waistcoat kept the knife from penetrating deeper." She applied a new poultice while she talked, then wrapped a clean dressing around him to hold it in place.

He gritted his teeth, fortifying himself against the prickles her gentle touch sparked. When she finished, she draped the shirt across his back.

"Ye must wait for the poultice to close the wound before trying to move your arm."

"What is in the poultice?"

"Yarrow and chickweed. Drink this."

He gave the proffered remedy a skeptical glance.

"Not a verra trusting soul are ye, Duncan? I willna poison ye. 'Tis tea from the bark of the willow. 'Twill ease your pain, lessen your fever, and calm your sleep."

He swallowed the warm unpleasant-tasting liquid and returned the cup to her. While she cleaned up, he pondered the complications he faced in marrying her. First, she was a MacGregor. Second, she was Thistle. Third, she was a folk healer. Even among the least superstitious of his clan the combination could prove volatile. He thought of the gruesome image of an old woman that had haunted his dreams as a young lad. Fear stabbed his heart. He did not wish to ask, but knew he must.

"Rory, has anyone died from your healing cures?"

The hue of her eyes changed from the brilliant blue of sapphire to the pallid blue of pale flax. Dread filled him.

"Are ye fearing I practice *buidseachd?*" she asked.

Witchcraft. She had risked much to rescue him and bring him amongst her people. If he could, he would spare her the sorrow his question brought her, but he dared not. He caught her hand and pulled her closer. "It pains me to cause the sadness I see in your eyes, Rory. I have no right to intrude on your hospitality, but…"

She tilted her head and stared into his eyes. Hers narrowed, then closed. She twisted the hand he held until her palm touched his. When she opened her eyes, she placed her other hand atop his. "What do ye fear, Duncan? They struck down the laws against witchcraft nine years ago."

"Laws canna stop people from fearing witches."

"Ye witnessed their madness then?"

"When I was a wee lad, a sickness fell upon the people of my *clachan.* A kind old woman was our folk healer. She cared for the afflicted, but one by one they died. I dinna ken how the rumor started, but witnesses soon came forth swearing they saw her converse with the devil. They claimed she cast spells so the sick died. Fear overwhelmed their good sense, and they arrested her. They scored her brow with crosses to draw off the devil. When the witch-pricker came, he stripped off her clothes and shaved the hair from her body. He drew a rope around her neck, and searched for the Devil's Claw."

"I suppose he found at least one mark on her flesh that proved the devil possessed her soul."

"From the number of times he pricked her with a long brass pin, I would say he found many. Had she screamed from the pain, or bled from the punctures, they would have declared her innocent. Her silence and the lack of blood condemned her."

Rory turned her gaze to the fire. Her long slim fingers played with the unbound ends of her braided auburn hair. A resigned sadness crept into her voice. "She did not cry out because she felt no pain, Duncan. 'Tis the trick of the witch-prickers. The pin's handle is hollow, so when they press the pin against the skin, it retracts into the handle. Since the pin does not pierce the flesh, there is no blood. What happened after they had their confession?"

He curled his fingers into tight fists. How many other innocent women had perished because of the witch-prickers' deceptions? Men who used such means to justify their desired ends sickened him.

"They bound her to a stake and strangled her. When she was dead, they burned her. I have seen men die gruesome deaths, but nocht compared to watching them kill that woman. I doubt I shall ever forget."

Rory squeezed his hand. "Dinna fash, Duncan. No one has died while under my care. Since ye introduced the subject, I have a question."

His relief was fleeting. "Aye?"

"Do ye consider those who have *Dà-Shealladh* to be witches?"

He let out a deep sigh. She gave him a quizzical look, so he smiled to reassure her. "Have ye ever heard of Ewen Dubh, Lochiel's grandsire?"

"The man who killed the last wolf in Scotland? The man who saved himself from certain death by sinking his teeth into his enemy's throat and saying 'twas the sweetest bite he ever tasted? Aye, I have heard of him."

Duncan laughed. "I canna say the first story is true, but I ken the second one is."

"What has he to do with *Dà-Shealladh?*"

"Lochiel once told me his grandsire had the Two Sights. No one accused him of being a witch, so no, I dinna consider it witchcraft."

His answer seemed to satisfy her. What had made her ask about people who saw things before they happened? Then he knew.

"Ye have the gift."

The noise she made was halfway between a grunt and a laugh. "I would not call it a gift, Duncan. My first vision was of a winding sheet around my father's feet. When I told him, he said my mother had the Two Sights, which passed to me upon her death. Since all men die, he did not fash on what I saw. That vision visited me often. Each time the winding sheet came closer to his head. Then I saw a corpse candle. The quivering blue light followed the path to our burial grounds. By evening next, Father was dead. 'Tis a terrible sorrow to foretell a loved one's death or the evil wrought by men."

"Does it come upon ye often?"

"'Tis random and I have no warning before it visits, though it seems to favor thunderstorms."

The mischievous twinkle had returned to her eyes.

"Like last night's storm?"

"Aye."

"What did ye see?"

"Yourself, a weapon, and the color red."

"And from this ye kent what the caterans intended?"

She laughed. "My visions are not so precise."

"Then how did ye ken they would attack?"

"What I kent was a stranger faced peril. The lightning showed what the caterans planned." She stood. "'Tis time ye rested."

He yawned, knowing she was right. The loss of blood and his long journey had weakened him. He must rest if he wanted to regain his strength in time to wed Rory and return to Lochaber before the first snow.

At the doorway she paused. "I did see one other thing last night, Duncan."

"What was that?"

"I stood at your left hand. Whatever do ye think that means?"

Her expression told him she knew precisely what the vision meant. If she had seen herself at his left hand, then they were destined to wed. His promise to Angus, though, required that he not reveal the truth of the prophecy. He decided to play along with her teasing.

"Dinna it depend on whether ye were Rory, or Thistle?"

She winked at him. "Aye, it does."

CHAPTER THREE
THE CLACHAN

Soon after Duncan snapped at Mairi, loud crashes resounded through the cottage. He considered covering his ears, but discovered the clamor suited his mood. Trapped. Restless. Ready to pounce. Yes, those words best described how he felt. He would stand for it no longer! It was time to show *her* who was in charge. He tossed the blanket aside, swung his legs over the side of the bed, and stood.

"And where might ye be going, Duncan Cameron?"

At the sound of Rory's voice, he made no move to cover his nakedness.

"Outside."

She crossed the room, retrieved the blanket, and threw it at him. "I suggest ye clothe yourself first."

He wrapped the plaid around his waist, tucking in the loose end to secure it. It pleased him to see she tapped one bare foot against the earthen floor. Was she irritated with him? Was she angry? He hoped so. A fight was just what he craved. With the stealth of a hunter closing on its prey he crossed the room. He bent close to her ear.

"How dare ye keep me bedfast for five days! Ye treat me no better than a caged animal."

She poked his chest. "'Tis an apt description I think. Ye surely have the manners of one. Your snarling put Mairi in a fine mood. Then Angus complained to me. Well, I willna have it, Duncan Cameron! Ye will apologize to my foster parents immediately."

He scowled.

"No woman tells me what to do."

"This one does and she expects ye to do her bidding."

"I am thinking 'tis time someone showed ye your place, Rory. Women dinna give men orders."

He grabbed for her. She ducked his grasp. He stalked her. She backed into a corner.

"Angus was right. 'Tis a sound thrashing ye need."

"Ye best think again, Cameron. If ye lay a hand on me, 'tis the last ye will lay on another."

"If ye dare lay a hand on our chieftain, I will kill ye."

The menacing voice enunciated each word, making the threat ring true. Duncan pivoted to confront a short stout man who reminded him of a bear. Duncan had met men like him before. When faced with danger, his gentle façade manifested into a ferocious and agile lethalness.

Intent on meeting this new challenge, Duncan failed to comprehend what the man had said. When his words finally sank in, Duncan froze. *Chieftain?* Confused, he flicked his gaze from Rory to the man, then back to Rory. The swiveling made him dizzy. Queasiness rolled in his stomach. He groaned, and sank to his knees.

"Help me get him to the bed, Malcolm," Rory said.

The man wrapped an arm tight around his waist, squeezing harder than necessary. Duncan winced.

"Gently, Malcolm. I dinna want him injured anew."

Duncan cradled his head, hoping to still the spinning room. Sweat trickled down his neck.

"Away with ye now, Malcolm," Rory said. "I will handle this."

"I canna leave ye unprotected. He threatened ye."

"I dinna think he will be laying hands on anyone. 'Twas his temper speaking. He did not mean what he said."

Malcolm grumbled, but obeyed.

"Duncan?"

He opened one eye a crack. When the room remained in place, he opened both eyes. Rory knelt before him. The concern clouding her eyes filled him with chagrin. Already, he rued the words spoken in anger and frustration. When he thought of how he had threatened her, he groaned. "Och, Rory, 'tis sorry I am. I dinna usually act like an oaf."

"I accept your apology if ye accept mine."

"Your apology?"

"For not considering what it must feel like to be bedfast so long. Let me change the dressing on your wound, then we will take a wee stroll. Is that to your liking?"

"Aye."

She retrieved what she needed from the other room.

"Who is Malcolm?" he asked.

"My foster brother and the older son of Angus and Mairi."

"Is what he said true?"

She paused in her ministrations, resting her hand on his uninjured shoulder. "Aye, Duncan, 'tis."

"I—"

Uncertain what to say, he began anew.

"How—"

Again he halted. He did not know how to vent his bewilderment. Men were chiefs, not women.

Rory chuckled. "Do ye find it a wee perplexing, Duncan?"

He exhaled a long audible breath. "Aye. A chief sees to the needs of his people. He settles their disputes. He leads them in battle. He is their father."

"And canna a mother do the same?"

"A mother provides for her children and settles their arguments, but she dinna leave home to fight."

"True, but who defends the house against those who attack when the men are away?"

The women. Rory had outmaneuvered him.

"I see your point, but what of loyalty? A chief commands loyalty from his kinsmen. They follow where he leads."

"Then we differ on our opinions of loyalty, Duncan. I believe he earns loyalty after winning their respect. His deeds show why he is a good leader. He takes the fore, and guides through thought, not just action. He does what is right and best for the majority, but he also kens how to sway to his side those who are undecided or even against him. If wise, he listens to their objections and explains his reasons so they will do his bidding."

"Ye used 'he' throughout your explanation."

Her smile reminded him of his mother when she explained something he ought to have already learned. With a slight shake of her head, Rory said, "We can continue this discussion later. 'Tis a manly form ye have, but I dinna think ye want to be showing yourself off to my kinfolk. Mairi mended your shirt and I found a purple and black plaid amongst your belongings. Will those clothes do?"

"Aye, but I canna fold the plaid or belt it."

"I will help, or if ye prefer, I can fetch one of the men."

"After what has passed between us, Rory, I dinna mind if ye do it."

He grunted once or twice while she eased the shirt over his head. Since the garment reached mid-thigh, he discarded the blanket and watched her. She wore a sleeveless waistcoat and matching plaid over a long-sleeved linen shift. The moss green color suited her auburn hair and the indigo sett of the plaid darkened the sapphire blue of her eyes. A daisy adorned her waistcoat.

She retrieved the wool from his satchel and spread the cloth until it covered most of the floor. She pleated the center portion, but left the ends undisturbed. When she finished, she slid his leather belt beneath the plaid and motioned to him. He lay down on the cloth so the belt was aligned with his waist and the bottom hem touched the top of his knees. She knelt beside him, then draped one end of the plaid over him. When she reached across him for the other end, he smelled the sweet scent of soapwort in her hair. He felt a sudden unexpected urge to pull her down and kiss her, but forced himself to keep his hands still.

After she buckled his belt, she spread her feet to anchor herself and managed to get him to his feet without much assistance from him. She drew the top half of the plaid over his uninjured shoulder. He stood six feet in height, and her height almost equaled his. Her eyes were level with his, so he peered at them while she pinned the plaid in place. A shiver passed through him. Again he fought the urge to kiss her.

"'Tis a bonny plaid, Duncan. It matches the purple of your eyes. Are ye wanting your brogues or your boots?"

"My feet will do."

When he emerged from the cottage, he shielded his eyes from the bright sun until they grew accustomed to the change in light. For a second he stopped breathing. An arc of MacGregors surrounded him. He reached for his sword, but it was not there. To hide the gesture so they did not take offense, he continued to lower his arm until he held it at his side.

They peered at him with wary eyes. The faces of the men displayed no emotion, but they carried an assortment of tools they could use to attack him. The women gathered their children and eased them behind their skirts. Angus stood at the center of the group, his stance portraying anger. Mairi was beside him, her head held high. Duncan could almost see the daggers in her eyes when she looked at him. Malcolm waited by the door, his posture taut and louring. A lean, tawny-haired man stood by Malcolm's side. No one uttered a sound.

Duncan had no doubt he was responsible for the assemblage. He had threatened their chief. He had disabused their hospitality. If he failed to set things aright, he would also have to answer to his chief, assuming he survived punishment at the hands of the MacGregors.

"May I borrow your flower, Rory? I promise to replace it."

"I dinna ken what ye want with it, but ye are welcome to it." She removed the daisy and gave it to him.

He walked over to her foster parents. "I owe ye an apology, Angus, for upsetting your wife. 'Twas rude and thoughtless of me. Mairi, I am sorry for my harsh words. Ye have been most kind, and I repaid your kindness by thinking only of myself. I hope ye will find it in your heart to forgive me, and that ye will accept this as token of my sorrow for causing ye pain."

The lines in Mairi's face softened, and she smiled. She took the flower, then touched Angus' sleeve. She gestured to him, then he interpreted.

"We accept your apology, Cameron. My wife hopes the din this morning dinna pain your head over much."

"'Tis only what I deserve."

A ripple of laughter passed through the crowd. Duncan sensed his worth had risen in their eyes, but hostility lingered. He had no idea how long ago they had gathered, but he had a fair idea. His argy-bargy with Rory had not been a quiet one. They had both shouted in anger, so the MacGregors had heard most of the exchange. He stepped back to see more of their faces. When he extended his hand to Rory, she frowned but came to stand beside him. He addressed her people. "I already begged Rory's forgiveness for my harsh words. I ask now for yours, for violating the rules of hospitality and for threatening your chief."

Silence greeted his apology. Finally, the man beside Malcolm stepped forward. He glanced at Angus, who nodded. Then he turned to Rory.

"Have I your leave?"

"Aye. Duncan, this is Jamie, Angus' other son. He speaks for all."

Jamie extended his hand. "For a man to humble himself before others and seek their forgiveness for his transgressions takes rare courage. Ye have the stance of a warrior, but speak with the wisdom of a king. The Gregorach accept your apology, and welcome ye to our *clachan*."

The crowd dispersed and returned to their work. Jamie stayed while Rory spoke with those who sought her.

"I must say, Duncan, ye look a sight better than the last time I saw ye."

"'Twas ye in the cave, was it not?"

"Ye have a keen eye."

"Do ye help Rory because she is chief or because she is your sister?"

"The latter. She is, and always has been, a rebel, in case ye had not noticed."

"I have. I assume it has gotten her into trouble before."

Jamie laughed. "She was never one to stay with the lasses. Malcolm and I could go nowhere without her trailing after us. Every day her father warned her to stay away from the sea cliffs, but she did not heed him. If we went, she followed. One day she lost her footing and fell."

"Did he punish her?"

"He never knew. I rescued her and kept my silence."

"Ye two look like ye are conspiring against someone," Rory said, joining them.

Jamie hugged her. "'Twas speaking of your rebellious tendencies we were."

She pushed him away. "Have ye no work to do?"

"I do." He brushed her cheek, then extended his hand again. "Duncan, I hope we can talk later."

After Jamie left, he said, "I like your brother."

"Everyone likes Jamie."

"The same canna be said for his brother. Malcolm is verra protective of ye."

She smiled. "He has been so since I was wee. When fearsome dreams plagued my sleep, Malcolm cradled me until I slept again. When I was nine and he was fourteen, we vowed to always be together."

"But he married someone else?"

She nodded. "I love Malcolm, but not the way a wife loves her husband. When he met Fiona, I released him from our childhood promise. He is my brother, though we share not the same blood. He willna allow harm to befall me."

"I believe ye promised me a walk." Duncan offered her his arm. He counted thirteen long houses and two cottages, one of which belonged to Angus. All were kept neat and clean. "How many families live here?"

"A score."

"Where do ye live?"

She pointed to the other stone cottage situated between Angus' and a long house. "'Tis the chief's abode. Father built it with his own hands. There were only the two of us so we had no need for a larger one. Angus and Mairi built theirs so Malcolm and Jamie and their families had more room in the house they share."

"How do ye provide enough food for everyone? The earth is not verra arable."

"We plant oats and bere, and tend sheep for wool and goats for milk. Most of our meat comes from the sea. Uncle Iain provides what we lack."

"I would like to meet him."

"Och, ye are out of luck. He was here the night the caterans attacked, but has since returned home."

"He dinna live here?"

"No, he fled to France after the 'Fifteen."

"Did he fight for King James?"

"He hoped the Stewarts would lift the proscription against our clan. When they lost their bid to reclaim the throne, he could not abide the injustice any longer. He went to sea, and now owns several ships."

They fell into a companionable silence as they passed a group of men working in a field. Duncan compared them to his people, and realized they led a similar existence. Like most Highlanders, the MacGregors lived a simple but exacting life. The surrounding country was serene and beautiful, but the fickleness of nature could turn it into a harsh and savage land. A gentle breeze quickly became a forceful gale. A fine mist changed to a deluge in the blink of an eyelid. The warm summer sun rose early and set late while cold darkness ruled the long winter.

Rory stopped at a stone structure with rounded corners and thick walls. Rocks tied with rope secured the heather thatching to its roof. The steady clamor of metal against metal echoed within the dim interior. A brawny man with sinewy arms swung a hammer against the iron lying on the anvil.

"Welcome, Rory," the blacksmith said, setting aside his work and wiping his hands on his leather apron. "Ye must be Cameron. I am Andrew. I have seen to your horse. 'Tis a rare one he is."

Duncan stepped forward to shake the smith's hand. A dark blue-gray hound sprang from the shadows, its keen eyes tracking his slightest movement. The deerhound's fierce snarl revealed long sharp teeth.

"Tam!"

At Rory's command, the dog ceased its growling and bounded to her.

She scratched its long ragged coat. "Dinna mind Tam. When strangers are about, he is like Malcolm, a wee overprotective. 'Tis all right to shake hands with Andrew now."

Duncan did, then the smith returned to his work. Tam, in the meantime, ventured closer. The hound sniffed him, then pushed his hand with its nose. Duncan patted Tam's neck.

Rory pointed to where Duncan's blue-black stallion grazed with several heavier and shorter dun-colored garrons. He whistled. The Highland ponies raised their heads, but the horse trotted over to him.

He stroked the stallion's forehead. "Did ye think I forgot ye, Midnight?"

The horse nickered and turned its attention to Tam. It seemed the two animals had become fast friends while he convalesced.

A dull ache settled around his shoulder. He flexed his arm. A jolt of pain shot through him. He grunted.

"Take it slow, Duncan," Rory said. "Give the muscles and skin time to heal. Before long, the discomfort will fade."

~*~

Each day Duncan grew stronger. Once Rory pronounced the wound healed, he began to exercise his shoulder and arm until he regained full use of them. In the early morning he rode Midnight, then helped the MacGregors prepare for the upcoming winter. He deemed it important to make their acquaintance and earn their trust. He wanted them to acknowledge Rory's safety and the rightness of his union with her.

Jamie's outgoing manner helped dispel much of the men's latent hostility. Although Duncan held no illusions of having acquired their complete trust, they treated him with less wariness and conversed more readily. The exceptions were Angus and his elder son, Malcolm.

Malcolm's foremost objective was to protect Rory. He waited for Duncan to make a mistake akin to his threat to thrash her. The moment he did, Malcolm would swoop down with the controlled swiftness of a hawk and strike a fatal blow. Conversely, Angus scrutinized him with the sleepy intensity of an owl. His attack, should he side with his son, would come without warning and with devastating celerity.

After three weeks of enduring their ever-vigilant gazes, Duncan decided to confront them. He heard their voices raised in anger before he saw them. While he was too far away to hear all they said, what few words he heard explained Malcolm's animosity. To avoid the appearance of spying, Duncan retraced his steps and circled around the stable. The instant Malcolm and Angus saw him they ceased their conversation.

"What do ye want, Cameron?" Malcolm's tone made it plain that he intruded.

"If 'tis a fight ye are wanting, so be it, but I hoped to settle our differences without one."

Malcolm's eyes widened in mocking surprise. "Differences? What differences?"

"I can think of several. One, your opposition to my presence. Two, your dislike of my keeping company with Rory. Three, your disapproval of my wedding her. Four, your overprotectiveness of her."

Malcolm's lips thinned. "Aye, I protect Rory. Before her seventh birthday, she saw Campbells slay her mother and witnessed their brutal abuse of mine. I consoled her night after night, so dinna tell me I have no right to shield her from further harm."

Malcolm's revelation caught Duncan off-guard. Rory had mentioned the dreams, but not their cause.

"I dinna dispute your right. I am glad she has ye to watch over her."

The other man blinked in surprise, then his eyes narrowed with suspicion. He clearly had not expected this tack.

Rather than let Malcolm gain the upper hand, Duncan continued. "Is honor important to ye?"

Malcolm straightened. "Of course."

"And if your chief, to whom ye swore allegiance, told ye to carry out an order, would ye obey?"

"Without question, else I shame her and myself."

"Then ye will understand why I came."

A puzzled frown appeared on Malcolm's face. "What are ye after saying, Cameron?"

"My chief chose a bride for me. I had not thought to marry yet, but what could I do? I swore on a dirk to do his bidding. If I refused, he could end my life. When the time comes for me to die, I would rather do so with honor than with dishonor. That is why I came to your *clachan*."

Malcolm weighed his words. When he spoke, Duncan knew he began to succeed in his endeavor. "I see ye had no choice. I would choose honor over dishonor myself. Still, Rory dinna ken why ye came. By keeping your silence, ye deceive her."

"That is your father's doing not mine."

Malcolm glanced at Angus, then said, "So ye abide here and wait."

"Aye and no."

"Explain yourself."

"I stay because Rory's family and clan are important to her, and she is important to ye. My duties within my clan prohibit me from living here, so your sister will accompany me to Lochaber. Whenever she leaves your *clachan,* she leaves its safety. 'Tis one reason ye protect her, is it not, Malcolm?"

"Aye."

"By giving ye and the others the chance to become acquainted with me, I hope to allay your misgivings. I also want ye to ken I will protect her once we leave here. I thought 'twould ease your minds if ye choose not to join us."

"Are ye after saying I can go to Lochaber with ye?"

"Once Rory and I wed, anyone in the *clachan* may change their allegiance from the Gregorach to the Camerons. Ye can take our name and live free from persecution."

"Ye would welcome my presence, even though we have our differences?" Malcolm asked in disbelief.

"Aye. Should Sir Donald require my presence, I would wish for Rory to have someone she trusts to be there for her. As Jamie says, Rory is a rebel. Should ye come with us, Malcolm, mayhap between the two of us we can keep her out of trouble." Not knowing whether his words were enough, Duncan extended his hand.

The other man stared at it. "I canna call ye friend."

"I ken that, but hope ye will in time."

Malcolm shook his hand. "My brother was right, Cameron. Ye do have the wisdom of a king."

Duncan had succeeded in winning over Malcolm, but still had Rory's foster father to confront. He turned to Angus. "Time grows short. Dinna ye think Rory should ken the truth?"

The old man gave an enigmatic smile. "I ken ye leave anon, but the time for telling has not come."

Duncan disliked the answer, but could not force the issue. Not yet anyway.

"My answer displeases ye, lad, but I am thinking ye want something more of me. Out with it."

"Where do ye stand on my wedding Rory?"

"I told ye before I willna stand in your way. My objections to this affair have nocht to do with ye, Cameron. They never have. Ye have proven yourself worthy of Rory. Your decision to learn about us shows that others dinna sway your thinking. Ye admit your mistakes, and dinna fear asking for forgiveness. Ye dinna mind dirtying your hands and are willing to learn from those who dinna have the book learning like yourself."

The older man wiped his brow. "Rory is a rebel, but ye have the temperament to tame her without destroying her spirit. If 'tis my blessing ye seek, I willna refuse it. Ye will be a good husband to my daughter, but whether she weds ye or not, 'tis her decision, not mine."

CHAPTER FOUR
THE CLANS

Rory hugged the stone wall, inching along until she judged herself at a point perpendicular to where the target slept. She hitched up her skirt and crept forward. When she crouched less than half an arm's distance from the prone figure, her lips twitched into a smile. She stabbed the air with her fist. She had won the dare!

She started to rise, but a hand clutched her ankle and twisted. A startled cry escaped her lips as she collided with the hard ground. She winced at the jarring sound of her spine cracking. Legs straddled her waist, pinning her arms to her side, while a dirk's blade pricked her throat.

Roars of laughter filled the quiet. Two men emerged from the shadows, halting a safe distance from her. One of them said, "Dinna let her up, Duncan. Rory has a grand temper when nettled."

Their teasing goaded her. "Cowards," she taunted, miffed by her brothers' trickery. Anger blended with humiliation. Curses flew from her lips. A hand clamped over her mouth. She glared at her captor.

"If ye promise to hold your tongue, I will remove my hand."

She nodded. The instant she could speak, she shouted, "When I get free, Malcolm and Jamie, not even Saint Andrew and the Archangel Michael will save ye."

Duncan's hand silenced her before she could utter another sound. He addressed her foster brothers. "If ye value your lives, I suggest ye make yourselves scarce. I will deal with Rory."

When Duncan sheathed his dirk, she renewed her struggles. He squeezed his knees, tightening his hold on her waist. She stilled. His bare calves hugged her naked thighs. He bent forward and placed his hands on the ground on either side of her head. When he spoke, his warm breath tickled her nose. "I thought a chief's word was sacred."

She tensed. His body quivered with suppressed laughter. Her skin tingled from his closeness. His finger traced her jaw. She gazed into eyes that sparkled like amethysts and swallowed.

"The jest is done. Dare I release ye?"

She wet her lips. "Aye."

"I canna hear ye, Rory."

His teasing broke the spell. She wriggled one arm free and swatted him. "Aye!"

With a final chuckle, he rolled off her. She scrambled to her feet and ran. He caught up to her, grabbed her around the waist and drew her against him.

"Leave go of your anger, Rory. Jamie and Malcolm were having a wee bit of fun. 'Tis proof of their love for ye."

The truth of his words cooled her anger. She relaxed against his hard body. His hold on her gentled.

"They have done this before?" he asked.

"Forever."

"And do ye retaliate in kind?"

"Of course. Have ye never teased your sisters or brothers?"

"Not in a long time, Rory."

She heard the sadness in his voice.

"I apologize if I stirred up unhappy thoughts, Duncan."

"I was thinking of Tòmas."

"Is he your brother?"

"He was my twin. He and my parents died when I was twelve." After a brief silence, he cleared his throat. "I am thinking 'tis time I dress. The darkness is nigh gone."

Rory flushed. She had forgotten he wore only his shirt. Since he slept out of doors, he had unbelted his plaid to use for a blanket. When he ensnared her, he tossed it aside. She turned away from him and watched the gray clouds hovering over the mountaintop. Rain scented the air.

"Are ye ready to face your brothers, Rory?"

"I shall let them ponder their fate a wee longer. Would ye care to accompany me to where I go when they vex me?"

She heard a low rumble. When Duncan refused to meet her gaze, she burst into laughter. "If ye wait here, I will return with some bannocks. I would not want ye to starve. 'Tis a wee walk to the cliffs, and ye will need your strength."

He grunted, and sat down to wait. She returned a short time later carrying a *cuach* of milk and a small bundle of oatcakes. He drank from the large cup, then handed it to her. They ate their meager meal in silence.

When she finished, she brushed off her skirt. "Are ye ready?"

"After ye, my lady," he said, giving a low bow. He fell into step beside her, matching his long strides to hers.

"Why have ye come, Duncan?"

"I canna say. I gave Angus my bond."

Honor was sacred to a Highlander so she did not pursue the matter. Angus' gloom had led her to surmise that her guess was correct, but so far he had thwarted her from discovering what the secret pact entailed. How much longer would he keep the truth from her? She sighed.

"I am sorry, Rory."

She waved her hand. "Dinna fash, Duncan. I ken my foster father. He prefers to choose the time for the telling and no one can budge him until he is ready. I wonder, though, dinna Lochiel expect ye to return soon?"

"Before the first snow falls."

Tomorrow was Michaelmas. After the celebration, the MacGregors would prepare in earnest for the onset of winter. Snow often arrived by the time they lit the sacred fire of *Samhein,* the night when spirits of the Otherworld roamed the land. That meant Angus had four sennights left to reveal the truth.

"How did ye come to be *leine-chreis* to your chief?"

"I won the baldric at a wappenshaw my clan holds once every three years near Achnacarry, Sir Donald's home. Have ye ever attended a great gathering?"

"No, but I ken of them. 'Tis where men demonstrate their prowess and loyalty. The strongest, hardiest, and most clear-witted vie for the honors. What did ye do to win your baldric?"

"I traversed a ben, put the stone, wrestled an opponent, hurled the hammer, and tossed a cabar."

"And would ye toss a cabar for me?"

"Have ye a log of pine about twenty feet in length and eight inches in diameter?" he asked, a sly grin on his face.

"Not with me."

"No matter. Watch and I will show ye."

She stepped to one side, crossing her arms in front of her. She tried to suppress her laughter.

Duncan squatted. He linked his fingers so his palms faced up. He knitted his brow and nodded. A second later, his hands lowered as if they held a heavy object. He took an awkward step backward and grunted. With great care, he stood. His shoulders bobbed and his feet moved constantly to keep the cabar upright. Once he had his balance, he trotted forward, gave a great yell, and heaved the pole.

Rory pretended the cabar flipped over so the end he had held pointed away from him. She clapped. "Congratulations, sir. 'Twas a fine toss."

He bowed low. "Thanks, lassie."

They laughed and resumed their walk. When a fine mist began to fall, Rory pulled the top of her plaid over her head. She slipped on wet scree, but Duncan caught her and did not release her until they reached a cleft carved into the granite rock by melting snow.

He peered over the edge into the black chasm. "Where do ye suggest we cross this clough?"

"There." She pointed to a ledge where the two walls of the cleft were at their narrowest point.

With great care he tested the spot to see if it would support his weight. Satisfied, he straddled the clough then helped her jump to the other side. Once he joined her, he asked, "Will ye tell me of the proscriptions, Rory?"

"Now why would ye be wanting to hear about our miseries?"

"'Twill help me better understand who the MacGregors are."

Since his arrival at the *clachan*, she knew he strived to do what few did. They had preconceived notions about the MacGregors. To them, the Gregorach would always be thieving murderers. Duncan was different. He chose not to judge them by what others said, and this demonstrated to one and all that her trust was not misplaced. Still, she wondered at his incessant curiosity.

"'Tis the unspoken rule of the Highlands that hospitality be given to any who seek it whether they be friend or foe. 'Twas what two kinsmen sought from an ancient enemy of our clan, the Colquhouns. What they received were doors slammed shut. Their hunger compelled them to slaughter a sheep. When the Colquhouns discovered the deed, they refused compensation and slew the MacGregors.

"The Gregorach retaliated by reiving nine hundred cattle and sheep. Two Colquhouns were killed during the raid. Their clan beseeched the sixth King Jamie for permission to pursue the MacGregors. The two clans fought a fearsome battle at Glen Fruin. Alasdair of Glenstrae, our chief, entered the narrow defile with half the Gregorach, while his brother's men hid themselves. Ten score were slain that day.

"The Colquhoun chieftain gathered a hoard of his kinsfolk and descended on Stirling Castle. The women and bairns hung the bloodied shirts of their dead on long poles and demanded the right of satisfaction.

"King Jamie, who could not stomach the blood, issued the *Dìteadh gu bàs*, abolishing our name and condemning us to death. MacGregors were executed without trial. Any criminal who desired a pardon had only to bring in a certain number of MacGregor heads, and he was a free man! MacGregor women were branded with hot irons and whipped naked through the *clachan._*Bairns were torn from their mothers' arms and delivered into slavery."

Rory fell silent. As if sensing her need for quiet, Duncan refrained from further conversation. She was grateful for his understanding. When she reached the top of the sea cliff, she stared down at the churning waves that rushed to meet the shore. With each swell came an unbidden and cruel image from the past. With each ebb the picture faded, only to be replaced by a more barbarous one with the next swell. She had hoped the passage of time would dull the nightmarish memories, but they remained ever vivid. She shivered, but not from the cold rain seeping through her clothes.

A warm hand clasped hers. "Ye are chilled, Rory. Come with me."

Duncan led her to a protected outcropping of rock. He sat, then pulled her into his lap and sheltered them with the upper half of his plaid. With his strong arms wrapped around her and his warmth melting the coldness in her, she felt safe—a rare feeling. As chieftain and Thistle, she protected others. They relied on her strength, so she hid her doubts, her fears, and her loneliness from them.

Duncan, on the other hand, was a kindred spirit trained to fight and defend. She had seen how he despised his inability to do for himself while recuperating from his wound. Once healed, he always led; never did he follow. When he thought she needed comfort, he gave it freely. She cherished the security he offered, and leaned against his chest.

"'Tis good to feel ye relax, Rory. I fear I caused ye pain with my question. 'Twas not my intent."

"I guess ye can liken what I feel to the sorrow ye experience when ye think of Tòmas. It dinna matter how much time passes, some pain remains."

"Aye, it does. I have another question, but dinna ken whether ye will answer it."

"What is it?"

"Have ye no one special ye care for?"

"Are ye meaning a man?"

"Aye."

"Ye forget that I stood at your left hand. If I marry, 'tis ye I will wed."

"'Tis a serious question I ask, and ye tease me with your vision."

"If 'tis a serious answer ye want, Duncan, then 'tis no."

"Why not? Most lasses are long married at your age."

"I was raised to lead my people. The oath that binds me to them stipulates that when I wed, the chieftainship passes to another."

"Is there no exception?"

"There are two, but 'tis unlikely a man would agree to either of them."

"So ye willna wed?"

"Not until I can do no more to help my people, and there is no need for Thistle to roam the braes and glens."

Duncan leaned forward, pressing his chest against her back. He bent one arm behind his back, while he held tight to her with the other. After a few seconds, he straightened. He showed her a jagged stone before he tossed it into the sea. "'Twas like a thorn pricking my back."

"Then I am glad ye removed it."

"Do ye remember the first time we spoke, Rory?"

"In the cave or at Angus'?"

"Angus'."

She nodded.

"Ye said Lochiel had chosen well, but ye called him *Mac Dhòmhnuill Dhuibh,* son of Black Donald."

"'Twas what I called him long ago."

"Then ye have met him before?"

His question caught her off guard. Bloody images of Rannoch Moor surged forward again. She covered her ears to block out the screams, the howls, and the sickening thud of swords rending flesh from bone.

Duncan caught her hands in his. "'Tis all right, Rory. I willna let any harm befall ye."

In contrast to the thunderous roar of the waves below, his soothing words washed over her, stilling the raging storm within.

She opened her eyes and saw a single white flower amid the lichen, clinging to the granite rocks. Silhouetted against the bleak sky and stormy sea, the star-shaped blossom struck a chord of familiarity with her. It must have weathered much in its struggle to survive in this desolate spot, and she understood the effort that required. Its solitariness emphasized the despair and sadness she felt.

She blinked several times, trying to keep back the tears that stung her eyes. A haunting wind whistled through the rocks above. She trembled and Duncan drew her close.

Tell him. Trust him.

The words came unbidden into Rory's thoughts. She had told no one of what she witnessed, not even her father.

Tell him. Trust him.

The words came again, compelling her to answer. "I met Lochiel sixteen years ago after—"

"Rory." He whispered her name and stroked her hand. "Ye dinna have to tell me."

"'Twas not a good day for the hunt with a chill mist hovering over the moor, but we had little food left. Father sent Angus with a score of men to search what remained of the ancient forest for rabbit or fowl or deer. Jamie, Malcolm, and some of the other lads accompanied the men. I was always after thinking the lads had more fun than the lassies, so I trailed them. Angus doubled back and caught me. Since my mother had forbidden me to leave the *clachan,* he ordered me home with a warning of punishment if he learned I did not heed him.

"I had almost reached home when I heard the fevered barking. My parents had warned me what to do if strangers came, so I slipped into a peat bog. The Campbells came unheralded with their *coin dubh.* With great savage shouts of *'Cruachan! Cruachan!'* they drew their broadswords and let loose their hounds.

"I slithered forward to warn my parents and friends, but too late. The *coin dubh* chased down wee bairns like rabbits. Two hounds fought over a babe, ripping him to shreds like a sack of grain. The women and what few men remained fought with poles and pointless dirks. The proscription forbade us weapons. Father separated one Campbell from the others, but had no chance of defeating him. The stranger clutched his great sword with two hands and severed the bones in Father's shoulder. He stumbled and fell. Blood gushed from his wound.

"I screamed without uttering a sound. I could not cover my ears. I could not close my eyes. The dead littered the bloodied ground. Those still alive, including my mother, huddled together while Campbells pillaged our homes and set the *clachan* ablaze with the flames from our hearths.

"The Campbell leader went from corpse to corpse making certain each was dead. He had the look of the devil about him, and showed no mercy to those still alive. When kicked, Father moaned. The Campbell raised his sword, but Mother flung herself across Father's chest. She ignored the order to get out of the way, busying herself instead with stanching the bleeding. Incensed, the devil cleaved her in two with his sword.

"Mairi pummeled the Campbell with her fists, but he swatted her aside. His men grabbed her. He took his *claidheamh mòr* and rent her clothes with that great sword. They pinned her to the ground and had their way with her. Before the devil raped her, he thrust his sword into the flames. When he finished, he plunged the white-hot steel against Mairi's cheek. A shrill, keening wail more terrifying than the Campbells' yells pierced the air and set the *coin dubh* to whimpering. The butchers gathered their meager plunder and disappeared.

"Malcolm found me lying atop my parents, but I dinna ken how I got there. He carried me to where Angus held Mairi. He had washed her and covered her with his own plaid. Jamie sat beside his father, holding his mother's hand. When I clasped her other hand, Mairi turned tormented eyes on me. She freed her hand from Jamie and reached for me. I looked to Angus. He nodded, so I crawled into Mairi's lap.

"With his sons and me to tend his wife, Angus helped the others bury our dead. Later, he took me to Mother's grave. He told me Father lived, and that she had given her life to save his."

Like the mountain rivers swollen with melting snow in spring, the tears streamed down Rory's cheeks. She made no effort to brush them away. She sought the solace Duncan offered with his silence and his gentle rocking.

~*~

A grating cry startled Rory awake. Duncan rubbed her arm.

"'Tis just a kittiwake. He did not ken ye slept."

She blinked, trying to get her bearings. The earlier rain had vanished. A warm sun brightened the gray cliffs. She yawned and stretched.

"Would ye mind if I stretched too? My legs are cramped from sitting so long."

"Och! Duncan, 'tis sorry I am." She scrambled from his lap.

While he paced to ease the stiffness in his legs, she looked out at the great expanse of ocean. The waves no longer roiled. They washed ashore with a seductive calm similar to the peace that had settled over her. The confessing of her secret had stilled the storm of guilt and pain. When Duncan came to stand beside her, she glanced at him. The gentle breeze blew the brown curls from his face. He smiled. She knew then that she had been right to trust him.

A white gull with black tipped winds glided on the breeze. When it screeched, Rory thought of what her uncle believed.

"Uncle Iain says the call of the kittiwake is the haunting cry of someone lost at sea. Do ye think 'tis true?"

"I dinna ken, but it does sound like a spirit."

"And how would ye ken that? Ye have communed with them, have ye?"

He winked at her. "I have it on good authority. The Queen of the *Daoine Sith* told me herself."

"The Queen of the fairy folk? Go away with ye, Duncan. Ye spend too much time with my brothers. Their teasing rubs off on ye."

"Speaking of Jamie and Malcolm, I think we should return. 'Tis several hours since we left the *clachan*. Before we go, though, I want to do something."

"What?"

He knelt by a puddle and wet the corner of his plaid. He wrung it out, and crooked his finger for her to come near. When she hesitated, he said, "I dinna think ye want anyone to see that ye shed tears, Rory."

He took her chin in his hand and wiped her face. "Malcolm mentioned the attack, but I did not ken its details. Ye never told anyone what happened before, have ye?"

She let out a long breath. "No."

"How old were ye?"

"Six."

"Do ye ken ye could do nocht to prevent what happened?"

"Aye."

He offered her his hand. She relished its warmth and its strength. While he led her along the narrow path, she thought of the simple gifts he gave her. He listened without judging. He absorbed her pain. He soothed her guilt. He provided a safe haven where she could rest her weary spirit. He had asked one question of her, but she had not answered him. She knew she could do so now without fearing the memories.

"I never said how I met Lochiel. Do ye still want to ken?"

He searched her face. "If ye wish to share it with me. I dinna want to restart tears flowing."

"I promise no more tears, Duncan."

When the track widened, they walked side by side and she began the ending to her tale.

"The Campbells left us nocht but bitter, painful memories. We could not stay in Rannoch Moor, so we fled. It took two days to reach your clan's lands. Lochiel granted us sanctuary until Father healed or died."

"Your father survived his wound?"

"Aye. The afternoon before we left Lochaber, Lochiel returned. While he spoke with Father, I wandered over to his guards. I had never seen the like of their horses before. One man lifted me so I could pet his magnificent steed. A dog barked. I screamed and kicked. The guard dropped me, but Lochiel caught me and spoke soothing Gaelic words to calm my fright.

"When the guard explained what happened, Lochiel ordered him to bring the pup. Your chief, he is insistent. He told me to take the pup, but I cringed and tried to burrow under his plaid."

"I suppose he did not hold with your hiding."

She smiled. "We stared at each other for a long time, for I would not do what he wanted, and he would not accept no for an answer. 'Twas then he spoke, treating me as an equal rather than a wee bairn.

"'Hounds are like people, Rory,' he said. 'There are good ones and there are bad ones. Dinna judge them all because of what the *coin dubh* did. I understand your distress. Hounds can terrorize even a man like myself. When I was wee, my grandsire told me never to show fear to others else I lose honor. Ye are a chieftain's daughter and I am the grandson of one, so I ask the same of ye, Rory MacGregor. Set aside your fear and take the pup.'

"My father taught me to be proud I belonged to the Gregorach. I kent what I had to do. I stepped forward with my arms outstretched and said, 'I am not afraid, *Mac Dhòmhnuill Dhuibh,* son of Black Donald.' Before he could give me the pup, the rascal wriggled free and knocked me to the ground. He clambered onto my chest and licked my face. When I giggled and hugged the pup, everyone cheered."

"Is Tam that dog?" Duncan asked.

"No, 'twas Tam's sire."

Duncan squeezed her hand and brushed a stray hair from her face. "Thank ye for trusting me enough to share your story."

They walked the rest of the way in silence, but Rory enjoyed the quiet. It was neither awkward nor oppressive. It was a silence between friends.

CHAPTER FIVE
REVELATIONS

Rory took advantage of a lull in the races to scan the wind-battered cliffs where puffins nested. With triangular bills of red, yellow, and bluish gray, and teardrop eyes swamped by large patches of white, the black and white birds reminded her of the buffoon at a French fair she had attended with Uncle Iain.

Children's laughter drew her attention back to the stretch of wet sand where the MacGregors celebrated Michaelmas. She had lost count of the number of horse races held so far, but had no trouble remembering the winners. There had been only one—Duncan. While the children ran alongside the horses, she and the other women cheered their men to no avail.

"Rory can best him!" one MacGregor said, pointing to Duncan.

Others echoed Gunn's challenge.

Rory appreciated their confidence in her, but knew she would lose like the others. For her to win, Duncan must relinquish the blue-black stallion on which he sat. His plaid had inched up to expose the bare skin of sinewy thighs. How far up did the bronzed coloring extend? When she lifted her eyes, he met her gaze with a teasing grin. He had guessed her thoughts and was issuing his own silent challenge, but did he dare her to a horse race or to satisfy her curiosity? She averted her gaze and responded to the challenge issued by her kinsman.

"If 'tis winning ye want, Gunn, ye give me a great responsibility. While I would gladly accept it, I would not want to disappoint ye. None of ye lost because of your skill with the sure-footed garrons. Duncan's is no greater than your own. I believe 'tis Saint Michael himself who gifts Midnight with the swiftness of his steed."

The men and women conversed with each other over this revelation. They began to nod in agreement.

"Are ye refusing to race, Rory MacGregor?" Duncan asked.

"I am."

"And 'tis not because I am more skilled than the others?"

She put her hands on her hips. "With my own eyes I saw many who wielded more skill with their garrons than ye did with Midnight."

Guffaws greeted her barb.

Duncan jumped onto the wet sand. "Then ye must ride Midnight. Shall I assist ye in mounting my fine steed?"

While she had achieved her goal of switching mounts, Rory had the uncomfortable feeling the outcome of the race was not assured. Perhaps she had been too quick to cast aspersions on Duncan's horsemanship.

"I can manage." She hitched up her skirt higher than necessary, grabbed hold of Midnight's mane, and swung up on its bare back. The stallion pawed the sand, backed up, and started to rear on its hind legs. She whispered soft words of Gaelic to gentle the horse, and after a moment or two, Midnight nickered and calmed.

Duncan drew alongside her on a brown mare. She noted surprise and admiration in his glance. He started to speak, but she got her words out first.

"Are ye ready to race or are ye wanting to change your mind?"

"Whenever ye are ready."

She kicked Midnight with her bare heels. The stallion took off at a full gallop. She clung to its mane, savoring the rush of the wind on her face and the spray of cool water against her bare legs. She dared to glance behind her. Duncan was nearer than expected, and closing the distance fast.

"Faster, Midnight. Faster."

Neither horse nor rider gave an inch. One second Duncan's garron held the tiniest lead, then Midnight stole it. Rory scrunched closer to the stallion's sweaty neck so her body did not slow them. Lather from its mouth flew past her. Hooves pounded the earth, flinging wet sand in all directions. When they crossed the finish line, she did not know who had won. All she knew was that she had given her best.

"Rory! Rory! Gregorach! Gregorach!"

Her kinsmen's triumphant shouts reached her ears. She slipped from the stallion's back. Andrew handed her a carrot, which she fed to Midnight while she stroked its glistening coat.

"Congratulations, Mistress MacGregor!" Duncan said, coming up behind her. "Ye ran a good race."

She curtseyed. "Ye willna hold my winning against me?"

"'Twas a fair contest. Ye have a way with animals. I thought Midnight would unseat ye. He dinna let others ride him."

"I ken that, Duncan."

The amazement on his face made her laugh.

"Ye forget I rode Midnight once before."

He frowned for a minute, then his expression brightened. "After the caterans attacked me."

She nodded.

"What did ye say to calm him?"

"'Tis between Midnight and myself. I have no intention of sharing our secret."

He laughed.

"I willna pry it from ye, Rory. "

Someone yelled. She glanced toward the great fire fueled by the nine sacred woods: oak, rowan, elder, hazel, birch, willow, alder, yew, and bramble. "Come, the special bannock the lads cooked is done."

After the meal, young couples began to approach Rory. Michaelmas was the time when those who wished to marry announced their intentions and sought her blessing. She did not see Duncan again until after she exchanged gifts with her nieces and nephews.

He stood with his back to her watching the sun sink below the watery horizon. Without waiting for him to acknowledge her presence, she slipped her arm beneath his and turned over his hand. When he looked askance at her, she put her gift in his palm.

"I found this yesterday after we spent the morning on the cliffs."

"Do ye ken the meaning of the carrot's forked end?"

His husky voice raised goose flesh on her arms and sent waves of warm tingles rippling through her. Again, she saw herself standing at his left hand—a sign of marriage foretold. Could the vision be true? Did Duncan feel the same stirrings? They were comfortable in each other's presence. She trusted him, and thought she could call him friend. Did she dare hope there could be something deeper between them?

"'Twill bring good luck and whatever ye sow will be fruitful and grow strong."

"Thank ye, Rory, for your gift. 'Twill be interesting to see if I have many sons and daughters after I wed."

She felt herself flush, and averted her eyes. When she turned back to him, she found him rummaging in his sporran. He handed her a small knife.

"Before Tòmas died, he gave me this *sgian.* I want ye to have it."

Awed by the giving, she traced the intricate carvings of knotwork on the wooden hilt. "'Tis a rare gift, Duncan, and I thank ye for it, but I canna accept it. Tòmas meant for ye to have it. 'Twould be wrong to take it from ye."

He captured her hand in his and closed her fingers over the *sgian.* "'Tis not a taking, but a giving. What my brother and I shared is more precious than his knife. I have my own, and someday will give it to my firstborn son. Ye gave me your trust and your friendship, Rory. These, too, are gifts I will cherish. Ye live with danger, and I willna always be here to protect ye. 'Twould ease my mind if ye accept the *sgian.*"

His words gave Rory hope, but they also brought her sadness. She would miss him when he returned to Lochaber. She blinked away a tear. "I will treasure it always."

The skirl of Jamie's bagpipes filled the air. Duncan tucked her hand in the crook of his elbow. "'Tis time for the dancing. If ye celebrate as the Camerons do, the chief leads the first dance."

"'Tis our custom to begin with the *Cailleach an Dùdain.* Do ye ken it?"

He nodded.

"Would ye do me the honor of dancing with me?"

"Ye are certain ye want me for your partner, Rory? The music and dance weave a spell of their own. I canna promise to do what is proper."

"Fate brought us together, Duncan. Whatever is between us is meant to happen. Neither of us can change that. Whether the magic of the *Cailleach an Dùdain* separates or joins us, 'tis fated to be."

"Then I will dance with ye."

MacGregors formed a wide circle around the sacred bonfire to celebrate the harvest and the promise of renewed life after the passing of winter. Duncan accepted the *Slachdan Druidheachd* from Angus, then held the wand over his head with his right hand.

Rory swayed to the uneven rhythm played by Jamie and the fiddlers. She circled Duncan, moving close then drawing away. He echoed her movements. Several times she extended her hand to caress his face, but drew back when he reached for her. They played a taunting game of cat-and-mouse—weaving in and out, crossing back and forth—until she grew careless. He caught her. She struggled to break free, but when he waved the wand over her head, she collapsed onto the warm sand.

Duncan tried to revive her. He raised her arm, but it fell limp upon release. When he tried her other arm, the same happened to it. He moved behind her, grabbed her about the waist, and lifted her to her feet. She dangled motionless in his embrace.

Resigned to her death, he lowered her to the sand. She peered at him through slit eyelids. His shoulders sagged and his head dropped to his chest. He covered his eyes as if he wept. A white shroud was placed over her, and woeful laments rent the air. The piper played a melancholic dirge while Duncan knelt beside her prone body. He took her hand from beneath the shroud and cradled it against his cheek. She felt dampness on her palm. He did not feign weeping. His tears were real!

Did he weep for the death of all living things or for the loss he would feel upon parting from her? A tear slipped from Rory's eye and her heart ached, knowing she would experience a similar loss.

He squeezed her hand, then ripped the shroud from her body. With the wand lifted toward the night sky, he danced around the circle. He knelt and raised her left hand to his lips. Heated breath whispered across her palm, then the hard wood of the *Slachdan Druidheachd* touched her. Her arm jerked from side to side, then up and down. She slowed the twitching to a graceful sway.

Overjoyed, Duncan leapt over her. He breathed on her right palm, then touched it with the wand. He also tapped her legs. Again, she twitched until the movement of each limb grew more refined.

Several loose strands of wavy brown hair tickled her nose. Tiny droplets of perspiration fell from his chin onto her neck. He brushed his lips against hers, startling her with his hot ragged breath. The searing intensity in his purple eyes held her spellbound. Heat radiated from his body, fanning flickering flames deep within her. He lowered his head and kissed her.

The crescendo of music and cheering clan shattered the magic. Duncan touched the wand to her heart. She leapt to her feet. Those around them joined in the dance, celebrating her miraculous rebirth, a promise that spring would return.

When the music ended, Duncan disappeared into the darkness without a word. Saddened yet irritated by his sudden departure, Rory trembled. She still felt his heated breath on her lips and the warmth of his body pressed against hers. She yearned for solitude to sort through contradictory sensations and emotions, but duty required her to stay.

~*~

Malcolm slammed his fist down on the table in Rory's cottage. His scowl and the growled words he uttered further proclaimed his disapproval. "I dinna like it. One of us should go with ye."

"It canna be helped. With Jamie and the others not yet returned from their fishing, ye must divert Duncan so he and the others dinna suspect my absence. Should I be taken, none can confess to what they dinna ken. Can I depend on ye to do what I ask?"

He stiffened. Hurt flickered in his eyes, and she regretted offending him.

"Forgive me, Malcolm. Ye have never let me down before, and I ken ye willna do so now."

"I will do what ye ask, but I willna be liking it."

He left, grumbling words too low to understand. Although she would prefer his companionship on this trip, their earlier investigation of the tatterdemalion hovel an hour north of the *clachan* had revealed that she could handle the drop alone. Whoever sought refuge in those ruins was either on the run or in desperate straits. He needed food and clothing to survive on that isolated moor, which Thistle could provide.

Since neither she nor Malcolm had detected any sign of soldiers or the Watch, she had little to fear from that quarter. Her long absence from the *clachan,* however, would make Duncan suspicious. If her foster brother failed to distract him, Duncan might find some means to thwart her.

She peered through the window. When she saw Malcolm engage Duncan in conversation and lead him toward the stable, she gathered her things and slipped outside.

~*~

To the east of the hovel was a bog. Ahead and to the west, bramble and moor grass covered the uneven ground. Thistle inched forward, murmuring a silent prayer of thanks for the overcast night that camouflaged her movements. The faint echo of pebbles skipping across stones reached her ears. She froze. The hair on the back of her neck bristled.

Perhaps a hare hopped or a shrew skittered across the narrow moor. Thistle listened. The wait seemed eternal crouched in the open as she was, but she doubted more than ten minutes passed. When the sound did not come again, she crept forward and deposited the bundle against a dilapidated stone wall. She listened again. Nothing.

Twenty paces into her retreat the moon emerged from the clouds. The sliver of light illuminated a lad dressed in a scarlet uniform. If she saw him, then she too was kenspeckled. His momentary surprise at finding himself face-to-face with a notorious smuggler provided her with the advantage. She pivoted and fled toward the bog. Fear of being sucked into the black mire would stay the soldiers, but she knew a secret trail through it.

"Halt! In the King's name, halt!"

She ignored the shouted command. Her heart pounded in her ears. Her chest constricted with each breath. She paused to get her bearings at the lone rock that afforded her any protection. Bent at the waist with hands on thighs, she gulped air. Beads of perspiration trickled down her face beneath the mask.

"Over here!"

More shouts and the crunch of running boots drew near. Thistle ran.

"Fire!"

The thunderous volley echoed over the moor. Hot searing pain tore at her side. She stumbled and fell.

Get up or be taken!

She struggled to stand, then wasted precious seconds waiting for the dizziness to subside. She gritted her teeth and hobbled toward the bog.

"Thistle!"

Like leaves rustling in the wind, she heard her name. The barely audible whisper came from in front of her, not behind. Should she continue? The clatter of priming muskets permitted no other option. Capture meant torture and death, and would give the government reason to resume their persecution of the Gregorach. She would not allow her stupidity to hurt others.

The apparition thundered from the depths of the gray mist hanging over the bog. No, not a ghost! A shaggy white garron!

Strong hands propelled Thistle onto the pony's back. Pain speared her, but she bit the inside of her cheek to keep silent. The wraith-like shroud swallowed them before more musket fire shattered the night.

The sure-footed garron wended its way through the mire that concealed the path. Upon reaching firm ground, the rider spurred the pony into a gallop. Fiery spasms radiated outward from Thistle's midsection. In rhythm with their mount's gait, blood pulsed from her wound.

~*~

The echo of hooves striking stone woke Rory. Dried blood knitted cloth to skin, and she knew the bleeding would begin anew once she removed her shirt. With her left hand, she untied the lacings of her mask and pulled it free. Cool sea air hit her heated face. She wet her lips and tasted salt. She was in the smuggler's cave beneath the broch.

She slid from the garron's back, keeping herself upright by leaning against the wall. She fought the blackness that threatened to engulf the dim light of the gray dawn seeping into the cave. When her head cleared, she turned her gaze to her rescuer.

Duncan bolted from the garron's back. In two strides he covered the distance separating them. His anger hit her with the force of a gale toppling the sturdiest home.

"Have ye no brains at all, woman? Why ever did ye put yourself and the others at risk?"

She flinched, from the coldness in his tone and the fists he clenched and unclenched.

"Ye are gifted with the Two Sights, Rory. Why did ye not use them? A bairn would have sensed the trap laid for Thistle."

The memory of ignored warnings flashed through her thoughts. She could berate herself for her stupidity, but *he* had no right to castigate her.

Angry with herself and with him for hitting too close to the truth, she lashed out at him. "What right have ye to concern yourself with the Gregorach? And dinna forget to whom ye speak! Ye are a messenger. I am a chieftain. Ye will treat me with respect or return from whence ye came."

She tried to sidestep past him, but he seized her wrist and spun her around to face him. Pain shot through her like a bolt of lightning. She gritted her teeth, refusing to succumb to the dizziness that swept over her.

"I leave when my business is ended and not before, my bonny lass. I may not hold the same rank as ye, but the message I bring gives me the right to speak in whatever manner I deem proper." He grabbed her head and brought her face close to his.

She struggled to free herself, but his grip was like iron. The danger in his dark eyes stilled her. Without warning his lips crashed down on hers. The swiftness of the kiss startled her, and she leaned against him. His arms encircled her, and his lips softened. Enveloped by an overwhelming sense of security, she snuggled closer and returned the kiss.

He trailed his fingers down her side. She felt as if someone had thrown scalding water on her. The burning jarred her into a clear awareness of what she did. She had allowed him to sway her resolve, to rob her of her will. Angered by the ease with which she had succumbed to such a tactic, she struck him. The sharp crack reverberated through the cave. She raised her hand to slap him again, but he pinned her to the wall. Blood oozed beneath her shirt.

"One strike I deserved, but not two. Ye willna ever again raise a hand to me. Is that clear? And ye will also heed me on this. Never again will Thistle roam the Highlands. Thistle is dead!"

Like a cat, she arched her back in undisguised fury. She spat out her words. "Ye canna order me about, Cameron!"

"Aye, I can. Your father and my chief gave me that right."

She stopped breathing. A sick fear clutched at her stomach. "What do ye mean?"

His smile did not warm her. Instead, she felt chilled.

"Within a fortnight I take ye to wife."

Dumbfounded, she stared at him. His outline grew fuzzy. The room began to spin and she felt herself falling.

CHAPTER SIX
THE TRUTH

Blurred images flashed like lightning. Garbled voices rumbled like thunder. A man hovered in the shadows. Who was he? What did he want? Why did he frighten her?

Exhausted by the effort to remember, she sought the tranquil serenity of the loch. The still water glistened with a looking glass reflection of blue sky, verdant hills, and snow-capped bens. Butterflies with peacock eyes on rust-colored wings drifted over rosy willowherbs and blue forget-me-nots. Robins warbled. She knelt by the loch's edge and dipped her hand in the cool water.

The birds fell silent. She tensed then turned, sensing a presence behind her. The witch-pricker stood in somber garments, his hands clasped together as if in prayer. He raked her with cold haughty eyes, and she recognized the condemnation in them.

Cold hands lashed her wrists with coarse rope, then secured her arms to a tree limb. Her toes barely touched the ground. She wrestled with her bonds. The rope chafed and gnawed until the flesh bled.

The witch-pricker's hands clutched the neck of her chemise and yanked the worn cloth free. He squeezed and prodded her naked flesh. His tongue darted out to wet thin parted lips. He slipped another rope over her head, then drew the noose tight until it prickled and choked. He extracted a brass pin from an inner pocket of his coat. Bony fingers caressed its gleaming length.

He plunged the instrument into her breast. She screamed, but no one heard. Again, she felt the sting of the brass pin, then the noose tightened around her throat. The pattern repeated—a sharp prick, a silent scream, a pulled rope. Sweat beaded her brow until it flowed like rushing rivers of melting snow. She gasped for air, unable to breathe.

The torture ended, but she still felt the jabs. Tears stung her eyes. After slicing the rope binding her to the tree, the witch-pricker dragged her toward a boat. The rough ground tore at her bruised and battered body, but she was too numb to feel the pain. He rowed to the center of the loch, tied her feet together, and then dumped her overboard. She sank below the shimmering surface of the loch into its murky depths. Spiny tentacles undulated around her.

Rory screamed. She tried to sit, but her body refused to obey. A burning pain sliced her waist.

"Och, lass 'tis all right. 'Tis a dream. Please, Rory, please wake up."

Something warm and rough touched her face. A drop of water fell on her lip. When she licked it, she tasted salt. Her eyelids fluttered open. She lay in the sleeping room of her cottage. Someone sat beside her, but the sun was behind him. She recalled the man in the shadows of her nightmare and shuddered.

"Rory?"

A familiar voice! She tried to speak the man's name, but her throat ached and her voice cracked. He fumbled at something above her head. When he finished, she could move her arms. He lifted her head off the pillow, then brought a scallop shell to her parched lips. She sipped the whisky, letting its warmth soothe her. "Malcolm?"

"Aye. Let me loosen the binding around your ankles."

"Why am I tied to the bed?"

"'Twas the fever, Rory. Mother feared ye would tear out your stitches and start to bleed again. Ye had already lost so much blood."

His words stirred a memory. She had escaped the soldiers, but they left their mark—a permanent reminder of her stupidity.

"Duncan…"

"He waits outside. I will fetch him."

"No!" She had not meant to speak his name.

"Lass, did he hurt ye?"

"No." *At least not the way ye mean.*

Malcolm leveled narrowed eyes at her. His lip was cracked and his face bruised. She touched his unshaven cheek. "Did Duncan do this?"

"Aye." He rubbed his jaw. "Next time, find someone else to distract him. I dinna wish to tangle with him again. He fights like a she bear protecting her cubs."

"Since he kent where to find me, I assume ye lost."

"I am not one to yield, Rory, and I willna apologize for the telling. Ye would be dead or in the clutches of the Sassenach had I not done so."

She squeezed his massive hand. "How long did I sleep?"

"Three days. 'Twas a bad grazing wound Mother sewed up. Father wants to speak with ye."

"Not now."

"He—"

Rory cut him off before he could finish. Angus had waited too long. "Tell him I already ken of the marriage."

"Duncan told ye."

Tears welled in her eyes. Angus had confided in Malcolm, but not her, his chief. She slammed her fist into the heather mattress.

"Rory?"

"Go away. I dinna want to see anyone."

~*~

The hand over Rory's mouth woke her. Light cast by the embers of the fire neither dispelled the darkness of the sleeping room nor illuminated the intruder. She started to struggle, but a commanding voice whispered in her ear. "Listen!"

She heard shouts, followed by boots marching over stone. Soldiers searched for Thistle! She glanced at Duncan. He put a finger to his lips. When she nodded, he removed his hand from her mouth. "Malcolm suggested a plan that might work. There is no time to explain. Just follow my lead."

Rory watched dumbfounded as Duncan discarded his plaid. When he unlaced his shirt, she grew alarmed.

"What do ye do?"

"Undress."

"I can see that. Why?"

He crawled under the blanket beside her and drew her against his naked body.

She seethed at such brazenness. "Get out of my bed, Duncan Cameron! Ye go too far."

"We are newly wed, *m'eudail.* Where else should a husband be, but in bed with his wife?" He grinned.

She rolled her eyes. This was Malcolm's plan? She bit her lip to keep from cursing her foster brother for thinking of this and Duncan for agreeing to it. He was enjoying himself a bit too much for her liking. "If ye think I will tolerate—"

He sifted strands of her hair through his fingers. "I ken ye are nettled with me, Rory, and I am sorry for hurting ye, but this canna be helped. If ye willna do it for yourself, think of your kin. What happens to them if the soldiers discover your wound?"

Their innocence would not matter. They sheltered a smuggler, one with a price on her head. Those not killed would suffer the persecutions again. She could not allow that to happen. She sighed, and Duncan wrapped his arms around her.

"Search the house. Leave nothing unturned. Thistle hides somewhere, and I will have him!"

She stiffened on hearing the raucous voice.

"Who is it?" Duncan asked.

"Geordie Campbell. He willna be easily fooled."

Rory clenched her fists as she listened to the cacophony of sounds from the other room. Wood splintered, iron clanged, furniture crashed, cloth ripped. Campbell destroyed what little she owned because she had dared to rebuff him. His lechery had turned to hatred for all MacGregors, but the threat of a Mackenzie reprisal had stayed his hand. If he discovered her wound, he would have the proof he needed to pillage, rape, and slaughter.

Angus' voice carried over the din. "Leave off, Campbell. There is nocht there to interest ye."

"I dinna take the word of one who belongs to the nameless, old man. Do ye hide Thistle in that room?"

"No."

"Then why dinna ye want me to enter?"

A silence fell in the other room. When Angus answered, Rory could tell he reined in his anger. He growled his words. "My daughter and her husband celebrate their recent marriage."

Duncan kissed her. The unexpected touch of his lips evoked ardent memories of the dance on Michaelmas. The door crashed open, shattering the sheltered tenderness.

"Well, is this not a pretty sight?" Campbell, a gaunt man with a hawkish nose, stood with arms folded, leering at her from hooded beady eyes. Mud speckled the green, blue, and black of his plaid, but his scarlet coat was spotless. A bony finger rubbed the jagged scar across his cheek while his upper lip curled into a sneer. "Rory in the arms of a naked stranger. Perhaps when ye are done with her, ye will give me a turn."

The knife in Duncan's hand appeared from nowhere. The menace in his voice chilled Rory. "Apologize to the lady."

"To one who dinna exist?" Geordie's laughter filled the room.

"I wait, Campbell." Duncan's finger stroked the dirk's blade.

The sergeant sobered. "Ye interfere in the King's business. 'Tis against the law for MacGregors to carry weapons. Disarm him, men!"

"If ye or yours lay hands on me or mine," Duncan warned, "ye will answer to Lochiel."

"Lochiel?"

"Aye."

"And how do I ken ye speak true?"

"Lochiel is my foster father and I am *leine-chreis* to him."

"So say ye."

"So says Lochiel." Duncan pulled a ring from his finger and tossed it at the intruder. "What crest do ye see, Campbell?"

Geordie opened his fist and held up the gold band. "'Tis that of an arm holding a sword."

"And the motto over it?"

The sergeant snorted. "Why dinna ye tell me and I will say yes or no."

Duncan threw back his head and laughed. "Is it the Latin ye canna read or the words, Campbell? *Pro Rege et Patria,* for king and country. Do ye ken to whom that belongs?"

"Lochiel."

"'Twas himself who gave the ring into my hands. Now, are ye wanting to start a feud?"

"I beg pardon. 'Tis plain Thistle is not here." Geordie turned on his heel, but Duncan stopped him.

"Campbell, I will have the ring back or Lochiel will be paying an unwelcome visit to your chief to discuss stolen property."

The sergeant threw it at Duncan, then stormed from the room.

Laughter bubbled inside Rory. Before it escaped, she burrowed her face against the dark curls of Duncan's chest. She laughed then, ignoring the stab of pain from her wound.

Duncan lifted her chin with his finger. "'Tis good to hear ye laugh, *m'eudail.* I like it better than the fretful face ye have worn the last few days."

Her mirth died. Before she could speak, though, Angus appeared in the portal.

"I must check on the others," he said. "I expect to see ye clothed and on two feet when I return, Cameron."

For an instant Rory thought she saw regret flicker in Duncan's eyes. With a sigh, he rose from the bed. She missed his warmth, but the chill proved the catalyst she needed to prepare for the confrontation to come. The time had come to hear the bitter truth.

While they waited, Duncan studied the vessels of dried herbs and plants that lined the wall. She fixed her gaze on the mantel where she kept the box purchased from a tinker. In it she kept the few treasures she owned, like the pendant Iain had given her when he was chosen chieftain.

"Ye broke your word, Cameron."

Angus' sudden outburst caught Rory by surprise. He seemed to have aged during the past several days. He was two score and ten, but looked more like a man of four score years.

"I did," Duncan confessed, "but 'twas unintentional."

"Dinna blame Duncan, Angus," Rory said. "Had ye told me the truth earlier, we would not be here now. Why could ye not trust me?"

"Och, daughter, I thought to spare ye hurt. 'Twas not because I dinna trust ye. I would have told ye when the time was right."

His gray eyes pleaded for understanding, but she could not condone what he had done.

"The time to speak came and went, Angus. Ye forgot I am not only your daughter, but also chieftain of our clan. Ye betrayed me with your silence."

Her foster father muttered an unintelligible curse. "Since Cameron's coming, many are the days I wished for Gregor to live. This pledge was his burden to bear, not mine. I thought to spare ye more suffering, Rory. Can ye ever forgive me?"

"'Tis not my forgiveness ye need, Angus, but your own. No matter what comes between us, I always love ye. All I ask is for ye to remember I am no wee lass anymore. I am a woman who kens the sacred trust bestowed on her by the Gregorach. I willna fail in my duty to them. Now, tell me of my father's promise."

He retrieved the tin box from the mantel, and sat on the stool beside her. He lifted the lid and removed a heart-shaped brooch. "Do ye ken this?"

The image of a young woman with curly red hair filled Rory's thoughts. She took the pin from her foster father. "Father gave it to Mother on the day they wed."

Angus turned to Duncan. "Give Rory what ye brought."

He removed a thong of black leather from his sporran. The smoky quartz, also shaped like a heart, glittered in the firelight. "Lochiel gave this to me before I left Lochaber to prove he sent me. I think it belonged to your father."

She stared at the pendant he placed in her palm. "'Twas Mother's wedding gift to him. I thought it lost. Angus, how could—"

Understanding penetrated Rory's thoughts with a force akin to the musket ball that had pierced her. Lochiel had not proposed the alliance, her father had. Since he owned little and possessed no land, he had bartered her! Arranged marriages were commonplace, but the girls knew of them. Her father's deliberate concealment infuriated her. "Why, Angus? I was just a wee lass! Why negotiate for a husband and then keep silent about it?"

Her foster father cleared his throat. "We did not ken what brutality ye witnessed when the Campbells attacked, but we saw the results. Gregor vowed ye would never again suffer such horror. Your father wanted ye to grow old without fearing for your life. He could teach ye to defend yourself, but to escape the proscription and its terror, he kent ye must marry into a powerful clan. The Camerons lack the strength of force that the Campbells can muster, but they are the fiercest of all the clans. They command the respect and honor the Gregorach does not.

"Yet, I believe Gregor regretted the promising before his death. Ye had learned your lessons well, and with peace between the Mackenzies and us, the need for protection was none so great. Mayhap 'tis why he left the telling to me."

Duncan placed his hand on Angus' shoulder. "Permit me to share this burden. 'Tis the least I can do to mend my broken pledge. Rory, there is more to the promise than just our wedding."

His tone forewarned that she would not like hearing the rest.

"Tell all of it, else I canna decide whether to abide by promises given."

"Any MacGregor who lives here may come to Lochaber with us and swear allegiance to Lochiel."

Her father had thought of everything. His machinations unleashed a flood of hurt, resentment, and betrayal. For the first time, she understood how trapped Duncan had felt cooped up in Angus' home. She was caught in a snare from which there was no escape.

~*~

Rory did not stoke the smoored embers in the cottage's hearth. If anyone saw the blue smoke, they would come to inquire after her health or to keep her company. They meant well, but she needed to think. She had tried to come to some resolution regarding her future, but memories of her father in this place intruded into her thoughts. Her anger toward him threatened to overwhelm her good sense. The solitude of the sea cliffs would bring her solace.

She eased open the door, making certain not to alert her self-appointed guardians. Ever since Duncan had brought her home, he and her foster brothers took turns sleeping outside the cottage. She had lost track of whose turn it was to watch over her, but if he discovered her intentions, he would prevent her from leaving.

With the top half of her plaid wrapped around her shoulders like a shawl, she stepped from the cottage into the brisk early morning air. Her first tentative steps tired her, but she was resolute. She garnered her strength, glanced around to see if anyone followed, and then set out on her trek to the sea.

Halfway to the cliffs, the sun broke through the twisting mist that encircled the craggy mountain peaks. She smiled. This was her favorite time of year. Purple and crimson heather, white fairy flax, yellow lady's fingers, and red violet thistles carpeted the rugged landscape, softening it for a brief span of time. A solitary golden eagle soared over her head.

She envied its ability to look down at the world from a distance. She wished she could take flight and leave behind her cares.

The long hike tired her. After easing herself onto the rocks, she leaned back and closed her eyes. All was quiet except for the waves lapping the sandy shore, but even their susurration failed to soothe the hurt, the anger, or the betrayal that roiled inside her. The tranquility she so often found here eluded her.

She stared at the spot where she had sat within the shelter of Duncan's arms. In him, she had recognized the kindred spirit of an ancient warrior trained to fight and protect. His gentle manner and respect for her people had drawn her to trust him. Yet in the blink of an eye, he had sullied that troth by withholding the truth and demanding obedience from her. She had thought him warm and sensitive, but he was like all men—expecting a wife to be obedient and docile, quick to heed his every command.

Her fingers curled around a stone. That despicable image was not the one she had envisioned. She thought marriage a partnership, one in which she and her husband shared joy, sorrow, pain, and pleasure. She had hoped to marry the man she loved, but her father had shattered that dream. While allowing her to spread her wings like an eagle and fly, he evaded the truth, breaking her heart and tarnishing her love.

"How could ye betray me like this, Father? Why could ye not trust me with your plan? Why did ye let me believe I could make my own choices without fearing ye would interfere in my life?"

Her questions went unanswered, and she hurled the stone into the air. It arced out, then sank into the sea near several razorbills floating on the waves, their tails pointing skyward. Already their black throats had turned white, a sure sign of winter's approach. Their dumpy bodies reminded her of Angus.

How did she feel about him? It hurt to realize Angus lacked confidence in her leadership abilities. She appreciated his desire to safeguard her, but his reluctance to impart what he knew had led Duncan to violate his word. Had either thought to trust her, she might not feel so deceived.

She sighed, knowing her feelings were incidental in this quandary. No matter her decision, someone would be hurt. To return to his chief unwed would shame Duncan and cause irreparable harm. If she sacrificed her dreams to secure her people's welfare, she was the loser. By not marrying, she condemned her kinsmen to a continued life of constant fear and dread.

Her eyes strayed from the sea to the ruins of the broch. The builders had layered the heavy stones one by one until they reached more than five times her height. Within its walls, people had sought sanctuary from raiders. The walls her father had built, however, provided no safe haven. Rather, they immured her.

"Rory?"

The mellifluous voice sent ripples of delight and annoyance through her. She resented his intrusion, yet expected it. Confronted with the inevitable fact that she must confront him, she faced Duncan.

He and her brothers waited a short distance from her, relieved to find her safe, but wary of her reaction to their presence. Jamie winked and smiled. No matter how serious the problem, he always made the best of the situation. Furrows of concern marred Malcolm's face. She sensed his frustration at being unable to shield her this time. Duncan leaned against the rocks with his arms folded across his chest. He watched her through half-closed eyelids, content to wait until she was ready to talk.

She nodded to him, but addressed her brothers. "Jamie. Malcolm."

"Willna ye come home, lass?" her older brother asked. "Father and Mother are worried."

"I am fine, Malcolm. Take Jamie and return to them. When I am ready to leave, Duncan can be after escorting me."

That suggestion did not set well with Malcolm. "Rory—"

She put a finger to her lips. "Will ye sit with me before ye go?"

He shuffled over and squatted beside her.

She looked at the others, and tilted her head to indicate she wanted privacy. After they retreated, she spoke. "Do ye remember what I said when ye told me of Fiona?"

"I was to think of her before ye because she was the one I wished to take for my wife."

"And I released ye from the commitment we had made to each other. 'Tis time for ye to grant me the same courtesy."

"Why? Your father is dead. Ye are not bound by his promises."

She reached for Malcolm's hand. "Did ye not join the others in choosing me for your chief?"

"Aye."

"And do ye ken what it means to be chief?"

He did not answer.

"I am responsible for all our people. They look to me to guide them and to see to their safety. Malcolm?"

When he looked at her, his eyes glistened with unshed tears.

She pretended not to notice, and continued her thought. "Duncan and I need to discuss things without ye or Jamie or anyone else around. No matter how much ye love me, this is something ye canna help me decide. What ye can do is accept whatever decision I make. I need ye to stand with me, Malcolm, not against me."

He extracted his hands from hers and stood. Though his back was to her, she saw him rub his face, and heard him sniff several times. He had to clear his throat before he answered. "I will abide by your decision, Rory, but ken that should ye ever need me, I will come. Promise ye will send word."

"'Twill be our new vow, and if ye or Fiona need me, ye have but to ask."

He nodded, then trudged down the slope toward his younger brother.

Duncan waited until they were out of sight before he crouched beside her. He offered her the hilt of his dirk. "I brought this in case ye wished to use it."

She laid the weapon on the rocks within easy reach. "While I am sore tempted to heed your suggestion, I will keep it for another time."

"I suppose I deserve that." His tone sobered. "I am sorry, Rory, for all the hurt I caused. I allowed anger to rule me rather than heed the good sense God gave me. I never should have attacked ye with my words or my deeds."

"'Twas not your orders or your kiss or even the telling of why ye came that wounded me, Duncan. What hurt was learning of a friend's falsity."

"I never lied to ye, Rory. I did not ken ye when Angus asked for my bond, and once given, I had no reason to think he would keep silent."

She rubbed her forehead. "Why did ye not confront him?"

"I did, but he counseled patience. I intended to force his hand the night Thistle roamed the moor."

"Why did ye change your plans?"

He shrugged. "I trust my instincts. All day I felt uneasy. When I could not find ye and Malcolm kept his tongue, I kent ye were in danger."

"Thank ye for saving my life, Duncan. I wish, though, ye had told me the truth from the start. 'Twould have caused less pain for all of us."

"I regret my silence, Rory. Someday, I hope ye find it in your heart to forgive me."

She was taken aback by the unexpected request. Men who demanded obedience rarely sought forgiveness. The contradiction between words and actions confounded her. Which man was the true Duncan? The gentle-hearted warrior or the wrathful tyrant? It mattered not, for she could not grant him pardon.

"Perhaps one day, Duncan, but I make no promises."

An awkward silence fell between them, so different from other silences they had shared. Several times he started to speak, but each time he changed his mind.

"If we canna say things that need saying, Duncan, ye should leave for Lochaber now."

He cleared his throat, then asked, "How can ye remain chief should we wed?"

Again he surprised her. She expected him to demand her answer, not look for a compromise.

"Ye can swear an oath to obey me," she said, "or ye can take the MacGregor name. If ye do the latter, we serve together as chief."

He sifted a handful of scree through his fingers. "'Tis the rare man indeed who takes orders from a woman, and I dinna think I am he."

She pursed her lips together.

"Dinna take offense, Rory. I was just being honest with ye. We are both strong-willed people who can talk to each other and decide on what needs doing, but I willna take orders from ye."

"Ye expect me to heed yours."

He frowned. "Where would ye get an idea like that?"

"Yourself."

His eyes widened. "Me?"

"I recall your exact words. 'Ye willna ever again raise a hand to me. And ye will also heed me on this. Never again will Thistle roam the Highlands. Thistle is dead! Your father and my chief gave me that right.' The last refers to your ordering me about."

Duncan ran a hand through his thick curls. "I was sore afraid and vexed that night, Rory. If I could take back those words, I would. My wife will be no servant, and I willna treat ye like one if we wed. Will that satisfy?" He waited for her nod before he continued. "As for forswearing the name of Cameron for that of MacGregor—"

She held up her hand. "I dinna expect ye to relinquish a respected name for a proscribed one."

"Rory, what next I ask of ye is not an order but fact. Ye canna ever be Thistle in Lochaber even though the people lose their crops and suffer the harsh winters. 'Tis horrible to see their limbs covered with pus-filled, itchy sores because they are starving."

"Dinna fash, Duncan. Thistle's place is here and now. There is no need for him amongst your kinsmen."

"Why?"

"Because I willna be MacGregor." When she saw his perplexed look, she elaborated. "Ye misunderstand the reason for Thistle. He allows me to help those less fortunate without hurting their pride. When he leaves a parcel of food, the folk consider it a gift from God. If I, Rory MacGregor, do it, the kind ones consider it charity while the others spit in my face. They willna touch what a MacGregor touches."

Duncan glanced at her, then rose and turned to look upon the sea. His stiff bearing and flexing fingers made her think him troubled. Since her wounding, she had come to rue the day she saw herself standing at his left hand. She had concentrated on the imminent danger he faced rather than the fierceness of the storm. Nature had spoken of the tumult he would bring into her life. He faced her again, looking at her with pleading sorrowful eyes. He meant to reveal another truth, one she did not want to hear.

"From the day we first met, Rory, ye told nocht but the truth. Ye entrusted me with your life and your suffering. I repaid ye with secrecy and deceit. The arrangement between us demands a true kenning of what wedding with me means."

"There is more than leaving this place and protecting my people?"

He nodded. His words, when spoken, were whispered. "For ye there is hurt and betrayal."

Her anger flared. "I already kent that. 'Tis my father's doing, not yours."

"No, 'tis mine and Lochiel's."

"Explain yourself."

"I am of Clan Cameron, but Campbell blood flows through me."

He wielded his words with the deadly efficiency of a *claidheamh mòr*. They cleaved her in half as the Campbell's two-edged great sword had cleaved her mother. Her father had sought to protect her by entering into an alliance with the powerful Camerons, yet their chief repaid his efforts by selecting a husband with ties to the clan that had murdered her mother! She stumbled backward, stunned by the betrayal.

"Rory, I would cut out my tongue to spare ye this treachery."

She stared at him, unable to bring him into focus. The screaming of one word echoed in her head. *Why?* In answer, she heard Lochiel speak, imparting words similar to those he had uttered many years ago. *There are good men and bad in each clan, lassie. Dinna judge one by the deeds of another. An evil man murdered your mother. A good man offered ye sanctuary.*

Duncan's soft voice replaced the one that echoed in her head. "Lochiel is after doing what he thinks is best for us both. I canna go against the wishes of my chief. Will ye marry me or not, Rory?"

He offered her a choice, an honorable way to escape. Duty provided no such refuge. She was chieftain of her clan and must look first to her people's welfare. Dignity, however, compelled her to add stipulations to this devilish arrangement.

"I will wed ye on two conditions. The marriage will last but a year and a day."

"And the other?"

"'Twill be in name only.

CHAPTER SEVEN
THE HANDFASTING

The young girl glanced up from her work in the field. Her eyes widened. A shriek escaped her trembling lips. The half-bundled sheaf of grain spilled from her hands. She stumbled backwards. Men ceased their work. Children quieted. Women gathered around the stricken girl.

Rory stomped across the arable earth at the southern end of the *clachan.* "What are ye doing, Cameron?" she demanded through pursed lips.

"Harvesting the bere."

She scooped up a handful of cut grain. "This looks more like ye mauled it."

Duncan glanced at the narrow blade in his hands and realized he wielded it like a sword. No wonder the girl was afraid of him. He handed the sickle to Rory, then knelt before the tremulous girl. He offered her a coin from his sporran. "Will ye forgive me, Mistress Anna? I did not mean to frighten ye."

She eyed his peace offering. "What is it?"

"A penny. The next time the tinkers visit, ye can buy a ribbon for your hair."

"Can I keep it, Rory?"

"Ask your father."

Anna scampered over to a balding man with a frizzled beard.

He turned the coin over, then bit it. Satisfied with its authenticity, he nodded. "I will keep it for ye, daughter. Go finish your work."

With matters settled, the others also returned to the task at hand. Rory returned Duncan's sickle. "'Tis twice ye have won over the MacGregors."

"Jealous are ye?"

She rolled her eyes. "Dinna flatter yourself. Do ye think ye can cut the bere rather than attack it?"

"I willna be frightening Anna again, *m'eudail.*"

Rory bristled at the endearment, but held her tongue. What would she say if he told her that she was responsible for this incident? His thoughts had strayed to her rather than concentrating on the cutting. Why had he allowed a woman to dictate to him? Why had he agreed to her accursed conditions? His anger chafed and vexed him. His acceptance bewildered and incensed him.

Duncan shook such thoughts from his head while he bent to cut another armful. The thistles and thorns growing amid the grain scratched him. Specks of blood dotted the back of his hands and his bare arms. Seed and dust coated the sheen of sweat on his bare torso. After a dozen swings of the sickle, the ache in his back returned. He finished the row, then began another. When Anna did not keep pace with him, he locked his fingers together and stretched his arms over his head. His gaze lingered on Rory's trim calves, bared from tucking up her plaid while she toiled. Ever the rebel, she wielded a sickle rather than bundle grain as the other women did.

Her penchant for defying tradition was what bewitched him, he realized. She possessed none of the womanly attributes he loathed—shallowness, timidity, and meekness. Rory's sagacity sustained and shielded those under her vigil. Honor and duty held sway over personal wants. She provided succor instead of wreaking vengeance, yet she wielded the dirk or blade as well as any warrior, including himself.

She examined a situation from all sides before proposing a solution. When riled, she unleashed her fury with the vehemence of a thunderstorm, but once spent, she discussed the issue. Although they did not always agree, Duncan was nevertheless intrigued and confounded by her arguments. She thought like a man, yet he never forgot she was a woman.

The first condition of marriage that she set resulted from the proscription. Since a priest was forbidden from sanctifying their union, they would declare their intentions before witnesses. Under the rules of handfasting, their marriage would not be binding until after the passage of a year and a day. Before that time, Rory could leave without dishonor.

Then why set forth the requirement that he wed her in name only? Perhaps honor and duty played significant roles in this stipulation. To lay with a man who claimed kinship with a murderer would desecrate her mother's memory, which Rory would not do. Resolute in her duty to her kinsmen, she would wed him, but not risk conceiving a child. Custom dictated that any child born of such a union must remain with the father.

To preclude her from abandoning her child, Rory demanded abstinence from him.

There could be only one reason that explained his acceptance of these despicable terms—love. He loved Rory. He wanted to live with her. He wanted her to bear his children. He wanted to share the good times and the bad with her. He wanted to grow old with her.

"Did ye hear me?"

Duncan blinked and looked around. The cutting was done. Families headed home.

"Sorry, Jamie. I was thinking of your sister. What did ye say?"

Rory's foster brother laughed. "She can have that effect on a man. Malcolm and I go to wash. Would ye be wanting to join us?"

"Aye. Your sister would never forgive me if I came to the *rèiteach* looking like this."

When they reached the stream, they stripped off their plaids. Jamie splashed cold water over himself, then sat on a rock still warm from the sun. Malcolm dunked himself three times, then sprawled on the mossy bank with his eyes closed. Duncan bathed in waist-deep water.

"Ye mentioned the *rèiteach* earlier," Jamie said. "Have ye ever done the asking for a lass' hand in marriage, Duncan?"

"Once, so I am glad not to be doing the asking this night. I would rather fight a whole army than face a lass' father."

"'Tis a wonder a lad gets married at all." Malcolm opened one eye. "My brother, here, chose me to do the asking for Sàra. Words are Jamie's strength, not mine. I did not eat or sleep for a sennight trying to think of what to say."

"And ye took twice that long to actually speak the words! My wife thought I would die of old age before ye ever spoke the last word. Have ye someone to stand for ye, Duncan?"

"Ye called me friend from the start, Jamie. I would be honored if ye would."

"'Tis an honor I will gladly accept if ye will tell of your experience."

"Aye, Cameron, enlighten us!"

"Rory!"

While Jamie and Malcolm scurried to cover themselves, their sister tapped her foot. Since her glare matched the temperature of the water, Duncan stayed where he was.

"What do ye do here, Rory?" the younger MacGregor asked.

"Dinna look so surprised, Jamie MacGregor. Sàra kens how ye love to talk, so she sent me to fetch ye home. Since ye are already late, I canna see how a wee bit more blather will matter. Ye were saying, Cameron?"

She feigned rapt attention, but Duncan guessed her true thoughts from her patronizing tone. Like other women, she deplored the idleness of men. No matter how hard he worked, if he rested or played in some game, women thought men slothful. Rather than engage in a futile argument, he humored her. "Red Pàdraig asked me to speak with Morna's father and her other male kin."

"What did ye talk about?" Rory asked, a smug look on her face.

"Everything except what we came to discuss."

"Och, men! Think how much more ye could accomplish, if ye spoke your mind instead of going all around it."

Duncan winced at the barb. "Morna's family abides by the old rituals passed down from one generation to the next. Women do women's work and men keep to theirs. Shall I finish, *m'eudail,* or have ye heard enough?"

She flicked her hand at him.

He assumed the gesture meant he should continue. "Once a suitable amount of time had passed, I spoke of Pàdraig's wish to wed. Morna's father sat like a great standing stone, giving no sign he heard what I said. After reciting Pàdraig's good qualities, I explained why the joining made a suitable match. Morna's father belched, then he and his kinsmen haggled over the marriage terms. Once we agreed, we sealed the bargain with whisky."

"Sounds like ye wasted considerable time and energy when ye already kent her father would not refuse."

"Mayhap, Rory, but tradition demanded I adhere to the ancient customs of the *rèiteach.*"

"Ye seem to like doing so, Cameron, for our marriage stems from an older custom—one where a woman is no more than property to be bartered. She has no voice because her father arranged the union before she was old enough to even understand!"

Duncan almost flinched from the way she spat out those words, but he met her gaze without blinking. Her eyes, sparkling with unshed tears, impaled him with the sharpness of blue icicles plunged into his heart. The intensity of her anger forced him to draw a breath. If he could go back in time, he would spare her the hurt and betrayal. It was a whimsical notion, though, so he accepted her rage and frustration.

~*~

While the women prepared the meal, the older children kept the younger ones from under foot. Duncan joined the men around the hearthstone of the largest house. He tried to focus on the conversation, but his gaze kept straying to Rory. Malcolm poked him, then nodded toward his brother.

"Father," Jamie said, "I am after wondering if ye might listen to a request I wish to put before ye."

Angus studied his son. "Another one? I thought I was done with your questions once ye married Sàra."

Chortles of laughter flowed through the circle of men.

"'Tis not for myself I ask this, Father. I make this request on behalf of another."

"Who?"

"Cameron."

Angus looked Duncan square in the eyes. When he spoke, however, he addressed his son. "What request canna he ask himself?"

"He heard ye have a grand filly who tends to wander. Glad he would be to take her so ye dinna fash about her safety. 'Tis a protected home he has for her."

A hush descended over the assembled clan. No one stirred. Each held his breath. The wait seemed immeasurable, but Duncan tried not to show his impatience.

"'Tis happy I am to let him have the filly," Angus said.

A collective sigh issued forth from those gathered, then everyone started to nod and speak in muffled tones. Normally, Duncan would shake hands with those present without acknowledging Rory's presence or she his, but not so this time. Since she was chieftain, her acceptance must also be witnessed.

"Quiet I will be having!" Angus waited for the chatter to cease. "Daughter, come here."

Those in her way parted to let Rory pass. With a tone of playful indulgence, she asked, "And what are ye wanting, Angus?"

"To be having a word with ye, lass."

"And what word is that?"

Duncan bit his lip to conceal a grin. Rory's polite irreverence at such a solemn occasion dispelled the taut nerves of her clansmen. They knew what was at stake, but having witnessed their strained relationship, they might wonder whether she would abide by her father's agreement.

"Have done with your teasing, daughter. Show a wee more respect for your elders."

"Aye, Angus."

"Did ye hear what Jamie asked, and do ye ken his meaning?"

"Cameron wishes to marry me."

"And were ye after hearing my answer?"

"Ye gave your blessing."

"Now, lass, ye must give yours. Will ye wed the man?"

Duncan waited. Did she smile for the benefit of those around them? Or had she changed her mind, and wished to prolong his agony? Manipulated into a union she opposed to a man whose mother was born a Campbell were reasons enough to forswear the alliance. Memory was long lasting in the Highlands, and the MacGregors would never forget or forgive what the Campbells had wrought. Should Rory refuse to wed him and reveal his kinship with their enemy, he might forfeit his life although no blood stained his hands.

A bead of sweat trickled down Duncan's back beneath his shirt. His whole body tingled with dread and anticipation, while he prayed for her acceptance.

"I will wed him."

A great roar echoed through the long house. Duncan swore he felt the timbers shudder.

~*~

"No!" Rory's low voice slashed the air like the honed blade of a great sword. "I am chief for one day more, Angus MacGregor, and until I wed my word is law. I willna wear the *bréid.*" She executed a sharp turn on her heels and left the cottage.

Angus shrugged. "Ye wed a rebel, lad. 'Tis sacrilege to refuse to cover her hair with the linen kerchief. Others will think she dinna heed God in the ways of a good wife. Mayhap ye can make her see reason."

Duncan shook his head. "Are ye hearing what ye say, Angus? 'Tis tradition, not duty. Rory wants no part of what is expected unless 'tis her duty. Ye canna expect her to cease being the rebel just because we are to wed."

"'Tis the husband's right to demand obedience."

"Ye assume I want her to wear the *bréid.*"

"Ye agree with the lass?"

"When the sun shines on Rory's hair, 'tis like gazing upon the leaves after they turn brown and red and gold."

"What nonsense are ye spouting?"

"Not nonsense, Angus. 'Tis a pleasing sight of which I willna deprive myself. Mayhap, though, she refuses to wear the *bréid* because 'tis a symbol of what her father wrought. She sacrifices much for your safety, but ye and I hurt her by concealing the truth. If I lessen her pain by granting this wish, then 'tis a wee thing she demands."

Angus rubbed his scruffy chin. "I take your point, but 'twill be a terrible sorrow for Mairi to bear. My wife dreams of the day when she will bestow the *bréid* upon her daughter, even though she did not birth Rory."

"Bide a wee before ye tell her. Mairi may yet get her wish."

Angus gave him a quizzical look, but Duncan chose not to explain. Instead he hurried after Rory. "Wait!"

She stopped, but did not turn to face him. She spoke with a trace of anger in her tone. "I willna change my mind, so dinna waste your breath."

He caught her plaited hair between his fingers. It felt soft like a rabbit's fur. "If ye dinna want to wear the *bréid,* 'tis fine with me. 'Tis Mairi I wonder about."

"Be off with ye, Cameron." Rory pulled free of his grasp. "I dinna need ye to be after making me feel guilt."

"Ye misunderstand, *m'eudail.* If ye will but listen, I ken how to satisfy ye and please your foster mother."

"What are ye after suggesting?"

He stooped to pluck a handful of daisies. He offered her the bouquet. "I once promised to return the daisy ye lent me."

She tilted her head and reached for the blossoms. "Has your idea to do with flowers?"

"It does. Would ye wear a chaplet of wild flowers at the handfasting instead of donning the *bréid* on the day after?"

"Ye mean let Mairi place a crown of flowers on my head after we exchange vows?"

"Aye."

She smiled. Her eyes sparkled like sunlight on morning dew. "'Tis a grand idea, Duncan. Thank—"

Someone grabbed him from behind. An empty grain sack was pulled over his head. Rory screamed. He kicked at those who held him. They grabbed his legs, hoisted him into the air, and carried him a short distance. He heard rushing water and assumed they neared the stream. They stripped off his brogues and stockings, then plunged his feet into the cold water. His arm slipped free. He made a tight fist and swung. Someone groaned.

"Mercy, Duncan, mercy. 'Tis just a wee bit of fun we are having."

"Jamie?"

Someone removed the blindfold.

"Where is she?" Duncan demanded.

Jamie rubbed his chin and pointed downstream. Rory sat on the bank, a resigned expression on her face. Giggling and chattering maidens surrounded her, washing her feet. The *Glanadh-nan-cas*! Duncan groaned. How had he forgotten the ritual footwashing on the eve of his wedding?

Malcolm attacked the rite with enthusiasm, scrubbing one foot with the besom until Duncan found it difficult to stand. Once both feet were purified, the men dumped him on the moss-covered bank. Jamie dipped a rag into a bucket. Duncan renewed his struggles, but the men held fast.

"'Twill go easier if ye let go of your stubbornness. Would ye wish ill fortune to visit on the morrow?" Jamie asked.

After painting Duncan's feet a reddish-brown, he handed the bucket to Gunn who delivered the henna dye to the women.

Duncan breathed on the light frost coating the window of Angus' cottage. Outside a thin layer of fog blanketed the *clachan,* but he could see light where the sun tried to burn through the shroud. It was mid-October, and today he would take Rory for his wife at the handfasting.

He slipped a white linen shirt over his head and tied its lacings. Since Rory had admired his deep purple plaid, he belted it on. He shrugged into a blue velvet waistcoat, then draped the upper portion of the plaid across his chest and secured it with his mother's silver brooch that held the white pearl his father had found while fishing in the River Tay with Sir Donald.

"Ahem." Angus stood in the doorway, surveying him from head to toe. "'Tis time."

Duncan adjusted his blue bonnet and followed Angus outside. With the bag of his pipes tucked under his left arm, Jamie lifted the drones to his shoulder. He fingered the bone chanter, wet his lips, and blew into the blowpipe. After a single loud squawk, a flourish of high lingering notes resounded through the glen.

Two lads appeared on either side of Duncan. With Jamie leading them, they headed for Rory's cottage. She wore a belted white *arisaid* with thin crisscrossing lines of yellow, purple, and blue. Pinned over her heart was her mother's brooch of smoky quartz. Flanked by two lasses, she took her place behind Duncan and his escort. Jamie led them from one home to the next until the entire clan had joined the procession. When they reached the stable, they walked sunwise around the structure three times for luck.

Andrew, the blacksmith, ushered them inside. The MacGregors formed a circle around the anvil. Andrew indicated to Duncan that he should stand to the right of the anvil. Once Rory took her place opposite him, Mairi loosened each knot in her foster daughter's attire, starting with the one at the neck of her linen shift and ending with the leather straps of her deerskin shoes. When she finished, the older woman turned to Duncan.

He watched her fingers move with calculated swiftness. When she ceased her gestures, he frowned. He knew she desired something of him, but had no idea what. With a shrug of his shoulders, he looked to Rory.

"My foster mother wants ye to untie the knots in your attire. We canna exchange pledges until ye do." As if sensing his question, she added, "'Twill prevent evil from befalling the marriage."

He loosened the the lacings of his shirt and the knots of the ribbon garters holding up his woolen hose. After he untied his shoe straps, Andrew placed Rory's hands in his and motioned for him to begin.

Duncan had lain awake long into the night trying to decide what to say. He must say nothing to contradict her kinsmen's belief that she entered into this union without reservation.

"Marriage seals the bond between two people. Rory, ye and I honor the wishes of your father, Gregor of Rannoch, and my chief, Sir Donald Cameron of Lochiel. I came to this *clachan* because of an oath given. Ye did not ken me, a wounded stranger, but ye took me into your home and cared for me. I cherish your gifts of friendship and a warm heart. Today, before your kin, I pledge to honor, shelter, feed, and clothe ye. I gift ye my heart, for I love ye, Rory MacGregor. I take ye for my wife, but willna hold ye to my side should ye wish to leave."

Although they might never share the joy of being one, he had no regrets. When she did not answer, he wondered if he had said too much. He searched her glistening sapphire blue eyes.

While his thumbs stroked her knuckles. She wet her lips and spoke, her voice strong and clear. "I have kent ye but a short time. Ye were a stranger when ye came, but no longer. Ye are friend to the Gregorach. I take ye, Duncan Cameron, for my husband. We ken not how the future will unfold, but while we bide together, I will stand with ye, honor ye, and care for ye."

By naming him friend, she solidified his standing within the clan, but the generality of her declaration hurt. Were a year and a day enough time to win her trust anew and overcome her hatred for a clan to which he claimed no allegiance? He hoped so, but had no doubt she would teach him to master patience and forbearance while he wooed her.

Rory extricated her hands from his to kneel before a radiant Mairi, who crowned her foster daughter's auburn tresses with a chaplet of yellow tormentil, white daisies, and purple gentian. The older woman brought Rory to Duncan's side and placed her left hand in his.

"From my father and his father I learned the mysteries of wedding two metals into one," Andrew said. "With this kenning comes the right to wed two people. I canna think of anyone more deserving of each other than ye, Duncan, and ye, Rory. Like the sheath that protects the sword, ye guard each other's weaknesses while nurturing your strengths."

The blacksmith swung his hammer down on the anvil. The clang reverberated through the stable. "Ye are now husband and wife, Duncan and Rory. May God bless this union and all the sons and daughters ye will raise."

A rousing cheer shook the rafters. The men and boys tossed their bonnets into the air. The women and girls pelted them with flowers.

"Kiss her! Kiss her!" they shouted.

Duncan gave his bride a chaste kiss. He considered stealing another, but Mairi tapped his sleeve. She pointed to him, then to a corner. With her left fingers touching the palm of her right hand, she moved one finger then another across her palm.

"Ye wish me to walk over there?"

Mairi nodded.

"And why would I be wanting to do that?"

The older woman exhaled a long breath, then touched the lacings of her chemise.

"Ye want me to retie my knots?"

Again she nodded.

"Shall I take Rory with me?"

Mairi's eyes grew large and her head shook. She pointed to the opposite corner.

"Rory is to go over there and tie her knots?"

Mairi smiled.

"Why do we do this?"

"To be fruitful and blessed!" the women of the clan shouted as one.

A rosy flush colored Rory's cheeks. Duncan laughed, then bowed. Once they stood in opposite corners, the MacGregors filed from the stable.

"Ye had to ask, did ye not?" Rory asked.

Duncan glanced up from his tying. "Aye, I did."

She glared at him, then whirled to face the wall.

With a silent reminder to have patience, he walked over to her and placed his hands on her shoulders. They trembled. "I am sorry, *m'eudail.* I did not mean for my jest to hurt ye."

She stepped back and wiped her eyes with the back of her hands. "My hide is not fragile like glass, Duncan Cameron."

He smiled, preferring her anger to her tears. "I ken your strength, Rory. Are ye hurt? Is that why ye weep?"

"Ye willna leave it be, will ye?"

He leaned against an empty stall. "Whether ye tell me or not, 'tis your decision."

She stooped to tie her shoes. "'Tis nocht but the day and your words. Ye promised not to lay with me, so why speak of love?"

"I ken what I promised, Rory. Once I held the truth from ye, but willna do so again. I will honor my vows and release ye from this handfasting because I love ye." But not before the allotted time. Until then, he intended to woo her. He offered her his arm. "Shall we join the others?"

"Aye."

The MacGregors gathered at Malcolm's long house to await their arrival. Her elder brother greeted them with a two-handled wooden *cuach* filled to the brim with *uisge-beatha,* the water of life.

"To your health." He drank a generous portion of whisky. After wiping his mouth on his sleeve, he held the large drinking bowl while Rory took a sip. He passed the *cuach* to Duncan, who in turn handed it to Angus who passed it to the man beside him. In short order every MacGregor, young or old, had toasted their health.

Jamie guided Rory to Mairi. He and his older brother lifted their mother until she stood taller than Rory. The young lads and lasses gathered around them, their hands raised in eager anticipation. Mairi prolonged the suspense for a moment, then broke shortbread over Rory's head. The lasses and lads scrambled to catch the crumbs.

When they compared sizes, Anna shrieked with delight. She held the biggest piece, which meant she would marry next. She did a slow pirouette, surveying the unattached young men. Her gaze settled on a lanky lad of seventeen with fair hair, a stark contrast to her ebony tresses.

When she offered him her prize, he reddened. He broke the piece and offered her half.

"What do ye smile at, Duncan?" Rory asked.

"The lass and her new found swain."

"Did no lass ever offer ye the shortbread?"

"None I care to recall. Do ye think they will marry?"

"Anna is her father's bane and joy, for she flirts with all the lads. Since ye gave her the penny, though, she has wealth. Mayhap that will attract more suitors. On the other hand, mayhap young Neil will prove the anchor she needs to settle."

Angus approached. "'Tis time to feed your guests."

Duncan escorted Rory to the head of the table, then served the food. Although they lacked wealth, the MacGregors had searched their secret caches and raided the stores of Iain MacGregor's smuggled goods. They hunted deer, partridge, and grouse. They fished for salmon. Mairi had mixed the ground heart, liver, and lungs of a slaughtered calf with suet, onion, and oatmeal. She seasoned the mixture, then stuffed it into the stomach and boiled it. Haggis was a special dish served on rare occasions, and everyone savored the delicacy.

After dinner the women cleared the dishes while the men stacked the tables. Two MacGregors brought out their fiddles. The first reel was reserved for the wedding couple, so Duncan led Rory to the center of the room. Jamie and Sàra, Malcolm and Fiona, and Angus and Mairi joined them. They danced in time to the music, shifting from their toes to the balls of their feet and swinging each other by the arms. With each repetition of the melody, Duncan found himself paired with a different partner. When the music ended, he faced Rory again.

Thirsty from the exertion, he drank whisky while he watched other couples dance to an unfamiliar tune. With arms raised, the men wove between the women until they reached the spot from which they had started. The women took up the dance, while the men stood with their hands resting on their hips. When each woman faced her original partner, the man swung her around, passed her to the next man, and the sequence began again.

When Rory appeared at his side, Duncan said, "I dinna ken this reel."

"A MacGregor first danced it with his lady long before the proscriptions began."

"When the Gregorach held a respected place amongst the other clans?"

"Aye. A MacGregor loved the daughter of a neighboring chieftain who possessed great wealth. He wanted Isobel to wed him, but her father wished to ally himself with the Robertsons. Isobel disliked her father's choice, but agreed to the courting if MacGregor could also woo her. She hoped to persuade her father that her poor piper was a better choice than his landed gentleman.

"Spurned by Isobel, Robertson allowed his dislike for his rival to grow to jealous loathing. He schemed with her brother to slay MacGregor. One evening while Isobel walked with MacGregor, Robertson and his men attacked. The couple fled to a nearby stable, where MacGregor searched the rafters for sword or dirk. He found musket and ball, and killed Robertson and Isobel's brother. Elated at escaping death, he seized his pipes and devised this tune and dance."

"I suppose they lived happily ever after?"

Rory shook her head. "Not at all. Angered by his son's death and at having his plan thwarted, Isobel's father executed MacGregor. A gillie delivered the severed head to his daughter. Grief killed her."

Duncan wondered if Rory had suggested the fiddlers play this particular tune to demonstrate the consequences of a father interfering in his daughter's life.

"Do ye speak true or do ye weave a tale?

She gave him an enigmatic smile.

Before he could pursue an answer, Malcolm appeared. "Sorry to intrude, but I am wanting Rory to dance the next reel with me."

Duncan went outside for some fresh air. Reddish-orange rays of sunlight illuminated the mountains. The trees with their golden brown canopies cast elongated shadows on the ground. With mixed emotions, he watched the sun set and the time for the bedding approach. The thought of spending the night alone with Rory did not trouble him, but they would do so with only a blanket to cover their nakedness. The night chill would require them to keep close together. Although the thought of holding her enticed him, it would also try his patience.

"'Tis time to usher the bride and groom to their bed, Duncan," Jamie said, a teasing glint in his green eyes.

Tradition held that if the bride and groom spent their first night with the animals, luck would visit the marriage. *I will need all the luck I can muster to restrain myself from bedding my wife,* Duncan thought.

When they reached the stable, Jamie joined the men. The women appeared leading Rory. They formed a circle and placed her in its center. The men encircled the women, then turned so they stood back to back with the women. Mairi and her two daughters-in-law, Fiona and Sàra, entered the inner circle. In the dim light of gloaming, they undressed Rory while Duncan remained outside both circles by the stable door.

Mairi hugged her foster daughter and kissed her brow. Sàra and Fiona, their arms laden with bridal attire, bestowed their kisses and departed the circle. Rory offered her cheek to each woman in turn until all the women had returned to Angus' home. As the men turned to face Rory, Duncan clenched his fists. Although the darkness hid her nakedness, the thought of their eyes on her body irritated him. The men bestowed their kisses in silence. Angus was the last to honor the bride. Without a word, he handed her to Duncan and returned with the others to continue with the feasting and toasting.

For a long moment Duncan and Rory remained where they stood. When she shivered, he ushered her inside. He closed the door, but did not secure the latch. Once morning came, the clan would assist them in greeting the morning.

The glowing embers of a smoored fire lit the stable. Duncan removed his waistcoat and pulled off his shirt. He placed his shoes under the pile of clothes. He unbelted his plaid and carried it to the fresh pallet the women had prepared for them. Although he tried not to look at his wife, his eyes did not heed his wishes. She made no move to shield herself from his gaze. He thought her beautiful, and the urge to gather her to him hit with an unexpected swiftness. His pulse quickened and a burning desire filled him. He gritted his teeth and swore under his breath. The night promised to be long and agonizing.

"Remember your vow, Cameron."

Irritated by her admonition, he longed to escape to the ben where the autumn night would quench the fire she stirred in him. He would not leave, though. To walk out on their wedding night would shame Rory, and no matter how much he wished himself away from here, he would not hurt her.

"I dinna need reminding, Rory. I gave my word and willna break it." He lay down on the feathery softness. The sweet scent of heather filled his nostrils. He made room for his wife beside him. "Come to bed."

"I willna sleep with ye."

The dam that stayed his anger burst. He grabbed her wrist and yanked her down beside him. Caught unawares, she did not stop him from turning her on her side with her back facing him. He wrapped one sinewy arm around her waist and drew her close against his length. She struggled against the embrace, but he draped his leg over hers to prevent escape. She continued to fight, and her movements aroused him.

"Enough! Dinna try my patience, Rory. I gave ye my sacred bond. If I break it, slit my throat."

She stilled.

"I hold ye not to have my way with ye, but to keep away the chill. With only my plaid to warm us, we must stay close to pass the night in comfort."

When Rory did not renew her struggles, he permitted himself a slight smile at the small concession he had won. Although it would torture him, he intended to relish cradling her. He had a year and a day to change her mind, and would do nothing to jeopardize his chances. Once he felt her slow steady breathing, he brushed his lips against her silky tresses.

"Sleep well, *m'eudail.*"

He closed his eyes, but several hours passed before he slept.

CHAPTER EIGHT
SLÀN LEAT AND *FÀILTE!*

Rory snuggled into the warmth radiating from the inner folds of the plaid. Something soft tickled her cheek. Her fingers brushed against silky curls. *Curls?* She blinked, instantly alert. Her head rested on Duncan's hairy chest. She swore and tried to jerk free of his embrace, but he held fast.

With a muted chuckle, he put a finger to her lips and whispered, "Listen."

From outside the barn came hushed giggles and murmurs. High-pitched squeals pierced the air, but were quickly silenced.

"Dinna give them fodder to feed the gossip, *m'eudail*," Duncan said. "The blanket canna cover us both unless we cuddle, and I guarantee I willna be the one standing before them unclothed."

While the darkness had concealed Rory's nakedness from her kin last night, the same no longer held true. Although she stifled her retort, she vented her frustration with a jab to Duncan's ribs. He winced, but swallowed his rebuke.

The stable door creaked open.

"Make no move to rise, or else, wife."

The ease with which he dictated raised Rory's vexation to a new level. She longed to scratch him with her nails, but if challenged, he would carry out his threat and she would embarrass herself in front of the others.

Forced to do his bidding, she feigned sleep. Duncan tucked the blanket around her neck, then rested his free arm on her waist. The simple gestures caught her by surprise, for they demonstrated his vow to protect. That realization disquieted her, but at the same time she felt gladdened.

A cow mooed. Brogues shuffled. A garron nickered. Plaids swished. Muffled footfalls neared the spot where she and Duncan slept. She shifted within his embrace.

A collective drawing of breath echoed through the rafters, then silence descended. No one stirred. None uttered a sound. It was as if bitter cold wind from the north had gusted through the stable, freezing every person and animal into statues. Laughter bubbled in Rory's throat, but the velvety strokes of Duncan's fingers circling her skin bewitched her into muteness.

Rustling sounds warned that someone drew nearer. The scent of porridge, pine, and fish identified Jamie. A feather tickled her ear. When she failed to stir, he leaned closer. Duncan grabbed the hem of her tormentor's plaid and yanked hard, spilling Jamie onto his rump. Those gathered erupted in laughter. Duncan grumbled.

"Why can a body not get a decent rest after a long night?"

Rory's face grew hot. She tried to hide the blush with her unbound hair, but Duncan brushed it from her face, exposing her reddened cheeks for all to see. Her kinsmen laughed louder.

"Sorry we are, lad, to hear ye did not get much sleep," Angus said.

The men hooted and whistled. The women tittered and clapped. Their good-natured teasing brought a smile to Rory's lips.

"Since we canna rest any longer," she said, "my husband and I shall rise, but not until ye return to your homes."

"Och the wee filly speaks!" Jamie teased. "And how are we feeling this fine morning?"

Rory pursed her lips and gave a piercing whistle. A low deep growl emanated from the shadows. Tam advanced with teeth bared, halting an arm's distance from Jamie. Rory snapped her fingers. The hound ceased snarling, but remained ready to pounce.

"Jamie MacGregor!"

"Aye, Rory?" he asked. His voice squeaked.

The men and women laughed at his unease.

"Tam sounds a wee bit hungry this morning, dinna ye think?"

Her brother nodded.

"Ye are done with the teasing?"

"Aye."

"Then I suggest ye take your friends and leave. My husband and I prefer to be alone, if ye understand my meaning."

Jamie chortled. "Aye, Rory, I believe I do. Come all, the fun is ended."

The others complied, uttering ribald comments with their farewells.

"Your clothes are by the anvil," Jamie said. "Food warms at the fire, and I brought water for washing. When ye are ready for the council to meet, Rory, send Father word. Come, Tam, our presence is not wanted here."

Jamie followed the hound out, closing the door behind him.

"A most effective means to rid us of unwanted guests, *m'eudail.*"

Duncan's incessant habit of calling Rory "my treasure" nettled. How could he cherish her when he knew this marriage obligated her to tolerate their union for the sake of her people? Although she handfasted with him, she would never forget that enemy blood coursed through his veins. Yet, he was Cameron, not Campbell, and a man held in high regard by his chief. Was Duncan friend or foe? That question might take her the pledged year and day to answer. Perhaps it was wiser to pick the battles they fought. To war with him over endearments would sap energy she needed for venturing amongst strangers.

Her husband stretched his arms above his head. His embrace no longer captured her, but her resolve to keep peace between them stilled the urge to distance herself from him. He inhaled, but did not release the indrawn air.

"Breathing is best, Duncan. I prefer ye alive to dead."

"Why?"

She shifted onto her stomach and rested her chin in her hands. "Why do I prefer ye alive or why dinna I scurry away?"

"Both."

"Loyalty to the clan above all else is one lesson all Highland laddies and lassies learn. 'Tis what fuels the feuds. Ye claim blood ties with the Campbells, long an enemy of the Gregorach. I once vowed to avenge my mother, but with age came wisdom. 'Tis harder to let an enemy live than to slay him."

"Am I the enemy?"

"I have not decided, but one thing speaks to your favor."

"And that is?"

"'Tis not your face that haunts my sleep."

"My death would simplify matters."

"True, but I am not so heartless that I wish death on another. If 'twas so, Thistle would be wanted for murder not smuggling. I dinna ken if I can befriend an enemy, but I seek a truce between us. Will ye grant it?"

Duncan laced his fingers behind his head. "I agree to your truce, Rory, but ask for truth between us in return." He freed one hand and lifted her chin until her eyes met his. "I lost your friendship because I kept a secret from ye. I compounded the hurt by telling ye of my mother. I hope to reclaim our friendship, but I ken I must earn your trust anew. Without truth between us, the truce willna work and friendship will be forever lost."

She squeezed her eyes shut. Could she renew what he had betrayed? Dare she rely on a possible enemy to provide support and encouragement? Would he speak true to her whether in accord or discord? Once, he had been such a bulwark and confidant. Perhaps he could be so again, but she would not heedlessly trust him as before.

"Aye, truth between us in all things," she said.

"Then why did ye not leave when Jamie departed?"

"Dinna misconstrue my words."

"I will accept what ye say without thinking ye mean to avow more."

She searched his face for duplicity, but he met her gaze without blinking. "For three years I shouldered alone the burden of caring for my people. Now, I relinquish those duties and leave the home I ken for one I dinna ken. I am stubborn and strong-willed, but today I need ye to shield me with your warmth and fortify me with your courage."

"If the shelter of my arms gives ye these things, Rory, then I give it freely."

Troubled by the uncertainty of her future, she laid her head on his chest. He wrapped his arms around her and held her close.

~*~

Rory placed the black bundle on the stool by the hearthstone of the cottage. She propped the black longbow against the wall. From her head she removed a blue bonnet adorned with two quills from a golden eagle and stroked the brown feathers one last time. Since she no longer had the right to wear the emblems of a chieftain, she pulled them from the bonnet and set them on the mantel with great care.

A gust of icy wind stirred the fire. She glanced over her shoulder.

Duncan slammed the door shut. "Have ye another plaid, Rory? 'Tis getting colder. I willna be surprised if it snows before we reach Lochaber."

She turned toward the sleeping room. "I left a package by the hearth. Dispose of it as ye see fit."

When she returned with the extra blanket, Duncan crumpled Thistle's mask in his fist. A range of emotions played across his face. "Why? 'Tis not like ye to give up without a fight, Rory."

"I gave my word. Thistle is dead."

"Ye are Thistle. I canna change what is part of ye."

"I have no wish to incite your wrath, but ye are wrong. I agreed to renounce my rank and clandestine activities after we wed. To seal my fate, I give ye the trappings of Thistle and thus slay him."

She noted Duncan's anger in his glance, his face, and his stance. He muttered a curse under his breath, snatched up the clothes and longbow, then stomped from the cottage. The trip south would be a long one and she had not shortened it by provoking him. Perhaps she should have disposed of the items herself, but could not bring herself to do so. Besides, submissiveness suited her mood, for by irking him, he experienced some of the hurt and anger she felt.

A sudden urge to leave pushed her outside. She walked the length of kinsmen who chose to swear allegiance to a new chief rather than remain behind. Although Angus and Mairi were not among them, their sons and their families were. Like her, they carried only what they could use to build new lives.

When she reached the head of the line, she stood leeward of Midnight so the stallion shielded her from the harsh wind. Concerned about the weather, she glanced at a sky swirled in darkness and light. It was the time between night and day when the hills were most beautiful. Stray tendrils of orange vermilion lanced pewter clouds gathering overhead. She tasted the moisture in the air. The first snow would blanket the *clachan* soon after their departure.

"Rory." Angus' gruff voice brought flashes of memory to mind. He had taught her wisdom and patience, and was more a father to her than Gregor had ever been.

She brushed a tear from her eye. In an unusual display of affection, he hugged her tight. She clung to him.

After a long moment he set her from him, then cleared his throat. "*Slàn leat,* daughter."

"Farewell, Father."

Duncan appeared at her side. He extended his hand. "I promise to keep Rory safe, Angus."

"I ken ye will. Besides, my sons will see ye dinna fail in your duty."

"Should ye have need of us, send word to Lochiel."

Angus waved his acknowledgement.

Rory watched him head toward his sons. Mairi was absent, having bidden farewell the evening before rather than embarrass her husband or sons with her weeping.

"Come, Rory. We must go."

She looked at Duncan who sat his steed like a proud warrior from times past. He scooped her up with one arm and settled her close in front of him, wrapping one plaid around her shoulders and draping another across her legs. Malcolm and Jamie, mounted on the two garrons the men of the *clachan* had decided they could spare, signaled their readiness. Duncan spurred Midnight to a trot. As the column of families departed, those huddled in their portals shouted farewell.

"*Slàn leat!*" Rory mouthed the words, not trusting herself to speak. Tears clouded her sight. She loved them all and it hurt to leave them behind. Who would lead them? Who would see to their safety? How many would still be here when she returned in a year's time? She asked God to protect them from sickness and danger.

For the first hour of the journey Rory's attention alternated between her surroundings and her people. She might not hold the rank of chieftain any longer, but the MacGregors continued to look to her for strength and guidance. She glanced over her shoulder. Jamie rode at the center, talking with those around him. Malcolm rode at the end of the line, urging the stragglers to hurry their pace. Rory returned her gaze to the path in front of her, but glanced back again a short time later. After several repetitions of this, Duncan chuckled.

"What amuses ye?" she asked.

"Ye do. Like a mother wolf intent on kenning where her pups are, ye are, *m'eudail.* Dinna fash so. I will protect your kin as I will protect ye."

"I canna help the fashing, Duncan. After three years, 'tis second nature."

"Would it ease your mind if we switch places with Jamie?"

"'Twould."

Duncan turned Midnight.

"Is there trouble?" Jamie asked.

"No. Can ye take the lead while on Mackenzie land?"

Jamie glanced at Rory. "Fashing, is she?"

"Aye, and if she dinna sit still, we will be camping for the night before we go far."

Rory stiffened at the implication of Duncan's words. Had they been alone, she would have spoken the words that roared in her head. She was not, so she feigned the embarrassed bride. It was not difficult to do because she could feel the warmth in her cheeks.

Jamie laughed. "'Tis no problem. I have followed this track before."

Rory's spirits lifted and her unease quieted as she spoke with her kinsmen. Her nearness seemed to encourage them. They began to laugh and chatter. When they reached a lochan, Duncan called a halt. He handed the reins to a lad who agreed to feed and water the stallion.

"Why do we stop?" Rory asked.

"Come."

"Where do we go?"

"I want to consult with your brothers."

They collected Malcolm and Jamie, then walked a short distance from the others.

"What troubles ye, Duncan?" Rory asked.

"How far do ye trust the Mackenzies?"

Her eyes widened with surprise. "They have never given us cause to doubt their friendship. Do ye suspect trouble from them?"

"No, but when traveling with so many, 'tis best to be cautious. Your *clachan* is fair isolated. Where we go, there will be more people. Ye ken the law better than I. MacGregors may not gather in groups greater than four. We number far more than that."

Malcolm scowled. "Ye are right. The Mackenzie gave leave to bide on his lands, but not all may agree."

"'Tis better to be wary," Jamie added.

Rory nodded. "How do we travel to Lochaber, Duncan?"

"The easier way would be to follow the shore of Loch Maree," Duncan said, "then head south through Kintail until we reach Glengarry."

"'Tis not the way ye suggest we go, is it?" Rory asked.

Duncan shook his head. "I prefer to be cautious. If we keep to the high ground, we can see danger before it sees us. Fewer strangers will ken of our presence."

"I agree, but what of the MacDonells of Glengarry?" she asked.

"They willna ken ye are MacGregors unless ye tell them," Duncan said. "My clan and theirs have been friends for hundreds of years. If we encounter trouble, I will explain I do Lochiel's bidding. They willna risk bloodshed."

The Cameron chief's influence extended far, Rory knew, but she had had no dealings with Glengarry. Duncan seemed to trust the MacDonells as she did the Mackenzies, but experience had taught her to err on the side of caution. "We shall keep to the high ground. I ken we will be Camerons once we swear allegiance to Lochiel, but until then we are MacGregors. I think it best to travel the tracks through the bens in Glengarry, too."

Duncan looked to her foster brothers. They nodded their agreement.

"All right." Duncan turned to her brothers. "Malcolm, return to the end of the line. 'Tis important no one lags too far behind the others. Jamie, take the lead."

"This land is unfamiliar, Duncan. Should ye not lead us?

"Rory and I will scout ahead. All ye need do is follow our trail."

~*~

On the second day of their journey, the air warmed but Rory could still see her breath when she blew on her hands to warm them. The gray sky had lightened, but the unending clouds remained. When she inhaled, she smelled the snow. Duncan must have noted these warnings, too, for although they rode in the van as usual, he kept the others in sight.

She exchanged few words with him, but the silence between them was not stilted. His constant nearness, however, proved nettlesome. His touch raised gooseflesh on her skin in spite of the wool plaids wrapped around her. She sat straighter to distance her body from his. He permitted this without argument. He even released his hold of her waist. Fate, however, refused to comply with her wishes. The uneven track flung her against Duncan, and more than once she clutched his arm to keep from being unseated. Another drawback of separation was the loss of his heat. He warmed her more than the extra blankets. She acknowledged the futility of her efforts and leaned against him.

"'Tis glad I am ye decided 'tis all right if we touch, *m'eudail.* I feared ye would fly over Midnight's head or I would be battered black and blue from ye bumping against me. It feels right for us to ride this way."

It felt more than right, and this irked Rory more than his touch. She pulled away again, but a chill gust of wind ended the struggle. She allowed Duncan's arm to encircle her waist while the steady gait of the stallion soothed her. Midnight seemed impervious to the buffeting wind and rugged terrain. Not once did the horse stumble, and its surefootedness astounded her. Had she ridden a garron, this would not be unusual. Midnight, however, was not a garron.

"'Tis rare for a horse not bred in the Highlands to be surefooted. Ye must have spent long hours training Midnight."

"'Tis fairy magic that he walks like a garron."

Rory suspected he teased her with a boast. "Are ye saying 'twas the *Daoine Sith* who blessed Midnight with surefootedness?"

Duncan nodded.

"How did ye convince them to bestow such a gift?"

"I was kept late in Inverness on Lochiel's business, but its import precluded my staying the night. Fearing Midnight would stumble and break a leg, I kept to General Wade's road. I had just passed the ruins of Castle Urquhart on the shore of Loch Ness when I heard weeping. 'Twas not a night for a woman to be out, so I ventured from the road to search for her. I followed the sound until I found her. I asked what was wrong, and she said she had nocht to warm the wee babe she cradled. I cut a length of cloth from my plaid to give her. She looked hungry, so I offered what little food I had. The instant she accepted my gifts a dazzling light of gold and silver blinded me.

"When my sight returned, an army of fairy soldiers dressed in green surrounded me. They parted to reveal a white stallion. His coat shimmered like moonlight on water and tiny silver bells adorned his mane. A lady arrayed in a mantle of green velvet rode him.

"The woman with the babe bowed low before her. She spoke of how I had helped her, and then she vanished. The lady in green thanked me for my kindness and said my wish was granted. I started to ask what wish, but there was no one there. Ever since, Midnight travels the bens with the surefootedness of the garron."

Rory clapped her hands with delight. "Ye have the gift of the *seanchaidh*."

"Thank ye, *m'eudail*."

A drop of moisture landed on her nose. Another hit her eyelid. Snow! She tried to catch the tiny flakes with her tongue. Duncan chuckled. She ignored him. She had seen snow before, but each time she felt like a child caught up in the wonder of seeing snow for the first time and understanding what it was.

Her joy did not last. More and more snowflakes fell. Duncan pulled the reins and Midnight veered left. Soon, swirls of snow rose and fell with the wind, obscuring Rory's view of the others.

She could not keep fear from her voice. "Duncan?"

"Tie this rope around your waist." He dropped to the ground. "Whatever happens dinna let Midnight stray from this spot."

He took the other end of the heather rope and headed toward the spot where she had last seen Jamie. Snow danced like wraiths twisting and bending to the macabre strains of the haunting howls of the buffeting wind. Rory searched for Duncan, but could not see him through the curtain of white. Since the rope remained taut, she knew he was all right. Time passed slowly. Her eyes ached. Her arms and back grew stiff. Her fists cramped around the rope.

"Give me the reins."

The unexpected voice startled her. When a white snow creature rubbed her leg, she jumped.

"Sorry, Rory. I did not mean to startle ye."

Duncan's voice brought tears of relief. She wanted to alight and hug him.

"Give me the reins, *m'eudail*. I will lead Midnight to a cave I ken not far from here. 'Tis deep enough to shelter all of us."

There was a tug on her waist. She glanced over her shoulder. "What of the others?"

"They hold tight to the rope. 'Tis like a long chain."

Although thankful for Duncan's familiarity with the terrain, she was baffled by how he knew that he headed in the right direction. The going was slow and treacherous, but within the hour they arrived at the cave.

~*~

Rory listened to the snores of sleeping friends. She extricated herself from the mounds of damp wool and crumpled bodies littering the cave floor. A few little heads popped up when they heard the rustle of her skirt. She put a finger to her lips and motioned for them to follow her outside.

Bright sunshine reflected off the snow-clad mountains. She licked a handful of fine powdery snow, delighting in the cold crystals that melted on her warm tongue. After everyone took care of his or her needs, she broke apart several bannocks and shared the oatcakes with the children.

The brisk air invigorated her. She yearned to explore this foreign land, but dared not do so. She had to mind the children's safety. Someone yanked on her plaid.

"'Tis cold, Aunt Rory."

She knelt beside Malcolm's youngest son and brushed reddish curls from his blue eyes. "'Tis best not to complain, Conn. Ye ken your father dinna approve of it. If ye and the others are cold, ye must think of what we can do to keep warm."

Connor frowned, crossed his arms, and rested his chin in the palm of his hand. Rory shook her head in amazement, and wondered if Malcolm and Fiona had seen him do this. He looked just like his father, only smaller. His eyes grew wide and a grin spread across his wee face.

"Ye have thought of what to do, Conn?"

"Aye, Aunt Rory."

"Whisper it in my ear."

He did so, and she smiled.

"'Tis an excellent suggestion."

She shaped three clumps of snow into spheres, then divided the children into three groups and handed each a fragile white ball that they pushed through the snow. When the older children finished making the largest mound, the others rolled theirs over to them. Rory helped them place the second ball of snow atop the largest one. Connor held onto the one made by his group, and she lifted him. He affixed the smallest ball to the middle one.

"'Tis a fine start, but 'tis not yet a man of snow," she said. "He needs a few more things to make him real. Can ye think of what we must collect?"

"Branches could be his arms!" Connor shouted.

"And stones for eyes!"

"Rope for his belt and pine branches for his hair!"

"Red oak leaves for his mouth!"

"And he can wear my bonnet until we leave!"

The children scoured the area for what they needed. By the time Connor placed his bonnet on the man's needle hair, Rory was amazed at their creativeness. An unsuspecting passerby might well mistake this man of snow for a real person.

"Has he a name?" she asked.

"Of course!" the children shouted. "'Tis Duncan!"

She blinked. "Duncan?"

The children laughed.

"Aye, our man looks just like Duncan did when he appeared like magic from the snow," Conn said.

Rory remembered how snow-covered her husband had looked when he reappeared at her feet, and thought their choice of name ideal. "Then Duncan he is!"

"Did someone call my name?" the real Duncan asked.

The children covered their mouths to hide their giggles.

"'Twas not ye we called, husband." She led him to the man of snow. "Duncan Cameron, may I present Duncan of Snow."

Her husband doffed his bonnet and bowed low. "'Tis pleased I am, Duncan of Snow, to be after making your acquaintance."

The children doubled over with laughter.

Duncan clapped his hands to gain their attention. "Back to the cave now. Your mothers have cooked porridge to warm ye."

Groans and protests greeted his announcement.

"Get on with ye. We canna be staying for the winter." He dusted the snow from Connor's bonnet and returned it to the lad's head. The children returned to the cave without further protests.

"Would ye be wanting to warm yourself by the fire, *m'eudail?*"

Rory had enjoyed the morning's play, but it was time to continue their journey.

"How did ye ken of this cave, Duncan?"

"Rain plagued me the whole of the ride to your *clachan*. I was so concerned with keeping Midnight and me from washing into the river and going over the falls that I paid no heed to the storm. A bolt of lightning struck a tree, startling Midnight and unseating me. I was soaked from the dunking, so I searched for a place to build a fire. 'Tis how I found the cave. I marked it in case I had need of it again."

"I am glad ye did so. We might have lost some of the wee bairns or the old ones otherwise."

"Well, I dinna think we need fear more snow squalls. We have another three days to travel before we arrive where your kin will be welcomed."

"Will we stay there, too?"

"No, Rory. I promised Lochiel I would return with ye to Achnacarry. 'Twill take another day to reach there."

~*~

After warming herself by the fire and eating hot porridge, Rory helped the women gather their belongings and their children. They reformed the line. She and Duncan rode in the van, while Jamie led the MacGregors and Malcolm brought up the rear. By mid-afternoon,

Duncan pointed out the towering barren mountains of the Five Sisters just before they descended into the wild forest of Kintail. They sheltered for the night in a gloomy hollow overlooking a deep defile shadowed by jagged mountain peaks.

The next day they entered Glengarry, but met no MacDonells. After stopping for the night on the edge of Glenquoich Forest, they crossed the Gearr Garry, then followed the River Kingie around Beinn Bheig to a glen sheltered by rugged mountains. Rory counted fifteen stone and turf huts near the pebbly shore of a small lake. Smoke filtered through holes in a third of the heather-thatched roofs.

An old man emerged from one hut. He squinted against the bright sun. "Good day to ye, Duncan."

"And to ye, William."

"These are the folk Lochiel spoke of?"

"Aye, they are kin to my wife and have sworn allegiance to Sir Donald. How many huts are habitable?"

"We thatched half and the women cleaned them."

"Ye will find these folk are hard workers. They will help repair the rest."

"Will ye and your wife be staying?"

"No, Lochiel awaits us."

William nodded. "Is this bonny lass your wife?"

"Aye." Duncan lifted her from Midnight.

"Rory, this is William."

Their host pulled the bonnet from his head. "Welcome to our *clachan*. Dinna fash about your kin. They are welcome here."

"Thank ye, William. Ye are most gracious to allow my kin to live with ye."

"'Tis we who are grateful. Those huts have lain empty these past two years after famine took most of us. 'Twill be good to have more hands to do the work. Duncan, will ye rest the night before ye go on to Achnacarry?"

"We will help everyone get settled, then say our farewells."

~*~

"If ye look through the ancient firs, *m'eudail*," Duncan said, "ye can see your new home. Achnacarry has been the seat of Clan Cameron for nigh on a century."

"Where was it before?"

"Ewen Dubh, Lochiel's grandsire, lived atop the cliffs that overlook the River Lochy. He decided the garrison at Inverlochy was too close to Torcastle for his liking, so he built Achnacarry."

82

The fir-planked house with a central stone gable faced the River Arkaig, which connected Loch Lochy with Loch Arkaig. A cauldron of feelings roiled inside Rory—relief, disappointment, sadness, uncertainty, anger, trepidation, and resolve. Her arrival consummated the agreement between her father and the man who lived here.

She waited while Duncan stabled Midnight, then he guided her toward the house.

Five children, ranging in age from ten to two, ran toward them, shouting, "Duncan!"

"It seems ye have your own welcoming committee," Rory said.

"Aye, well, I guess they are like Jamie and Malcolm. I am foster son to Lochiel, and these are his sons and daughters so they are my foster brothers and sisters."

The youngest girl pulled free of her sister's grasp, and toddled toward them. She stopped and frowned, looking first at Duncan, then at Rory before returning her gaze to Duncan. She flung herself against his leg and wrapped pudgy arms around his knee.

"Good day to ye, little dormouse." He swept the girl into his arms, then tickled her stomach. She squealed with delight.

"Ye have snitched from the sweets again." He tapped her nose, then turned to his wife. "Rory, may I introduce Henriet. She is the youngest, but is by far the most ticklish."

"Hello, Henriet. I hope we can become friends."

Duncan stroked the girl's golden hair. "Would ye like to hold her, *m'eudail?*"

Rory nodded. He whispered to Henriet, who cocked her head, then stretched out her arms. She rested her head on Rory's shoulder.

The others arrived and greeted Duncan.

The tallest lad stepped forward, and addressed him in a low tone. "This is your wife?"

"Aye."

The lad bowed. His younger brother did likewise, and the girls curtseyed.

"Welcome, Rory. I am James, and these are my brother, Charles, and my sisters, Isobel and Janet. On behalf of our father, Sir Donald Cameron of Lochiel, and our mother, Lady Anne, I welcome ye to Achnacarry."

"Thank ye, James. 'Tis a pleasure to meet all of ye."

"Where are your father and John?" Duncan asked.

"Who is John?" Rory asked.

James answered. "My older brother. He and Father went to Paris to confer with our grandsire. They willna return till year's end."

An elegant, middle-aged woman awaited them at the door. She wore a forest-green woolen overdress with a quilted brown underskirt. Lace ruffled sleeves protruded from the shawl draped over her shoulders that partially concealed the low, square neckline of her bodice. A cap with braided ribbons of green and brown covered soft golden curls.

"Welcome home, Duncan."

He twirled the woman around as if she was a young lass.

When he set her down, her hands flew to rosy cheeks. "Ye are lucky my husband did not see ye do that."

Duncan grinned. "Sir Donald would not object, Lady Anne. He would spin ye around himself."

She shook her head and smiled. "I dinna doubt it at all, my dear. Ye are forgetting your manners, Duncan. Willna ye introduce me to your bonny companion?"

"Lady Anne, may I present my wife."

"Welcome, Rory. We have looked forward to ye joining us. I, too, was a stranger when I set foot in Achnacarry, so I ken the awkwardness ye must feel for not yet belonging. Just remember this is your home. Ye are welcome to explore it to your heart's content."

Rory curtseyed. "Thank ye, Lady Anne."

"Give Henriet to Marie, then I will show ye to your husband's room. Are ye coming, Duncan?"

"No. I have a few matters to attend." He kissed Rory's cheek and winked. "I will see ye later, *m'eudail.* Try to stay out of trouble until then."

She swatted his shoulder. He strode from the hall, laughing.

"Pay no heed to his teasing." Lady Anne headed for the wide polished staircase. "'Tis the curse of the Camerons, I fear. Archie and Sandy, two of my husband's brothers, are the same."

Rory retrieved the satchel Duncan had left and followed, feeling somewhat adrift in her new abode. She was more at home in the simple stone huts of the *clachan* than here amid the grandness of Achnacarry. Life amongst the Camerons would take getting used to.

At the top of the stairs, Lady Anne turned left and headed down a long hall. She swung open a heavy oak door. The spacious corner room reminded Rory of a one-room cottage. A fire crackled in the hearth. A small high-backed bench was to one side, while an animal skin carpeted the planked floor in front of the fireplace. Opposite the hearth was a canopy bed with ornate carvings decorating the dark wood. She crossed to one of the large windows and looked down on the River Arkaig.

"I hope ye like the room, Rory."

"I do, Lady Anne."

"Shall I have the men bring a tub of hot water?"

"I would like that."

Lochiel's wife reached for the door handle, then paused.

"Is there something else, Lady Anne?"

The older woman faced her. "Donald thought I should say nocht of this, but having met ye, I must do what I feel is right. I ken who ye are, Rory. My husband told me of the attack on your people when ye were but a wee bairn. I am sorry for what happened and for the sorrow and pain it brought ye."

"I thank ye for your kindness, but 'twas not your fault."

"No, but the horrible deed shames me though I had no hand in it."

Rory stiffened. "Ye are of Clan Campbell?"

"Once, before I wed Donald."

Ye thought to keep me safe by wedding me to a Cameron, Father, but your scheming was for nocht. He had sought protection from the fiercest of the clans, but the reach of the most powerful clan was long indeed. The Campbells had amassed their power by manipulating the law to favor them. They seized forfeited land by obtaining royal charters. They kidnapped the daughters of other chiefs and forced them to wed their sons. They bought markers signed by chiefs and forced them to deed over their lands. None dared to gainsay them, for they could summon five thousand men to arms and had allied themselves with king and crown since the days of Robert the Bruce.

To call Clan Campbell friend meant peace. To call them enemy meant death. Rory had learned this truth the hard way, as had the MacDonalds of Glencoe. How could she blame Lochiel, who favored peace, for seeking an alliance with the clan who had massacred a people for declaring their loyalty to King William too late?

"I think 'tis best if we forget what lies between the clans of our sires, Lady Anne. Ye are Campbell by birth, and I, MacGregor, yet we are both Camerons by marriage. Ye are wife to Lochiel, and 'tis to him ye swore your allegiance. 'Tis the same for me."

"Ye are wiser than your years, Rory Cameron. I am thankful for the hand that guided Donald and your father to arrange the marriage between ye and my foster son. He has long needed someone like ye, even if he dinna ken the fact. I pray ye and Duncan will share the same happiness Donald and I do."

Rory nodded, although she knew they would not.

~*~

Rory felt like throwing the pitcher against the bedroom door. She could abide the walls of Achnacarry no longer. She grabbed the extra plaid from the bed and stormed from the room. Halfway down the stairs, she bumped into Duncan.

"Where are ye going?"

Rather than answer, she shoved him aside and fled down the steps. She flung wide the door and ran to *An t'seinn Frith* with its ancient firs that touched the sky. She ran from frustration, boredom, insignificance, and idleness. When she paused to catch her breath, vaporous white frost clouded the air with each exhalation. She found solace in the beauty around her. Emerald pine needles pitted the crisp blanket of snow. Sunlight shimmered on icy boughs of bramble, birch, and oak that crackled in the light breeze.

A whoosh came from the towering crag overhead. A wave of snow rushed toward her. She ducked, covering her head with her arms. The inconsequential avalanche soon ended. She shook the snow from her hair and brushed it from her clothes. Curious to see what had caused the ledge to release its burden, she lifted her eyes to the crest of the monolith. Duncan stood watching her, a mischievous grin on his face. Her irritation returned.

"Leave me be!"

Instead, he scrambled down from his perch. "I thought to bring ye this. Would it please ye more to use it on me or to hunt a stag?"

She stared at the proffered bow. "I am sore tempted to do the first, but think the other suggestion meets with your approval more."

He threw back his head and roared. "Aye, it does. Might I suggest we go a wee farther into the forest? Ye are well-skilled with the bow, and I would not wish others to guess your secret."

They kept on a course parallel to the southern shore of Loch Arkaig. By the time they reached a spot Duncan deemed a safe distance from Achnacarry, Rory was starving. When her stomach rumbled, he dusted the snow from a fallen tree and offered her a seat. From his sack he pulled roasted ptarmigan left over from the evening before.

"Ye are short-tempered of late, Rory. Have I done something to annoy ye? Do ye so regret our bargain that ye need to run?"

"I was not running from ye, Duncan. When I make a promise, I keep to it no matter how I feel about it."

"Then ye do regret wedding me."

"What would ye have me answer? The blood of my enemy flows through ye, yet duty binds me to ye. The handfasting belongs to the past and it does me no good to dwell on it."

"Then why flee?"

"'Tis the predicament I find myself in because we wed."

"I dinna understand."

"I have no patience for idleness!"

Duncan took a last bite, then tossed the bone aside. "Explain what ye mean, Rory."

"At the *clachan* I never wanted for some task to do. The sick and injured had need of me. My kin sought my counsel or asked me to settle their argy-bargies. I helped with the shearing and the sowing, the weaving and the reaping. I gathered the herbs and cooked the food."

"Ye dinna mention the smuggling."

She hit his arm, but smiled. "Aye, and smuggled the goods brought by Uncle Iain."

"'Tis different for ye here?" Duncan asked, warming her hand in his.

"Lady Anne has servants who cook, who clean, who tend to all the needs of the household. The tutor teaches the older bairns while one of the women cares for the babes. Dr. Archie tends the sick, but until Lochiel returns, he willna permit me to help for fear folk will call me witch. Sandy teases me to no end to lift my spirits. We talk, but he must heed his brother's wishes not to preach. While Lochiel is in France, ye are kept busy into the wee hours with your duties.

"'Tis fine for ye, who have spent most of your life at Achnacarry, but I canna live this way. I am used to a simpler life. Life at the *clachan* was hard, but 'twas better than my life here. I have no purpose, and without one I willna survive."

"I canna argue with most of what ye say, Rory. I wish ye had spoken of it before now. Since ye can read and write, I would welcome help with Sir Donald's affairs. And dinna fash about Sandy's preaching. Since ye are Papist like him, his brother willna object to the preaching. 'Tis only his desire to convert others that raises Sir Donald's ire."

Rory's spirits soared. "Lochiel willna mind if I help ye?"

"He canna say no, and when he returns, 'twill be too late to object. Enough talk. I came to hunt with my wife. The day passes and we have yet to catch our prey."

~*~

The hour of midnight fast approached. Rory descended the stairs eager to see how the Camerons greeted the New Year. Earlier, Lady Anne and the servants had banished every speck of dust from Achnacarry. Now, candle flames danced throughout the drafty halls. Green holly bedecked with red berries decorated windows and doors to prevent unwanted fairy visits. The music of harp and fiddle wafted through the lofty rafters of the great hall where a cheerful fire crackled in the hearth. Family and friends gathered in small groups, talking and laughing.

The sound of musket fire startled Rory. She tensed, wondering what danger the noise brought. A second volley echoed outside. Should she alert Lochiel? She searched the room for him and frowned. No one else seemed to have heard the din. They continued their conversations, and one group began to sing.

Rough pounding replaced the musket fire. At first, no one heeded this noise either. When the banging persisted, Lochiel excused himself and went into the entrance hall. Curious to see who knocked and fearing for his safety, Rory followed. When he threw open the door, she was amazed by the spectacle that unfolded.

A score of flickering torches turned night into day. They ran the length of the house in two rows. Between them strode a piper with bagpipe skirling. Gathered in an arc in front of the door stood a small band of men. They stomped their feet, rubbed their arms, and blew clouds of white vapor to warm their hands against the frigid air. No one moved to enter the hall. Instead, they seemed to wait for something or someone.

A hideous bellow echoed in the darkness. A two-legged creature with sharp horns and swinging hoofed arms charged through the men. They whipped out sticks from beneath their plaids and chased the beast sunwise around the house. As they struck the creature, they chanted incomprehensible rhymes. After the third circling, the bull bellowed again. With frightening speed it headed for the door. Rory stopped breathing. Inches from Lochiel, the beast halted and removed its fearful head.

Duncan! The men gathered close behind him, slapping his back and praising his performance. Then Rory understood. He and the others were First Foots. Who would cross the threshold first? He must be dark-haired and tall like Duncan and without deformity, otherwise bad luck would visit the house and its occupants during the coming year.

"Sir Donald," Duncan shouted, "we bring peat to warm ye, bannocks to stave off hunger, salt to weight your purse, and this pine branch to give long life to ye and yours. May ye have a bountiful New Year!"

Lochiel raised a *cuach* of whisky. "*Slainte Mhor!* Good health!"

The First Foots raised a cheer and followed Duncan into the house. They wished their chief and his lady a joyous New Year, and nodded to Rory as they passed into the gathering room. When all were reassembled, Lochiel placed a chair in the center of the room. Rory assumed it represented the traditional spot occupied by the hearthstone in olden times. Duncan appeared, wearing the breast skin of a deer across his back. He circled the chair while everyone struck his back with sticks. This drumming noise, like the beating of the bull, helped to keep fairies and evil from the house. He repeated the revolutions twice more before handing the skin to Lochiel. He, in turn, singed the hide in the flames of the fire. Afterward, he also walked three times around the chair holding the deerskin to each person's nose. The fumes had the power to impart good health to all who sniffed. When the ritual ended, he spoke.

"Father Alex will give us the blessing."

Sandy stepped forward. He nodded to his brother, then bowed his head. "Let us pray. On this first night of the New Year, Holy Father, we ask ye to bless this house and all who dwell within. Favor all who claim allegiance to Clan Cameron with good health, full bellies, and merry days. Grant our prayers for a prosperous and safe year. In the name of the Father, the Son, and the Holy Spirit, amen."

"Amen."

He raised his cup high. "To your good health!"

Rory joined the toast, then set aside her empty cup. Lochiel rapped on the table with a stick and waited for the assemblage to quiet. "'Tis a special time not only because we celebrate Hogmanay, but also because my foster son has brought home a wife to live amongst us. Duncan, bring your bride before us."

Duncan escorted Rory to the hearth. "Here she is, Sir Donald."

"How do I ken this bonny lass is your wife?"

In answer to the question and the taunting of his kinsmen, Duncan swept her into his arms. The kiss caught Rory by surprise. Emboldened by the festivities and the drink, she relinquished her control and returned his kiss with equal ardor. When they parted, he had a puzzled look on his face.

Lochiel raised his pewter *cuach* in a salute. "*Ceud mìle fàilte,* Rory! A hundred thousand welcomes to Clan Cameron!"

A thunderous "*Ceud mìle fàilte!*" resounded through the hall. For the first time since her arrival, Rory no longer felt like a stranger.

PART TWO
1745

CHAPTER NINE
LOCHIEL

Rory climbed the worn steps to the garret. She breathed on a frosted window, then rubbed it with her sleeve until she could see the landscape below. Thick ice concealed the murky depths of Loch Arkaig. Snowflakes floated like feathers, winding their way toward the powdery blanket that covered the bens and glens. Blue green pines with red fissured trunks dared to disturb the monotony of white, but even they wore crowns of snow.

A desolate whistling echoed through the empty space beneath the huge roof beams of Achnacarry. The sound reminded Rory of the wailing rock in the sea cliffs. Emptiness enveloped her, and she sighed. As if to comfort her, Tam put a paw on her lap. She scratched behind the hound's small ears. "It does no good to think of what was, Tam, does it? I canna yet return, so I must put aside such thoughts. I just canna abide the idleness. 'Tis sinful."

Since Lochiel's return from France, he had again assumed control of his affairs. With the winter snows, he forbade women and children to venture outside, thwarting Rory from joining Duncan on the hunt. Frustrated, she slammed her fist against a timbered plank. She winced.

"Did ye break it?" a man asked.

The deerhound stood and growled.

"Whist, Tam!"

Rory's visitor wore an amused expression on his thin face. The few priests she had encountered favored black cassocks, but not this one. He dressed in plaid and waistcoat like other Highland gentlemen.

"Are ye meaning the wall or my hand, Father Alex?"

"Sandy, my bonnie lass, and I mean your hand."

"I told ye before, Father, I willna call ye by your Christian name. Ye are a priest and due more respect. No, I did not break my hand."

"And this from one denied the sacraments! Since I canna change your mind, I will cease trying."

She gave him a smirk. "Now, why dinna I believe ye?"

He laughed. "Ye listen too much to Anne. My sister-in-law says teasing is the curse of the Camerons."

"I ken. 'Twas she who said so the verra day I arrived. Did ye follow me here for a reason, Father Alex, or were ye just wanting to escape the din of your nieces and nephews?"

"They do make the noise, dinna they?" He sat beside her and peered out the window. "Did ye ken Donald often came here in his youth?"

"No."

"Aye, he did. Grandsire, may God rest his soul, believed in testing the mettle of a man, and he spared no one, not even his sons or his grandsons. I remember one tale Father oft told of a winter like this one. Grandsire decided to hunt and took Father with him. A fierce blizzard blew up, so they sought shelter in a cave on those bens." Sandy pointed toward the western end of the loch where a cowl of pearl gray clouds concealed the jagged peaks of the tall snow-covered hills. "Tired from the unrelenting pace Grandsire set, Father mounded snow into a pillow and laid his head upon it. When Grandsire saw him, he lost his temper and smashed the pillow with his foot. He accused Father of turning soft like a woman. For a sennight they would not speak to each other.

"'Tis why Donald sought refuge here. He would give Grandsire time to cool his ire before facing him. Later, after Father was attainted for raising the clan to restore King Jamie to the throne, Donald realized he would succeed Grandsire in the chieftainship. 'Tis a task of great responsibility, as ye well ken, and he did not wish to lead in the manner of those who came before him. 'Tis here where he decided to end the feuding and to better our peoples' lives."

"So his coming here was a way to escape and to rebel?"

"Aye, in a manner of speaking. For which reason do ye come, Rory?"

She knew the priest's question signaled some wisdom he wished to impart, so she waited.

"Your silence surprises me, lass. Rebels oft speak without forethought."

"They do, Father? And do ye ken this because of *your* wild ways?"

He wagged his finger at her. "A rebel who kens when to hold her tongue."

"'Tis a wee lesson I learned long ago. When I dinna answer, folk tend to dislike the silence and thus reveal more than they should."

"So ye use what they say against them?"

"If need be."

"Ye are too young to ken such tactics."

She shrugged. "Circumstance kens no person's age, Father Alex. 'Tis the fool who dinna learn from the experience."

"How true are those words! Unlike ye, though, I did not do the learning when I was your age. I was like a wild beast, ever restless in my wanderings. I fought with the French. I worked our Jamaican estate with my brother Ewen. I frolicked in Rome at King Jamie's court. Yet, peace eluded me until I submitted to God and joined the Jesuits. 'Tis been fifteen years since then and I have never kent such contentment and happiness. Ye dinna possess them, do ye? 'Tis why ye come here as Donald did."

Rory averted her gaze.

When she did not answer, he stood. "Never mind, lass. 'Tis not my way to meddle where I am not wanted. I ken ye will speak of it when it suits." He started for the steps, but snapped his fingers and turned back to face her. "I nearly forgot, Donald sent me to fetch ye."

Since Lochiel had not spoken to her since Hogmanay, she was both surprised and disturbed by the summons. He was aware of her presence, for she had caught him watching her. She had had the uncanny feeling that little escaped his notice. Why did he wish to see her now after all this time? She frowned.

"Do ye ken the story of King Solomon and the two women who claimed to be the mother of the same infant, Rory?"

"Aye."

"My brother is like King Solomon. He considers all sides before pronouncing judgment. He prefers peace, but will use force to settle a dispute, if he must. Ye have nocht to fear from him so long as ye speak the truth."

With Tam at her heels, she descended the staircase to the main floor. Sandy knocked on the library door, then stepped aside to allow her entry.

Sir Donald Cameron of Lochiel, chief of Clan Cameron, sat at his desk, writing. He glanced at her. "I will be with ye in a moment, Rory."

She crossed to the hearth and held her hands in front of the flaming oak logs that crackled in the fireplace. Tam clicked his way across the wooden floor and curled up at her feet. Rory studied the portrait hanging over the mantle. The swarthy young warrior clad in black armor peered down at her with shrewd, piercing eyes. Thick waves of ebony hair dusted his shoulders and a thin cusped mustache crowned his unsmiling lips.

"They say my grandsire could frighten the boldest of enemies with a single glance," Lochiel said, handing her a pewter *cuach* containing whisky.

"He does have a menacing look about him. Duncan says there was one soldier Ewen Dubh did not frighten."

"What did my foster son tell ye?"

"I canna say whether 'tis true or not, for my husband has the gift of the *seanchaidh* when he tells a story. He wove a fearsome tale of how your grandsire ripped out the soldier's throat with his teeth."

"Duncan can spin the tale, Rory, but never doubt him. When he gives his oath, he is steadfast and honorable. The deed he told of Grandsire is true. 'Twas how he escaped with his life."

"'Tis evidence of a quick mind, Sir Donald. I would like to have met Ewen Dubh."

"I would have enjoyed attending such a meeting. He admired the lasses, and ye would be no exception. Though ye are wise, loyal, courageous, and fearless like himself, he would not have tolerated your tendency to stray from a woman's proper place. He loved the hunt, and respected any who bested him. Since I witnessed your skill with the longbow, I believe ye could have done so."

Rory's eyes widened with surprise. She and Duncan had traveled far to make certain they encountered no other person on their hunts. How had they failed to detect this man's presence?

"Dinna fash, lass." Lochiel motioned her toward a chair. "I grew curious by Duncan's frequent disappearances, so I followed him. I did not ken he went to meet ye. I must admit the hunt surprised me, for I thought 'twas a lovers' tryst. What I witnessed astounded me. Ye heard the stag long before ye saw it, but ye did not pursue it. Your eyes tracked the red deer until the moment came to release the arrow. 'Tis a rare talent ye have with the bow and I congratulate ye for bringing down your prey. I canna explain my reasons, but would ye humor an old man and forego further hunts?"

Old man? She saw flecks of silver in Lochiel's fair hair, but did not consider him old. Like Angus, he had survived fifty winters, but the simple elegance of his attire spoke of a gentler life than her foster father had known. Frilled lace cuffs edged the sleeves of his green velvet short coat. The blue, green, and white of his woolen hose matched the sett of his red belted plaid. Large silver buckles adorned brown leather shoes with flat heels.

"Has Duncan not told ye he wed a rebel?"

"He mentioned it." Lochiel winked at her. "If ye remember our last meeting sixteen years ago, I witnessed the rebel for myself. Are ye saying ye willna heed my wishes?"

"Father Alex counseled me to speak the truth, so I will. When I came to Achnacarry, I found servants enough to fetch, clean, and cook. Duncan saw to your affairs while Dr. Archie refused my offer of aid. My hands were idle ones, and that never happened before. When Duncan understood what caused my unhappiness, he asked me to help him. We hunted too, and 'twas good to have a purpose for being again."

"And when I returned home, ye could not help Duncan any longer. By asking ye not to hunt, I make ye feel feckless again."

"Aye. Whether I agree to your request is a moot point. I am a woman and ye forbid us to venture outside."

"Does the rebel intend to obey that edict?"

Rory shrugged, refusing to divulge her intentions.

"If ye disobey, ye ken there will be consequences."

"I have been a rebel most of my life, Sir Donald, and ken there is a price to pay for disobedience."

"Aye, 'twas a lesson ye learned long before ye should have."

He refilled his *cuach,* then offered her more whisky. She shook her head.

"Duncan tells me your word is your bond," he said.

"If I give my promise, I willna break it."

"Then I ask ye again, Rory, will ye forego the hunt?"

"'Tis that important to ye?"

He nodded. "I canna explain my reasons, but assure ye 'tis verra important."

She was curious to know why he asked this of her, but knew he would not divulge his reasons anymore than Angus would.

"Then I willna hunt."

"I thank ye for your promise, and in return, I vow that if my fears dinna bear fruit, I will release ye from the pledge. Now, regarding my affairs."

"Did I err in what I did?"

"Not at all. 'Tis rare to find a lass who has learned her letters. Where did ye get your education?"

"Most of my book learning comes from my uncle. I dinna ken the *Sassenach* tongue as well as Duncan, but I ken the French from my aunt."

Lochiel stroked his chin. "Tell me what ye learned from helping Duncan."

"Ye ken we must end the feuds. There will come a time when the Crown willna stand for it, and ye prefer your kinsmen to change before they are forced to do so. While the soil is more fertile here than in other parts of the Highlands, it dinna yield much. Ye try to change this by introducing new crops. Ye dinna tolerate cattle lifting or collecting the blackmail. To compensate for those lost revenues, ye sell timber for shipbuilding. When the men fell the trees, though, ye make certain the forest will grow anew. What remains of the cuttings is burned into charcoal to fire iron furnaces."

"Ye learn well, Rory. Do ye approve of these changes from the old ways?"

"I dinna ken if ye will succeed in ending the feuds, but I support your attempts. I suppose 'tis why ye allowed my people to travel through Lochaber unmolested, especially when most prefer a dead MacGregor to a live one."

Lochiel sighed. "No matter the clan, there are good and bad men in them all. I believed ye and yours were honorable MacGregors who did not deserve what befell ye. While there are alliances that bind my clan to the Campbells, I do not condone what they did."

"But ye could condone the request Father made of ye."

Lochiel folded his hands together, extending the first finger of each to form a triangle. He propped his elbows on the arms of his chair, rested his fingers against his lips, and studied her. She had not spoken in anger—the passing of time had cooled that fire—but she wanted him to know of her displeasure at his having arranged her life. Other women might not object to such an alliance; in fact, they would expect it. She, however, had lived a far different life from most women.

"Ye canna blame me because Gregor declined to explain our pact."

"What I hold against ye is your decision to honor it. Ye could have forgotten and left us alone."

"No, Rory, I could not. Ye ken a chief must see to the welfare of others. Once we give our word, honor demands that we see the promise through. I thought of the wee lass, and kent I could not let her suffer more than she already had. 'Twas within my power to offer her a new life, free of fashing whether she would see the sun rise on another day. Canna ye understand that?"

"'Twas why I agreed to wed Duncan. As chieftain I could not deprive my people of the gift ye offered them. Whether 'twas my wish to marry your foster son or not did not matter."

Lochiel released a long breath. "When I sent Duncan, I did not ken ye were chieftain. I was a wee surprised when he told me this because 'tis men who hold that rank. Then I remembered the fiery and determined lass I had met and kent ye possessed the makings of a leader. I agreed to your father's wishes and acted on them because of ye."

"Me?"

"Ye were wee, but fierce and bold. Ye accepted my gift of a hound of the chiefs, though ye feared him. By trusting a stranger, ye showed the kenning to do what is right."

Her anger flared. "Though he be of Campbell blood?"

Lochiel winced. "He told ye."

"How could ye send my enemy to wed me? 'Twas not what Father wanted."

"Duncan is no more Campbell than ye are. He is Cameron and 'tis to me he pledges his allegiance. As for your father's wishes of who ye should wed, he left the choosing to me. Canna ye trust me now and believe that Duncan and ye are meant to be husband and wife?"

Rory walked across the room and gazed out the window without seeing the landscape before her. Her Two Sights had revealed that she was fated to marry Duncan. What they had not shown was the pain and discord such a union would bring.

"Did ye think I would not learn of it? Duncan is a man who values truth. He confessed, though he kent how I would feel. 'Tis why we altered the pledge between my father and ye. I willna explain the events that led to the bond Duncan gave, but ye have the right to ken what it entails because ye are his chief."

"I am listening, Rory."

"The law willna allow a MacGregor the holy sacraments. We exchanged promises at a handfasting."

She saw understanding dawn in the Cameron's eyes. "Then ye intend to leave him?"

"I do."

"And if ye bear him a son or daughter, willna ye change your mind? If ye declare the marriage ended, the babe must remain with Duncan."

"I ken the rules of handfasting, Sir Donald. Before I agreed to the union, I set one condition before Duncan. 'Twas his choice to agree or refuse. Since I am here, ye will ken he accepted it."

"Tell me," he said with a hint of sadness in his tone.

"Duncan promised we will have no bairn."

Lochiel closed his eyes. While Rory knew she disappointed him, she felt it necessary that he understand why she had given her consent. This time she had won the confrontation, but garnered no joy from that knowledge.

~*~

Rory smiled when she saw the cloudless blue sky and brilliant gold sun. Her wait had ended. She sneaked down the stairs and eased open the door. She peered out, but saw no one to prevent her escape. Without a backward glance, she hurried around Achnacarry and through the garden to the frozen river. Sunlight shimmered on crystals of ice coating the rocks near the water's edge.

"I see ye continue to disobey your elders, *m'eudail.*"

She whirled. Duncan stood a short distance away, his hands clasped behind his back. His devilish grin made her suspicious.

She took a step backward. "And how did ye reach that conclusion?"

"Ye ken Sir Donald forbade ye to come outside. I suppose ye have good reason to disobey him."

Duncan took a step toward her. Her senses warned her not to allow the distance separating them to lessen. She backed up a step. He inched closer, but she maintained an equal distance from him.

"'Tis a rule meant to be broken unless I am a prisoner and Achnacarry is my jail. Is that what I am, Duncan?"

"Ye are not a prisoner, Rory, as ye well ken. Ye should have asked permission before ye came here."

"And risk denial?" She shook her head. "No, Duncan. To do so would warn him of my intent and he would order ye to stop me. Once I could have slipped away without anyone seeing me go. Idleness dulls my nimbleness, else ye would not have discovered my absence."

"'Twas coincidence, *m'eudail,* not the blunting of your skills. I rounded the corner as ye ducked out the door, so I followed to see where ye might go."

"Am I to be punished then?"

"Sir Donald will forgive this wee transgression. I, on the other hand, am your husband and canna allow ye to disobey our chief at your whim. Ye must be punished."

She was about to tell him what he could do with his punishment when she noticed he no longer held his hands behind his back. Instead, he held them in plain sight, tossing a snowball from one hand to the other. She ran. Snow tugged at her skirts, slowing her.

"Run all ye like, *m'eudail.* Ye canna escape. Sooner or later ye must accept your fate."

The snowball hit her shoulder. She stumbled and fell facedown in the snow, her hand beneath her. She clawed for a fistful of snow before ceasing all movement.

"Rory?"

She kept silent and still.

"Rory?"

She heard concern in Duncan's voice. She heard him trudge toward her. He knelt, blocking the sun's warmth. When he turned her over, she stuffed the handful of snow down his shirt. He growled and jumped about to dislodge the cold, wet mass. She scrambled away, laughing.

"So, ye wish to play, do ye, *m'eudail?*"

She dodged another snowball then stooped to make one of her own. Before she threw it, another hit her skirt. She hit him square in the chest. They attacked each other with equal fervor in an attempt to outdo each other. Before long Rory was damp and weary.

She sank to her knees. "Och, Duncan, I give up! Ye win this time."

He dropped his projectile and lifted her to her feet. He brushed snow from her hair.

"Duncan!"

The shout came from the river. Rory turned with him to see who called. Seven men stood on the ice. One waved.

"Aye, Fergus. What are ye wanting?"

A towering man with flaxen hair said, "If ye have strength left after that fierce battle, we are a man short for the curling. Will ye join us?"

"I think I can find the strength. Do ye mind, Rory?"

She shook her head.

"The match may go on for hours. If ye get cold, promise ye will return to the house. I dinna want ye to fall ill."

"I promise."

He stepped onto the slick black ice.

"Duncan?"

"Aye?"

"Good luck."

He winked, then joined the others. Fergus drove an iron rod into the thick ice. Another man scratched a circle around it with his dirk. Once completed, the men divided themselves into two teams of four men each. Duncan examined an assortment of heavy irregular-shaped granite stones with iron handles affixed to them. He selected two, then picked a scraggly bundle of twigs fashioned into a broom. He and his teammates huddled together to discuss strategy. With a loud shout, they separated and took up their positions.

Duncan aimed a stone at the house, the center of the circle where the iron rod protruded from the ice. When he released it, the spinning stone sailed across the frozen surface. His teammates skated ahead, brushing the ice to make it faster while exercising care not to touch besoms to stone. It came to rest just inside the circle's edge.

The other team took its turn, following the same procedure. Their stone bumped Duncan's farther from the center of the circle. The game continued in this manner, each team trying to knock the other's stones from the circle while putting theirs closest to the iron rod. The stones hummed across the ice. The men shouted taunts to each other.

Rory jumped to keep warm, cheering for Duncan's team and hissing at the other one. She shouted until her throat felt raw and her voice was no louder than a whisper. In spite of her antics, the cold seeped into her bones. She shivered. The time had come to keep her promise. With a reluctant sigh, she headed back to Achnacarry.

When she reached the room she shared with Duncan, she found a tub of steaming water and a roaring fire. She discarded her wet clothes, stepped into the bath, and savored the warmth. After drying her long tresses at the hearth, she yawned. Unable to keep her eyes open, she rested her head on her arm while the fire's heat lulled her to sleep.

A slamming door startled Rory awake. She stretched and rubbed her eyes. Duncan towered over her, his legs braced apart and his arms held stiff at his sides. He clenched his fists so tight his knuckles turned white. A scowl marred his face and his dark eyes gleamed with anger. She shrank back, but the unyielding bench prevented her retreat.

"What did ye say to Lochiel, Rory?"

Duncan's cold tone sliced through her like the honed blade of a sword. She tried to fathom the reason for his anger, but his question made no sense.

"I said nocht at all. I have not seen him. Why are ye angry, Duncan? What have I done?"

"Lochiel said he spoke with ye two days ago. Now, tell me what ye said to him."

"I did not—" She stopped, recalling her exact words. *I ken the rules of handfasting, Sir Donald. Before I agreed to the union, I set one condition before Duncan. 'Twas his choice to agree or refuse. Since I am here, ye will ken he accepted it.* She could understand if she had angered Lochiel, but why did her revelation rile Duncan?

"I asked a question, Rory Cameron, and I demand an answer!"

She felt the first stirrings of her own temper, but fought to control it. She counted to ten, refusing to attack him as he did her. "If ye canna speak with a civil tongue, I have nocht to say to ye."

Duncan wrenched her to her feet.

"Take your hands off me!"

Without warning, he complied. She stumbled, clipping her ribs on the sharp corner of the bench. The stabbing pain knocked the breath from her. She clutched her side and collapsed. Duncan reached for her, but she kicked him. He sat on the bench and dragged her onto his lap. He tried to wipe her tears, but she slapped away his hand.

"Please, Rory. I did not mean to hurt ye. 'Twas an accident."

The anguish in his voice drew her eyes to his. Moist with unshed tears, they mirrored her pain. Her anger dissolved.

"Ye affect me to extremes, Rory."

She smiled. "'Tis the rebel's way."

He returned her smile, then sobered. "I am sorry for hurting ye, *m'eudail.*"

"I ken." She felt the dampness of his plaid through hers and stood. "'Tis time to shed what ye wear. The water has cooled, but ye are welcome to bathe before I call to have it removed."

Without a second urging, he began to disrobe. She busied herself elsewhere until she heard him settle into the tub.

"Duncan, what riled ye so? It canna be what I said to Lochiel, for I told him nocht that ye dinna already ken."

"He ordered me from Achnacarry. I am to return home."

Confused, she turned to look at him. "I thought Achnacarry was your home."

"'Tis when I am with Sir Donald, but I have a cottage not far from where we left Jamie and Malcolm. I seldom have the chance to go there."

"But why does Lochiel say ye must leave?"

"He is after ordering me to take ye there. I canna return to Achnacarry until ye change your mind."

Duncan's words angered Rory. Lochiel might be the Pope himself, but she would not bend to his wishes in this matter nor should he punish Duncan for the promise she had extracted. A MacGregor chieftain took her own punishment. She did not hide behind the coattails of another. This chief deserved to be taught a lesson, and she knew just where to find him.

"Change your mind about what, Rory?"

She heard Duncan's question, but was already heading for the stairs. When he realized she was no longer in the room, he would pursue her so she did not have much time to carry out her plan. Outside the gathering room, she halted for a moment to listen for Duncan's footfalls. When she did not hear them, she burst through the double oak doors.

Her quarry sat in a high-backed chair near the hearth. In one fluid motion, she extracted a *sgian* from the folds of her plaid and threw it. The whistling blade drew the guards' attention, and those in the room fell silent. The dull thud of steel hitting wood echoed in the silence.

The door crashed open, breaking the spell. Men drew their dirks and rushed her, but someone grabbed her from behind. "Halt! She is my wife and I claim the right to bring her to judgment."

One by one the guards sheathed their weapons. Peals of laughter resounded through the room. Surprised, Rory and the others looked toward the hearth.

"She put the blade less than an inch from your right ear, Donald!" Sandy slapped the arm of his chair. He turned to a middle-aged man with prematurely gray hair. "I fear he beats ye again, brother."

"All right, Donald, ye win the wager," Archibald Cameron said, his blue eyes twinkling with amusement.

"Aye, Archie, and I expect ye to supply the promised whisky." Lochiel extracted the *sgian* from the wood and traced the intricate carvings in the red bog oak hilt. He flipped the knife so he held it by the blade. "I believe this belongs to ye, Rory. Duncan, release her. Had she intended to slay me, I would be dead. She kent where the *sgian* would land."

Her husband did as commanded, but stayed close at her side. Her eyes traced the path of a glistening bead of water that slid from his wet hair down his bare chest and disappeared under the carelessly wrapped plaid around his waist. The flush of heat that crept up her neck caused her to refocus her wandering gaze on the *sgian* Lochiel handed her. Unable to hold her tongue, she lashed out at him. "I thought ye a fair and honest man, Sir Donald, but I was wrong. Ye punish Duncan because of me. If ye think to change my mind because of this, ye are mistaken. I ken my rights and I willna allow ye to sway me from my chosen course."

"Like a Highland wildcat ye are, lass, fierce and fearless." Sandy stroked his smooth chin. "I am glad 'tis yourself, Donald, who feels her claws."

Rory glared at the priest. She was in no mood for his teasing. Serious business was at hand. She considered giving a retort, but Lochiel held up his hand to stop her.

"Pay no heed to Sandy. I assure ye, Rory, what I do is not to punish Duncan. He has done nocht wrong. I ken he loves ye, and perhaps the day will come when ye will return his love."

"Then why banish him from your home? Ye told him he could not return unless I change my mind."

"To test ye."

Understanding dawned. He had told Duncan what he did to see how she would react. Again, her temper seethed. She opened her mouth, but Lochiel silenced her.

"Ye are a rare lass, Rory. Ye have the right to be angry, but I have my reasons for what I do. I ask for your trust in this, for I canna divulge them to ye at this time. I would also make another request."

For the second time in two days, he asked for her trust without offering explanations. She wondered if the requests were linked in some way and if she would ever learn the reasons behind them.

"What would ye have me do, Sir Donald?"

"Go to Duncan's home. There, ye will have the freedom ye seek. I also believe ye will have plenty of work for those idle hands ye spoke of. While ye are gone from Achnacarry, explore all of Lochaber and the Cameron lands. Meet your new kinsmen. Learn how they live and what they think. Duncan will ride with ye. If ye have questions, he can answer them. 'Tis mid-March. At summer's end return to Achnacarry and tell me all ye have learned. Then I will explain why I ask ye to go now."

Her frustration was so great Rory knew she would agree. Away from Achnacarry she would prepare their meals, mend their clothes, clean the house, gather her herbs, and tend to any other needs they had. She might also have the opportunity to visit with her brothers and their families whom she missed.

"If Duncan dinna object, I will do your bidding."

"If we stay, Sir Donald, I dinna want the responsibility should my wife decide to aim truer."

Lochiel and his brothers roared with laughter. Rory shook her head, certain the whole family had gone mad.

CHAPTER TEN
NEW FRIENDS

Wind gusts whirled powdery snow across the rippled ice on Loch Arkaig. The frozen crystals shimmered like diamonds in the bright sunlight. Midnight shook its mane and snorted, spewing white vapor into the air. The image of a winged dragon expelling fiery breath popped into Rory's thoughts. She rubbed her arms, wishing she had the fire to warm her, while Duncan tied down the last bundle of supplies.

"Are ye ready to leave, *m'eudail?*" he asked.

She nodded. He mounted Midnight, then lifted her in front of him and enfolded her within his great cape. Heat radiated from his chest and arms, swathing her in a silky cocoon of warmth. He tightened his hold on her and spurred Midnight forward. They followed the narrow winding loch for six miles, then headed northwest into the hills.

"Did we not come this way when ye brought me to Achnacarry?" she asked.

"'Tis so."

"How far is your home from Jamie and Malcolm?"

"The eagle flies there directly, but we must travel several hours to reach them. The cottage lies in a corrie halfway up a ben. To get to your brothers, ye descend the ben for a ways, then climb another till ye reach the lochan where they live."

"How many families live in your *clachan?*"

"'Tis just the cottage and a wee byre for Midnight, Rory. The *clachan* where your brothers live lies closest to the corrie."

"Why did ye choose so isolated a spot? Is it not dangerous?"

"'Twas not I who did the choosing. Grandsire brought Grandmother there after reiving her from her parents."

"Are ye telling me your grandsire kidnapped your grandmother and forced her to wed him?"

Duncan chuckled. "I dinna believe she objected since Father was born seven months after they took their vows."

"Then why did your grandsire not ask permission to wed her?"

"Grandmother was not of Clan Cameron. She was a Macintosh lass, and for over 350 years her clan fought the Camerons in the bloodiest feud in all the Highlands over ownership of the Disputed Lands. Although Macintosh and Ewen Dubh ended the dispute thirteen years before my grandparents met, bitter memories lingered in the minds of both clans. Grandmother's father hated all Camerons because he lost many kinsmen in the feuding, including two sons. He vowed to slay any he encountered, so 'twould do no good to ask for his blessing.

"Suspicioning pursuit from her kinsmen, Grandsire searched for a spot that provided a good view of the land below and where no one else lived. Thus, few would know where they hid and they would have warning of any who approached."

"Did your grandmother's father come after her?"

"Grandsire suspected Ewen Dubh and Macintosh intervened to prevent a rekindling of the feud. The year after Father's birth word reached Grandmother that her father had disavowed her. No one, not even her mother or sisters, were ever to speak her name. 'Twas as if she had never been born." Duncan reined Midnight to a halt at the crest of a hollow.

Nestled amongst the blue-green firs was a small white cottage with a byre attached. Whispers of smoke curled up from the chimneys at either end of the stone and wood structure. Shuttered windows flanked a sturdy door to the right of which lay the *clach an t'seabhdail,* a turf-covered boulder where weary travelers could rest.

"That is the cottage your grandsire built?"

"Fire destroyed that one. Lochiel ordered this one built after Father saved his life during a hunt. When my parents died, he gave it to me in exchange for a yearly rent, though he waives the ferme while I guard him."

He guided Midnight down the steep track leading to the cottage. As he helped Rory alight, the door opened and a plump woman emerged. Wisps of hair escaped the thick plait of silver hair draped over her shoulder. Deep creases etched the corners of her red lips and violet eyes. "Duncan!"

He swooped the old woman up in his arms.

"Och, lad! Put me down. I am too old for such foolery." When she regained her feet, she straightened her shawl and smoothed her skirt. "Ye never brought home a lass before, Grandson. Did ye do the Cameron's bidding and wed?"

"Aye, Grandmother. I would like ye to meet Rory."

Rory stepped forward and curtseyed. "I am pleased to—"

"Dinna be curtseying to me, lass," the old woman said. "I am your elder, not your better. Since ye dinna wear the *bréid,* I can see ye are a lass after my own heart. Did ye have much trouble convincing Duncan of your decision? No matter, I am happy to meet ye, Rory. I have waited a long time to see my grandson wed. Ye may call me Nannag or Grandmother."

The whirlwind of words spewing from Nannag made Rory dizzy. While the woman had lived for eighty years, time had not slowed her. There was nothing wrong with her eyesight either. Rory was certain she would enjoy getting to know this woman. She yearned to call her "Grandmother," for she had never known her own grandparents, but Nannag's forthrightness and the temporal union with Duncan advised against it.

"I am pleased to make your acquaintance, Nannag."

"Come along, Rory, 'tis too cold and my bones are too old to be standing out here. Duncan, see to Midnight." Nannag slipped her arm around Rory's and led her inside. The instant the door closed, Duncan's grandmother resumed speaking. "'Tis not so grand a house as Achnacarry, but 'tis cozy nonetheless. The ladder leads to the loft where Duncan and his brother slept. Do ye ken of Tòmas?"

"Duncan told me when he gave me Tòmas' *sgian* on Michaelmas."

"If my grandson gave ye what he treasured most, then ye are a rare lass indeed."

"'Tis exactly what she is, Grandmother," Duncan said, entering the cottage. "Mayhap one day she will tell ye how we met. Had the fates not revealed to her what they did, I might well be dead."

Nannag reached out to stroke Rory's cheek. The gnarled finger felt warm against her cold skin.

"Though I ken ye might think it a curse, I am grateful for your Two Sights. I dinna ken what I would do if I lost my Duncan." Without warning, Nannag pulled aside a curtain at the rear of the alcove to reveal a wooden shelf. "'Tis a bed for visitors who stay the night, though there are few who visit. Last week when William came to check on me, he brought along two delightful lads, Jamie and his nephew."

"Ye saw Jamie and Connor?" Rory asked, eager for news, but sorry to have missed seeing them.

"Aye. The lad told me a tale of Duncan of Snow. Said he got the name from my grandson."

Duncan smiled. "Connor and the other bairns built a man of snow and dubbed him Duncan of Snow because of the coat of white I acquired during a blizzard. Ye must tell Rory how he and Jamie fare. His father and Jamie are Rory's foster brothers."

"They do well. 'Twas a delight to have someone to cook for and to have a wee lad about the place. This door leads to my room. Duncan will show ye the other soon enough, my dear." Nannag patted Rory's arm. "Come warm yourselves by the fire."

With her head spinning from the rapid changes in conversation, Rory followed Nannag into the kitchen and gathering room. Wooden benches with high backs and curved arms framed either side of the stone hearth. A table and several small kists for storing meal and other food occupied the center of the kitchen area. Along one wall a rack held mixing bowls, plates, and several wooden bowl-like drinking cups. A knocking stone and wooden mallet for beating oats lay beside the hearth. A milk cog and butter churn were in one corner. Baskets of various sizes hung from the rafters. Two wooden pails were beside the door.

While she warmed her hands over the fire, Rory noticed a *cuach* of light and dark wooden staves fastened together with cane on the mantel. She picked up the cup to admire its fine workmanship. Encased between the two pieces of glass that formed the base was a lock of black hair.

"'Tis beautiful."

Nannag came to stand beside her. "I gave it to my husband a year and a day after we said our vows. When my son wed, his father gave it to him. 'Tis Duncan's now, and one day he will use it to toast his love for ye, Granddaughter."

The revelation was delivered with subtle grace. Had she paid less attention to Nannag's words, Rory might have missed the silent message. Like Duncan and herself, Nannag and her husband had wedded by handfasting. This meant Duncan's grandmother knew she was a MacGregor. Nannag seemed to accept this fact, and hoped things would work out between her and her grandson.

"Duncan?"

"Aye, Grandmother?"

"Have ye given your wife what is her due?"

He frowned. Nannag rolled her eyes.

"'Tis your house, Duncan, and Rory is your wife."

"No, Grandmother. We just arrived, and I could not give her what I did not have." He stooped by the peat fire and retrieved a pair of jointed iron tongs. "Rory, I welcome ye to my house. My cottage is also yours, and this gift is but a wee token of my love."

She understood the intent of the gift and was reluctant to accept it. By taking possession of the tongs, she agreed to be mistress of his house.

With Nannag watching, however, she could not refuse. To do so would reveal the truth of their marriage. As he had not shamed her on their wedding night, she could not shame him in front of his grandmother.

Nannag clapped her hands. "Welcome, Granddaughter, to your new home. I hope ye willna mind my presence, and if ever I am in your way, ye must speak of it. Now, while I prepare the meal, Duncan can be after showing ye your room."

With equal reluctance, Rory ventured into the sleeping room. To the right of the hearthstone was a loom for weaving. She stared at the paneled box bed in the opposite corner, wondering if she dare extricate herself from the sleeping arrangements on which Duncan insisted. To lie beside him was difficult enough, but to do so in such close quarters could fray what remained of the taut control she strove to maintain. And what of him? He played with fire, skirting the edges of the flame while holding to his promise. If they slept within the box bed....

"There is no escape, Rory, and I willna tolerate your defying me again."

She jumped at the words whispered in her ear. The hand on her shoulder kept her from stepping away from him.

"If I choose to sleep on the floor, ye canna stop me, Duncan Cameron."

"Aye, I can. If ye dinna believe me, think back to our first week together at Achnacarry. Every night ye lain by the hearth, and just before ye drifted off to sleep, I picked ye up and dumped ye on the bed. I guarantee this bed is not so soft."

Rory bit her lip, remembering the constant battle they had waged. Once she ceased defying him, he stopped pinning her against him. She had no desire to renew the struggle, and truth be told, was thankful for his presence. The extra warmth warded off the bitter chill of long winter nights. She faced him. "I have no intention of altering our sleeping arrangements if ye honor your promise and dinna touch me."

He folded his arms across his chest and leaned against the wall. "If memory serves me, Rory Cameron, the promise I gave was that I not be after consummating our marriage. Nocht was said about touching ye."

"'Tis fire ye play with!"

"If I wish to have ye, ye canna stop me, but after all this time ye must realize I willna break my oath."

She cast down her eyes, feeling ashamed of her doubt.

He nudged her chin until her gaze met his. "Before all else, Rory, ye are my friend. I love ye with all my heart and willna force ye to seal our vows, but I never swore not to try to change your mind. I pray one day ye open your heart to me. If that is not to be, then at least let us part friends. Ye must live as my wife for seven more months. During that time, I will treat ye as a husband should treat his wife. 'Tis why I gave ye the tongs. While here, ye are the mistress of this house."

~*~

A sennight after their arrival, Duncan decided it was time to carry out Sir Donald's wishes. They traveled the length and breadth of Cameron lands from Loch Quoich in the north to Loch Eil and Loch Leven in the south, from Glen Pean in the west to Carn Dearg and Glen Gloy in the east.

Rory met Camerons, MacSorlies, MacMillans, Macphees, MacLachlans, MacMartins, Macgillonies, MacMasters, and Cummings, all of whom followed Lochiel. Wherever she went, people welcomed her. She was touched by their generosity, for even those who had little enough for themselves shared their food and hearth. These cherished offerings were rare gifts that erased earlier memories of barred doors, threatening insults, and derisive rudeness that greeted a MacGregor.

She learned when to be forthright and when to hold her tongue. Where men accepted her as Lochiel's emissary, she listened to their thoughts, their wisdom, and their criticisms. Where men held with tradition, she garnered information from their wives while helping with their work. Always, Duncan stood beside her, offering advice when asked and counsel when needed.

He introduced her to men deputized by Lochiel to render judgments against criminal or thief. Alexander Cameron of Glennevis, leader of the MacSorlies, sided with the Camerons whenever he deemed it best for his clansmen. He made a good ally, but Rory concluded she should watch him with a wary eye. Allan of Callart was descended from the younger grandson of Donald Dubh, the first chief of the clan. Although loyal to Lochiel, he would first protect himself and his own in a fight. Donald of Clunes held a large tack of land near Achnacarry with a grand view of the austere and majestic Ben Nevis. Old Clunes was a leal kinsman who had known Ewen Dubh, as well as Lochiel and his father.

The others Rory met had stronger ties to Sir Donald—those of blood and marriage. Alexander of Dungallon was a grandson of Ewen Dubh and cousin to Lochiel. His sister, Jean, was Dr. Archie's wife. John Cameron of Fassifern was Sir Donald's brother. Whenever Lochiel traveled, John served as chief. A cautious and prudent man, he wasted no time on sentimentality. Common sense ruled him, and although loyal to his family, he never involved himself in the intrigues that had resulted in his father's exile. His business acumen provided him the financial means to secure his family's future and to loan money to his older brother for his improvement projects.

Lochiel's uncle, Ludovic, lived in Torcastle, the former home of the Cameron chiefs. He was the son of Ewen Dubh and his third wife, and therefore half-brother to John, Sir Donald's father. He prized honor but followed his conscience, adhering to the old ways by demanding the blackmail or reiving the cattle, even though this put him in direct opposition with his nephew. He was polite, but made it clear that he despised wives who meddled in the affairs of men, and distrusted husbands who permitted it.

Dr. Archie, whom Rory had already met, welcomed her to his tack in the hills north of Loch Arkaig and introduced her to his wife and four sons. He lived by his faith, thinking of others first and treating friend and foe alike.

By the time she and Duncan bid him farewell, they had crisscrossed Cameron lands for five weeks. She longed for the solitude of the corrie where she would have time to assess the importance of all she had learned. She was also eager to see Nannag.

"Are ye certain this is the way to the corrie, Duncan? Though it be night, I canna locate one of the landmarks ye pointed out on our way to Glendessary."

"And here I thought ye were after trusting me!"

She thought to give a retort until she felt his chest muscles ripple with amusement. She jabbed his ribs with her elbow.

"Ye wound me!"

"And I will again, if ye dinna cease. This is not the way to the cottage. Where are we?"

"Ye have the eyes of a wildcat, *m'eudail,* so dinna be telling me your instincts have dulled."

His praise pleased her. The constant visiting and assessing of each situation had honed her wits anew until she saw and heard what most did not.

"We dinna return home then?"

"I have business to attend to for Sir Donald. Once 'tis done, I promise we will go home to stay for a time."

Rory sighed in disappointment, but did not complain. Duncan's insight and assistance had proven invaluable during their many visits. He probably missed the cottage and his grandmother more than she did.

They followed a rough overgrown track for another hour. Jagged peaks rose around them like pointed teeth. The moon seemed to bounce from one *sgòrr* to the next as if being swallowed whole by a twisting serpent. They stopped at a stream to refresh themselves and let Midnight drink. When they resumed their journey, Duncan followed the water's edge. The farther northeast they rode, the wider the stream grew and the greener the land became.

She discerned the outlines of clustered buildings that soon became thatched hovels that edged the lower rim of a lochan. The lapping water and the clatter of Midnight's hoofs echoed through the sleeping *clachan*. Duncan alighted in front of one stone hovel. Shuttered windows and a closed door greeted him.

"Are ye in?" he shouted, pounding on the door. "Open up in there."

Rory wondered what the occupants thought of a stranger rousing them from their sleep in the middle of the night. Had it been herself, she would answer with sword drawn.

The door swung open and the silhouette of a man barred the entrance. In the darkness, Rory could not make out any distinctive features, but could tell he was broad-shouldered with short massive legs. When she heard his unintelligible growl, she knew where Duncan had brought her.

"Malcolm!"

"Rory?"

She slid from the stallion, and flung herself at her foster brother. He gathered her close and hugged her with the gentleness of a mother bear tending her cub.

"Take her inside, Malcolm," Duncan said. "I must tend to Midnight."

~*~

With the first rays of dawn the rooster crowed, awakening the *clachan*. Rory uncurled herself and stretched. "'Tis morning, Duncan. We promised to help with the peat cutting."

He groaned and rolled onto his back.

After their morning ablutions and a meal of oatcakes, they joined the others. Rory noted how MacGregors and Camerons greeted each other, exchanging news and gossip or giving opinions on numerous subjects. Since her last visit, they had completed thatching and repairing the abandoned hovels. Red buds blanketed the trees. Flower blossoms peeked through dried leaves. An air of hope and life—rather than the despair and death she had sensed before—permeated the *clachan* and its inhabitants.

Within the hour they arrived at the bog, eager to start the day's work that would provide fuel during the coming year. The men waded into the mire and began to skim the top of the peat with their spades. When they finished, they divided into teams of two. Since Malcolm paired with Duncan, Rory joined Fiona on the bank above. Her brother sank a small flat blade with a flanged side into the peat, working the wooden haft to cut the soft block which Duncan lifted onto the bank for her and Fiona to spread under the sun to dry. Connor and his siblings helped them. After an hour, Malcolm and Duncan switched tasks.

When the sun reached its zenith, the work halted. Rory's arms and back ached from the constant lifting and bending. With hands on her hips, she leaned back, then to each side. Nearby, the youngest children, who went naked to spare their few clothes from the filth, chased each other around the drying peat.

"Ye are quite a sight, *m'eudail*. Dirt covers ye from head to toes," Duncan said, joining her. He nodded toward the squealing and laughing children. "Perhaps ye should follow their example and work naked."

"Before ye start offering advice, heed it yourself." She swatted the backside of his plaid to brush away peat.

He laughed. "I suppose I deserved that. Shall I pay ye the same compliment?"

"Dinna even think about laying a hand on me, Duncan Cameron."

He clutched his chest and staggered backward. "How could ye think ill of me, *m'eudail?* I never even considered it."

"And the trees have leaves the color of your twinkling eyes."

"To be sure, wife, to be sure. Would ye be needing help with your bathing later this evening? I would be—" He broke off abruptly.

One glance told her she no longer held his attention. Instead he studied something on the hill behind her. Curious, she turned.

Half a dozen armed men stood on the ridge, swords drawn, targes at the ready. Rory stiffened, remembering the Campbells who had charged over a hill and slaughtered her mother. Duncan placed himself in front of her, shielding her with his body. If these men attacked, he would sacrifice his life to save hers.

The chatter ceased. Women gathered children to them, while men formed a protective arc in front. Like Duncan, they stood at the ready with hands on dirks. A few retrieved shovels or peat cutters and waved them menacingly.

The leader of the intruders appeared to be a strapping man of average height. He sheathed his sword and slung his targe over his shoulder. The others imitated his gesture. Then the man raised his bonnet and waved it over his head. Even from this distance Rory could see the flaming red hair that covered his head and face. Duncan relaxed his stance. "'Tis all right," he said. "I ken him. He is of our clan."

With wariness, the men from the *clachan* lowered their weapons and tools. Duncan returned the stranger's greeting and headed toward him. When Rory saw her husband grab him in a bear-like hug and clap his back, she deemed it safe to approach. She had a fair idea who the man was, and wanted her curiosity satisfied.

The stranger, whose face was stained brown from constant exposure to peat smoke, noticed her first. With a twinkle in his green eyes, he asked, "And who is this bonny lass?"

Duncan put a protective hand on her shoulder. "Rory is my wife. I trust ye will remember that, else I shall speak of it with Morna, and ye ken what her father will do to ye."

"Aye, I do. He warned me about my wandering eye. Said if he dinna slit my throat, I willna be leaving the house until the bruises heal. I have no wish to test him."

Rory heard the hint of humor in his voice, but the brightness of his eyes dimmed and she suspected there was an element of truth to his words.

"Ye must be Red Pàdraig. My husband has spoken of ye."

"Right ye are, lass."

"What brings ye here?" Duncan asked.

"I heard ye traveled the braes and bens on Lochiel's business. Since I desired to meet your bride and ye had not yet visited us, I thought to invite ye to celebrate Beltane. Will ye honor us with your presence?"

"At the moment we visit Rory's brothers. When we finish the peat cutting, I promised we would return home. We have not seen Nannag in awhile."

Rory tapped Duncan's arm. "If ye wish to visit with Red Pàdraig and his wife, 'tis all right. William can send word to Nannag and see that she wants for nocht until our return."

"Then ye will come?" Pàdraig asked.

"Aye, after the peat cutting. Will ye and the others share our meal before ye return home?"

A nod sent Rory off to prepare for the extra mouths to feed. As she left, she heard Duncan ask, "Why the weapons, Pàdraig? Ye were prepared to attack." She did not hear the response, but wished she had. She had wondered the same and would like to have known the answer.

When Rory saw how far they traveled to reach the *clachan* where Red Pàdraig and Morna lived, she was surprised. It lay almost on the western boundary that bordered land belonging to Clanranald. What had Duncan's friend and the others been doing in the Disputed Lands? She doubted they had come searching for Duncan, especially since they initially suspected danger when they encountered the peat cutters. Although she wondered about this, she refrained from asking Duncan. He seemed preoccupied with concerns of his own.

He reined Midnight to a stop along a stream where the stallion trotted over to drink the cool mountain water. Duncan also drank, then cupped his hands and offered some to Rory. After drying his hands on his plaid, he led her to a grassy spot shaded by a tall oak. Tam, who had been off chasing rabbits, burst from the trees and bounded over to her.

She patted the earth and the hound settled beside her. "What fashes ye?"

Duncan jerked his head as if startled to find her near. "Huh?"

"Your thoughts are somewhere else today. Do they concern Pàdraig?"

He rubbed his hand over his mouth and chin. "Aye."

"What was he doing near the bog? 'Tis a far distance to travel to see ye. And if he came to visit a friend, then why was he armed to fight?"

"They were reiving."

"Against Lochiel's orders?"

"Aye."

"What will happen if he catches them?"

Duncan shrugged. "'Tis hard to say. He willna tolerate it. They misjudge him if they think otherwise. Whatever punishment he metes out, 'twill be swift and harsh to teach others a lesson."

"Will ye inform Sir Donald of their reiving?"

"No, but I warned them I could not hold my tongue if I learned of it again. Pàdraig is a friend, but I swore allegiance to Lochiel. My loyalties must be to him first."

Rory smiled. "Ye would not have come to the MacGregor *clachan* otherwise. What else distresses ye?"

"Did ye not notice the clover stuck in their bonnets or the red thread tied to their belts?"

"Aye, I saw. They ward off evil and protect them from witches."

"Pàdraig also watched ye and Tam. He asked many questions trying to discover who ye are and from whence ye came."

"How did ye answer him?"

"I said ye lived with the Mackenzies where your family fished the sea."

"Did he believe ye?"

"Not completely. I overheard him ask William what he kent of ye, but he learned nocht else."

"Ye seemed surprised by what he did and what he wore. Why?"

"I met Pàdraig while I fostered with Sir Donald and he with his uncle who worked in the stables. Since we were of an age, we became friends, and later, I arranged for his marriage to Morna."

"I remember the tale ye told of it. 'Twas not an experience ye ever wished to repeat, is that not what ye told my brothers?"

"Aye." A smile formed on his lips. He pointed a finger at her. "Ye distract me, *m'eudail.* How can I warn ye, if ye willna heed what I say?"

"I am listening. I assume Pàdraig was not one to tarry over superstitious charms."

"Ye deduce right."

"Since he asked all manner of questions, I also assume he is curious about those he dinna ken."

Duncan nodded. "Pàdraig watched ye while he helped Malcolm and me. Once or twice he frowned with disapproval when ye helped William with the cutting."

"He is like Ludovic of Torcastle, is he not?"

"Aye. A wife tends to her work and should not cross into the world of men."

"Tam follows me wherever I go whether I am in the fields or under a roof. If Pàdraig learns I am of Clan Gregor and not Mackenzie, coupled with Tam and my penchant for not minding my place, he may—"

"Think ye a witch," Duncan finished for her. "Since he did not hold with superstitions before, then I assume 'tis a fear he acquired after wedding Morna. If I am right, the others in their *clachan* must also believe as he does."

"'Tis a fair assumption." Rory petted the hound, which wagged its long curved tail. "What do ye think, Tam? Are ye the devil?"

"Rory!"

She looked at Duncan, and saw fear in his eyes. "Dinna fash so. I will come to no harm."

He snatched her hands in his and held them to his chest.

"What if he shares his suspicions with the others? I canna protect ye against a mob."

His words brought to mind the story of the old woman he had seen tortured and killed because people thought her a witch. Rory suspected those memories fueled his foreboding.

"Duncan, listen to me." She waited until she held his gaze before continuing. "I dinna fear death. Being a MacGregor cured me of that. I will do nocht to raise Pàdraig's suspicions. I ken the strikes against me— my birth, the Two Sights, my healing powers, and Tam—and promise to take extra caution whilst we visit."

"I fash like a foolish old woman about what I am powerless to change."

"I like kenning ye willna let harm come to me."

He enfolded her in his arms. She made no move to separate herself from him although her head warned her to do otherwise. It was the first awareness she had of the subtle change in her feelings. She forced herself to pull away from Duncan. "Dinna ye think we should go?"

"Aye."

They reached the hamlet of drystone hovels before dusk. Grayish brown branches of rowan adorned doors made of animal skins stretched over wooden frames. Long considered sacred, the rowan prevented evil from entering the dwellings. Men with dour faces and women with deep lines etched on theirs watched their entry in wary silence.

Red Pàdraig emerged from a crude windowless hovel with a bracken-thatched roof in need of repair. Wisps of smoke escaped through the hole in the center of the thatch. He strode forward, leaving a tiny woman heavy with child standing by the entrance.

"Welcome." He helped Rory dismount, but spoke to Duncan. "I see ye brought the hound."

"Aye."

Tam approached the woman, who seemed to shrink as she backed into the stone wall, a terrified look on her face.

"Whist, Tam!" At Rory's command the dog sat. She approached the woman, taking care to speak in a gentle tone. "I apologize if the hound startled ye. I am Rory. Ye must be Morna."

Pàdraig's wife dragged her eyes from Tam. She twisted a corner of the *bréid* that covered her raven black hair. After the stoic greeting they had received, Rory was glad she had fashioned one from Duncan's extra shirt to cover her own auburn tresses. Had she not worn the kertch, she would have drawn undue attention to herself by flouting custom.

A hulking man with narrow eyes and a pockmarked face blocked her. "What are ye doing with the hound of royalty?"

His sudden appearance and snarled question startled Rory. Before she could answer, Duncan insinuated himself between them. With his hand resting on the hilt of his dirk, he addressed the stranger. "Evening to ye, Douglas. If ye have something to say to my wife, then ye must speak to me first. Is that not the custom here?"

The man grunted. "How does your wife come to have the hound of royalty?"

"'Twas given to her by Lochiel."

A collective gasp came from those who gathered to watch the confrontation.

"Why would he?"

"Are ye questioning my word, Douglas?"

Rory knew it was a challenge. She had no desire to cause discord here of all places, but kept her silence because she knew to interfere would compound the problem.

Pàdraig intervened. "Morna's father meant no insult, Duncan."

"'Tis concern for my daughter that causes me to speak."

"When I am summoned from home," Duncan said, "there is no one to protect my wife and my grandmother. Kenning this, Lochiel offered Rory what protection he could. Tam will rip the throat of any who dares to lay a hand on her in the same manner that Ewen Dubh bit the throat of his enemy."

Douglas nodded, then disappeared with the same swiftness as he had appeared.

"Morna, take Duncan and Rory inside. I will see to Midnight," Pàdraig said.

When her husband rounded the corner of the hovel, Morna spoke in a soft, nervous voice. "I welcome ye, Rory. Please dinna take offense at my father's transgression."

"I understand his concern, Morna. Is this your first babe?"

"Aye. Come, ye and Duncan must be hungry after your long ride." She entered the hovel.

Rory stooped to follow, but the foul stench emanating from inside made her step back. She bumped into Duncan who steadied her.

"Sorry, *m'eudail.* 'Tis been a while since I visited. These people live like their forefathers."

"Will we rest here?"

"Dinna fash about the accommodations. Our bed will be the soft green earth with trees and stars for our roof. Now, in with ye before Pàdraig returns."

She ducked inside, trying not to think about the smell. Clucks and moos, bleats and crowing assaulted her ears. Once her eyes adjusted to the darkness, she saw beasts occupied the smaller room at the far end of the structure while the family lived in the larger one. A low wattle divided the living quarters into two sections, the smaller portion being used for sleeping. While the animals provided extra warmth during the winter, they also added to the odors that fouled the air.

At the center of the hovel on the hard earth floor, flat stones surrounded the peat fire. A hole in the thatch above served as the chimney. Its ineffectiveness was visible by the smoke, which many believed prevented fever, blanketing the room. Since Rory preferred to breathe smelly but clean air, she seated herself on a low three-legged stool.

Morna stirred the cooking pot that hung from the *slabraidh.* A rope secured the iron chain to a wooden crosspiece in the roof. She brought whisky to drink. When Pàdraig joined them, she ladled stew into a dirty wooden dish that she set on a stool in the center of where they sat. All four of them dipped horn spoons into the bowl and ate.

"'Tis good," Rory said. "Ye added meat to the greens and oats."

Morna's face brightened. "Venison."

"Is the baby due soon?"

"In a month's time."

"Perhaps while we are here, ye will allow me to help with the work."

"I can always use another pair of hands, Rory. Thank ye."

~*~

The day after next signaled the seasonal change from dark to light. Beltane, a time of celebration, marked the season when women and children left their winter hovels to accompany the animals onto the mountain where the beasts grazed during the summer months. The men stayed behind to work the fields and repair their winter homes.

Rory assisted Morna with preparations for the move. She gathered eggs laid by the kain hens roosting in the rafters. She shooed the fowl from the house, and helped place the dirty straw and dung into two creels. By the time they finished, it was midday.

"Morna, I will check to see if the men are ready for the manure."

"Take this basket to them, Rory. 'Tis laden with cheese, bannocks, and whisky."

She walked the short distance to the field where the men prepared the earth for sowing. While the land was not the best for growing crops, it was more fertile than the soil around the MacGregor *clachan.* She set down her basket to watch Duncan.

His bare limbs glistened with beaded sweat. Wet curls clung to his forehead and smudges of dirt streaked his face. He thrust the iron-tipped end of a *cas-chrom* into the ground, then stepped on the peg at the curve of the birch shaft. With a jerk to the plowing implement, he turned over a clod of dirt. When he stopped to wipe his brow, he saw her and waved. She returned his greeting.

"How long were ye watching me?" he asked, coming over to her.

"For a wee bit. I brought food for ye and the others."

"Will ye sup with me?"

She shook her head. "I promised to return to Morna. I think her time will come before a fortnight passes, and she worries about the birthing."

"Shall we stay till the babe is born then?"

"I think that would please her. Are ye ready for the dung?"

"By the time ye fetch the women and return, the field will be done."

When Rory arrived back at the hovel, Morna was delighted with the news that Duncan had agreed they could stay. The two women shared a simple meal, then Morna fetched a girl to carry her creel. When they reached the furrowed field, the men lounged on the ground, eating.

The women worked in pairs. Rory carried the creel, while Morna opened the hinged bottom to let manure drop. They worked it into the soil using a spade and a *ràcan* that had a triangular blade at the end of a wooden haft. Rory insisted on doing the more strenuous work, and by evening her back ached.

Exhausted from the day's toil, she and Duncan bid goodnight to their friends and walked to where they slept. After washing in the stream, she stretched out on a plaid and rested her weary head on her arms. Duncan rubbed her back, legs, and arms.

She sighed. "That feels good. Thank ye."

"'Twas a kindness ye did for Morna. I think she is glad ye came."

"She is a quiet one who fashes, but she has a kind heart. I like her."

"How did she take the news of our staying?"

"She is delighted. I think it eases her mind to have a friend amongst the old women."

"Ye spoke to her of your folk healing then?"

"No, but I think 'twill be needed. The midwife died three days before our arrival, and the lass she was instructing lacks the kenning should the birth be a difficult one."

"And ye fear 'twill be so?"

"'Tis Morna's first. The babe is big, but she is wee." Rory got to her knees. "'Tis your turn."

Duncan lay on his stomach, and she kneaded the muscles in his back and shoulders. "Have ye heard talk of me or Tam?" she asked.

"Not since Douglas accepted our tale of Lochiel's gift. 'Twas a wise thought ye had."

He caught her hand and pulled her down beside him. She settled herself in his arms and fell asleep.

~*~

Rory accompanied the women to the stream to wash clothes. All work had to be finished by nightfall. There would be no toiling on Beltane.

"Give me your things," she said, seeing the exhaustion on Morna's face. "I will wash them. Ye should rest."

"Thank ye. I do feel a wee weary today."

Rory helped Morna find a shaded spot to sit, then gathered their soiled garments and headed for the water. She kept her new friend within eyesight while she chose a spot to the left of the others. She tucked her skirts high and waded into the stream. Stunned by the coldness, she bit back a shriek.

After soaking the homespun garments, she beat them against the rocks. She was half done with her work when she became aware of movement to her right. She glanced in Morna's direction. What Rory saw sent chills down her spine. On the opposite bank sat Bean-nighe, the Fairy Washerwoman, washing shirts and singing a lament for the dead.

CHAPTER ELEVEN
OMENS

A buzzing sound penetrated the fog clouding Rory's head. She lay still, uncertain if bees swarmed near her. When the mist dissipated, she realized the sound was the murmuring of nervous women. Although she could not make out their words, she knew they debated what calamity her fainting foretold.

"Rory?"

She recognized the worried voice and tried to rouse herself. Morna peered at her with anxious eyes.

"Can ye sit, Rory?"

She nodded, thankful that someone had pulled her from the stream. Lightheaded still, she rested her head atop folded arms and bent knees. The speculative chatter began anew.

"Is it a sickness she has?"

"'Tis with child she is."

"Mark my words, she saw an ominous sight."

Rory swallowed a gasp. What had the woman seen? How did she know?

The women fell silent. Rory dared not look to see why. She heard the rustling of cloth, then a calloused hand touched her hand. She lifted her head to gaze into pools of shadowy amethyst. In answer to the unspoken question in Duncan's eyes, she gave a slight nod.

He squeezed her arm, and asked, "Is it not easier to wash your clothes after shedding them, *m'eudail?*"

The women tittered with laughter.

Duncan addressed them. "Ye can see my wife suffers no ill effects from her dunking. Since ye have much to finish before the sun sets, we willna keep ye."

Reluctantly, the women returned to the washing, muttering to each other in muted tones while casting furtive glances in Rory's direction. A few crossed themselves; others hastily tied bits of red thread to the tails of their kertches.

"Duncan, take your wife to the hovel so Morna can tend her," Pàdraig said.

Rory shivered, dreading confinement amidst fetid darkness.

"'Tis kind to offer, but I will tend her."

Pàdraig furrowed his brow. "'Tis woman's work to tend the sick."

"She suffers no sickness, so she has no wish to burden Morna needlessly."

"'Tis no trouble, Duncan," Morna said quietly. "Rory has done much to help me. Caring for her is the least I can do to repay her kindness."

Rory sensed trouble brewing, for Duncan's proposal had caused another cessation of the washing. His desire to help stemmed from his concern for her, but by announcing his intentions for all to hear, he committed a gross transgression. In this *clachan* husbands never stooped to do their wives' menial chores unless necessity required it.

Duncan might be Pàdraig's friend and Lochiel's emissary, but his acceptance by these people was tenuous at best. If she did not intervene, their superstitious tongues would wag, spreading rumors borne with the swiftness of an eagle. With more poise than she felt, Rory stood. "I apologize for causing everyone such a fright. 'Twas my own folly that caused the faint. No one need attend me."

"Ye are certain, Rory?" Morna asked.

"I am fine. If ye dinna mind, though, I will change from these wet clothes before continuing my work."

Her friend smiled. "Should she not take Duncan with her, Pàdraig?"

"Since Duncan prefers the open sky to a dry roof over his head, aye. 'Twill be forever my shame if evil befell ye during your visit."

"I willna keep him longer than necessary," Rory said.

"Kenning Duncan, 'tis he who will do the keeping, lass," Pàdraig said with a wink.

Rory felt herself blush. Her host laughed as he headed back to work.

"Come, *m'eudail*," Duncan said. "Ye have kept Morna from her work overlong."

Rather than show weakness, Rory walked without Duncan's assistance. Once away from the women, though, her legs buckled. He caught her before she fell, then carried her the rest of the way. Tam barked and jumped in greeting.

Duncan snapped his finger. The hound heeled.

"Guard."

The single word brought Tam to his feet. With ears raised and stance alert, the hound entered the woods.

Surprised by the animal's quick obeisance of Duncan's command, Rory eyed her husband. He refused to look at her, but the slight quiver of his bottom lip betrayed his impassivity.

"So that is where ye and Tam have disappeared to of late. Ye were training him to heed your commands."

Duncan set her down on the soft heather. "Aye, and before ye start with your objections, I did so to ensure ye come to no harm. I dinna trust Douglas, but canna always be present to guard ye. Tam keeps to the trees, watching ye. Should Douglas come near, Tam will protect ye as I would."

"Do ye think Morna's father means to harm me?"

"'Tis his suspiciousness that fashes. Accusations of witchery will come from him or a woman like the old one who thinks ye saw what the others did not."

How had the woman guessed the truth? Was it because of her inherent distrust of strangers, or had she seen Bean-nighe too? These worrisome questions seemed inconsequential when compared to one of greater import. Rory failed to silence a gasp before it escaped her lips. What if the Fairy Washerwoman washed Duncan's shirt?

"What is it?" he asked, touching her cheek.

Her fingers flew to her lips. She averted her gaze and shook her head, unable to speak of such a possibility.

Duncan squatted in front of her. He gripped her chin, forcing her to look at him. Whatever her face revealed convinced him not to pursue the matter, for he changed the subject. "Thank ye for rescuing us from an awkward situation. I spoke without thought to the consequences."

"Ye seemed a wee distracted."

"I fear 'tis been so ever since meeting ye, *m'eudail.*" A broad grin curved his lips. "Do ye wish help in shedding your clothes?"

Rory did not want his help, but doubted she possessed the strength to accomplish the task herself. "If I accept your offer, will your hands mind themselves?"

"Ye dash my fun before it starts."

The twinkle in Duncan's eyes betrayed him. Perhaps if she joined in the teasing, her trepidation would ease. If nothing else, it would turn her thoughts away from death.

"Would a hug appease the wound, kind sir?"

He cast an appraising eye the length of her while rubbing his chin. "Holding ye is a grand prize, *m'eudail,* but not while ye drown in soaked wool. The stench reminds of wet sheep."

She glanced down at her dripping plaid. "Then ye must settle for the undressing alone."

With a sigh, he left her to retrieve their satchel from its hiding place. Upon his return, he set aside the blanket, shirt, and chemise he carried to unwind her plaid. She loosened the ties of her shift, letting it fall to her ankles, then placed her hand on his shoulder. His jaw clenched, but she detected no other sign of how her nakedness affected him. After patting her dry with the shirt, though, he handed over the clean chemise then busied himself with spreading out the wet clothes on bushes.

Rory picked up the blanket, but Duncan took it from her. He stepped behind her, draped the unfolded blanket over her shoulders, then hugged her. His embrace soothed her disquiet. His warmth dispelled the coldness. His gentle rocking made her drowsy. She closed her eyes.

"What did ye see?"

Rory started at the whispered words, but susurrus Gaelic assuaged her. She exhaled a long breath. "How did ye ken?"

"Ye are not given to swooning, *m'eudail,* and when first I saw ye, your skin was as white as snow. Ye also stiffened at the mention of seeing what others did not."

"Who else noticed?"

"None that I ken, too busy they were suspicioning the why. Did the Two Sights come upon ye?"

"I saw Bean-nighe."

He turned her toward him. "The Fairy Washerwoman? Are ye certain?"

"The wee woman was washing bloody shirts and singing dirges. With the clans at peace, how can she be foretelling death?"

Duncan uttered a mild oath and ran his hand through his dark curls.

"What ken ye that I dinna?" Rory asked.

"Four years ago Lochiel pledged men to restore King Jamie to the throne if France supplied soldiers, arms, and gold. Nocht came of it, so I had forgotten."

"Do ye think war comes now?"

"'Tis unlikely, but one never kens with the Stewarts. They have attempted thrice before to reclaim the throne since Parliament welcomed first William and Mary, then Anne, and now the Hanoverians to rule over us."

"Would Lochiel come out for King Jamie?"

Duncan shrugged. "The Camerons have long supported the Jacobite cause. 'Tis why Sir Donald's father, attainted for participating in the 'Fifteen, lives in France. If James means to try again, though, he must bring with him the promised items, else the Highland chiefs willna heed the call to rise."

~*~

"Will ye carry the basket of bannocks, Rory?" Morna asked. "I have just to douse the hearth fire, and then we can head for the shieling. 'Twill be good to leave the darkness of the hovel. I do so prefer the long summer days, and this time I shall have a wee one to fuss over."

Rory waited at the door. When Morna joined her, she held two red threads in her palm.

"I noticed yesterday ye must have lost yours when ye fell in the stream. 'Tis not a day to be without protection from the witches. Shall I tie one to your *bréid?*"

"Thank ye." Rory hoped the gesture would allay the apprehension caused by her fainting. "Who is the other one for?"

"Tam."

Aware of Morna's mistrust of the hound, Rory was surprised and touched. She doubted her friend was prepared to attach it, though.

"Shall I bind it to his tail as we did the cattle?"

Relief spread across Morna's face. "Aye."

Rory whistled and Tam bounded from the woods. She knelt beside the hound, speaking while she worked. "Look what Morna gives ye, Tam. 'Tis certain now the witches willna bother ye. Would ye like to pet him, Morna?"

Her friend wrung her hands together. "Will he bite?"

"No. I will hold him while ye pat his back."

Morna reached out a tentative hand to stroke the hound's wiry coat.

"Daughter!"

She jumped at the snarled word, snatching back her hand.

Tam gave a low growl, but Rory silenced it. She met Douglas' hostile gaze. A tense silence fell between them.

Morna's father looked away first. "Gather your baskets and get on with ye, Morna. It willna do for Gerald and the other lads to reach the need fire while the bannocks are still in the *clachan.*"

"Aye, Father." Without another word, she picked up her basket and headed up the ben.

Rory followed with Tam at her side. If not for her promise to Morna, she would leave on the morrow. Douglas' open hostility reminded her too much of the past, and living in this *clachan* was oppressive.

On the outskirts of the village, Rory passed Gerald and his friends gathering the cattle and other animals into a herd. Within the hour, they would begin the slow trek up the mountain to the sweet grass pasture. Gerald, a fair-haired boy with freckles, and the lads shouted greetings, which she acknowledged before hurrying to catch up to Morna.

At the crest of the hill women and younger children gathered to watch the men cut a large circular trench into the earth. They removed the outer sections of turf before piling logs to either side of the center, creating a narrow passage between the two stacks of wood.

Duncan strained along with Pàdraig and several others to cart an axletree into the trench. To this they affixed a square frame of green wood. A score of men filled in vacant spaces around the frame. In one voice, they counted aloud—*aon, dà, trì*—and pushed. Slowly, frame and axletree turned. As the speed of the rotations increased, friction kindled sparks to light the need fire. Those not in the trench tossed dried mushrooms gathered from birch trees onto the wood to assist the sparks in igniting the logs.

By the time Gerald and the lads arrived with the herd, two huge bonfires greeted them. All persons and animals circled the trench sunwise three times, then the boys drove the herd along the passage between the Beltane fires to purify the beasts from sickness and protect them from fairy arrows. On the far side of the trench, several men assumed the driving duties from the lads.

Gerald approached Rory. "I come for bannocks to offer fox and eagle so they willna harm our cattle. Have ye one to give?"

"Here is one from Morna and Pàdraig, and another from my husband and myself."

Gerald accepted the offering with a slight bow. "Thank ye. This evening I come to the shieling with a torch lit at the need fire for lighting your hearth fire."

He set off down the hill, tossing pieces of oatcake over his shoulder and chanting rhymes to the predators. Rory watched his descent until Duncan and Pàdraig joined her and Morna for the rolling of the bannocks, an event used by the villagers to divine the future. Each round oatcake had two sides, one of which was marked with a cross. After being rolled down the hill, the cake either bespoke good health and fortune or ill health and calamity, depending upon which surface showed.

Pàdraig and Duncan hunched over their bannocks beside the other participants. Morna's father strode behind them, checking to see that all were ready. Satisfied, he gave the signal to start. Pàdraig took the lead, rolling his cake with expert grace. He avoided patches of rough ground and hidden objects. The bannock slowed, then spun around several times on its rim, before coming to rest on a soft tuft of grass.

Duncan guided his bannock with great care, taking every precaution to insure its safe arrival. When it hit an unexpected dip, the oatcake wobbled and fell flat. His grimace told Rory he saw the cross. If the divination held true, the year would be fraught with peril.

She looked to Pàdraig, who seemed bewildered. Since the outcome of the rolling allowed for one of two options, she went to see what puzzled him. His bannock had cracked into many pieces. A feeling of dread enveloped Rory like a shroud.

~*~

The shieling had just come into view when an agonizing scream pierced the air. Rory dropped the basket, scooped up her hem, and ran. By the time she reached the summer dwelling, other women had arrived. She pushed through them and went inside.

Morna lay on the hard straw-covered shelf. Sweat beaded her forehead. Huge frightened eyes pleaded for help.

"Ye and the babe are fine." Rory kept her tone soft and steady. She pried the crumpled *bréid* from fisted hands, then brushed damp curls from Morna's brow. "I ken it hurts, but 'tis the way of things. Before long, ye will have a new son or daughter to treasure."

"But there is no midwife!"

"Dinna fash at all, Morna. These women will help ye. Most have borne at least one babe. And dinna forget I am here. I dinna have bairns of my own, but I have helped birth a few."

"Ye are a midwife then?"

Rory turned to a dour-faced old woman. "A folk healer."

Another contraction seized Morna. She screamed.

"I dinna trust ye, but the lass does. 'Twill do the babe no good to upset her by banishing ye from the shieling. Collect your herbs, but remember we watch. If anything happens, 'tis on your head."

Rory felt the hair on her neck rise. This was what Duncan had feared might happen. She had promised not to endanger herself, but friendship bound her to help. She nodded her acceptance of the condition. If fate decreed she face punishment at the hands of these people, she would do so with honor.

"'Tis done then. Ladies, prepare the shieling. We must guard the babe against the magic of the *Daoine Sith* and the veil of witches." The woman fixed her gaze on Rory as she spoke the last.

Rory ignored her. A search of her herbs revealed she had left the needed one in Duncan's satchel. She scanned the room for someone to fetch it. A girl with red hair and freckles stood near the door watching the women work. She had the look of someone who wished to help, but no one paid her any heed. Rory approached her. "Would ye go to my husband for me?"

The lass straightened. "Aye, Meg will do your bidding."

"Ye must be swift like the hawk."

"I run faster than anyone."

"Good. Tell my husband 'tis the time of the crying and I need the small bundle I left with him. Can ye do this?"

With a nod, Meg dashed from the shieling.

"Rory?" Morna's whispered plea returned her to the bedside. She soaked coarse linen in cool water and placed it on her friend's brow.

"Rest while ye can. There is nocht to fash about. These ladies and I will tend ye. See the preparations they make to safeguard ye and the babe?"

Morna turned to watch. One woman hammered a nail into the wooden bed while another put an iron chain beneath the shelf. A cross of rowan was placed on a stool beside the bed. The old woman who had confronted Rory lit a splinter of wood. The other women formed a circle and passed the fir-candle around the sleeping shelf three times. The taut lines of fear and panic faded from Morna's face.

A loud commotion outside drew Rory's attention. She identified two of the voices. Meg entered carrying a carefully tied bundle. "Is this what ye wanted?"

"Aye. Has Pàdraig come?"

The girl nodded. "And your husband and Morna's father with him."

Rory withdrew a small vial.

The old woman appeared at her side. "What do ye give her?"

Rory counted silently to ten, trying to cool her impatience before she answered. "'Tis extract of shepherd's purse. 'Twill ease the birth."

Under the woman's watchful eye, she lifted Morna's head to administer the liquid. "Drink just a wee sip."

Morna complied, then sank back onto the bed. Rory wiped her brow then turned to Meg. "Thank ye for bringing this. Mayhap ye will stay with Morna while I speak with her husband?"

Meg nodded.

The instant Rory stepped outside, Douglas accosted her. "What have ye done to my daughter?"

Before she could answer, Duncan whirled Pàdraig's father-in-law around. "I warned ye before, Douglas. If ye wish to speak to my wife, ye must seek my permission."

"'Tis my daughter in there!"

"Aye, man, and she is having Pàdraig's child. 'Tis what women do. They have no need for us to interfere."

A scream came from the shieling. Pàdraig and Douglas paled.

Rory laid a hand on Pàdraig's sleeve. "Morna is fine. 'Twill be a while before the babe comes. Ye must stop your fashing."

She let him compose himself, before making a request. "I need three things from ye."

Pàdraig gawked at her. "What?"

"Your shirt, dirk, and bonnet."

"My shirt? My dirk? My bonnet?" With each repetition of her words, his voice grew louder.

Duncan intervened. "Calm yourself, Pàdraig. Rory but asks for what the women need. The shirt is to swaddle your son in once he is born. The dirk will lie in the cradle to protect him from the wee folk until the kirking. The bonnet is for Morna's bed to keep them away during the crying."

Pàdraig laughed to cover his chagrin. He doffed his bonnet and unsheathed his dirk. Rory held them while he removed his shirt.

"I apologize. 'Tis my first bairn, and I am a wee nervous."

"Dinna fash. If ye wish to help, walk sunwise around the shieling seven times to ease Morna's pain."

While she doubted the validity of this, Rory nonetheless counseled new fathers to follow the custom. If nothing else, it eased their anxiousness and kept them from underfoot.

"She gave your wife a potion."

On hearing the old woman's pronouncement, Douglas exclaimed, "She is a witch!"

Duncan put himself in front of Rory. His hand rested on his dirk. "My wife is no witch, Douglas, and I willna tolerate ye saying otherwise."

The old woman spoke again. "She claims she is a folk healer."

Rory wanted to throttle the woman, and suspected Duncan was tempted to, too. She had to end this before matters escalated to where she would be banned from Morna's side.

"Ye have no midwife to tend your daughter. Since I have attended cryings before, I offered to help. I gave Morna a sip of shepherd's purse to ease the pain. Dr. Archie uses the same."

"Is it Lochiel's brother ye speak of?" Pàdraig asked.

"Aye."

Pàdriag turned to Duncan. "Does she speak the truth? Is your wife a folk healer? Has she spoken with Dr. Archie?"

"Aye, to all your questions. While I have not seen her at a crying, I ken of her healing. 'Twas she who healed the scar ye questioned me about."

"Dinna fear, lad," the old woman said, a satisfied gleam in her eyes. "If any harm befalls Morna or the babe, 'twill be on *her* head."

"So be it, then. If my wife or son dies, ye will answer for it."

Rory sensed rather than saw Duncan's alarm. She stepped close for him to hear her whispered words. "I willna allow myself to suffer the same fate as the woman ye saw. 'Tis my pledge, Duncan."

He swallowed. His eyes bespoke the words he thought. *I expect ye to honor your word.* She prayed for guidance, asking God to bring them all safely through this.

In the hours that followed, Morna's contractions grew stronger and more frequent, but the baby did not come. With the pain upon her, her face reddened. When it ended, she paled. She writhed, then collapsed. Her screams waned to whimpering moans.

The women huddled near the cradle, crossing themselves. They glared at Rory, blaming her for Morna's suffering. Their censure provoked vivid images of a witch-pricker jabbing his needle into her naked body.

She shook her head to scatter such cluttering thoughts. She must concentrate. Why could she not see the babe's head? In considering the possibilities, a sickening realization came to her. If right, the infant would be born dead and Morna might well follow. Rory felt along the outside of the womb, using her fingers to identify the babe's head, back, and buttocks. The examination confirmed her worst fears.

"What do ye do?" the elderly woman shrieked, grabbing her hands.

Rory shrugged her off. She had no time to placate her or the others. She must turn the babe before it suffocated.

"I asked ye a question and demand an answer!"

The apprehensive women drew closer. One muttered "witch."

"'Tis a footling. Morna is too wee for the babe to be born backward. If ye can save Morna and her babe, then do so."

She waited, wondering if any would take up the challenge. None did.

"Ye told me to tend Morna, and I am doing so. If ye dare interfere again, I will banish ye all from the shieling. Do ye understand?"

"Aye, I understand," the old woman said through clenched teeth. "Just remember I am watching. Ye will answer for what ye do here."

Rory ignored the threat. She placed her hands on her friend's lower abdomen and gently tried to turn the footling. The going was slow and painful. Morna whimpered from the discomfort, so Rory cooed calming words while she worked. She pushed and kneaded, feeling slight movements that strengthened her resolve. Morna's whimper grew louder and she clawed Rory's arms. Rory continued to push. Morna screamed, and Rory felt the baby shift position. She also felt Morna's body tense with another contraction.

"The babe will come now, Morna. Push! Push!"

A fuzzy head appeared between the mother's thighs.

"Again!"

Where Morna found the energy, Rory never knew, but with heels braced against the wood her friend pushed. The baby slid into Rory's waiting hands. The elderly woman snatched away the child. While she washed him with cold water, he squealed in protest. She wrapped him in Pàdraig's shirt, then presented him to his father, who stood at the door. He carried his son up the mountain to insure the infant enjoyed good health and prosperity throughout his life.

In their absence, the women shoved Rory aside and set about bathing and dressing Morna. Rory hovered near the door, waiting to be certain that her skills were no longer needed. By the time they finished plaiting Morna's hair, Pàdraig had returned. The old woman laid the babe in the cradle. Six women formed a ring around the infant to protect him from fairies who thought to exchange him for a changeling.

Morna and her son were healthy and safe. Rory slipped from the shieling. She refused to face the superstitious villagers and their heathen accusations. Her pledge to Duncan required that she keep herself from danger. She climbed the ben until she lost track of time. Paying little heed to her destination, she strove to distance herself from those who meant her harm. When she could go no farther, she curled up on the ground and fell asleep.

Tiny droplets of ice stung her skin. Swirling mist cleaved to her plaid. Cold wind drove her forward. She stood on a moor that was draped half in scarlet, half in blue.

A barrage of rumbles assaulted her ears. Black smoke drifted over tussocks of brown heather that seemed to ebb and flow like the tide. A blue wave swept over the moor, then receded. Steel clanged. Again the blue wave surged and waned. Again steel clanged. The red wave swelled to towering proportions before engulfing the blue.

Silence descended, eerie and utter. Corbies circled a field of severed limbs, headless torsos, and mangled corpses. A blue-black stallion reared. Heedless of the carnage, compelled by black foreboding, she looked down and screamed.

"Rory! Wake up."

Strong arms held her. She flailed, trying to escape.

"'Tis all right, *m'eudail.* Shh! There is nocht to fear. I will protect ye. Shh!"

Duncan's soothing words and gentle stroking of her hair splintered the remnants of the dream. A sob escaped her lips. She clung to him, trembling with fear.

"What is it, Rory? What is wrong?"

Afraid to speak of what she had seen, she shook her head. He lifted her and began to walk. She cared not where he took her. She wanted only to feel his reassuring arms around her.

The cold water hit like a slap across the face. She sucked in deep gulps of air. She slipped on moss-covered stones, but Duncan pulled her to her feet. He crossed her arms in front of her, binding them to her sides with his. He continued advancing into the stream until rushing water swirled around her waist. She squirmed, trying to escape. Why did he wish to drown her?

"Be still, Rory! Look at yourself!"

His tone compelled her to obey. When she ceased struggling, he eased his hold on her. The water around her turned pink. She glanced at her clothes and arms. Duncan must have sensed her panic.

"'Tis not your blood, Rory. 'Tis from the crying."

He enunciated each word until the meaning penetrated her fear. The crying. Not his blood. Morna's. Rory sagged against him.

Ye do not drown me."

"No. If I thought to drown someone, 'twould be Douglas. I wanted only to wash away the blood."

"'Twas the dream, Duncan. I kent not what was happening."

"'Tis no wonder after the foolery at the shieling."

Accusations of witchery! She remembered all now. She had weathered one ordeal only to face another—the examination.

"When do we return?"

"We stayed until the babe was born as ye promised, but no longer. I have had my fill of the whole lot of them."

"But the denunciations, Duncan. What of them?"

"I sent Gerald to bring Dr. Archie and Sandy to the shieling. They will quell the idle tongues that talk of witchery."

Rory expelled a long breath. "I am glad. I would rather face a whole army of Campbells than return to the shieling."

"So would I. Now, shall we see to your bath?"

"I can wash myself."

"'Tis more fun to soap than to watch."

"If 'tis soaping ye wish to do, ye can wash my clothes."

He sighed. "If 'tis all ye will allow."

"Aye, 'tis."

She unbelted her plaid and handed it to him. He offered her soapwort, then concentrated on rinsing the blood from the wool. She rubbed the lather into her linen shift, over her bare skin, and into her hair.

"Hold me, so I can rinse."

Duncan slung the soapy plaid over his shoulder, then placed his hands under her arms and lowered her into the burn. The force of the water from the melting snow pushed against her, trying to sweep her from his grasp, but he held fast. He dunked her several times until she had rinsed the suds from hair and clothes. He deposited her on the bank, wrapped a blanket around her, and then resumed his washing. After he wrung out her plaid, he gathered her in his arms and headed into the woods. Too exhausted to ask where he took her, she laid her head against his shoulder and slept.

~*~

Pinprick rays of sunlight dotted the dirt floor. From the lack of furnishings in the rough-hewn room and the soft furs that warmed her, Rory guessed that she lay in a shelter used by hunters caught in winter snows. She reached to scratch her back, and discovered her nakedness.

"Dinna be saying words ye might regret later."

She tempered her anger as she rolled to face Duncan. He lay on his side with his head propped up by his hand. His free arm rested atop the fur.

"Why do I wear nocht?"

"The blanket was soaked by the time we reached this shieling. I held ye by the fire while your hair dried, but your shift remained damp. Fearing ye might take ill, I dared not leave ye to sleep in it. I hung your clothes with mine to dry while we slept. 'Twas all proper, I assure ye, though seeing all of ye again was enough to warm me."

The mischievous glint in his eyes and the devilish grin on his face irritated her. When she raised her hand to slap away his smugness, he rolled onto his back. She paled. His thumb brushed a teardrop from her cheek.

"What is it, Rory? What makes ye so sad?"

When she did not answer, he propped himself against the wall and gathered her to him. "Tell me, *m'eudail*. What did ye see?"

"How did ye ken?"

"'Tis the only time ye willna talk to me. Did I do something to remind ye of the dream?"

She nodded.

"Ye canna bury what ye saw, Rory. Share it with me."

"No."

"Because the dream involves me?"

She nodded again.

"I canna imagine what 'tis like to ken what will happen before it does. It canna be a blessing, especially if ye care for the one seen. I dinna ken whether I believe what ye see is preordained, that it canna be changed. Mayhap 'tis God's way of warning ye. If ye share your kenning, I may be able to safeguard myself. If not, at least I willna be surprised when it happens and I might be able to thwart the seriousness of it."

Pay him no heed. 'Tis Campbell blood that runs through him.

Duncan is no more Campbell than ye. He is Cameron.

Rory clamped her hands over her ears to shut out the warring voices. The din faded, and a calmer voice echoed in her thoughts. *Dinna judge one by the deeds of another.*

A young Lochiel had spoken those words, but guilt and anger had prevented her from understanding his wisdom at the time of their utterance. Later, she acknowledged the rightness of them and allowed the adage to guide her in her dealings with others.

Except Duncan.

Except Duncan. She acknowledged the truth without understanding the why of her actions. He belonged to Clan Cameron, not Campbell. He was not her enemy. He deserved better than what she had given. He had acceded to her demands, asking one thing from her in return—the truth. To give him less would compound the dishonor she did him.

She lowered her hands and closed her eyes. Once again, the horrid images revealed themselves. She licked dry lips and spoke of what she saw. "I stand in the midst of a frightful battle between two armies. Smoke blackens the sky and clanging swords reverberate through the glen. Twice the blue repels the red. On the third meeting, 'tis the red that prevails to slaughter the blue. Black corbies circle the heaving bloodied ground. A stallion, black as night, stands over a fallen warrior."

"'Tis me, is it not?"

She nodded.

"Am I dead? Think before ye answer."

His command took her by surprise. She had assumed him dead, but he had awakened her before the dream ended. She stared at the rough thatching overhead. The scene unfolded a third time.

She knelt beside Duncan, moving her lips in silent prayer. She touched his neck, then his chest. Each time, she felt the steady beating of his heart.

"Wounded!" She gasped out the word.

Duncan brushed away her tears. She stiffened, not from his touch, but from the hairs rising on her neck. He withdrew his hand, but she clutched his arm. She no longer lay beneath the furs. She stood amongst slain warriors littering a moor red with blood. Danger, unseen and dreaded, lurked nearby. She searched for it, but a brilliant light flashed, shattering the vision.

"Ye can release your claws, Rory! Ye said I was wounded, not dead."

She looked to her hands, and saw her fingernails dug into Duncan's arm. She withdrew them, leaving deep grooves in his skin.

"Och! Sorry."

He rubbed his arm, then turned her until he could peer into her eyes. "What else, Rory?"

She frowned. "I canna say."

"Canna or willna?"

"If I could tell, Duncan, I would."

"Then what did ye feel?"

"Danger. Your life is in jeopardy, but I canna say from whom."

"I will remember your words, *m'eudail.* I dinna ken what the future holds, but after the omens we have witnessed, I ken trouble brews."

"Ye are a warrior, Duncan, but I ask ye to take special care."

"I promise."

His purple eyes studied her, while his finger caressed her cheek. Finally, he set her aside. He rose from the furs and gathered up his plaid and shirt. "Get dressed. I wish to return home in time to taste Nannag's fine cooking."

She shook her head. "I dinna take orders, Duncan Cameron. 'Tis a warm soft bed ye made me, so 'tis here I will stay."

She curled up with her back facing him. He grunted and slapped her backside. When she heard the door close, she dressed. She extinguished the fire, straightened the room, then closed the door behind her.

CHAPTER TWELVE
CONFRONTATION AND THE CROSS

"Grandmother, could ye be after sparing my wife for a wee bit? From the looks of her, I think there is more flour on her than in the mixing bowl."

Irritated by Duncan's teasing, Rory stopped stirring long enough to shove stray hairs from her forehead. "Go away with ye, Cameron! We have no time for your jests."

Rather than heed the reprimand, he picked up the wet cloth draped over the rim of a bucket near the hearth and attempted to wipe her face. She jerked her head away, but he held her chin still. With gentle swipes he rinsed off the dust.

Nannag dried her hands on her apron. "I seem to recall a wee lad who decided to help his mother and me with the cooking. By eventide, there was more on him than 'twas in the pot."

"Ye have a mischievous twinkle in your bonny blue eyes, *m'eudail,*" Duncan said, dabbing the tip of her nose. "What are ye thinking?"

Rory feigned innocence. "Whatever do ye mean? 'Tis only enjoying the tale of a wee lad I am. Are ye saying, Nannag, that Duncan can cook?"

The old woman's face crinkled with laughter. "His skills are better put to warring, but his cooking is edible."

"Mayhap then he should toil at the hearth fire while we tend to the work outside."

"'Tis a grand idea, Rory. Did I not tell ye, Duncan, your wife and I would become friends?"

"I dinna ken whether I like the turn this conversation takes. It sounds like the stirrings of a rebellion. And I thought I had tamed my two favorite rebels."

Rory smirked. "Never! Nannag and I will forever be rebels."

Duncan caught her from behind and pulled her against him. She pushed against his arms to free herself, but they held like iron bars.

"I would not have ye any other way. Rebels make life interesting."

"Unhand me!"

Although he adhered to the exactness of her request, she still found herself imprisoned. He had shifted his arms from holding her to leaning against the table, capturing her between them. Blocked on four sides, her only route of escape was to crawl under the table or under one of his arms.

Before she decided which option to try, he moved forward, pinning her against the table. "Grandmother, ye did not answer my question."

Nannag pursed her lips and thought. "Och! Can I be after sparing Rory, do ye mean?"

"Aye."

"To be sure. When ye are gone, 'tis myself who does all the work so I can manage without her."

"I think there is one less rebel here than a wee while ago," Rory said. "Have I no say in this?"

"None at all." Duncan unhooked a basket from the rafter overhead. "For our supper."

Resigned to the fact that he meant to take her somewhere whether she wanted to go or not, she crammed fresh-baked crusted meat pies, apples, and whisky into the small creel, then shoved the basket into his chest. Amused by her irritation, he winked at her while his lips fought to contain a grin.

She huffed, then sought a reprieve from his grandmother. "Nannag, are ye certain ye dinna mind?"

"Not at all, Granddaughter. Enjoy yourselves."

Rory ignored the hand Duncan extended and dodged his reach to exit the cottage. Once outside, she was forced to look at him because she had no idea which direction to take.

Laughter shimmered in his purple gaze as he nodded toward the burn. At the water's edge, he swept her into his arms and carried her across the ankle-deep water. When he set her down, he said, "I have a vague memory of a bonny lass asking for a truce. I wonder when she changed her mind."

He was right, but his teasing sometimes nettled and when nettled, she tended toward anger. Perhaps she would do better to ignore his teasing. Resolved to try this, she tucked her hand around his arm to climb the hillside.

When they reached the crest, Duncan stopped. "Close your eyes, Rory."

"I dinna want to play games with ye."

"'Tis not a game. Willna ye do what I ask?"

She closed her eyes.

He took her hands in his to guide her down the hill. When she slipped and lost her footing, he righted her. "Ye kept your eyes closed!"

"Did ye not ask for my trust?"

"I did."

"Then why open my eyes until ye say 'tis all right to do so?"

"I was not certain ye would ever trust me again." Hope laced his whispered words.

"I canna say that I trust ye in all things, Duncan, but in this I do. Ye have kept me safe from harm without thought to yourself."

"Always. Shall we continue?"

"Aye."

"Put your hands on my shoulders. I will walk ahead, so ye dinna fall again."

Rory heard thunder, but the sun warmed her face. She listened to the unceasing noise. The rumbling neither started loud nor faded away. It did not cycle through again and again. Rather it remained steady, soothing in its constancy.

She smiled. "'Tis a waterfall, is it not?"

"Open your eyes and see for yourself."

A canopy of silver-white birches and red-fissured pines sheltered a narrow glen ringed by snow-capped peaks. Water cascaded over gray rocks flecked with pink granite to form a pool of clear water. Scattered amongst dried pine needles and emerald green moss grew clusters of blue hyacinths and purplish foxglove. Furry blurs of creamy yellow and rusty brown darted through the bracken. The two pine marten kits caught a whiff of a new scent and disappeared behind bushes covered with ripening raspberries.

"'Tis a special place," Rory whispered. "Thank ye for bringing me here."

"It has its own magic that quiets the most troubled soul. Shall we feast beside that hoary oak?"

"Aye."

After the meal, Duncan stretched out on his back with his hands clasped behind his head. Rory walked amidst the trees, where discovered a drift of sweet-smelling meadowsweet that could be used to flavor stew or dye cloth. If she dried the leaves and flowers, she could make an infusion for colds. The rose-colored flowers of woundwort were useful in healing wounds while goldenrod knitted broken bones.

A green cone-shaped flower with a red-violet tuft stirred a flood of memories and made her heart ache. Three and a half months remained before that sorrow would ease. She touched the thistle.

"Ouch!" Rory sucked on her sore finger, chiding herself for forgetting the thistle's spiny bracts.

"Allow me," Duncan said, taking her *sgian* from her.

She held her palm steady while he worked to remove the embedded prickle. When he finished, she dipped her hand in the pond.

"Thank ye." She watched his finger trace the carved hilt. "Tell me about Tòmas."

"My brother and I were a wild pair," he said with a smile. "Mother and Nannag were forever telling Father we were in need of the belt. Our favorite game was fighting the Sassenach. We drew straws to see who played the foul enemy."

"Who lost more?"

"Tòmas. His displeasure made him quite fearsome, and he oft won our tussles. 'Twas he who first broke my nose when we were pelting each other with stones. I could never decide whether he missed his target or if he aimed true.

"When we were ten, Father took us to the gathering of the clan. Ewen Dubh had devised a test for those who vied for the baldric, but no one had passed it before he died. Folk said a champion would at last be named at this wappenshaw."

"And what was this grand feat of strength?" Rory asked, intrigued at the thought of two boys dreaming of the day they might participate. Whatever Duncan had seen at the games had piqued his interest enough for him to master the skills of a warrior.

"He called it a stone of strength, and claimed 'twas the true test of a man. He put a new baldric under a great stone. Whoever lifted it off would win the belt and the honors that went with it."

"Who won?"

"No one. The baldric still lies beneath the stone."

Rory laughed.

"I believe this is yours." Duncan handed her the *sgian* hilt first. "'Tis not a sport oft taught to lasses, but since ye are a rebel, I was wondering if ye can swim?"

"Uncle Iain insisted I learn so I could save myself if washed overboard or the ship sank."

"Would ye join me for a dip in yonder linn?"

"Will the midges not bother us?"

"The wee tormentors would not dare disturb this magical spot."

"All right. I will go swimming with ye."

Duncan unbelted his plaid and stripped off his shirt. With a great yell, he dashed into the water. Rory shook her head, amused by the boy inside of the man.

"I thought ye said ye would join me."

She motioned with her finger for him to turn.

"Ye have nocht that I have not seen, *m'eudail.*"

"While ye speak the truth, if ye want me to join ye, ye will do what I ask."

He rolled his eyes, but acceded to her request.

In a less hurried pace she folded her plaid and stepped out of her chemise. Once submerged in the cold water, her teeth chattered and goose flesh dotted her skin. She dove beneath the surface, then swam the width of the pond while Duncan swam the length. Once or twice they met in the middle, but he glided past without a word.

When she felt warm, she stopped to push hair from her eyes. She glanced around, but Duncan was nowhere to be seen. Something nipped at her ankle. She gave a gentle kick, but the creature nipped again. Then it grabbed her ankles and tugged, pulling her under. Water rushed into her mouth and up her nose. She thrashed about trying to escape, but it took several hard kicks before she broke the surface, coughing and gasping for breath.

"How dare ye, Duncan Cameron!"

"Ye look like a drowned puppy," he said, laughing.

She raised her hand to strike him, but he grabbed her wrist and dragged her against him. She felt the pulsating beat of his heart against her palm. Their eyes met, and the searing intensity of his gaze made her heart skip a beat. Her chest tightened and prickles of goose flesh made her shiver. She tilted her head; he lowered his. An ember deep inside flared. He kissed her again, and the ember ignited into flame. His tongue teased her lips while his fingers trailed her spine. He trickled water down her neck, then blew a puff of air. She shuddered and arched against him. His hands cupped her buttocks. She went rigid.

Shocked by his falsity and her body's betrayal, she staggered from his grasp. "No!"

"Rory, I—"

Tears slid down her face. "Ye promised, Duncan. How could ye break your oath?"

~*~

A radiant beam of moonlight illuminated the *clach an t'seabhdail* by the cottage door. Rory sank onto the turf-covered stone, then tucked her legs beneath her plaid. With eyes closed, she leaned against the stone wall. Her body and mind felt numb. She could wander no farther; she could think no more. All she wanted was to sleep until the anniversary of the handfasting, then walk away from *him* without a backward glance.

A loud thud jarred Rory. She blinked several times to get her bearings, then realized she had dozed. She stiffened at the flurry of loud curses that came from inside the cottage.

"Leave off, Grandmother! What happens between my wife and me stays between us."

"When Rory wanders the bens alone and does not come home until the wee hours of the morning, 'tis my concern. She is dear to me, Duncan. Dinna ye care about her?"

"Of course I do. She is my heart."

Rory squeezed her eyes tight against stinging tears. She did not want to hear such words.

"Then why are ye angry with her?"

"'Tis not Rory who raises my ire. 'Tis myself."

A long silence followed. When Nannag spoke, Rory strained to hear her muted words.

"Och, Duncan, what have ye done to vex yourself so?"

"I made a promise before we wed, and today, I almost broke my word. 'Tis twice I have hurt her, and this time I fear I canna repair the damage."

"Go to her, Grandson. Ask her forgiveness."

"'Twill do no good. I have lost her. I willna ever change her mind now. She will leave me."

His words devastated Rory, and she did not understand why. She had made clear her intentions from the start. Then why did it feel like Duncan had just ripped out her heart?

He appeared in the doorway beside her. With shoulders slumped, he walked to the byre and saddled Midnight. After mounting, he rode to her. When she met his gaze, she found herself drowning in his despair.

"I am sorry, *m'eudail*."

With those whispered words, he rode away. Rory sensed he would not return. The thought filled her with profound sadness. When she finally dragged herself inside the cottage, she curled up inside the box bed and cried herself to sleep.

~*~

"'Tis a fine day to dye the wool we carded and washed," Duncan's grandmother said, emerging from the cottage. "Will ye fetch the plants from the chimney, Rory?"

"Have ye chosen the colors for your threads?"

Nannag shook her head. "'Tis for ye to choose. The cloth we make is yours to give or keep. Mayhap ye will give Duncan a new plaid upon his return."

Rory looked in the direction he had gone. How many times had she done so in the past fortnight? He had left before she could tell him that she bore equal blame.

Nannag laid a weathered hand on her arm. "Lass, what fashes ye?"

"Nocht. I will fetch the dyes."

Inside, she removed the plants Nannag had set to dry over the hearth. Rory examined the contents of each parcel, selecting three and returning the rest to their niche within the chimney. When she reemerged, she saw Nannag struggling with an iron pot and hurried to help. The old woman placed a hand to her lower back.

"'Tis too old I am for such weights. 'Tis a chore for the young."

Rory laughed. "Ye may have the face of an old woman, but in your heart ye are forever young."

"Bless ye, lass. Now, shall we set the fire?"

They built three slow-burning fires. While Nannag tended them, Rory carried buckets of water from the burn. She also collected two more pots. Opening the parcels retrieved from the chimney, she put a layer of gean bark into one vessel. Nannag laid wool on top, then Rory added more bark. They repeated this pattern several times before switching to the second pot. Into it went layers of wool and the root of sundew, while wild hyacinth and wool occupied the third.

When they finished the layering, Nannag added a mordant of moss to each to set the colors. Rory poured water into each pot before placing them over the fires. While they waited for the water to boil, they satisfied their parched throats with heather ale. Occasionally, Rory stirred the contents of the pots and checked to see if the wool had turned the hues she desired.

"What colors do ye want for the cloth, lass?"

"'Twill be a plaid of purple and blue with cream."

Nannag furrowed her brow. "Is there a reason for choosing those colors?"

"None at all."

Rory noted the skepticism in the old woman's eyes, but Nannag did not probe. Rory checked the pots again, then finding the wool the desired shades, she carried each vessel from the fire. After removing the wool, they laid it out to dry.

Over several days, they combed the dyed wool with bristly withered teasel cones. When Nannag deemed it soft enough for spinning, she located two distaffs. "Hold it under your left arm like so. Now, attach a wee wool to the split at the top of the spindle."

Rory inserted the cream-colored thread onto the small tapering piece of wood.

"Good. Ye must spin the spindle while letting it recede from ye by drawing the thread between finger and thumb while the spindle twists."

Nannag watched Rory work the distaff and spindle. After she had a length of yarn, she wrapped it around the base of the spindle. The old woman nodded her approval, then took up her tools and began to spin the purple wool into thread. During the long hours of dusk, they spun the wool and within a fortnight they had completed the task.

"Have ye a pattern for the wool, Rory?"

On a piece of wood, she sketched the desired pattern, including the number of threads for each stripe.

"Which color will run the length of the cloth, lass?"

"Purple."

She watched Nannag set up the warp on the loom. The old woman worked in the morning to take advantage of the sun. Seated on a stool, she wove the shuttle in and out of the warp to create the weft.

"Do ye ken where my grandson went?"

The mention of Duncan broke Rory's concentration. She dropped two plaits of heather from the rope she wove.

"He did not say."

"When do ye expect him to return?"

"I doubt Duncan will return before I leave."

Nannag set down the shuttle. "Why did ye marry my grandson, Rory?"

"My father never wanted me to suffer the fire and the sword so he arranged for me to wed a Cameron."

"Ye did not agree with his wanting to protect ye?"

Rory gave a rueful laugh. "I was never consulted. 'Twas revealed to me when Duncan broke his promise to my foster father."

"Is that how he first hurt ye?

She nodded. "If I wed Duncan, my kinsmen could swear allegiance to Lochiel. Duty gave me no choice but to agree to the handfast."

"But in exchange ye extracted your own promise from my grandson."

"Aye."

"Duncan loves ye, lass."

Rory's gaze dropped to her idle hands.

"I think ye return his love."

She shook her head in surprise. "No, Nannag. I canna love him."

"Why?"

"He has the blood of Campbell."

Nannag's eyes narrowed. "And what has that to do with anything?"

"Campbells murdered my mother! They raped my foster mother! They burned our *clachan!*"

"Och, Rory!" Nannag took hold of her hand and rubbed her thumb over the knuckles. "I would take the pain from ye if I could. 'Tis frightful to ken what comes from the feuding. It destroys folk, not just the sword, but the hatred. 'Twas so with my father, and I suffered because he could not forgive. Dinna be like him and let the past rule ye. 'Twill rob ye of your true love."

"I dinna love Duncan."

"Are ye so certain of this, Rory?"

"Aye."

"Then why do ye look for his return? Why choose these colors for the plaid?" Nannag asked, slipping her fingers between the threads of the warp and weft. "They match the hues of Duncan's eyes and your own."

Rory stared out the window, unwilling to concede that she might have chosen them for that reason. She murmured her answer. "I dinna ken."

"Your heart kens, but ye willna heed what it tells ye. There is but a wee time left before ye decide your fate, lass. Before ye do so, Duncan and ye must settle the anger that separates ye. Dwelling on it will cause it to fester. My husband and I argued often, but we kept one rule between us. Duncan and ye would be wise to heed it. Never let the sun set on your anger."

"I am not angry with him, Nannag."

"Then ye must tell him so."

"I canna do so if he is not here."

"Dinna fash. He will come."

Tam's incessant barking brought a swift end to the conversation.

"Is anyone to home?"

The familiar voice jarred Rory. She had not heard it since leaving Achnacarry.

Nannag, on the other hand, seemed unperturbed by their visitor. "We are in the front sleeping room, Sandy."

"Good day to ye, Nannag," the lean brown-haired priest said. "And to ye, Rory."

"Father Alex. 'Tis good to see ye."

"I thought to visit earlier, but Duncan and ye were forever traversing the bens and glens on my brother's business."

"What brings ye now, Sandy?" Nannag asked.

"A bonny raven-haired lass needed an escort, so I volunteered."

"Where is she? Ye have not lost her, have ye?"

"Not at all, Nannag." He stepped aside and motioning someone to come forward.

"Hello, Rory. I was not certain ye would wish to see me again."

Surprised by such a thought, Rory set aside her work and went to her friend. "What happened at the crying was not your fault, Morna."

"I told her so myself, but she insisted she must apologize to ye," the priest added.

"Rory," Nannag said, "we have forgotten our manners. Morna, ye and the babe must be tired after your long walk. Come and sit in the gathering room. Will ye be staying long, Sandy?"

"A few hours. Pàdraig brought Morna and their son to Achnacarry to receive Donald's blessing. The ceremony is on the morrow."

"Then ye have time for a wee bite."

"'Tis the true reason for my visit, Nannag," Sandy said with a wink. "There is no one else whose cooking compares."

Duncan's grandmother dismissed the priest's flattery with a wave of her hand. "No amount of your honeyed words will sweeten the offering, Sandy. 'Twill be no feast ye get."

"My bonny lass, I would settle for porridge if 'twas cooked by yourself. 'Tis fit for a king."

Rory did not hear Nannag's muttered answer, but the banter between the priest and Duncan's grandmother gladdened her heart. While Father Alex helped Nannag, Rory turned her attention to Morna, who seemed ill at ease.

"Has he a name yet?" she asked, nodding at the cradled blanket.

"Aye, Brandubh. Father Alex performed the kirking when he came to the *clachan.*"

"May I hold him?"

Morna handed over her son.

Rory lifted the blanket. Sparkling green eyes stared up at her. He stretched out his hand and grabbed hold of her finger. "He has Pàdraig's eyes and your hair."

"My husband never saw hair so black except on the raven. 'Tis why he named our son Brandubh."

"'Tis a good name and he is strong like his father."

"Pàdraig will be pleased to hear that. Rory?"

She glanced up to find Morna looking at her with a solemn expression on her face. "Aye?"

"Thank ye for what ye did. 'Twas a true act of friendship. Ye offered help though ye kent what the others would say. Brandubh and I would be dead had ye not risked your life to save ours."

"I did what needed doing, Morna, nocht else."

Brandubh began to cry.

"Bring the wee precious one to me," Nannag said. "I have a mind to fuss over him. Many a year has passed since the walls of this cottage were blessed with such a healthy voice."

After Sandy offered a prayer for the meal, he shared news of people and happenings. Too soon, the time came for them to leave.

"'Twas a pleasure to meet ye, Morna, and Brandubh is a fine son." Nannag handed her a small bundle. "'Tis a wee gift for the lad."

"Thank ye."

Sandy hugged Nannag. "Take care of her, Rory. This young lass is special."

"I ken, Father Alex."

"Now, dinna be listening to Sandy's teasing, Granddaughter. I am no more special than Morna, Brandubh, or yourself. Have a safe journey, Sandy."

While they watched their guests depart, Nannag said, "Morna is a quiet one, is she not?"

"She is."

"Well, I have weaving to attend. Will ye join me, Rory?"

"I think I will replenish my herbs and medicines. 'Tis a task I have sorely neglected of late."

"Will ye take Tam?"

"No, he can stay here. I am only going to the burn."

"Go on with ye then."

Rory ambled toward the stream, intent on enjoying what remained of a beautiful day. The late afternoon sun shone bright in a cloudless blue sky. A breeze whispered through the trees, cooling the air and stirring the pink bell-shaped flowers scattered amongst the carpet of dried pine needles. For a moment, she imagined she heard the foxglove tolling like kirk bells.

A feathery blur of white, orange, and brown swooped over her head and landed on a stone in the middle of the burn. The bobbing dipper flexed its legs, then plunged into the rushing water. With back slanted and head underwater, the small bird waded upstream in search of food.

"Hello, Rory."

Startled, she lost her balance and toppled toward the water. With deft agility, the speaker snatched her from a disastrous fall and set her on her feet.

"Have ye a particular fondness for the water, *m'eudail?*"

"Duncan!"

"Last time I looked upon my reflection 'twas I."

Rory swallowed. "I did not think to see ye again."

"'Tis my home, is it not?"

"Of course. Duncan, I—"

He put a finger to her lips. "Later we will talk. It has been a long journey and I am in need of nourishment."

"Nannag will be glad to see ye."

"And ye, Rory? Are ye also?"

"Aye, Duncan, I am."

He walked beside her, leading Midnight. When they reached the cottage, he stabled the stallion while she went to prepare his meal.

Nannag was delighted to see her grandson. "Then ye were at Achnacarry all this time, Grandson?"

"Not the whole of it."

While Duncan ate as if he had not done so in several days, Rory became aware of a dull drumming on the thatch. Peering out the open door, she noticed the sky had darkened and rain pelted the earth. When she rejoined Nannag and Duncan, she chose to sit across from her husband rather than beside him.

"'Tis grand weather for a story, is it not?" Nannag asked. "'Twas many the night, Duncan, your grandsire would weave the tales for your father, and later, for Tòmas and ye."

"I remember. He told of the great deeds of our chiefs or recited the legends of great warriors."

"So that is how ye came to have the tongue of the *seanchaidh,*" Rory said.

"Of course. Grandsire could persuade a fish to jump into his net, if he wanted. Have ye a story to tell, Grandmother?"

"Aye. 'Twas one of the first your grandsire told me. Before I begin, 'twould help my telling if ye poured a wee *cuach* of heather ale, Duncan."

"Are ye certain 'tis not whisky ye are wanting?"

"I am." Nannag sipped the drink, then licked her lips and began her tale. "Long before the time of Ewen Dubh, the Camerons swore allegiance to another chief who had many sons but only one daughter, a rare bonny lass named Seonag. One day a young warrior came to Lochaber. Coinneach accepted the Cameron's hospitality, and during his stay he fell in love with Seonag. Kenning the way of his heart, he asked her father for permission to wed his daughter. Now, Coinneach was chief of another clan. The Cameron had long wished to form an alliance with him, so he agreed to the union.

"Seonag kent the day would come when her father chose a husband for her, but she had hoped he would be of Clan Cameron so she need never be parted from her beloved Lochaber. 'Twas not to be, though, and ever the dutiful daughter, she obeyed her father and married a man she did not love.

"When the wedding feast ended, Seonag's father asked what she desired for a bridal tocher. She requested a guard of her own kinsmen, so twelve Cameron warriors rode with Seonag to her new home. They lingered there, and before long took wives of their own and settled down to raise families.

"Seonag took her place alongside her husband, running his home and bearing him sons. His love grew until it stretched the breadth of all Scotland. She came to love him, too, but the sadness in her deepened with each passing year. Coinneach tried to ease her sorrow, but there was nocht he did that cheered her. Seonag's grief over leaving Lochaber was too great; her beauty faded and her spirit withered until she fell ill. Her husband sent for the healers of his clan, but they could not cure her, for how does one mend a broken heart?

"Coinneach never left Seonag's side. He prayed for a miracle, but none came. One night, she asked him to grant one request. 'Ye have but to ask,' he said. 'Ye have given me all that I have without asking for anything in return.' 'When I die, bury me in my beloved Lochaber.' Unable to answer, for fear of weeping the tears he cried in his heart, he nodded. Before the night ended, Seonag left him.

"To an honorable man his word is his bond. Coinneach vowed to keep his pledge, but the land he must cross to reach Lochaber belonged to his enemy. This clan, who had no respect for the dead, attacked, and the fighting was fierce. Coinneach and his people won, but many were wounded or killed. He returned home, his promise to Seonag unfulfilled.

"One night while he slept, he dreamt he walked an earthen passageway. At the center of the underground chamber was a pit lined with stones. Seonag lay upon those stones. Men carried creel baskets of rich black soil that Coinneach sprinkled around her.

"Upon waking, he ordered his men to build such a tomb. Others he sent on horseback to fetch soil from Lochaber. On a moonless night, these men tried to cross the other clan's land, but the blackness failed to conceal them from their enemy. Two survived to return empty-handed. The Camerons, who had accompanied Seonag and settled amongst her husband's people, devised a plan to help.

"A warrior's wife must be strong and courageous, for she kens one day he willna return home. If there is love between them, 'tis a love that runs deep. There is nocht the husband willna do for his wife, nor she for him. And 'twas so with these Camerons and their wives. The women agreed to the plan without hesitation. They mounted garrons laden with creel baskets and set off for Lochaber without escort. They passed through enemy land unmolested, for true warriors dinna make war on women.

"A fortnight later, the wives returned with their creel baskets filled with Lochaber soil. In gratitude, Coinneach gave them land and the bairns of their bairns live there to this verra day."

Throughout the telling, Rory felt drawn to Duncan. Nannag's story was not about two people who had lived many years ago, but of him and her, and his love for her. Jumbled thoughts pulled her in opposite directions. She yearned for his lips to kiss hers, but at the same time she craved greater distance from him. His eyes captured hers, and she could not look away. Her chest constricted and her vision blurred. She tried to swallow, but it caused her pain.

A shout followed by an insistent pounding broke the spell. Rory ran to answer the knock. A stranger held aloft a small wooden cross, its two upper portions charred—the symbol of the fire—and bound by a blood-soaked rag—the symbol of the sword.

"Murlaggan in two days. *Chlanna nan con thigibh a so 's gheibh sibh feòil!*" the man shouted. Without waiting for a reply, he executed a sharp turn and disappeared into the darkness.

The Cameron rallying cry—Sons of the hounds come hither and get flesh!—echoed in Rory's ears. Visions of Bean-nighe and broken bannocks flooded her thoughts. Again, she witnessed the horrible bloodshed of her dream. Then, she remembered the fallen warrior.

"Duncan!"

Her cry brought him running. She flung herself against him. He stroked her hair and whispered calming words. He rubbed her cheek with his knuckle. "What did ye see, *m'eudail?*"

"The fiery cross."

CHAPTER THIRTEEN
TO ARMS

He has come! Rory did not know how she knew this, but she did. A chill threaded its way down her spine, and she shivered.

"Aye, *m'eudail.*"

Duncan's words caused her to blink. Had she spoken her thoughts aloud?

"The lass' hue is like cold ashes in the hearth!" Nannag pulled off her shawl and draped it over Rory's shoulders. "Bring her near the fire while I fetch her herbs."

Duncan laid a hand on his grandmother's arm. "There is no need for the remedies. They canna help, but the fire's warmth may do her good."

He guided Rory back to the bench in the gathering room. Nestled within his embrace, she let his warmth quiet her trembling while he explained about the omens and the fiery cross. The wrinkles on Nannag's forehead deepened with each revelation.

"There is something I dinna understand, though."

"What did I not explain, Grandmother?"

"Who comes?"

Rory moistened her lips. "Seumas mac Seumas."

Nannag's violet eyes widened with surprise. "King Jamie? Ye canna be serious. Why ever would he return to the Highlands?"

"'Tis more likely his older son, Charles Edward," Duncan said. "I doubt James would leave Rome and his court. He may be responsible for the intrigues behind the call for the clan to gather, but he is too old to lead us in a new rising."

"Is that why Sir Donald sent the runner with the fiery cross?"

Fire and sword. Rory shuddered. Those words imbued memories of the horrors inflicted by those who answered such a summons. Duncan stroked her arm. "'Tis not the same, *m'eudail.* Lochiel willna slaughter innocents. He may yet refuse to follow the Stewarts."

"When has a Cameron not followed a royal Stewart?"

"Rory is right, Grandson. Camerons fought for the Stewarts until Cromwell and his Roundheads beheaded the first Charles. When his son renewed the fight for the thrones of Scotland and England, 'twas Ewen Dubh who led the Camerons for the Stewarts. He fought for King Jamie's father at Killiecrankie and when Queen Anne died, he sent his son John to fight for King Jamie during the Rising of the 'Fifteen. And was not another son one of the King's most trusted agents? How can ye doubt his grandson willna support this Stewart?"

"Because Sir Donald is a man of peace. If Prince Charles has come and unless he brings the required arms, men, and gold, Sir Donald willna follow him." Duncan stood. "I must heed the runner and go to Achnacarry else my grandmother will curse me and my wife will despise me. Will ye stay here, Rory?"

"She will do no such thing. She goes with ye."

A smile played across Duncan's lips. "Grandmother, I love ye dearly, but ye canna be telling Rory what to do. 'Tis her decision to make. I canna say when I will return. If she prefers to stay here until she returns to her *clachan,* I willna object."

Truth between us in all things. Those words haunted Rory. How could she abide in safety while his life was in peril? He had risked his life to save hers. He had endangered his freedom to protect her from capture. He had jeopardized his standing within the clan to defend her against false accusations. The fiery cross might call him to arms, but it also called her. She had pledged to stand by him as long as they were wed. Friends did not forsake friends.

"I go with ye."

Duncan nodded. "Will ye stay, Grandmother? Sir Donald and Lady Anne would welcome ye to Achnacarry."

Nannag shook her head. "Your grandsire and I forged a new life here, and 'twas a grand time we had doing it. We shared good times and bad, joys and sorrows, but I dinna regret for one moment that I forsook my kin to follow Tòmas. This is my home. 'Tis where I belong."

Duncan hugged her. "William willna heed the call, so should ye need us, give him a message and he will find us."

Rory gathered medicines and clothes from the sleeping room. She fingered the soft threads of blue and purple strung on the loom.

"Ye chose those colors to represent Duncan and yourself."

"The why dinna matter, Nannag. Will ye give it to Duncan when 'tis finished."

"If ye wish him to have it, ye will have to do the giving yourself."

"'Twill be too late."

"'Tis never too late, Granddaughter." Nannag placed a small package inside the satchel. "Dinna open this unless ye decide to stay with Duncan. I ken ye think ye willna, but remember that fate brought him to ye. Much has happened since then, and what ye decided yesterday may not be the right choice today. In the tomorrows to come, promise ye will heed both heart and head before ye give Duncan an answer."

"I promise." Biting her lip to hold back the tears, Rory hugged the old woman.

Nannag patted her back, then eased away. "Go, now."

When Rory emerged from the cottage, Duncan stood on the traveler's stone with his hands buried in the thatch of the roof. He fumbled, grunted, and then extracted a basket-hilted broadsword that he handed to her.

"What is this?"

"'Twas my father's. He hid it when the Crown said we could not bear arms."

"Did he not turn it in like the others?"

"Not at all, and neither did they. What they delivered to the soldiers were broken swords and rusted dirks. They hid their prized weapons until the day came to retrieve them."

He tied her satchel behind the saddle, then took the sheathed sword from her. He pulled the leather strap over his head and slipped an arm through it. After mounting Midnight, he settled her in front.

"Take care of yourself, Grandmother."

"Ye do the same, Grandson. I want ye returning home the same way that ye leave—on your own two feet. I will pray for ye every day. Rory, I have a fond place in my heart for ye. Remember ye are always welcome."

"I will."

At the crest of the hill, Duncan reined Midnight to a halt and looked back at the cottage. Nannag stood in the doorway silhouetted by firelight. He raised his hand in farewell, and Rory did likewise.

~*~

Rory stood at the window of the sleeping room she shared with Duncan at Achnacarry. Everywhere armed men stirred around Loch Arkaig. Over three hundred Camerons had come in answer to the fiery cross. Two hundred more were expected within a sennight.

She had seen little of Duncan in the last two days. He returned to their room long after she retired, and rose before she woke. She craved word of what was happening, but all she knew for certain was that the clan gathered to join Teàrlach mac Seumas, Charles son of James, in a new rebellion.

Almost a hundred years had passed since the beheading of his great-grandfather, the first Charles, following the English Civil War. His son was proclaimed king, but did not reclaim the crown until three years after Oliver Cromwell's death. The second James succeeded his brother to the throne, but his adherence to the Papist religion and his belief in the divine right of kings conflicted with the views held by Parliament and most Sassenach. When the birth of his son ensured the prolongation of Papist rule, Parliament offered the crown to James's Protestant daughter, Mary, and her husband, William of Orange, forcing James to flee with his family to France.

When William died, his deceased wife's sister, Anne, ruled until her death twelve years later. Since her seventeen children had predeceased her and the Act of Settlement prohibited a Papist from ascending the throne, the crown passed to the Elector of Hanover, a German Protestant and great-grandson of the sixth James of Scotland and the first of England. His son, the second George, now ruled the united kingdoms.

The Jacobites, however, never ceased their efforts to restore the second James to the throne. Many Highland chiefs, including Ewen Dubh, assisted in these endeavors because James and later his son, the third James (so recognized by the Pope), were the rightful kings. Each restoration attempt—1689, 1715, and 1719—had ended in failure. Now another Stewart, Charles Edward, wished to try again.

Why did this prince think he would succeed where his father and grandfather had failed? Each defeat had brought with it retributions. The Highlanders were disarmed; General Wade built roads through the glens so troops could march unimpeded; and the garrisons of Forts William, Augustus, and George were strengthened. If this Stewart failed, Rory feared the vengeance inflicted on the Highlands would be too terrible to ponder.

The door latch clicked, and she turned. A weary Duncan closed the door behind him. He joined her at the window.

"'Tis an awesome sight to see so many gathered in one place!" she said.

"Aye, *m'eudail.* 'Tis not the same as the wappenshaw, though. This time there are few women and bairns who come." He sighed. "My feet ache from standing. If ye dinna mind, I shall sit on the bench."

"Have ye seen Prince Charles?"

"I willna set eyes on him until we reach Glenfinnan."

"Is that where he assembles his army?"

"Aye."

"How many soldiers and arms came?"

"That ship did not make it past a Sassenach warship."

"How many arrived with the prince?"

"Seven."

"Seven? Why ever did Lochiel agree to fight?"

"At first, he sent Archie to tell His Royal Highness to go home."

"And Charles' response?"

"Archie returned bearing two messages. The first one was that the prince was home. The second was a royal summons for Sir Donald to attend him."

"Lochiel obeyed?"

Duncan nodded. "On the way he visited his brother at Fassifern on the shore of Loch Eil. John feared the prince would sway Sir Donald to his cause, and he was right. Prince Charles reminded Sir Donald of the great feats accomplished by his grandsire, his father, and his uncle in the name of Stewart. He thought Lochiel a true friend on whom he could depend. If, however, Sir Donald did not wish to participate, that was his choice. The Prince, however, was resolute in his cause and would proceed without him. Lochiel could read of his venture in the newspaper."

"So Sir Donald relented?"

"Aye. He swore to share the prince's fate and pledged those who follow him to do the same."

"Och, Duncan, 'tis foolishness! The day will come when we rue his coming."

"Ye may speak the truth, Rory, but I gave my bond. If Lochiel follows Prince Charles, I must go with him."

"Would ye go had ye not sworn the oath?"

Duncan gave her a melancholy smile. "Though it pains me to leave ye, I would do so even then. I owe much to Sir Donald, for I would not be the man I am had he not taken me into his house. He brought us together, and for that alone I would not abandon him."

Rory saw the unspoken question in his eyes. She balled her hands into tight fists and turned her gaze to Loch Arkaig. The sun illuminated the dark water, creating a looking-glass reflection of verdant hills and tall pines outlined against a blue sky. A gust of wind sent ripples across the water, distorting the tranquil image. In its place she saw Duncan lying in a pool of blood. She leaned her forehead against the glass while tears slipped down her cheeks.

Nannag had seen what Rory refused to admit. While her mind remained detached and firm in her conviction to dissolve their union, her heart betrayed her. Duncan was more than a friend, and their lives were intertwined. Whatever the future held in store, they must face it together.

"*M'eudail?*"

Rory brushed away her tears, and turned. "Why do ye love me, Duncan?"

"Because ye are a warrior." He approached her. She started to speak, but he put his finger to her lips and smiled. "Dinna take offense. 'Tis a high compliment for a man to call a lass a warrior. 'Tis also the thread that binds us together."

He tapped her forehead. "Ye are a wise woman who thinks a situation through and considers all options before making a decision. While ye will ask for help when 'tis needed, ye can handle things on your own. 'Tis a sign of your independence, and it tells me that when Lochiel calls, I can leave without worrying how ye will fare.

"While ye are strong, ye are also gentle. Ye have a kind heart and care for others whether friend or foe. Ye speak your mind and do not hide the truth. I dinna like to argue, but I respect ye for differing with me.

"When I left after riling ye at the waterfall, I kept to myself high on the ben, for I was unfit company even for a wildcat. I missed ye something fierce, but thought ye lost to me. I never meant to hurt ye, and yet I had done so twice. Not until I plucked ye from the burn did I feel whole again. Whether we see eye to eye or whether we disagree does not matter. What matters is that I love ye and want ye for my wife." He smoothed new tears from her cheeks with his calloused thumb.

"Ye are my friend, Duncan."

"Friendship is not enough, Rory."

"I ken."

He released an exasperated groan and stepped away.

"Duncan, dinna leave." Her shoulders sagged and her hand fell to her side. "I am not explaining myself well."

"What are ye after trying to tell me?"

"While I ken ye want more from me than friendship, 'tis important that we be friends."

"Why?"

"Do ye remember Nannag saying she and your grandsire had weathered good times and bad, joys and sorrows? Friendship is the foundation upon which they built their love. If we dinna do the same, we willna survive the sorrows or the bad times."

Duncan drew a deep breath. With his hands on her shoulders, he held her at arm's length. "Are ye saying ye willna leave me?"

She nodded.

"What of my mother's blood, Rory? She was a Campbell, and there is nocht I can do to purge her blood from my veins."

"When first ye spoke of your kinship with my enemy, I thought wedding ye a sacrilege that would defile my mother's memory."

"But ye agreed to handfast with me."

"To protect my people, not because 'twas what I wanted."

"Then what has changed? 'Twas Campbells who murdered your mother. 'Tis their blood in me."

"'Twas your taking yourself away that taught me despair and loneliness. I kent ye loved me, so how could I condemn ye to that same anguish? In truth, I could not. While I am uncertain of my heart, I would rather stand with ye than against ye.

"'Tis time for me to let go of the past. What I experienced at the hands of the Campbells will never leave me, but they were evil men and my hatred is for them. It took courage for ye to tell me of your kinship, but I ignored the words of another who warned me against judging one by the deeds of another. 'Twas neither yourself nor your mother who attacked my clan, and I was wrong to condemn ye for it. Can ye forgive me?"

"There is nocht to forgive. Rory, what of the oath ye had me swear to before the handfasting?"

"I release ye from it, but—"

He tilted his head. His eyes clouded with wariness. "But what?"

"Have patience, Duncan. I want to love ye, but I must be certain before…"

"Before ye lie with me?"

She nodded, lowering her head, her face warm. He nudged her chin until their eyes met.

"When ye are ready, *m'eudail,* I will be waiting, but I ask something of ye in return for my patience."

"And what is it ye are wanting from me?"

"To kiss and touch ye without ye objecting. I willna force myself on ye, but I canna continue as we have."

In answer, she brought his face nearer to hers and kissed him. He fitted his hands around her waist and lifted her until his arms unbent. He laughed and spun around three times.

"Duncan, stop. 'Tis dizzy ye are making me."

When he lowered his arms, she slid down against him until her feet touched the floor. He held her close, then pulled her across the room to the hearth.

"Sit on the fur with your back against the bench."

The instant she settled, he sprawled on the rug and rested his head in her lap. He pulled her head down to kiss her.

"'Tis weary I am and ye shall do well for my pillow."

"Then I wish ye pleasant dreams, husband."

"I have no doubt 'tis what they will be, wife."

In seconds he was fast asleep. Rory noticed the dark shadows under his eyes. The muscles of his face relaxed and the creases faded. She brushed a few stray curls from his forehead, and smiled. He looked as peaceful as she felt. For the first time in months, the emotional maelstrom warring inside her had dissipated. She no longer felt pulled in two directions. While she understood how precarious her future with Duncan was at this moment, she no longer doubted she had chosen the right path.

Mairi and Angus had fended for themselves long before her birth. Since no one had heard from them in nine months, she knew they did not need her. She had provided a safe haven and protection for her kin by wedding Duncan, so they no longer needed her either. The man who rested his head in her lap, however, did need her and she needed him.

A light rap on the door interrupted her thoughts. Unable to rise, she whispered "Come" as loud as she dared. The door opened to reveal Sandy. She put a finger to her lips and pointed at Duncan. The priest eased the door closed, then sat on the bench beside her.

"Pardon my manners, Father."

"Dinna fash, lass," he whispered. "Kenning my brother, the poor lad has not had more than a few hours sleep since ye returned."

Have ye important business with him or can it wait?"

"My business is with yourself. Donald wanted me to ask a question, but I dinna think it needs asking."

"What question might that be, Sandy?" Duncan asked, his eyes still closed.

"Sorry, lad, I did not mean to wake ye. Donald is after wondering if Rory has changed her mind."

"Changed my mind about what?"

"He alluded to a handfasting ceremony. From the look of things, I gather ye have not reconsidered."

"She has not, Sandy. In less than three months, I will be free to flirt with the lasses again. Do ye wish to join me?"

The priest shook with laughter. "'Tis a tempting offer, but I dinna think the Lord would approve. How many lasses are lined up to help ye celebrate?"

Rory shoved Duncan from her lap. "I willna stay here and listen to your teasing. Father Alex, tell your brother that if the king himself sent ye, I would not give answer. 'Tis for him to do the asking, not yourself."

Sandy clicked his tongue. "She is a fierce wildcat. Ye best beware of her claws, lad."

Rory slammed the door on their laughter. She felt her anger rise, not from their good-natured teasing, but because she was no longer her own master. She was obliged to answer to another for her actions, but it was hard to accept. What she needed was a place where her anger could dissolve without her fearing she might lash out at any who crossed her path. It was too hot to climb to the eaves. There were too many men around for her to walk alone. She headed for the garden, but spied the stables and decided to visit Midnight instead.

The stallion nuzzled her when she laid her head against its neck. She picked up a comb and began to brush its coat. Her anger ebbed, but a new emotion appeared in its wake. Once Duncan departed for Glenfinnan, she had no idea when or if she would see him again.

They were not alone in this predicament. War tended to separate families. For the lucky ones, the parting was temporary. For others, it was permanent. Duncan did not fight because he believed a Stewart should wear the crown. He went because of his fealty to Lochiel. If he betrayed his oath, he lost honor, and without honor he could not live with himself. Men had followed her without question because they had sworn to heed and protect her. She could expect Duncan to do no less.

At least they did not war against each other. In this rising, men would take sides. Brother would fight against brother, father against son. No clan, including the Camerons, would escape unscathed. Already, a rift separated Lochiel from his brother, who refused to help raise the clan against King George. John would not risk his money, his land, or his family in a cause he deemed unwinnable. Neither would he lift his sword against his brother. He left his wife and son and withdrew to the home of his father-in-law, where he vowed to remain until the war ended.

A shadow fell across Rory. She supposed Duncan had come in search of her, but when she turned, she saw the silhouette of a tall gentleman leaning on a cane. The *cromag* symbolized the crook of a shepherd, and this man was the shepherd of his people.

"So ye willna answer my question."

"Dinna take that tone with me, Sir Donald! Father Alex is not my confessor, and ye had no right to include him in what was between ye and myself."

A low chuckle escaped the chief of the Camerons. "Ye are a welcome change, Rory. The handfuls of men who surround me are afraid to speak their minds, while ye have twice put me in my place."

"'Tis time someone did."

Lochiel guffawed. "Will ye walk with me?"

She set the brush aside, then gave Midnight a carrot before following her chief from the stable. His guards trailed at a discreet distance. He led her along a lane lined with new saplings.

"Ye planted these since the snows melted," she said.

"I thought 'twould be pleasant to have a shaded lane leading to the house."

"From the looks of them, ye did not take great care in the planting. They will grow crooked."

"An unexpected visitor required I hasten the task."

"Is he the reason for this walk we are having?"

Instead of answering her, Lochiel countered with a question of his own. "What do ye think of my uncle, Ludovic of Torcastle?"

"Are we to be playing word games, is it? I have but days left to spend with Duncan and I willna be wasting them. Good day to ye, Sir Donald."

She got halfway to the house before massive hands seized her waist and slung her over a shoulder.

"Put down my wife, Fergus."

Rory could almost look her husband in the eye. The brute who held her was a giant.

"I canna do that, Duncan. Sir Donald told me to fetch her back to him."

"If ye value your life, ye will put her down."

"Set Rory down, Fergus," Lochiel said.

"Gently."

"Aye, Duncan."

The flaxen-haired giant handled her as a father would a newborn babe. His gentleness surprised her. "I am sorry, Rory. I hope I did not hurt ye."

"Ye meant no harm, Fergus. Ye only obeyed an order."

"I would have thought ye learned your lesson the last time ye riled my wife," Duncan said, coming to stand beside her. "Ye came close to losing an ear then, Sir Donald, if I remember rightly."

Lochiel's hand went to his ear. "'Tis amazing I could forget such a thing. I must have too much on my mind. I suppose I also raised your ire?"

"Aye."

"When I proposed this union, I had no idea what a potent force I unleashed. Your father's reports, Rory, did not exaggerate. He wrote of your training and your learning. He also mentioned a wild rebellious streak that he could not rid ye of."

"My father wrote to ye?"

Sir Donald nodded.

"Once or twice a year I heard from him. 'Twas my condition for what he proposed. If I was to find a suitable husband for ye, I needed to ken of ye."

"Is that why ye chose me to wed her?"

"Aye, Duncan. No other Cameron has the temperament to tame an agile and ferocious wildcat. Nor would they tolerate her flouting of tradition. When I learned she had the Two Sights, I kent the husband I chose must be open to new ideas and willing to protect her from those who would not understand. Did I choose wisely, lass?"

Rory slipped her hand into Duncan's. He winked at her.

"Aye."

"Then ye willna end the marriage?"

"Not at all."

"Good. Then I have a question for ye, Duncan. Will ye permit me to decide what Rory does while we tend to other matters?"

A tight squeeze of her hand quieted her urge to object.

"While 'tis common for men to decide issues regarding their women, 'tis not the way between Rory and myself. I have learned to trust her with my life. She willna shame herself, the clan, or me, so there is no need for me to speak for her. If ye would have my wife do your bidding, ye must ask her yourself."

Lochiel drew circles in the dirt with his *cromaq*. He pursed his lips and glanced from Duncan to Rory before returning his gaze to his foster son. "Ye ken there are those who willna agree with giving women the right to decide their fate?"

"What is between Rory and myself has been hard earned. I value her wisdom and her canniness. Her skills as a warrior are akin to my own. I would give my life to protect her right to speak as men do."

"'Tis a rare compliment your husband pays ye, lass."

"I ken."

"And would ye defend him with equal vigor?"

"I already have."

Sir Donald's discerning gaze scrutinized her, but he refrained from quizzing her. "Ye are wildcat and rebel."

"I dinna deny it."

"Then how can I trust ye, Rory Cameron?"

"Just because I am not a man does not mean my word should carry less weight. I value my honor as much as Duncan values his or ye value yours. I dinna have the years ye have, Sir Donald, but I have *never* shamed kith or kin by breaking my bond."

"Then I put to ye the question I asked of Duncan. Will ye permit me to decide what ye do while we tend to other matters?"

"If it willna dishonor my husband, the clan, or myself, aye, I will do your bidding."

"So be it. I have called a meeting of the chieftains and leaders of the cadets and septs of Clan Cameron. I would have Duncan and ye attend me there."

"Father?"

Lochiel frowned at his thirteen-year-old son. "Is it important, John? Ye ken I did not wish to be disturbed."

"Aye, Father, but Uncle Archie sent me to fetch Rory. There are wounded soldiers in the hall who need tending."

Lochiel sighed. "'Tis started then, and there can be no turning back. We will finish our conversation later. For now, it seems we are needed elsewhere."

Sixty red soldiers sat on the front lawn, their arms shackled by heather rope. Half as many Highlanders guarded them. Rory recognized some Camerons, but the others wore the heath of the MacDonells of Keppoch and Glengarry in their bonnets. While she followed John into the hall, his father and Duncan remained outside.

Another twenty soldiers, suffering varying degrees of cuts and bruises, sprawled on the stairs or leaned against the walls. She went to tend to their wounds.

"Dinna fash about them, Rory. Lady Anne will see to their needs," Archibald Cameron said, glancing up from bandaging the head wound of one red soldier. "Give my nephew oil of Saint John's Wort and some bandages. He will help his mother. I need your help with the officer on the table in the gathering room. He has not drunk enough for me to tend him."

"Are ye asking me to see that he does?"

"'Twill do for a start. I have to remove a musket ball from his shoulder and stitch up his leg. One of the lads tried to sever it without much success."

The officer was about Duncan's age. Varying shades of rust-colored splotches stained the right shoulder of his red coat and the upper left leg of his white breeches. The pallor of his skin was ashen. Damp curls of black hair hung limp on his fevered brow. A young lad, one of the house servants, attempted to lift his head and hold a bottle of whisky to his lips. More liquid dribbled down his neck than entered his mouth.

"Ye hold the man's head, and I will help him drink," Rory said.

The boy handed the bottle to her. The soldier started to refuse, but she smiled and shook her head. "'Tis best to drink what ye can. 'Twill dull the pain while Dr. Archie tends your wounds."

He managed to swallow several gulps before refusing more drink. She dipped a linen rag into a bucket of water and wrung it out. She placed it on his forehead, then asked, "Ye are a captain of the Royal Scots, are ye not?"

He gave a slight nod.

"My name is Rory Cameron. Can ye tell me yours?"

"John Scott."

"Is he drunk yet?"

"He can take no more, Dr. Archie."

The physician frowned. "I must remove the ball from your shoulder and see to your leg, Captain. I fear the pain will be great. Are ye sure ye willna have more whisky?"

"Sure." Scott wet his lips. "It canna be worse than the trip here."

"Aye, well, we can pray 'tis so."

Rory held Scott's cold hand between her warm ones. He locked eyes on her rather than watch Archibald cut away the cloth around his shoulder. When the probing pain registered, he bit his lip and squeezed her hand.

"Tell me, Captain, whatever possessed ye to be after getting yourself into so much trouble?" she asked.

A rueful smile touched his lips. "'Twas not my idea. My men and I were minding our business when MacDonalds ambushed us while we crossed High Bridge. Do ye ken the place, Mistress Rory?"

"'Tis where Wade built his road over the rapids of the River Spean. And is that where ye came by your wounds?"

"Just the leg. The men who routed us numbered but twelve. 'Twas their leader's canniness that made us think they were a great host. His men darted back and forth through the trees and the infernal piping terrorized my men. The English lads are unaccustomed to the skirl of the pipes. They fled toward Fort Augustus. The MacDonalds followed and attacked again."

"How many did ye lose?"

"Six." A spasm of pain rippled across his face. The pressure of his grip increased, making Rory wonder if he would crush her hand before Dr. Archie finished his work. "Is it true?"

"Is what true, Captain Scott?"

"Has the Stewart prince come?"

"Got it!" Dr. Archie dropped a flattened ball of lead into the bucket. Water splashed onto the floor. "'Tis half done, Captain. Once I finish with the bandaging, I will have to sear your leg with hot iron. Would ye rather one of the lads knock ye out with his fist?"

"If I pass out, 'twill be a blessing. I dinna need a sore jaw to add to my pain."

"Who does my brother tend, Rory?" Sir Donald asked.

"Captain John Scott of His Majesty's Royal Scots."

"I am Sir Donald Cameron of Lochiel, Captain. I wish 'twas under better circumstances that I welcomed ye to Achnacarry."

"As do I, sir."

Rory caught movement out of the corner of her eye. Duncan and Fergus positioned themselves at Scott's feet while Lochiel shifted to hold fast the captain's shoulders against the table. When the hot metal touched the wound, his body jerked and he shrieked. His eyes rolled back into his head, and his hand went limp.

"How long will he be out?" Lochiel asked.

"'Tis difficult to say," his brother said.

"Will he be fit enough to travel?"

"To Glenfinnan?" Archibald snorted. "'Tis more likely to kill him."

"I ken ye would have him rest for several days, but 'tis best he not be found here. Do ye think he would survive the journey to Maryburgh?"

"If the going is taken with care, and Rory accompanies him. She kens what to do if the bleeding starts again."

"How soon can they leave?"

"Give him a few hours more to sleep, Donald. 'Twill be safer for them to travel in the gloaming. Fewer eyes will see them."

~*~

"He willna be riding with me!"

Rory jerked her head in the direction of the gruff voice. Two men stood in the shade of an oak tree halfway between Achnacarry and the loch. She edged closer, waiting until she was almost upon them before she spoke. "Ye dinna have the gentle touch of your brother so I willna allow it."

Startled, they whirled. The tawny-haired man said, "The lass looks a wee familiar, but I canna place where I have seen her. Can ye, Malcolm?"

"Not at all, Jamie. She is a buxom lass, though. Mayhap she will warm our beds while we are from home."

"If she does, your heads will be searching for your shoulders." Duncan shook each man's hand. "Welcome to Achnacarry."

"Aye." Rory hugged each foster brother. "'Tis a sorrow that ye visit under such circumstances. How are Fiona and Sarà and the bairns?"

"All are well, though Fiona was none too pleased with the messenger," Malcolm said.

Lochiel arrived, leading the contingent of bodyguards who carried Captain Scott.

"I see ye have met your escorts. Will they do, Duncan?"

"Except for my wife, I trust no one more."

"Good. Who rides with the prisoner?"

Jamie stepped forward.

"'Tis I."

"Mistress Rory?" Captain Scott asked.

"Aye?"

"Do ye go with me?"

"Until we deliver ye into safe hands that will see ye to Fort William."

"Mayhap I should warn ye, Captain Scott," Lochiel said, drawing nearer. "Dinna be getting too accustomed to Rory's company. She is newly wed and I think my foster son will have something to say should ye overstep yourself."

Duncan stood with his arms folded over his chest and a menacing glower on his face.

"Enough!" Rory said. "'Tis not fair to threaten a man who canna defend himself. If my husband canna trust me, then mayhap I should remain here."

"She will not!" Archie said. "I dinna approve of this, so if ye dinna want to be leaving this man here, there will be no more teasing. Am I clear?"

To a man they nodded.

"Good. Rory, I leave our patient in your capable hands. Run the lot through with Duncan's sword if they trouble ye again."

She coughed to keep from smiling. "If that is your wish, Dr. Archie, but 'twill add to the patients ye already have."

The doctor grunted and left.

"Captain," Lochiel said.

"Aye, sir?"

"While my brother mended your wounds, ye asked Rory a question I dinna think she answered. The man ye asked about has come home. At present ye are a prisoner, but I believe 'twould serve both sides if ye return to yours. I ask for your parole so ye willna lift the sword against us."

"'Twill be a wee while before I am fit to fight, so I give my word freely, sir."

"Duncan, make haste but dinna endanger Captain Scott or yourselves. When your task is done, return without tarrying. I will be with the chieftains on the morrow. I want the four of ye to report to me before the sun sets. Have I your word?"

"Aye, Sir Donald."

The small mounted group headed east, then turned south keeping parallel to the River Lochy.

"Do ye ken what Sir Donald wants from us, Rory?" Duncan asked.

"Whatever he is wanting concerns our being wed."

"Why do ye think that?"

"The first time he and I talked, 'twas what we spoke of. He did not like my answer, so he sent us from Achnacarry."

"So?"

"'Tis the same concern he had when we returned."

"He said nocht else?"

"He asked for my thoughts on Ludovic of Torcastle."

"Hmmm. I have long wondered something, *m'eudail,* and will ask your opinion if ye promise not to take offense."

"I willna."

"When Sir Donald had me take ye around Lochaber and introduce ye to the clan, I thought 'twas odd for him to place such importance on ye."

"Because I am a woman?"

Duncan nodded.

"I thought the same. As foster son and *leine-chreis,* ye rank high in the clan, but there are others, like Ludovic of Torcastle and John of Fassifern, with more influence. I may be your wife, but unless these men came to the cottage, there was no reason for us to seek them out."

"Rory."

Hearing Jamie call, Duncan spurred Midnight forward until they drew abreast.

"Have his wounds opened again?" she asked, noting the lack of color in Scott's cheeks.

"'Tis rest he is needing. The track is not even and the jostling canna be good for him. He tries hard to keep silent, but the wounds pain him. How far is it to Maryburgh?"

"We are half there." Duncan surveyed the area. He pointed to a thick grove of trees. "We shall rest there. 'Tis sheltered enough to build a wee fire so Rory can tend the captain."

While her husband and brothers hobbled the horses, lit a fire, and brought water from the river, she removed the bandage from Scott's shoulder and peered at Dr. Archie's stitches.

"How is it?" he asked.

"Bruised and swollen, but I dinna see suppuration." She poured oil of Saint John's Wort onto clean linen and re-bandaged the wound. When she examined his leg, she did not like what she saw. "Malcolm, have ye whisky?"

"Whisky, lass? I would never bring such along when I am heeding my chief's orders."

"And I am Queen of the Scots. Now, fetch me the whisky."

He grumbled, but complied.

"Captain," Rory said, "I dinna want to cause more pain, but if I dinna pour this on the wound, ye may lose the leg or die."

Jamie offered the officer a small piece of wood. "Open your mouth, man, and bite down on this."

Rory emptied the bottle onto the wound. Scott screamed through clenched teeth. His body jerked, but the others held him fast. When the pain eased, he opened his mouth and the branch fell to the ground. Jamie retrieved it.

"'Tis strong teeth ye have, Captain. Ye almost severed this into three pieces."

"Rest, Scott," Duncan said. "We will leave when the moon rises. I will take the watch."

Rory wiped her patient's sweaty face with a wet cloth. Malcolm and Jamie sat with their backs against two trees, and were soon snoring. She rested her head on her knees.

"'Tis time to move, *m'eudail,*" Duncan whispered, squatting next to her while rubbing her back.

"Let me check Captain Scott."

"He has a fever, but kens who I am."

In the wee hours of the night, they reached the head of Loch Linnhe. They skirted the earthen ramparts and stone bastions of Fort William, a garrison of twelve hundred soldiers. Duncan drew rein on the outskirts of Maryburgh, the village that lay south of the fort. He motioned for silence and dismounted. After helping Rory alight, he led Midnight to Malcolm. "Keep to the shadows. Make certain the horses stay silent."

At Malcolm's nod, Duncan went to Jamie and eased Captain Scott from the garron. He carried him to a darkened house. Rory knocked on the door.

"Who is there?"

"Open up, Neil. Himself sent me."

"Duncan, is that ye?"

"Aye, and if ye dinna open the door, I will!"

"Hold fast, lad."

The man inside slid back a timber, then swung open the door. Duncan motioned for Rory to enter and he followed. The smoored fire in the hearth gave off little light, but in the dimness she saw a man leaning on a crutch. The lower half of his left leg was missing. He sniffed the air.

"Ye have a lass with ye, Duncan."

"She is my wife."

Captain Scott groaned.

"Are ye hurt, lad?" Neil asked.

"No," Duncan said. "And dinna sit on your bed. I am setting Captain John Scott of His Majesty's Royal Scots on it."

"What is wrong with him?"

"He is twice wounded."

"How came he by the wounds?"

Rory recounted what Scott had told her.

"And what am I to do with him?" Neil asked.

"See that he is returned to the garrison," Duncan said.

"How should I explain to the governor how he came to be in my care?"

"I am certain ye will think of a reasonable excuse."

Neil harrumphed.

Rory went to Captain Scott. "'Tis time for me to leave ye, sir. Neil will see that ye get to the garrison."

"I willna forget your kindness."

Duncan drew her toward the door. "Neil, Lochiel wants ye to keep your eyes and ears open. Should ye hear any news of import, send word."

"'Tis the rising then, is it?"

"Aye."

"Good luck to ye, then, and God save King Jamie! And lad?"

"Aye?"

"I am glad ye are wed, but dinna bring the lass here again."

"'Twas Lochiel who sent her."

"Then give him my message."

Neil's comment puzzled Rory, but she waited until they distanced themselves from Maryburgh before pursuing the slight. "Why am I not welcome at Neil's?"

"'Tis not ye personally who is unwelcome. He objects to all women."

"Why?"

"Ludovic of Torcastle is not open about reiving the cattle, but rumors abound. Lochiel enlisted Neil to learn the truth of them because he has the gift of being able to blend in with those around him. 'Twas not long before he gained Ludovic's trust and accompanied him on two forages for cattle. After the second trip, Neil met up with a woman whom he oft bedded. I dinna ken how she learned of his spying, but she saw a chance to improve her lot and informed Ludovic of it. When Neil next went reiving, he fell before the cattle and had his leg crushed."

"Was he pushed?"

"Aye. While he lay there, one of Ludovic's men told him 'twas what traitors deserved. They waited until there was no hope of saving his leg before taking him to Dr. Archie."

"Was there nocht Lochiel could do?"

"He banished the woman and the man from Lochaber, but he had no proof against Ludovic. All he could demand of him was that he not lift any more cattle."

"But he does."

"And no one dares give evidence against him. They dinna want to end up like Neil or worse."

"And for this he has forsworn women?"

"Aye."

Malcolm drew up beside them. "Will we stop for the night or do we continue?"

Duncan rubbed the stubble on his chin and throat. "There is an old bothy deep in these woods where we can rest. I dinna ken what Lochiel has in store for us, but I think we should be fresh when we join him."

CHAPTER FOURTEEN
AN ENEMY WITHIN

While Duncan traversed the ten miles from Achnacarry to Murlaggan, he thought of little else but Lochiel's request to join the gentlemen of the clan at the grove of oaks at the western end of Loch Arkaig. Some of these lesser chieftains and leaders concurred with Ludovic of Torcastle, who preferred to live life according to the dictates of his father, Ewen Dubh, rather than heed his nephew's attempts to change long-held traditions. He believed women should not interfere in the affairs of men. His nephew's invitation for Rory to attend would stoke the ire of those with no tolerance for women who did not know their place.

With his fingers curled at the hilt of his dirk and his gaze darting from one man to the next, Duncan guided Rory through the throng to where Lochiel and his brothers, Sandy and Archie, stood.

"Did Captain Scott reach Fort William?" Sir Donald asked.

Duncan nodded. "We left him with Neil."

"Good." Lochiel turned to Rory. "Are ye ready?"

"Ready for what?"

"For whatever I ask of ye this day."

"I am."

Lochiel addressed the assembled men. "In two days we join His Royal Highness at Glenfinnan. While we endeavor to reclaim the crown for the rightful king of Scotland, our absence requires that I appoint another to act in my stead. Oft 'tis my brother, John of Fassifern, to whom such responsibility falls, but he has withdrawn to Glenorchy, and thus canna see to this duty. Archie and Sandy accompany me, as does my uncle.

"Times ahead are fraught with danger, both for ourselves and those we leave behind. My representative must act as counselor and judge, protector and guardian. I would choose someone who can handle my affairs while tending to the women and bairns, the aged and infirm. The one chosen must be adept in the use of all manner of weapons, be it sword or pistol or canniness."

Duncan suspicioned Lochiel's intent and stifled a groan. Ludovic of Torcastle, more than any other, would voice the first objection to the forthcoming proposal. Duncan glanced at Malcolm, then at Lochiel's uncle, hoping Rory's foster brother understood that trouble brewed.

"Have ye chosen your foster son, nephew?" Ludovic asked. "Be that why his wife attends him?"

Lochiel faced his uncle. "Duncan accompanies us. The prince has not men enough to spare one warrior. Rory is here at my request. 'Tis herself I propose to act in my stead."

Duncan spared his wife a glance, and noted her guarded eyes. She, too, must have deciphered the reason for her presence and realized the men would never accept her without proof of her competency. He held no doubts that she would best whatever test they put forth. What bothered him was that in doing so, she risked revealing a secret—one that could endanger her life.

The initial surprise wore off quickly, and the men grumbled. Instinct drew Duncan closer to Rory. Malcolm had maneuvered himself to flank Lochiel's uncle. Jamie remained beside Duncan.

Ludovic raised his voice to be heard over the others. "'Tis long I kent ye had peculiar thoughts, nephew, but before this, I never thought ye daft!"

All eyes focused on Lochiel to see how he would meet this challenge.

"'Tis no secret we often disagree, uncle. I am certain there are others who agree with your assessment, but my choice is a sound one."

"She is a woman!" Ludovic said.

Duncan waited for Lochiel to respond, but instead heard Rory speak. "Sir Donald, I would answer that, if ye dinna object?"

He motioned for her to do so. She stepped closer to Ludovic, and Duncan moved to protect her, but Jamie held him back. He mouthed a silent "Wait," before turning to watch his sister.

"Sir, I would have ye clarify your statement," Rory said.

Ludovic blinked. He seemed taken aback to find himself confronted by a female. The surprise was momentary. He regained control and spoke with sarcastic indulgence. "How may I be of service, my lady?"

"The reason ye dinna approve of your nephew's choice is because I am of the weaker sex?"

He nodded.

"And since I am a woman, I canna defend myself?"

Again he nodded.

"In that case, would ye agree to a wee wager?"

Ludovic's eyes narrowed. "Why should I waste my time wagering with a lass?"

"Then ye are afeared I might best ye?"

His face flushed red with anger. "How dare ye question my courage! Name your wager!"

"I will fight one of your choosing. If I win, ye will accept your nephew's proposal."

"And if ye lose? Will ye willingly come to my bed?"

A collective gasp echoed through the clearing, then utter stillness descended. Duncan heard only the blood rushing through his ears. He trembled with rage so intense he could slay every man present. Such an affront could not go unpunished. He made to draw his dirk, but strong hands stayed him. He glared at his foster father, who held his right arm, and at Fergus, who held his left. Jamie had disappeared.

"Regard your warrior, son," Lochiel whispered. "Ken she will dishonor neither ye nor herself."

How could he allow his wife to accept a challenge that would give to another what she denied him? Her sense of honor would compel her to go to Ludovic and subject herself to his lecherous touch.

Duncan looked to Rory. Her hand touched the intricate engravings on the silver brooch she wore. While he stared at the long slender fingers caressing the blue sapphire at its center, Duncan heard her voice even though her lips remained still. *Trust in me. Ye ken better than any the skills I have honed. Ye likened me to a warrior who is your equal. Could ye not best Ludovic or any man here present?*

The question startled him. Without looking away, he knew the answer and nodded.

Then trust me to do the same. I willna be alone in this, Duncan. I have your strength and wisdom, alongside that of Thistle's. Have I your leave to accept the challenge?

He could no more explain the words he heard in his head than he could explain his wife's ability to see the future. Since he knew her Two Sights to be true, he shook off those who held him. He crossed his arms over his chest and locked eyes with Rory, communicating the trust she asked of him.

"I accept your terms, Ludovic of Torcastle," she said. "Who is your champion?"

"Cathal."

A swarthy man with piercing eyes and chiseled chin stepped from behind Ludovic. His thick eyebrows and curled mustache lent him a sinister air, marring an otherwise handsome face. "Aye?"

"Teach this impertinent woman her place."

Cathal leered at Rory. "'Twill be my pleasure."

Duncan disliked Ludovic's choice. He claimed Cathal was his bodyguard, but Duncan suspected the man's duties went far beyond that of ensuring Torcastle's safety. In truth, he was more likely the one who carried out whatever nefarious command he received, including that of pushing Neil into the path of the cattle.

Lochiel stepped forward.

"Do ye interfere, nephew?" Ludovic asked.

"Ye chose who will fight Rory, uncle. I will select the weapon. Do ye object to this too?"

"Not if it has a sharp edge."

Lochiel snapped his fingers and Fergus brought forward two swords. Cathal took his and leaned the blade against his shoulder. Rory slipped her hand into the basket hilt of the other. Although the sword was meant to be employed with one hand, she seemed unable to grasp the heavy weapon without using both of hers. It wobbled until she managed to lower it point-first to the ground where the double-edged blade bore the brunt of the sword's weight. She held the weapon, which was half her height, like a cane.

"Look, she canna even hold the sword. Ludovic will feast on the spoils before he leaves."

The lewd comment brought nervous laughter from some of the men. Others voiced taunts of their own.

"A clever ruse."

The whispered words came from behind Duncan. Without taking his eyes off his wife, he answered in a similar fashion.

"'Tis. Where did ye go, Jamie?"

"To tend to Malcolm. Like yourself, my brother did not take kindly to Torcastle's insult."

Duncan glanced across at Rory's childhood protector. His lips were narrowed and he glowered at Ludovic's back as if to pierce the man's wicked heart.

"Dinna fash," Jamie said. "While he aches to slit the man's throat, he willna attack unless 'tis necessary."

"Ye seem amused, brother."

"My heart is in my throat, Duncan, fearing for my sister's life and her honor, but 'tis been there before and kenning her, 'twill be there again. 'Tis the rebel in her that makes her accept risks ye and I would avoid."

"She will best Cathal."

"If she does not, Torcastle willna live to savor his win."

Lochiel's voice interrupted their exchange. "Cathal, 'twill be a fair fight. If there be the slightest treachery on your part, ye will lose your hand to the blade and be banished from Lochaber forever."

"Why dinna ye threaten her?"

Lochiel laughed. "Rory is honorable. She willna resort to trickery to best ye. Prepare yourselves. When ye hear the skirl of the pipes, 'tis the signal to begin. 'Tis not a battle to the death. 'Twill end when one is disarmed or when first blood is drawn."

Rory leaned the sword against her plaid and struggled to tuck the cloth that covered her legs under her belt. A new round of ribald comments greeted the sight of her trim calves. When Cathal ran his tongue over his lips, Duncan resisted the urge to plow his fist into the lecher's face.

The piper blew into his bagpipes. Cathal, seeing Rory still unprepared, whirled around, his kilt swinging full. His sword, aimed at the sword still propped between Rory's legs, sliced the air. His intent was clear. He expected to knock her weapon to the ground, ending the duel before it began. His face registered stunned surprise when she hefted her sword with one hand and stepped back so his blade met only air. Propelled by the force of his attack, he spun around until he faced away from her. She tapped his shoulder with the tip of her blade.

"Are ye looking for me?"

The men howled with laughter. Cathal's sword slashed the air, and Duncan felt panic rise like bile in his throat. Riled by Rory's taunt, Cathal attacked like a rabid animal, cutting and thrusting in an attempt to cleave her head from her neck.

The clang of steel resonated through the trees. She parried his blow, then countered with a move of her own. She pressed her advantage, forcing Cathal to retreat. On her last lunge, he blocked her blade and feinted, drawing her parry. When she tried to defend herself, he brought his blade under hers and lunged. Without wasted movement, she stepped to one side, struck his blade with hers, and then reversed her movement with such speed that her blade sliced through Cathal's plaid. The draped portion fell from his shoulder, baring his chest. He roared with anger and charged. She twisted away from the thrust, but the blade ripped the sleeve of her shift.

Cathal slashed downward with his sword. Rory dropped to one knee and thrust upward under his slashing blade. He tried to step aside, but his momentum carried him forward. The sharp edge sliced his chest. He stared at the blood oozing from the wound, then raised venomous eyes. He wielded his sword like an ax and rushed her, but never reached his target. Instead he sank to his knees, a dazed look in his eyes. He dropped his sword and fell facedown on the ground.

Behind him stood Malcolm, grinning in self-satisfaction. He held a sword, not a basket-hilted one like Rory's, but a two-handed Highland sword, by its blade. The sight of the extended wheel-pommel and long quillons brought a chuckle to Duncan's lips. Rory's staunch protector had wielded the ancient weapon like a hammer, knocking Cathal senseless.

Lochiel stepped forward. "First blood is drawn. The duel is ended, and Rory wins."

A resounding cheer issued from the men. Ludovic made no attempt to hide either his displeasure or his disgust. With a snap of his fingers, two men emerged to drag Cathal away. Duncan stared at the one with flaming red hair. By casting his lot with Ludovic, Pàdraig chose a path that would lead him into trouble.

"Uncle, do ye abide by the wager and accept Rory to act in my stead?" Lochiel asked.

Ludovic spoke through clenched teeth. "I dinna hold with women who ken not their place, but I prize honor above all else and will accept her. I wonder, though, how ye think she can defend the clan against soldiers. They willna allow her to fight them with a sword. Rather they will laugh at her."

"Ludovic of Torcastle makes sense, Donald," Alexander of Dungallon said.

Others expressed similar doubts.

"I take your point, cousin," Lochiel said. "Rory, have ye strength to continue?"

She nodded.

"Fergus!"

"Aye, Sir Donald?"

"The weapons."

The giant brought forth a pistol, a *sgian,* and a longbow. Duncan wondered which weapon Rory would choose.

Instead of selecting one, she asked, "Is it more fighting ye are wanting, Sir Donald?"

"Not at all. Ye made your point with the men. 'Tis your skill I want ye to demonstrate."

"I can shoot, but willna do so unless ye insist. The garrisons at Fort William and Fort Augustus ken by now of the attack by the MacDonells of Keppoch and Glengarry. If there are soldiers near, we dinna want them to come upon us unawares."

"Ye make a valid point. Does any man here doubt my claim that she can load and fire a pistol?"

No one did.

"Then I choose the *sgian*," Rory said. "Have ye a target in mind?"

Fergus and another man brought a high-backed oak chair into the circle. They set it at the end opposite from where she stood.

"I need a volunteer," Lochiel said.

When no one stepped forward, Duncan sat in the chair. He winked at Rory. "I trust ye willna miss."

She smiled.

"Put the *sgian* near Duncan's left ear," Lochiel said.

"As I did to yourself, Sir Donald?"

He nodded.

Rory grasped the knife by its blade rather than the hilt. Duncan held his breath and counted. The wait tortured him, but he dared not stir. If he moved even a fraction, he might find himself pierced by the sharp blade.

She released the *sgian* with a deft throw. It cut the air with a shrill whistle magnified by the men's silence. All eyes, including his, stared at the blade. When he became cross-eyed by its closeness, he shut his eyes. The echo of steel slamming into wood rang in his ear. He expelled a long breath, extracted the *sgian,* and held it aloft. The men applauded.

"'Tis a dangerous woman ye wed, lad. Ye best not cross her."

Sandy's good-natured yell made the others laugh. While the banter continued, Rory reached for the bow Fergus held, but Malcolm brought forth another.

"Lochiel thinks ye might prefer this one," he said.

She accepted the finely crafted black longbow. Duncan met her gaze and understood that she expected a reckoning with him to explain why he had divulged her identity to another.

After Fergus set up a target, she pulled the bowstring taut and sighted along the arrow's shaft. Again, Duncan caught himself holding his breath and counting. From their hunts together, he knew she slowed her breathing and would not release the arrow until a serene calmness settled over her.

The twang of the bowstring broke the silence. A shrill hum pierced the air. The twirling bolt soared straight and true, flying farther and stronger because the shaft possessed four feathered sides instead of three. The humming ended with a sharp thud, and the men erupted in a thunderous roar. Rory bowed, acknowledging their approval.

"Well, uncle, do ye still think the lass canna defend the clan?" Lochiel asked.

Ludovic answered with a snort.

"Does anyone else object to my choice?" When Lochiel received no reply, he beckoned Rory forward.

With Malcolm and Jamie flanking him, Duncan watched her sink to one knee and bow her head. Pride and awe filled his heart. The first was for her skill and accomplishments. The second was because she was his wife. A scant few days ago, he had thought she would sever the ties that bound them together. Instead, she had followed the conviction of her heart.

"Rory, wife of Duncan, do ye swear upon this dirk to act in my stead and protect the people and lands of Clan Cameron?" Sir Donald asked.

"I do so swear." She took the dagger from Lochiel and kissed the blade.

"Do ye understand the penalty should ye break the bond ye give this day?"

"Death by the dirk should I betray my oath."

Lochiel extended his hand to help her rise.

"A toast!" He lifted a great *cuach.* "To Rory and to us. May we all succeed in our endeavors."

~*~

Rory dangled her feet in the rushing water that flowed from the upper to the lower Falls of Caig. Duncan grasped her torn chemise with both hands and ripped it. She sighed.

"What is it, *m'eudail?*" he asked.

"I kent I already had to mend the cloth. Ye dinna have to increase my work."

"I would rather have ye shed your clothes, but there are too many eyes in these woods. Now, hold your tongue while I tend your *scratch.*"

Surface wounds tended to bleed a lot, but the amount of blood concealed by the garment's sleeve was greater than he expected. He rent a strip from the discarded linen and dipped the cloth in the cool water. She winced once or twice, but held her tongue while he washed the encrusted blood from her arm. Once cleaned, he examined the wound. It was not deep enough to require stitches, for which he thanked God. He doubted he could pierce her soft skin with a needle, and would rather spend what little time they had left alone with her rather than hunting for Archie.

"I think all it needs is your medicines and a bandage," he said. "Until we return home, I will bind it with this."

"I wish we were back at the cottage."

"So do I, *m'eudail.* I would take ye to our waterfall where we could swim as before." He touched the brooch pinned to her plaid. "'Twas strange earlier."

"What was?"

"When ye touched this before the duel, I thought I heard ye speak to me, but your lips did not move."

"And what was I after saying?" Rory asked.

"Ye sought my leave to accept Torcastle's challenge. How could ye dare give him what ye deny me?"

"Never would I give to another what is yours."

"Dinna think ye are invincible, *m'eudail.* Ye could well have lost to Cathal. If ye had, ye would have gone to Ludovic's bed because honor demanded it of ye."

"Torcastle is a vile man, Duncan, and long before I went to his bed, ye or Malcolm or Jamie would have slain him. I ken I am mortal, but I also kent I would not lose this battle."

"How?"

"Ye forget I have lived long by my wits. What I did today was much like the chance I took when I revealed myself to ye. I canna explain how I kent I would win, but I did. Mayhap, 'tis the brooch that allowed me this kenning."

"Explain yourself."

"On the day I became chieftain of the MacGregors, Uncle Iain presented this to me. 'Tis an ancient brooch whose markings must have had some meaning once, but 'tis long since forgotten. By accident, I discovered that when I touch them and the stone, those bound to me could hear my thoughts. When ye gave your trust, I received a precious gift to cherish." She unpinned the circular brooch and handed it to him. "Ye will find a silver chain in your sporran."

"How do ye ken 'tis there?"

Laughter bubbled from her full red lips. He leaned close and kissed them, teasing them with his tongue.

"Ahem."

Annoyed that someone intruded, Duncan ended the kiss. Lochiel leaned against the abutment of the stone bridge that traversed the linn below the falls.

"Sir Donald."

"Ye always were resourceful, lad. I have searched for Rory and yourself for nigh on to an hour."

"We had matters to discuss."

Lochiel laughed. "'Tis one way to put it. Is the wound deep, lass?"

"Duncan says no."

"Good. 'Twas a fine display of cunning and skill ye showed, but ye ken ye made an enemy?"

"'Tis more likely two, Sir Donald."

He frowned for a moment before his countenance cleared. "Och, my uncle. Dinna fash about him. He willna be around to vex ye. He is ever eager to be feuding with someone, and if 'tis a Sassenach, so much the better."

"What of Cathal?" Duncan asked. He had no desire to leave Rory to deal with the scoundrel. Cathal would not hesitate to ambush her the moment Lochiel and he left for Glenfinnan. If he caught her, Duncan had no doubts of what Cathal would do to her before he killed her.

"His wound is not severe," Lochiel said, "but he canna go with us to Glenfinnan. I sent him under guard to my brother John. He will see that Cathal does not bother Rory or anyone else."

"Is there something else ye were wanting of us?" Duncan asked.

"I ken time grows short, and I willna deprive ye of your wife's company longer than necessary. Rory, 'tis an awesome burden I set upon your shoulders. Ye will need men ye trust to aid ye. I gave your foster brothers leave to remain in Lochaber. Sandy will stay for a wee longer to answer any questions. When I send for Lady Anne and our bairns, he will accompany them."

"Father Alex and I will manage," she said.

"'Tis a serious business we undertake. I ken what ye surrender by staying wedded to Duncan."

"I surrender nocht! I remain wedded to my husband because 'tis what I want. I did not do so to appease ye. If 'tis what ye thought, then ye dinna ken me as well as ye think."

Duncan squeezed his wife's hand. It was not a declaration of love, but it was the closest thing he was apt to hear from her before they separated.

"Then I will take my leave."

"Before ye go, Sir Donald, I would ask two promises of ye."

"I will grant them, lass, if 'tis in my power to do so."

"With Duncan to protect ye, I ken ye willna take foolish risks. Still, I ask ye to end this business with all haste. I have no wish to act in your stead over long."

"I will do my best. And the other request?"

"The kenning ye have of me is dangerous. Should the wrong person learn of it, 'twould mean my life and mayhap those of my kin. I would have your bond that ye will forget what ye ken."

"No one will learn of it from my lips. Ye have my word."

After Lochiel departed Duncan asked, "Would ye be wanting me to swear the same oath?"

"'Tis a wee bit late for that, husband. Ye told your foster father what I revealed to ye in secret."

"'Twas yourself who told him, Rory."

"I never!"

"Ye did not say the words, but ye told him nonetheless."

"How?"

"By your actions. Lochiel is no fool. He watched ye and puzzled it out for himself. I think 'twas the hunt that gave him the final clue. He merely asked me to confirm his hunch."

"Ye could have refused."

"Ye ken I could not do so. I am bound to answer him truthfully. If I dinna, ye ken what will happen."

She sighed and caressed his cheek. "Aye, I do. Never would I want to see the dirk slice your throat."

He caught her hand and held it to his chest. "And why is that?"

"Who else would kiss me?"

"Is that all I am good for?"

"Not at all, but 'tis a good place to start." Rory slid her tongue across her lips.

He cupped her head in his hands and gave her a gentle lingering kiss. He swallowed her moan, but gave one himself when she slipped her hands beneath the draping of his plaid and trailed her fingers down his bare back. He burned with need, but refused to take her where others might stumble upon them. He set her at arm's length from him.

Hurt and confusion clouded her sapphire blue eyes. "Did I do something wrong, Duncan?"

"Not at all. 'Tis our lack of privacy here."

"Oh."

He sensed her need for a distraction and held up a delicate strand of silver links. "Did a vision tell ye this chain was in my sporran?"

She laughed. "I put it there before we left with Captain Scott."

"And have I need for it in my travels?"

"Mayhap ye will. Mayhap ye willna."

"Would ye care to enlighten me further?"

She took the chain from him and hung her brooch from it. With the aid of both hands, she slipped the pendant over his head. "'Tis my gift to ye before ye go, Duncan. I ken the stone matches the color of my eyes. I thought 'twould help ye remember me."

"Och, Rory, never can I forget ye. Ye are my heart." He retrieved a ragged piece of linen from his sporran. He unfolded it, removed a silver brooch with a white pearl, and pinned it to her plaid. "This belonged to my mother. I wore it the day of our handfasting. I give it in pledge of my love and my promise to return."

A tear fell from the corner of her eye and slid down her cheek.

He brushed it away with his thumb. "No tears, Rory. 'Tis but a brief parting we endure. I will return before long and we can go home."

"I will hold ye to that promise, Duncan."

"Come, we should return to Achnacarry. Lochiel will want to confer with ye and I have my own affairs to put in order."

He stood, then held out his hands to her. She placed hers in his and he pulled her to her feet. After helping her over the roots and through the fronds of fern, he tucked her hand into the crook of his arm.

"Why did ye not destroy the bow, Duncan?"

"'Tis part of what makes ye who ye are. To destroy it would have been like severing your arm from the rest of ye. I gave it and the rest of your things into Malcolm's safe keeping."

"*He* is dead."

"The smuggler is, aye. The defender willna ever die. Ye ken better than I, Rory, what the future holds. The day may come when our people will need Thistle. I ken he will protect them while he shields himself from harm."

"If he is needed, he will come, but 'twill be *me* who greets ye on your return."

She winked at him, and he clipped her chin with his finger.

"I never doubted it at all."

~*~

Atop the craggy summit that overlooked Loch Shiel, Duncan swatted the pesky midges buzzing around his head. Rory's brooch bobbed against his sweat-soaked chest, and he smiled in spite of the miserable weather. Thick rolling clouds and light misting rain obscured the mid-August sun, but its heat turned the air into a steam bath.

Lochiel signaled for the pipers to announce their arrival at Glenfinnan. To the skirl of their war pipes, he led the clan in their descent, zigzagging down the sharp decline. The seven hundred men emerged from the low-hanging clouds into a glen of vivid emerald green strewn with gray rocks and tinged with purple heather. Ahead lay the cinder waters of the narrow loch. Two hundred men scattered in small groups waved their bonnets and cheered their arrival.

The sight of so few men dampened Duncan's spirits. This meager army had little hope of defeating the superior forces of the Crown. Many of King George's soldiers were seasoned fighters, having fought the French for the last several years over whether Maria Theresa or Frederick the Great of Prussia should rule Austria. Few Highlanders, including himself, had ever witnessed, let alone fought, another army. What battle experience they had came from feuding with other clans.

Although the majority of the Royal Army fought on the continent, King George could still muster a force five times greater than that gathered here. He could also arm his soldiers with better weapons than those carried by the clansmen. Duncan had pistol, sword, targe, and dirk—the weapons carried by Highland gentlemen who could afford to arm themselves well. He possessed them because of his relationship to

Lochiel and because he served as bodyguard to the clan chief. Most Highlanders, however, carried pistols or muskets and their dirks. A minority brought swords because they were dear in cost and few could afford to buy the blades. The poorest men armed themselves with pitchforks and scythes. Scattered amongst these, Duncan noticed two dozen who held long wooden shafts crowned by a sharp curved blade and hook. These two-sided weapons were Lochaber axes, and could be used to drag a rider from the saddle of his horse.

These images stirred a memory of words Rory had spoken. *'Tis a futile endeavor, this rising. Many will die. Little will be achieved.* He was inclined to agree, and wondered how different the situation might be had Lochiel heeded his brother's advice and refused to join in this undertaking. Although the clan was a small one, Sir Donald was well esteemed throughout the Highlands. His actions could sway others to follow his suit. MacDonald may have refused to bring out his men, but when other chiefs learned of Lochiel's participation, they might well choose to support the Stewarts. Duncan wished it was otherwise, but held no illusions. It was too late to turn back.

"Look!" Fergus shouted. "'Tis himself, Teàrlach mac Seumas!"

Duncan swung around to see a tall thin man, who looked to be a few years younger, dismount from a white horse. He wore a dun-colored coat over scarlet waistcoat and breeches. His mouth was small, his chin pointed. Flanked by advisors and chiefs, the prince climbed a hillock and stepped onto a flat rock protruding from the earth. He began to speak.

Fergus' mouth quirked to one side. "Whatever is he saying, Duncan? I canna understand a word."

"He does not ken our tongue."

"Ye have learning. Do ye understand his words?"

Duncan translated the French into Gaelic. "The Act of Union has not brought prosperity to Scotland as was promised. 'Tis the German Usurper who sits on the throne, not the *Ard Rìgh* of Scotland. We had no voice in choosing our high king. The time has come to change our destiny. The Stewarts are the rightful rulers of Scotland, descended from the ancient kings of Dalriada. God has sent himself, Charles son of James, to right this wrong. With our help, a Stewart king will restore our rights and bring new prosperity to the land. He will redress all grievances and rescind the heavy taxation. Our willingness to fight strengthens the Stewart cause."

Someone gave a derisive snort. "I was not asked to come. 'Twas fight or watch my home burn. Even then, I would still be here while my wife and bairns had no roof over their heads."

The sprig of oak that adorned the man's bonnet identified him as claiming kinship to Clan Cameron. While Duncan did not recognize him, he doubted Lochiel had employed threats to enlist the aid of his kinsmen. If the man spoke the truth, he lived on land held by Ludovic of Torcastle. Duncan could well imagine Lochiel's uncle or his henchmen coercing tenants into submission.

An armed escort bearing the standard of the Royal House of Stewart approached the prince. A soldier handed the banner to William Murray, the elderly Marquis of Tullibardine. The Jacobites recognized him as the rightful Duke of Atholl, but his brother held the title according to the Crown. Murray had participated in the 'Fifteen, and like Lochiel's father, had been attainted for doing so. For the past thirty years he had lived in exile, a member of the Jacobite court and trusted servant to King James. He held the standard while Bishop Hugh MacDonald blessed it, then unfurled the crimson and white silk banner with the help of two aides. The crowd cheered and tossed their bonnets into the air while brandishing their assorted weapons in a rousing salute. Brandy appeared from somewhere and Duncan joined the others in toasting King Jamie's health with cries of *"Deoch slàinte an Rìgh."*

A hard hand clapped Duncan on his back. Caught off guard, he would have stumbled had the man not steadied him.

"A wee while ago ye would never have allowed me to sneak up on ye, friend. Is it the lass who softens ye?"

"The whole of Highland cattle could stampede through the glen this day and I would not hear them for all the din, Pàdraig."

His friend laughed. "'Tis true enough. Your wife is a rare one."

The words were spoken with ease, but the tone made Duncan wary. Pàdraig had helped Cathal from the field at Murlaggan. If he had joined Ludovic's men, then he would not approve of Rory leading the clan.

Duncan kept his reply neutral. "Aye, she is."

"She heals the sick. She births babes. She fights like a man. 'Tis a strange upbringing for a lass."

"'Twas necessary."

Pàdraig cocked his head at that reply. "Was it now? I dinna remember your telling me of her clan."

"I am certain I did, Pàdraig. With the birth of your son, it must have slipped your mind."

"'Tis possible. 'Twas a good trick her brother played with the ancient sword. I had not seen the like since we were bairns. How do ye suppose he came by it?"

"It belonged to his father's grandsire."

"I noticed he wore a sprig of pine needles in his bonnet. Would he and Rory be Fergusons?"

"The pine is badge to many clans, Pàdraig. The Grants, MacAulays, and Mackinnons also use it."

Pàdraig nodded. "So do the Macfies and Macnabs. I believe the thieving MacGregors claim it as well."

Duncan stiffened. Tendrils of fear wrapped themselves around his heart. He did not know how his friend had learned the truth about Rory, but Duncan was certain someone had told Pàdraig. He lacked the means to discover it on his own.

"So what clan does Rory hail from?"

"Clan Cameron," Duncan said.

Pàdraig's lips formed into a thin smile. "'Tis good to hear. I did not think ye would allow a MacGregor to tend my wife." He waved his arm toward the gathered men milling around them. "'Tis a glorious sight, dinna ye think? Before long, we will meet the enemy and defeat them."

Pàdraig's enthusiasm for battle bordered on bloodlust, and they had yet to meet the enemy. In spite of the veiled threats he made against Rory, Pàdraig had befriended him at a time when the loss of his parents and brother cut deep. Until forced to choose between him and his wife, Duncan would not abandon their friendship.

"'Tis a serious business we are about, Pàdraig."

"Aye."

"Ye ken what will happen if we lose?"

"We will be victorious! 'Twill be a grand adventure I can tell to my son and his sons on long winter nights."

Would that it could be so. Rory's dream and the visit of Bean-nighe made Duncan think otherwise. Why would this time differ from the other attempts to regain a throne? If anything, the Stewarts had fewer supporters than before, and without the needed men and arms from France, they had little chance of success. Failure would deem them traitors. While Lochiel and the other chiefs would flee Scotland to live elsewhere, Pàdraig and he did not have that luxury. If they did not die in battle, they would suffer imprisonment or death by the hangman.

"If we succeed in our endeavor, Pàdraig, 'twill be because we ally ourselves into a united force. All clans must work together as one rather than continue the feuds that set one against another. Do ye think 'tis possible for us to set aside the anger and mistrust that has plagued the Highlands for hundreds of years?"

"If we are to fight the Sassenach, aye! They will have to withdraw and go home. 'Twill be a day to celebrate when the *gall* no longer linger on our lands."

Outsiders? Foreigners? Duncan heard the vehemence that Pàdraig directed toward the garrisons that stretched the length of the Great Glen from Fort George in Inverness to Fort William in Maryburgh. Some of the soldiers stationed at these strongholds were Scots. Lowlanders they might be, but they remained Scots. What right did Pàdraig and his cohorts have to drive them from their homeland?

~*~

Duncan lay on his stomach, his eyes glued on the stark stone edifice on the rise of the next hill. By the time of his departure from Glenfinnan, the army had swelled to twelve hundred men. While the majority of those had journeyed to Corrieyairack Pass in the Monadhliath Mountains, he attended Lochiel and Archie on the outskirts of Kingussie.

The main army intended to ambush the Royal Army commanded by Sir John Cope while the Camerons, along with the MacDonells of Lochgarry, prepared to take Ruthven Barracks, a redoubt built after the 'Fifteen to enforce the disarming and maintain peace.

"What think ye, Duncan?" Archie asked. "Can we scale it with ladders?"

"'Tis a fool's plan. That square fortress sits atop an isolated castle motte. The sentries who patrol along the high ramparts have a clear view of all who approach."

"'Tis just as well," Lochiel said. "Lochgarry's men found but one ladder in the village. Three hundred of us canna infiltrate the compound with a single ladder."

"Too bad we dinna have artillery. 'Twould not withstand a siege for long. The north and south walls are not thick enough to take the pounding."

"Ye can dream all ye like, Archie," his brother said, "but 'twould be the wishes of a fool. I dinna like the odds of storming the redoubt either."

"I count twenty gun loops on the wall with the three-story barracks and eight more on the south wall," Duncan said. "If the east and north walls are the same, the soldiers' muskets can pick us off with wee trouble."

"True, but I dinna see any other choice." Lochiel shrugged. "The prince ordered us to seize Ruthven. We are in need of the arms and meal stored inside. Prepare yourselves. We attack when the sun is straight overhead."

Duncan disliked the order. There had to be a better way to feed and arm a host of men than to participate in a suicidal storming of the redoubt. A successful Highland charge required surprise and strength. Ruthven Barracks presented neither. When the attack ended, good Highland men would litter the hillock.

Within minutes, thirteen Camerons and a score of MacDonells lay sprawled on the ground. After two hours and under a white flag, Lochiel accompanied the Lochgarry chieftain up two traverses to the main gate of the redoubt. A man on the sentry walk spoke with them, and a short while later Duncan helped carry off the dead and wounded.

"I tell ye, Donald, the plan has a chance," Archie said, while tending the last of the wounded Camerons.

Lochiel stroked his jaw. "Is what my brother says true, Duncan?"

"Aye, there is a wee sally port on the north wall that gives access to the dragoons' stable. No horses be there, and from the firing from inside the redoubt, I think 'tis but a handful of men who defend it."

Archie pressed his case. "All we have to do, Donald, is stuff a keg with materials that burn, place it next to the wooden door, and set it aflame. While the fire distracts them, I can lead a small band of men up the ladder onto the parapet. Once inside, 'twill take little to subdue them."

"The plan has merit, brother. I will give ye thirty men to assist ye. Keep to the shadows of the stable and dinna be climbing the ladder before the door burns."

Archie nodded. "Can Duncan accompany me?"

"Aye."

When the keg was ready, Lochgarry signaled his men to start the diversion on the south side while Duncan and the handpicked Camerons followed Archie. They reached their destination without hindrance. The keg was placed in position and set afire. From his perch under the staircase that led to the hayloft, Archie shook his head. "'Twill never catch. The keg lies too far from the door."

Duncan saw the problem. Three steps separated fire from fuel. He sent two men to remedy the situation.

"Point the keg toward the sally port. Dinna leave until it catches."

The draftees followed orders. No sooner had the door caught fire, though, than they heard a cry of alarm from inside the redoubt. Next, a cascade of water descended from the parapet, dousing keg and men alike. Muskets appeared through the gun loops.

"Get away!"

The Camerons heeded Archie's shout, but not soon enough. Duncan felt the musket balls sear his flesh as if he himself was hit. The men fell, and he choked.

After they buried the dead, Duncan felt Lochiel's hand on his shoulder. He wondered if his face looked as haggard as his foster father's. He was certain his eyes had the same haunted look. Until this day he had never sent another to do what he could do, and yet this day, he had ordered one man to his death without blinking an eye.

"I dinna ken what comfort 'twill be, Duncan, but ye are not responsible for what happened. Death is what war brings, a fact I chose to ignore when I agreed to this venture. 'Tis my responsibility. These men are kin whether by name or blood, and 'twas I who sent them to their graves. They were as dear to me as ye are, and I willna ever forget them. I will sacrifice no more in this futile endeavor."

~*~

Mid-September found the prince, Lochiel, Robert MacGregor of Glencarnaig, and several others enjoying the comfort offered by Lady Seton at the House of Touch, her home. While Duncan waited for his chief to emerge, he realized he felt more hopeful toward the success of their venture than he had after the debacle at Ruthven Barracks because of the two men Prince Charles had selected to command his forces.

In spite of his youth and frail health, James Drummond, the third Duke of Perth, possessed the gift of tact. With gentle words and a sweet nature, he could sway nobleman and peasant, Highlander and Lowlander, Irishman and Scot alike to support a common cause rather than fight amongst themselves. What he lacked in military genius, he made up for with courage and spirit.

Lord George Murray, one of the Marquis of Tullibardine's younger brothers, was Perth's exact opposite. His pride and fierceness brought quick acceptance from the Highlanders because he understood them and their ways. At fifty-one, he lost patience with those who questioned his orders or tarried in obeying them. His bluntness ruffled many feathers, but he had battle experience, an asset the Jacobite army lacked.

Shots rang out from the other side of the hill. Rather than race toward the sound, Duncan knew he must protect Lochiel. He pulled open the door and made to enter, but found his path blocked. His chief cocked an eyebrow in amusement. "Ye ken I dinna like ye underfoot, lad."

"That I do, but 'tis my job to see ye come to no harm."

"Is it red soldiers that attack?"

"I heard but two shots, so I dinna think 'tis them."

"'Tis the lads wanting a fine repast of their own," Glencarnaig said, cleaning his teeth with his fingernail.

"MacGregors thieving sheep is it?"

"Not at all, Lochiel. Most likely 'tis your own men."

Duncan prayed MacGregor erred in his assessment. Lochiel frowned on stealing, pilfering, and reiving. They were customs of times past, and he refused to tolerate their continuance.

"Mayhap the men claim kinship to neither Camerons nor MacGregors," Lochiel said.

MacGregor shook his head. "'Tis possible, but I doubt it. I have twenty merks in my purse. I would wager it against twenty of your own, Lochiel, that 'tis your men we will find on the far side of yon brae."

"Agreed."

The two men climbed the hill with Duncan running to keep up with them. He suspected thieves had fired the shots, but he could be wrong and dared not allow his chief to walk into a trap.

"What do ye intend, Lochiel, if I be right?" MacGregor asked, pausing to catch his breath. "What punishment will your kin suffer?"

"He will be shot."

MacGregor mulled that over for a few seconds. "'Tis serious ye are about pillaging then?"

"I am."

"Then should we find the Gregorach doing the deed, I will do likewise."

Duncan thanked the fates that placed him with his chief rather than on the brae. Lochiel and MacGregor drew their pistols. They watched a man swagger toward them, a ewe slung across his shoulders. Duncan recognized him, and felt no remorse. He wanted to shoot the man himself, not for stealing, but for injuring Rory.

"Hold!" Lochiel said.

"Is it me ye are wanting, Sir Donald?"

"What is it ye have there, Cathal?"

"'Tis but a sheep I found dead."

"How did it die?"

"I could not say."

"Then we willna find a wound from a pistol in it. Duncan, examine the ewe."

Cathal glared at him, but dropped the carcass to the ground. Since Duncan did not trust him, he dragged the dead animal a short distance away. Blood stained the ewe's chest near the heart. When he bent closer, he found an entry wound and stuck his finger into it. It matched the circumference of a lead ball.

"What killed it?" Lochiel asked.

"A pistol."

"Cathal, did ye not hear the law I set regarding pilfering?"

"I heard."

"Yet ye disregarded it."

"'Tis the way of Highlanders. What is one sheep to these people?"

Lochiel shook his head. "Did ye pay Lady Seton for it?"

"No."

"Then ye are guilty of taking what does not belong to ye. For that ye must accept punishment." Lochiel fired his pistol.

The shot hit Cathal in the shoulder. He staggered and fell.

"Help him to camp, Duncan." Lochiel returned his pistol to his belt. "If I catch ye again, Cathal, 'twill be your last day on this earth. Do we understand each other?"

"Aye," he said, through clenched teeth.

Duncan offered him a hand.

"Get away!" Cathal struggled to his feet. "Ye have not heard the last of me, Duncan Cameron. I will have my day of reckoning with ye."

Duncan watched Cathal's retreating back, and knew the threat was real. He had spoken against a kinsman. Added to the insult delivered at Rory's hand, Cathal's hatred would fester and putrefy. When next they met, one would die, of that Duncan was certain.

CHAPTER FIFTEEN
EDINBURGH

Flanked by two circular turrets and crowned by a spired square tower, Netherbow Port gave entry into Scotland's walled capital. Duncan approached the east gate feeling hobbled by the ill-fitting breeches that clung like manacles to his sinewy thighs. A hundred vigilant eyes bored into his back, but he shook off the urge to turn around. He would never see the watchers, for they hid in the shadows cast by the towering houses of Canongate. He should feel relieved to know they guarded his back, but he was not. Instead, he felt kenspeckle. He was too tall, too strong, and too brawny to play the part of a dragoon's manservant. Meekness and subservience were unaccustomed traits for him to portray with ease.

He pulled up the shabby collar of his riding coat, and scrugged the tattered hunting cap low on his brow.

One sentry glanced in his direction. "Who goes there?"

"I come to fetch Captain Smythe's sword," Duncan said.

The sentry raised a lantern and peered through the iron yett. Duncan kept his eyes downcast and his shoulders hunched.

"A captain without a sword?" The guard laughed. "'Tis a wonder he did not sack ye for lack of brains."

Duncan ignored the insult and waited, deeming it best to let the man have his jest. Soon enough he would be on the receiving end.

A second guard sauntered up to the gate. "Where is your pass?"

"Captain Smythe did not give me one," Duncan said.

The first guard shook his head, while the other said, "No pass, no entry."

"But I must enter. 'Twill mean my head if I return without the sword."

"Ye should have thought of it before ye left. We have orders to admit no one without a proper pass. Without one, ye must wait till morning to enter when no pass will be needed."

"'Twill be too late. I am to return posthaste."

The second sentry leveled his Land Pattern musket at Duncan's midsection. "I said *no*. Now begone before I settle the matter with this."

Duncan grumbled but retreated. The laughter of the two sentries rang in his ears. Although he had carried out his orders, he still felt the fool.

"Duncan."

His name was whispered, but the moonless night and narrow wynd caught the sound and magnified it. He cringed, but fought the urge to glance over his shoulder to see if the sentries had heard. He ducked into a darkened close, the private passage that led to apartments housing the wealthier citizens of Edinburgh. Three shadows converged on him.

He pulled off the cap and shrugged out of the coat. He flung both at the tallest of the men. "Where is my plaid?"

"Here."

He stepped out of the breeches and retrieved his belted plaid from Fergus. He spoke while he dressed. "They willna open it, Sir Donald."

"Did they believe ye were gillie to Captain Smythe?"

"I canna say. They will open the gate only for those with signed passes."

"Is there another way in?" the third man asked.

Duncan recognized the guttural voice of MacDonell of Keppoch. He and his men, along with those of Clanranald and Glengarry, had joined forces with the Camerons to breach Edinburgh's defenses.

"None that I recommend, sir. We could cross Nor' Loch, but the stench will likely defeat us long before we gain entry. The wall has surrounded the city since the time of the second James. While Edinburgh has been sacked before, we have neither time nor armament to do so now."

"His Highness suspects the provost and magistrates drag out the surrender negotiations," Lochiel said.

"To delay us until reinforcements arrive?" Fergus asked.

"Aye. We must get inside."

A noise distracted Duncan. He concentrated on the sound, then smiled. "Have the negotiators returned?"

"No," Lochiel said.

"Then 'tis likely their coach that approaches. The sentries will raise the gate for them."

"And we can slip in concealed by their conveyance." Keppoch chuckled. "I like your man, Lochiel. He may be young, but he has a head on him and kens how to use it."

The clatter of wheels on cobbled streets grew louder. When the hackney coach passed, Duncan fell into a trot behind it. Fergus and ten others followed, keeping low and quiet, then melting into the shadows while the driver waited for the sentries to open the gate. A crack of a whip and the clop of horses' hooves signaled them to reform behind the coach. They slipped inside Netherbow Port, and disarmed and silenced the sentries while the coach proceeded toward the castle. Those outside the gate hastened through the portal and scurried to their appointed destinations. By daybreak, the Jacobite Army controlled all of Edinburgh except for the magnificent fortress crowning the volcanic crag at the head of the High Street.

~*~

The hallowed ruins of the nave of Holyrood Abbey bore silent witness to the capital's turbulent history. Once the most magnificent church in Scotland, it reminded Duncan of the grievous destruction wrought by English invaders two centuries earlier. Beside it stood the former residence of the royal Stewarts. Within its gray walls Mary Queen of Scots had wed Lord Darnley and witnessed the brutal murder of her secretary, and her son, the sixth James, learned of the death of his cousin Elizabeth and his ascendancy to the British throne. Now, the Palace of Holyroodhouse was divided into apartments.

"God save the King!" the crowd chanted. "God save the King!"

"It seems the whole of Edinburgh turns out for this momentous occasion," Lochiel said, indicating the vast number of people gathered in the park that fronted the palace.

Duncan surveyed the assembly. "'Tis hard to believe the same town that ousted King Jamie and ransacked the abbey fifty-three years ago welcomes his grandson with open arms."

"Aye, 'tis, but ye must admit His Royal Highness is difficult to dislike, and few refuse him. I am proof of that. I intended to bid him farewell, but instead found myself agreeing to join him at Glenfinnan."

Duncan agreed. In spite of his qualms about the Rising, he had a begrudging respect for the young prince. Rather than hold himself aloof, Charles conversed with his men, ate what they ate, and often slept on the ground alongside them rather than search for more comfortable quarters. Although hardened by rough terrain, Duncan had to catch his breath from the prince's unrelenting pace of marching thirty to thirty-five miles a day. Their sojourn in Edinburgh was a welcome respite.

"God save the King! God save the King!"

"Look!" someone shouted.

A parade of gentlemen approached Holyroodhouse. The prince rode a bay gelding flanked by the Duke of Perth on his right and Lord Elcho, commander of a horse troop, on his left. Charles looked resplendent in red velvet waistcoat and breeches. Pinned to the blue sash he wore over a plaid short coat was the Order of Saint Andrew. A white cockade, fashioned after the white rose he had plucked from a bush at Fassifern, crowned his bonnet of blue velvet edged with gold lace.

He dismounted and walked through the crowd. The people pressed close to kiss his hand. Women swooned. A man held aloft an unsheathed sword and conducted Prince Charles into the home of his forebears. At the portal, the grandson of the seventh James turned and saluted his subjects.

~*~

"Do ye hear from Rory?" Fergus asked.

"I suppose she will send word when Sandy journeys to Edinburgh with Lady Anne," Duncan said, passing through Netherbow Port.

"Has she book learning like yourself?"

Ever since the giant had manhandled his wife at Lochiel's behest, Duncan had noticed that Fergus hovered around Rory whenever their chief did not require him. His manner betrayed no harmful intent, rather Duncan was reminded of the way Malcolm protected her. After spying Fergus giving her flowers, Duncan had questioned Rory and learned the giant asked countless questions. She surmised that he wished to emulate her husband.

"Aye, she does. Is there a reason for these questions, Fergus? Ye ken Rory is my wife."

The giant's Adam's apple bobbed and he crumbled his bonnet between his hands. "Womenfolk pay me no heed, excepting Rory. She treats me as she treats ye."

Duncan's eyes widened. "She does?"

Fergus' face reddened. "I did not mean—"

"I ken what ye meant. 'Twas teasing ye, Fergus, I was."

The giant expelled a relieved sigh.

"Is there a reason ye wish to ken about her book learning?"

"Do ye think Rory would teach me? After our business with the prince is ended, I mean."

"I canna speak for my wife, but I dinna think she will object. Shall I ask her for ye?"

"Aye."

"Then 'tis settled."

With the teeming throng in front of him stopped, Duncan looked to see how far up the High Street they had come. The crowning spire of the High Kirk of Saint Giles reached toward the heavens.

"It seems we are arrived, Fergus. Mercat Cross is to your left."

His companion turned and pushed his way through the crowd. One or two men thought to object until they found themselves staring at his chest. They tilted back their heads, swallowed, and stepped aside. Word passed quickly and the others parted like the Red Sea. A few muttered rude insults born of ignorance. To Lowlanders, who had adopted the ways of the English, Highlanders were barbaric uncouth warriors from centuries long past.

Duncan plowed into Fergus' back. Unable to gain the giant's attention, he stepped around him. Fergus' mouth gaped. Duncan followed the direction of his gaze, and saw what stunned him. Every town and village had its Mercat Cross where proclamations were read, merchants conducted business, and hangings occurred. A rock marked the spot in most places, but not in Edinburgh. Here, a wooden shaft carved with images of dragons and foliage and topped with the lion rampant stood in the middle of the High Street. An octagonal raised platform encircled it. A red and blue Persian carpet, draped from waist-high walls, concealed the wine spouts ordered by the second Charles in the previous century. Two soldiers guarded the door to the inner stairs that led to the rostrum where immaculate attendants stood at attention in five of the rounded corners.

"'Tis far grander than the one in Maryburgh," the giant said.

"Ye are in a royal city, not a wee village near a garrison, Fergus. Ye are certain to see many strange things here."

"Like the mass of people who wave from the windows?"

Duncan scanned the upper floors of the gray stone tenements. White cockades and plaid sashes adorned the pointed bodices of the female spectators. One woman wore a tartan overdress supported by wide elliptical hoops. The few males who peppered the crowd stood with arms crossed and wore sullen expressions. No sashes draped their knee-length coats. No cockades adorned their gartered stockings or tricorn hats.

A flourish of bagpipes followed the blare of a trumpet. Duncan watched the pipers surround Mercat Cross in a circle five men deep. A white horse advanced bearing a woman clad in a white gown with an unsheathed sword held aloft. She maneuvered her mount beneath an empty corner of the rostrum until she faced the townsfolk.

When the pipers expelled the last of the air from their bags, a distinguished-looking man stepped to the fore, unrolled a parchment scroll, and cleared his throat. "I proclaim James Francis Edward Stewart, King of Scotland. In his absence and in accordance with his wishes, the Regent will be his son, His Royal Highness Charles Edward."

The cheering deafened Duncan.

When the prince ascended the stairs of Mercat Cross, the din reached a crescendo that did not abate until he held up his hands for silence. "On behalf of your sovereign lord and my father, His Majesty King James the Eighth, we make this solemn pledge. Henceforth, those convicted of past crimes against us are pardoned. We have secured the crown taken from us so long ago, and will not relinquish it again. To this end, we promise a year's pay to any man who joins us in our war against those who would deprive us of our sovereign rights. Long have our beloved subjects suffered oppression and persecution for their devotion to Almighty God. From this day forward we will no longer tolerate suppression and maltreatment in worshipping the Lord. Finally, we denounce and deplore the Act of Union that makes Scotland a poor neighbor of England. We will endeavor to restore to her the wealth and status she so richly deserves."

Pandemonium erupted, but Duncan could not tell if those around him agreed or disagreed with the prince's pronouncements. Few would object to the first two, but the last ones would not sit well with everyone. Since the time of the Covenantors, Scotland had embraced the Presbyterian faith. Catholics, like Rory and Sandy, and Episcopalians, like himself and Lochiel, were in the minority, particularly in the Lowlands. In contrast to past edicts, Charles, also a Papist, would practice his faith while allowing his people the freedom to worship in theirs.

In 1707, in spite of violent opposition from the Scots, Queen Anne had signed the Act of Union, dissolving the Scottish Parliament and nullifying the Scots' right to accept or reject the English monarch. The promised prosperity and peace never materialized, although Lowlanders suffered less than Highlanders. Scottish ships no longer carried goods overseas for trade. The Crown imposed new tariffs on and discriminatory laws against the people, and sent soldiers to enforce them. After thirty-eight years, many still harbored deep feelings of resentment and betrayal.

~*~

Duncan stood a discreet distance from Lochiel while he consulted with Lord George Murray, co-commander of the army. After scouts had sighted the enemy eleven miles east of Edinburgh, Duncan hiked with the rest of the army to a spot south of the enemy and west of the small village Tranent. Dark clouds concealed the September sun, but there was sufficient light for him to survey the level expanse of open land before him. Lieutenant General Sir John Cope, commander of King George's Army in Scotland, had positioned his forces east of Preston House.

"What are your thoughts on the matter, lad?" Murray asked.

Startled, Duncan jerked his head around. Lord George and Lochiel watched him with amused expressions.

Lochiel crossed his arms over his chest. "A bodyguard should not slacken his alertness when the enemy could hold his chief in their sights, Duncan."

"I am innocent of the charge, Sir Donald."

"We surprised ye."

"Aye, but unless they wish to waste shot on one man, Cope would not give the order to fire. Ye are important to many, Sir Donald, but if he wishes to strike a fatal blow, 'tis Lord Murray he would shoot first."

The tall robust commander grinned. "He has ye there, Donald. What if I had brought your chief here to slay him, lad?"

"If ye meant to harm him, ye would not attack while we stand on high ground where all can see what ye do. Ye would fall on him when his guards do not surround him. He has nocht to fear from ye, though."

"And why do ye think that?"

"Ye and Sir Donald are of a like mind. Ye desire to improve our country's economy and our people's way of life through progressive ideas. Few men of station and wealth favor change unless 'tis in their best interest to do so. Why harm an ally who could sway others to embrace your ideas?"

"Your foster son, ye say, Donald?"

"Aye."

"He has a quick mind. Ye taught him well. Lad, what drew your attention so?"

Duncan nodded toward the Royal forces. "'Tis a good defensive position. With the Firth of Forth at Cope's rear, he willna fash about an attack from that quarter. We canna climb over the two stone walls that flank his right, and with the boggy marsh and a deep gully before him, we canna surprise his forces."

Murray nodded. "'Tis a keen eye ye have, but what if there was a footpath through the bog?"

"'Tis possible, although I would not attempt such a crossing unless I kent where it lay."

"A local visited early this morning and showed me. What think ye now of surprising Cope?"

"If done under cover of darkness and without sound, we have a good chance."

"Your foster son grasps well the situation, Donald," Murray said. "If ye ever decide ye dinna need his services, send him to me."

"'Tis not likely, George. I depend on Duncan, and kenning his wife, she willna go without a fight."

"An intrepid lass, is she?"

"Aye, and adroit with a blade." Lochiel rubbed his ear.

"She is not one to cross?"

Duncan smiled. "'Tis not advisable if ye cherish your life."

"I shall remember that should we meet. Let us return. We have much to do before the sun sets."

When they entered camp, a red-faced man, his lips tight with anger, accosted them. "I willna stand for it, Lochiel. Do ye hear me?"

Duncan moved to protect Sir Donald, but Lochiel stopped him with a wave of his hand.

"Of what do ye speak, MacDonald?"

"Ye ken well enough. 'Tis ours by right of the Bruce himself!"

"I have just returned and dinna ken what riles ye. If ye explain, I will do my best to right the wrong."

"He refers to my decision that you and he must draw lots to determine which clan takes the right when we attack," Prince Charles said.

Duncan turned his gaze on the royal speaker. His tactless issuance of orders was contrary to the way Lochiel handled conflicts. An insult to a Highlander, particularly a chief, often led to war. If the wrong was not righted, the feud could last for centuries. If MacDonald thought Lochiel was to blame, the two clans might find themselves on opposite sides. Duncan could not imagine a worse time for allies to bicker.

"Your Highness," Lochiel said, "I am honored, but MacDonald speaks true. Over four hundred years ago the second Edward sent twenty thousand knights to do battle against the six thousand who fought for Robert the Bruce. Weighted down by their heavy armor, the Sassenach knights foundered in the bog, and were slain by brave and loyal Scots like the MacDonalds. To honor them, the Bruce conferred upon their clan the right to lead all attacks by taking the right flank. 'Twould dishonor and insult them if Camerons usurped their position. Dinna we fight against a usurper who unjustly seized your crown?"

The prince considered the matter.

"You present a most persuasive and eloquent argument, Lochiel. I submit to your view. Since the first time we engage the enemy will be our most important engagement, you MacDonald, and your men, will take the right. Understand, however, that there will be more battles to come and you must share that position with others. All Highlanders are honorable, and it would cause unnecessary friction if I did not intercede on their behalf. Do I have your agreement on this matter?"

"Aye, Your Highness, ye do. I dinna like relinquishing what is ours, but I understand we must present a united front."

"Splendid!"

Duncan thought the matter settled until he saw the fury in Lord George's eyes. He braced himself for the coming storm, wondering what new cavil threatened.

"I ordered my men to prepare for maneuvers this night. Where are they?"

Charles bristled at Murray's offensive manner, but answered in a calm and quiet voice. "The Atholls? I deemed their work unnecessary and sent them to guard the road to Edinburgh. We must make certain the enemy does not cut us off from the capital."

"I command this army! Ye have no right to countermand my orders without consulting me. If ye dinna recall them, I willna ever draw a sword again."

Murray's wrathful words hung in the air. Duncan knew the threat was not an idle one. If the prince refused to rescind the order, the commander would resign. Without his experience and knowledge, the Jacobite army was doomed to fail. Duncan realized they could ill afford to lose such a strategist, but did Charles?

"Lord Murray, you command at my pleasure. I thought it best to protect our rear. I saw no reason to confer as you have weightier matters to attend to. If the Athollmen are needed for some detail of which I am unaware, I will concede to your greater experience and wisdom. Please replace them with others."

The blustering fury died. Lord George gave a curt nod and headed toward his tent with Lochiel at his side. Duncan followed, disturbed by what he had witnessed. When the officers should show unity and accord, they squabbled over petty matters in public forums. To display such behavior to the men they commanded provided the impetus for the rank and file to emulate their leaders. If they continued in this vein, dissension would defeat them long before the Royal Army did.

~*~

Bonfires flickered in haunting mockery to the martial air played by the pipers. The flames seemed to dip and whirl with every ebb and flourish in the gentle breeze that wafted through the Jacobite camp. Too early to assemble and too agitated to sleep, Duncan and Fergus followed the music. In days of yore the eve of battle was given over to a ritual of dance and music. Ever superstitious, the Highlanders kept to tradition.

"Is that not Red Pàdraig?" Fergus asked.

Duncan glanced to where the giant pointed. Seven men, each carrying two swords, took their places around the bonfire and faced the onlookers. The fiery red hair of the last man to enter the circle seemed like an extension of the flames rising behind him.

"Aye, 'tis. Did ye notice who leads them?"

"Cathal." Fergus spit in disgust. "Red Pàdraig follows a dangerous man."

"I ken, but I canna make him see reason. 'Tis glad I am that Cathal is where I can keep an eye on him, though. I would not rest easy if he remained behind in Lochaber."

"He would harm Rory?"

"She defeated him while his kinsmen watched. He is not a man to take such an insult. He will have his revenge."

"Does Lochiel ken this?"

"Aye."

"And yet ye bide here while Rory is alone at Achnacarry?"

"What danger she faces she can handle, especially with Malcolm and Jamie at her side. While Cathal stays with the army, he canna harm her. If I think her in peril, Lochiel has given me leave to go home."

"I would accompany ye."

Duncan smiled. "I ken."

The pipers ceased their music. The drummers beat a rapid tattoo, then fell silent. Ludovic of Torcastle stepped from the crowd.

"Legend tells of the Great Chief, Malcolm Ceann Mòr, who slew Macbeth, the slayer of his father the king. Malcolm coveted power and fought those who stood in his way. In one battle, he met a fearsome foe who gave no ground. Neither did Malcolm. History does not tell us how Malcolm defeated him, but the man died by Malcolm's blade. Exhilarated by his victory, Malcolm crossed his sword with that of the vanquished and danced between and over the blades. 'Tis tradition for warriors to seek the courage and skill of Malcolm Ceann Mòr on the eve of battle by dancing the *Gille Callum*."

With great ceremony, Cathal, Red Pàdraig, and the others crossed their swords and laid them on the ground. They lifted their heads high, placed their arms akimbo, touched right toes to left heels, and fixed their gazes on some point in front of them. When the pipers took up their instruments, each dancer sprang onto his toes and hopped on his right foot. While alternating feet, he raised first one arm and then the other or held both high above his head. He hopped over the blades and straddled the angles formed by the crossed swords. With each repetition of the tune, the tempo quickened. The dancers whirled and jumped, crossing both feet and weapons while hastening their steps.

In spite of his dislike of Cathal and his uneasiness about Pàdraig, Duncan marveled at their agility and dexterity. He was nimble when running and stealthy when sneaking, but neither attribute served him in this arena. He lacked the finesse to perform the dance under pressure and in front of others. It took only one misstep to make watchers think they were destined to lose or die.

The music ended with an abrupt flourish. Each dancer straddled the swords beneath him, his fists raised in triumph over his head. Silence hung in the air for a brief instant, then raucous huzzahs echoed through the camp. No one's feet had touched the sharp blades. While not given to superstitious beliefs, Duncan dared to believe he would not fall in battle on the morrow.

Several hours later he marched east with his comrades, skirting the village of Tranent before turning north. A chilling sea mist concealed their movements. In the wee hours before dawn, they crept single file through the knee-deep muck. The chirping of insects rose eerily around them, but it was the only sound that disturbed the night. Occasionally, dark shadows loomed on either side of the track. From their dwarfed sizes and irregular shapes Duncan concluded they were the hedges that rose from the murky depths of the bog.

He stole across a narrow plank that bridged the deep, wide trench that ran the entire length of the hill below the royal foot troops. He held his breath and waited for the challenge, but none came. Did Cope feel so secure that he had failed to post guards? Duncan shook his head. No matter the odds of someone breaching an impassable approach, he would never have left it unguarded. An enemy determined to fulfill his objective would discover a way to achieve the impossible, and Highlanders were such an enemy.

In the month since their departure from Glenfinnan, they had seen no action. They itched to do battle, and so had found the key they needed—a local who knew the secrets of the marsh.

Among the first wave of troops to reach firm ground, Duncan waited for MacDonalds, MacGregors, and Stewarts of Appin to form in a tight line to the right of his clan's position. Two hundred paces ahead lay the enemy. No one uttered a sound while they waited for the second line of Athollmen, Robertsons, MacDonalds of Glencoe, and MacLachlans to form.

With the sun peeking through the fog, sounds filtered down from the enemy camp. The white curtain that shielded the Jacobite army began to evaporate. Duncan saw the sentry with his head cocked to one side, listening. A sun ray struck a Highlander's blade. It glimmered with reflected light, revealing their position. The sentry raised his musket and fired a warning shot.

To the right, a sword slashed the air. The screech of bagpipes rent the stillness. Duncan pulled his bonnet low on his brow and cast off his plaid. His shirt flapped against his bare thighs. With his targe fastened on his left arm, he bent behind the shield until his body was almost horizontal. He emitted a bloodcurdling scream and joined the

Highlanders who rushed the enemy with the same force and speed of waves hammering the shore during a fierce storm.

Fifty paces from the enemy Duncan discharged then dropped his musket. He darted forward until twelve paces separated him from a soldier clad in a scarlet coat. Duncan fired his pistol, aiming at the man's chin but hitting him between the eyes. Without sparing him a second glance, Duncan clutched his dirk in his left hand, his sword in his right.

He caught a flash of movement to his right. He pivoted on his heel, bent his left knee, and deflected a thrusting bayonet with his targe. With swiftness born from years of training, he shoved his dirk into his attacker while his sword sliced the belly of another.

Somehow the thud of a horse's hooves filtered through the din of clanging metal and firing muskets. Duncan pulled his sword free then flipped his weapon, grasping it by the blade. When the horse came within striking distance, he slammed the sword's hilt into its nose. The beast reared, unseating the dragoon. The frightened animal whirled and headed back from whence it came. Before the dragoon scrambled to his feet, Duncan plunged his blade into the man's heart.

The frenzy of battle ensnared Duncan. Fever raged through him, thirsty for blood. He felt invincible amidst the carnage. He pursued the fleeing and confused red soldiers. Trapped between high stone walls and swarms of Highlanders, they discarded their weapons and scrambled over one another in a desperate attempt to scale the walls. A few dragoons held their positions and tried to give them cover.

Bright lights exploded in Duncan's head. His brow burned, his head throbbed. The enemy doubled in strength. Perplexed, he squinted. The numbers dwindled, then grew. He shook his head to clear the fog. Pain lanced deep within his temple, and he staggered to his knees. Firm hands guided him to the ground. They pried his hands from his head.

"'Tis the ball of a musket that grazed ye," a voice said.

"'Tis nocht." Duncan tried to rise, but the other man prevented him from standing.

"'Tis ended the fight for ye this day, friend."

The familiar label gave Duncan pause. "Pàdraig?"

"Aye. We routed the Sassenach and victory is ours! All that remains is to hunt down the scattered remnants of Cope's men, but others can tend to that. Ye need Dr. Archie's skilled hands. Sit there and rest while I fetch him."

Duncan crossed his arms on his knees and rested his head. He tried to block out the cries issuing from mutilated bodies lying on the field. *Wounded I maimed.* Their agony intensified the painful throbbing in his head. Black corbies circled, waiting to feast on the butchered. *Dead I slew*. His stomach churned and his insides cramped. He doubled over and retched.

"Ye must settle for my clumsy hands," Pàdraig said, returning from his search. "Dr. Archie has more wounded than he can tend to himself. 'Twill be hours before he can see ye."

Pàdraig's cheeriness irked Duncan because he himself felt remorse. Visions of the gore would plague his sleep for many nights to come. The pounding in his head worsened. His throat was raw. The foulness of vomit permeated his parched mouth. "Water."

He barely heard the plea himself, so was surprised when Pàdraig brought a cup to his lips. He swished around the warm liquid, then spit it out. He swallowed a second sip.

"Shall I tend to your head?" Pàdraig asked.

"There is oil of Saint John's Wort and clean linen in my sporran."

Pàdraig retrieved the items and set to work. "Dinna fash about the wound. 'Tis a wee thing, and the lasses will swoon when they see it. They will think ye a hero."

"I dinna care what they think."

"Why not? We fulfilled the old prophecy this day—victory at Gladsmuir! The lasses will want to honor us, and 'tis our right to take what they offer. For myself, 'twill be a buxom lass who warms my bed this night."

Gladsmuir? The hamlet lay four miles from here. Old prophesies? Duncan knew only of his wife's visions. To bed a woman other than Rory? Never! His head began to spin.

"What are ye saying?"

Pàdraig looked askance at him. "Ye have a muddled look about ye. 'Tis likely from the gash on your brow. Ye are forgiven for forgetting. Thomas the Rhymer foretold a great battle fought on the field of Gladsmuir. 'Twould be a glorious victory for a just cause. What he spoke of has come to pass. We fought and won the Battle of Gladsmuir! The enemy is met and vanquished!"

Duncan stared dumbfounded and dazed. "How can ye say that? This battle was no more than a slaughter. We may have routed the enemy, but they willna surrender. Both armies will meet again, and we may not win next time."

Pàdraig rose to his feet. He held his arms stiff at his side, his hands clenched into fists. Anger and disgust lanced his words. "They came at us with musket and sword, yet ye would have us shake hands and leave them to kill us another day? They slew our kin, yet ye forgive rather than seek vengeance? I thought ye a warrior, but I was wrong! Ye are nocht but a coward! The sight of ye sickens me."

Duncan watched him stomp away, knowing he had lost a friend. When had their differences become a chasm too wide to cross?

~*~

The approach of heavy footsteps stirred Duncan to lift his gaze from the campfire. Archibald Cameron collapsed beside him. The laughing twinkle in his blue eyes had disappeared. Deep lines furrowed his brow. He rubbed his hand the length of his face, scratched the stubble on his chin, and heaved a sigh.

Duncan knew Archie had not wanted to participate in the Rising any more than his brother, but loyalty and devotion ran strong through the clan. Although he fought beside Donald, his work began when the battle ended. Duncan wondered who ministered to the older man's heart and mind after witnessing so much death. Archie, though, wasted little time caring for himself.

"Ye do not accompany Donald to the ball, Duncan? I heard 'twill be a grand celebration."

"I have no heart for a fling."

"Is it your head that pains ye?"

"'Tis nocht."

"Then 'tis your heart that aches."

"I did terrible deeds three days ago, Archie."

"'Tis war, lad. What ye need is Rory's tender touch to ease the ache. I would bring the bonny lass to ye, if 'twas in my power to do so. Since I canna, mayhap a visit with her kinsmen would help."

The hair on Duncan's neck stirred. Why did he feel fear? Archie was like an uncle, and had never given cause to mistrust him before.

As if sensing his disquiet over Rory's safety because of her kinship with the outlawed Clan MacGregor, Archie said, "I am not Cathal, lad. Ye have my oath I would never betray her."

"I ken, and 'tis sorry I am that I dinna show ye the trust ye deserve."

The other man dismissed the apology with a wave of his hand. "In these troubled times, we must protect those we love as best we can. 'Tis difficult, though, when we are far from them."

"How did ye ken about Rory?"

"My brother confides in me. 'Tis a terrible burden for a chief to keep his own counsel all the time. One of my patients claims kinship with Clan Campbell, but he is of the nameless clan."

"Was his wound fatal?"

"The two balls of lead that pierced through him would have killed most men, but this one has the luck of his father. After he fell, he raised himself up for his men to see and warned that if any faltered, he would witness it."

"The Gregorach are a fierce lot. Who is this man ye speak of and who is his father?"

"The man's name is James Mòr. His father was Rob Roy."

"The great reiver and thief himself?"

"I would not speak those words to James' face, for he has a grand temper. He claims his father was after collecting the black mail in exchange for guaranteeing to protect cattle from reivers. 'Twas only those who refused to pay who lost their herds."

"Why does James Mòr fight for a Stewart? Rory claims 'twas a Stewart who proscribed the Gregorach."

"I canna answer your question, but while Rob Roy lived, he did much to further King Jamie's cause. Murray himself fought with MacGregor at Glen Shiel. Would ye like to meet James Mòr before I return to my work?"

"Aye, 'twill be a tale to share when I see Rory."

The closer they got to the MacGregor encampment, the more Duncan felt he was being watched. The darkness concealed the guards, but he knew they were there. While the Gregorach conducted themselves with honor and courage in battle, many continued to judge them by the deeds of their progenitors. Not only did the guards protect against a surprise enemy attack, but also one from those within the Jacobites' own ranks who would seek retribution for past transgressions.

The breeze carried raucous laughter to Duncan's ears. He discerned four men seated around a campfire. When they noticed his and Archie's approach, they fell silent. Wary looks passed amongst them. Their hands dropped to their weapons.

"I thought I told ye to rest, James Mòr!" Archie said.

The lean brown-haired man's mustached lips curled in a sardonic grin. "I am, Dr. Cameron. I sit."

The youngest of his companions howled with laughter. He had a pockmarked face and squinted when he spoke.

"James is not one to sit idle for more than a few minutes. He often makes us run alongside him with our drink sloshing over the rims of our cups!"

The others laughed, nodding their agreement.

"Ye showed me kindness, Dr. Cameron, so ye are welcome to share our fire. Your companion be a stranger and is not welcome," James said with unnecessary harshness.

"I apologize for offending ye, James Mòr, but Duncan has more right to sit than I."

"We MacGregors learned long ago we canna trust those we dinna ken. What proof have ye to back up your claim?"

"Ye trust and respect my brother, dinna ye?"

"Aye, Lochiel treats us fairly and with respect."

"Duncan is his foster son. My brother trusts him with his life."

"Then we must also trust him," a man with tawny hair streaked with silver-gray said. He was older than the others by a score of years. "Why does Duncan belong here more than ye, Dr. Cameron?"

"His wife is Rory MacGregor."

"From where does she come?"

Duncan answered the MacGregor chieftain. "Her kinsmen live on Mackenzie land in the north. Her father was Gregor of Rannoch.

The MacGregors conversed in low voices.

Finally, the tawny-haired man rose and extended his hand. "Welcome, Duncan Cameron. I am Gregor of Glen Gyle, cousin to James Mòr. The youngest here is Robin Og and the quiet one Ronald, Jamie's brothers."

The eerie squeal of a bagpipe made Duncan jump. The MacGregors laughed.

"The piper calls us to the dance," Gregor said. "Will ye and Dr. Cameron celebrate with us?"

"I thank ye for the invitation," Archie said, "but I must check the wounded. I fear more willna see the sun rise. 'Tis best that I do what little I can to ease their passing."

"What of yourself, Duncan?"

"I will stay."

"Good. Ye can help keep my cousin off his feet."

James Mòr scowled. "I have suffered worse and still celebrated our victory."

"Ye willna be dancing this night," Archie said. "If ye dinna heed me, James Mòr, I will have ye trussed like a boar before 'tis roasted."

A blaze of firelight caught the anger in MacGregor's eyes. Duncan feared for Archie's safety, but Gregor intervened.

"Ye will obey Dr. Cameron. We will need your courage another day. I willna allow ye to risk further injury to satisfy your vanity."

James' lips narrowed into thin slits. He glared at Gregor, but remained seated. He might dislike the orders, but the two eagle feathers adorning Gregor's blue bonnet meant that his position within the clan outranked that of his cousin.

"Would ye care to join Robin on a targe, Cameron?" Glengyle asked.

"Ye bestow a great honor on me, Gregor, but I must decline. I, too, was wounded, and Dr. Archie threatened me with worse than he did your cousin. He fears more injury if I black out."

Gregor nodded, then took his place beside a brass-studded oaken shield covered with cowhide and pierced by a sharp spike at the center boss. One false step would cripple him. At the first strains of music, he stepped onto the targe. With hands arced and thumbs joined to middle fingers, he raised his arms over his head, mimicking the antlers of a stag. He hopped on his left foot and bent his right knee while his ankle touched the back of his left calf, then kicked out his leg, pointed his toes, and moved his foot in front of his shin. He executed the distinct movements with fluid grace and vibrant speed, as if he performed one continuous step. Ever moving, he alternated between left foot and right, repeating the sequence while evading the dangerous spike. With a flourish he placed his hands on his waist and sprang onto his right foot. He touched his left toe and then his left heel to the targe. With his right foot, he repeated the steps until the music ended.

Astounded by the older man's stamina, Duncan joined the other spectators in a rousing cheer. Gregor wiped his brow with the back of his arm.

"Ye did that with more grace than I could have," Duncan said.

Gregor bowed. "Thank ye for your kind words, but I believe I grow too old for this. 'Tis for the young ones like Robin. Would ye join me in a wee sip?"

They returned to the fire. James had disappeared, and Gregor sent his brothers to track him down.

Duncan accepted a *cuach* and lifted it toward his host. "To victory."

"To victory."

Gregor tossed back the whisky. "Ye have the look of a man who misses his wife. Rory is it?"

"Aye."

"Are ye long wed?"

"Not at all. And yourself?"

"Since I was a young lad. Mary is my heart as I think Rory is yours."

"She is."

Gregor rummaged in his sporran and withdrew a gold locket. He snapped it open then handed it to Duncan. Inside was a portrait of a young girl with fair hair and blue eyes.

"She is lovely."

"My sister painted it of Mary soon after we wed. 'Tis so I can remember her when I am gone from Glen Gyle. Have ye one of Rory?"

Duncan shook his head. He pulled the pendant he wore from his shirt and slipped it over his head. "I canna imagine her sitting for one. She gave me this before we parted. When I look on it, 'tis like gazing into her sapphire blue eyes."

Gregor examined the hammered circle, tracing the silver etchings of wildcats and thistles with his slender finger. His thumb rubbed the blue stone. "It belonged to the ancients."

"So she thinks."

"It holds great power. She must love ye deeply."

Duncan sighed. "I wish 'twas so, for I love her more than life."

"She follows her head, then?"

"She does."

"'Tis the bane of the Gregorach. Living by our wits keeps us from death that all too often threatens. 'Tis a hard learned lesson, but I think the day will come when Rory will hear what her heart tries to tell her. Take care of her gift. 'Twill bring ye solace and might well save your life." Gregor returned the pendant. He stretched and yawned. "Ye must forgive an old man, Duncan. The day was long, and I am used to a softer life. I hope ye visit again."

"I will, and thank ye."

Duncan left the MacGregor encampment, but did not return to where his kinsmen rested. Stirred by a great longing to be alone, he climbed Arthur's Seat, a hill that resembled a sleeping lion but was all that remained of an ancient volcano. After he sat, he clasped the pendant between his hands and thought of Rory. A sudden need to hear her voice flooded through him. He clutched the pendant to his heart and rested his weary head on his knees.

"Duncan?"

He ignored the calling of his name. He did not want others to intrude.

"Duncan?"

The voice came again, but softer this time. A gentle hand touched his arm, and he lifted his head. His eyes grew wide, and he emitted an involuntary gasp. "Rory! How—"

He broke off, unable to finish his thought.

She smiled and knelt in front of him. *"Ye wished for me to come while ye held the brooch."*

"Is it really ye, Rory?"

"'Tis and 'tis not."

"I dinna understand. How can ye be in two places at once? Ye swore ye did not practice witchcraft."

"'Tis not witchcraft, Duncan, but the pendant ye hold. Remember how ye heard me speak before the duel?"

"Aye."

"'Tis like then. Ye wished to hear and see me with your heart. I remain in Lochaber, but I am also with ye."

"'Tis your *tamhasg* I see!"

"Aye. Our desire to be with each other forms a bridge that unites us. Remember, Duncan, I will come whenever ye have need of me." With that she faded from sight.

Was he asleep? Was it a dream? He rubbed his eyes. No, he was awake. Then how had he seen her? Was it her *tamhasg,* or had his weary mind tricked him?

"Ye seem lost, Duncan."

"Sandy! I thought ye were at Achnacarry."

"I was until Donald sent for Anne and the bairns. I accompanied them here, and 'tis glad I am that I did."

"Why?"

"The folk of Kirkintilloch are staunch supporters of King George. They attacked our coach, killing one gillie and wounding two others who died before we reached Edinburgh."

"What of Lady Anne and the bairns?"

"Rescue came before they were harmed. Anne is upset, but Donald will comfort her. The lads and lasses stood firm and rallied around their mother." Sandy sat beside Duncan. "Enough sad news. I bring a missive from a bonny lass dear to your heart."

Duncan grinned. "She sent a letter?"

Sandy nodded. The light of his torch caught the twinkle in his round black eyes. "Aye, but before I give it over, ye must confess your sins."

"My sins?"

"Ye gave a vow of faithfulness to Rory, yet I saw ye with another lass. If I did not ken that I left Rory behind, I would have thought 'twas her."

"Ye saw her too, Sandy? I thought I conjured her in my mind."

"Now why are ye after thinking that?"

"I canna explain, but 'twas Rory. Am I under a spell do ye think?"

The priest chuckled. "Aye, the spell of love. God does wondrous miracles when He answers our prayers. He kent of your yearning, so He allowed Rory to visit ye. Does your heart feel lighter?"

"It does."

"Good. Be certain to thank the Lord for answering your prayer."

"How is Rory?"

"She carries a great responsibility serving in my brother's stead, but she manages. She cares about our people, and sees to their needs. While she willna admit this, I ken she misses ye."

"I wager I miss her more."

"'Tis a wager I willna take." Sandy passed him the letter. "Donald sends a gillie back to Achnacarry at dawn, so if ye wish to write her, I suggest ye do so before ye sleep."

The priest left the torch, and made his way down the hill guided by the moonlight.

Duncan broke the seal and unfolded the letter. Tears clouded his eyes while he read.

Duncan, I am well and pray ye are safe and in good spirits. 'Tis hard work keeping track of everything, but Father Alex is patient with me. I will miss his wisdom and company. Midnight and I visit the clachans, going from one to another until we make a circuit. Nannag is well and sends her love. She also bid me remind ye to keep safe.

Should ye see Red Pàdraig, tell him Morna is also well. Brandubh is after growing more each time I see him. Greet Fergus for me. I had not realized how much I enjoyed our walks until after he was gone. Neil sends word when the patrols leave Fort William. 'Tis certain he is that they ken Lochiel has come out for the prince, but so far, they do no more than make their presence known.

'Tis strange lying abed without ye beside me. I wear your brooch and think of ye often. I pray for your safe and swift return. Love, Rory

Duncan reread the last two words. His heart soared and he let out a whoop. For the first time she had admitted she loved him. He folded the letter and placed it in the deerskin sporran that hung at his waist. Her words were priceless and he meant to cherish them always.

~*~

Duncan sat in the cramped office in the old Parliament House behind the High Kirk of Saint Giles. From here, Lochiel, newly appointed Provost Marshall, discharged his duties, or more accurately, had Duncan see to them. He put aside the latest report of deserters and rubbed his eyes. The momentum of the Rising had stagnated and the elation at routing the Royal Army had waned. Rather than capitalize on their victory, the Jacobites remained in Edinburgh while the prince and his officers attended nightly galas held by the gentry. Restive clansmen who felt they had achieved their objectives—the Jacobites controlled the capital, James had been proclaimed King and his son regent, and the Royal Army had fled—had returned to the Highlands to reap the harvest. With each passing day, more slipped away under cover of darkness until the number of soldiers had dwindled dangerously low. If the enemy attacked on the morrow, Duncan was uncertain whether the prince had enough men to repel their advance.

To compound the problem, the officer corps had split into two factions. The Highland chiefs aligned themselves with Lord Murray, while the Irish officers swayed the prince to their way of thinking. In the daily convening of the Grand Council little was accomplished except for heated argy-bargies over possible tactics. The discord filtered down into the ranks, resulting in frequent quarrels between Highlanders and Lowlanders, Protestants and Papists, and Scots and Irish.

The situation was untenable, but Duncan possessed neither the power nor the influence to alter it. Disgusted, he pushed back his chair and left the stuffy office. He threaded his way through men billeted in the straw-littered great hall and emerged onto a cobblestone street. He was about to head for a nearby tavern, when a patrol rounded the corner. One soldier broke from the others and approached him.

"Good day to ye, Pàdraig," he said.

His old friend nodded. "Is Lochiel in? We have deserters for him."

"He is with the prince." Duncan glanced at six disheveled prisoners, prodded and taunted by their guards. "Do ye ken their clan?"

Pàdraig spit on the dusty cobblestone. "At least two are Camerons! Cowards the lot."

"Take them to the tolbooth. Put a guard on them, and find them something fit to eat. When Lochiel returns, I will report this to him."

Pàdraig sneered. "Feed them? Whatever for? They dishonored the clan by fleeing before the battle. Death is too grand for the likes of them."

"'Tis not for us to say what punishment they deserve. Lochiel left orders that deserters are to be fed and imprisoned in the tolbooth. He will convene a court of officers to decide their fate upon his return."

Pàdraig muttered under his breath, but obeyed. Duncan thought he heard the word "coddle," but chose to ignore it. He waited until Pàdraig and his companions entered the Tolbooth with their prisoners before heading for the tavern.

The next morning a soft mist fell as Duncan exited the Tolbooth. What would Lochiel do when he heard there would be no execution?

Sir Donald narrowed his eyes. "I sent ye to fetch condemned prisoners, lad. Ye return empty-handed."

"They are no longer in the Tolbooth."

Lochiel's dark eyes turned a deeper shade of black. He clenched his fists until the knuckles whitened. His face took on a red tinge. "What do ye mean they are no longer there?"

Duncan swallowed. "The turnkey says His Royal Highness visited in the wee hours of the night. He promised to rescind the death sentences if the prisoners gave their parole not to desert again."

Had he not been watching, Duncan would have missed the relief that flashed in Lochiel's eyes. Since the men had shamed him, the clan, and their prince, duty compelled him to see the men punished, but the prince's intervention relieved him from rendering a sentence he accepted but did not concur with.

"Come, 'tis late and we have wasted enough time here. The Grand Council is already in session."

"Do ye expect a decision on what we do next?" Duncan asked. This was the first time his foster father had requested anyone attend with him.

Lochiel shrugged. "'Tis certain we canna continue as we are. If the prince does not make a decision, there willna be any men left to fight for his cause."

They hastened to the Palace of Holyroodhouse where a guard conducted them to the drawing room. Lochiel was the last chief to arrive. While he conferred with Lord Murray, Duncan leaned against the back wall where he had a clear view of all the participants, including the Duke of Perth, the Irish officers, and the quartermaster general.

A door opened and Prince Charles entered. Gold lace trimmed his blue grogram coat and red waistcoat and breeches. When he reached the fireplace, he set his white-plumed hat and silver basket-hilted broadsword on a gilt side table. He lifted his coattails and sat in a red damask armchair. His secretary called the council to order.

"The time has come to proceed," Charles said. "The army must march south."

Lord George rose from his chair. "I dinna agree, Your Royal Highness."

"Why ever not?" one Irishman asked, his tone condescending.

Murray ignored the slight. "When we did not march on England after Gladsmuir, we lost any advantage we gained by giving the Sassenach army time to gather strength. We canna match their numbers or their armament without France's help, which has not come. We dinna even ken if the Sassenach Jacobites will support us."

"I have letters pledging that they will," the prince said. "Once we are in England, they will declare themselves. Without further victories, the French will withhold aid, and we cannot win battles unless we move south."

As if doubting the veracity of those words, Lord George studied the prince before answering. "'Tis glad I am to hear of these promises, but how do ye intend to coordinate all this help?"

Rather than answer, Prince Charles countered with a question of his own. "Does anyone disagree with Lord Murray?"

Several gentlemen, including the Duke of Perth, murmured in the affirmative or nodded their heads. Duncan knew the two commanders often disagreed.

MacDonald spoke. "If we dinna move soon, the men will settle the matter for us because there willna be enough left to defend the palace let alone fight to keep Scotland for King Jamie. Each day we delay gives the Sassenach more time to prepare. If we are to succeed, we must swoop down on them like the hawk."

"*Exactement!*" Charles said. "We must instill the men with fervor. To accomplish this we must march without delay. We must regain the initiative."

"Sure and we need more money, else our coffers will be empty," an Irish officer said. "We cannot be mounting a war without gold."

The debate escalated until it reminded Duncan of the din Mairi had made with her pots. He would gladly suffer a sore head rather than listen to these men argue over what to do. This talk of marching into England bothered him. Many had assumed the prince's aim was to take Scotland from King George so his father could rule, but Charles did not seem to understand this. Now, he asked them to go south, and while some Lowlanders might have traveled from home, most clansmen never strayed far from the Highlands. How would they react to finding themselves in a country where no one spoke Gaelic and the people considered Highlanders akin to barbarians?

"Enough talk!" Prince Charles nodded to his secretary.

"Those in favor of marching on England, say aye." The man waited, then asked, "Those opposed?"

Duncan was unable to decide which side had the greater number of supporters. Apparently, so did the secretary, because he asked for a show of hands. Murray, Lochiel, and most of the other Highland chiefs voted against the motion. The Duke of Perth, the Irish, and the Lowland commanders sided against them. In the end, the matter was settled by one vote.

CHAPTER SIXTEEN
ENGLAND

Duncan propped the pickax against the trench. Rivulets of perspiration trickled down his back from hacking and digging in frost-hardened soil. Three days earlier he had experienced a similar sensation, but then the dripping wetness had come from fording the River Esk. After crossing into England, he had stood on the bank and faced Scotland. The unknown, a future fraught with peril, loomed behind him. Ahead, Rory waited. He yearned to return from whence he came, but his destiny lay elsewhere. He had drawn his sword from its scabbard and saluted his homeland.

"Digging is not for warriors," Fergus said, leaning on the handle of his shovel.

The other alternative, standing idle while blockading the roads into Carlisle, held little appeal.

Duncan grunted. "I would rather be warm from hard labor than shiver with cold from doing nocht."

The bright November sun glistened on the snowy fields. With the dissipation of the thick fog, the blurred shadows of Carlisle took color and form. A Scottish king, the first David, had completed the red stone fortification of keep and curtain that encircled the city. In the intervening six centuries, the second Alexander, William Wallace, and Robert the Bruce had stood where Duncan and Fergus did. The crumbling walls of the border stronghold bespoke years of neglect, but that did not mean the city and castle were indefensible. On the contrary, the militia had indicated its intent to fight when they unleashed their cannon rather than honor Prince Charles' request for quarters.

"Think ye they will surrender before we finish, Duncan?"

"I pray so, Fergus, for I am not looking forward to spending long frigid nights in the trench while we wait for them to change their minds."

A hail of musket fire issued from the castle. Cannon shot followed. Duncan and Fergus ducked to avoid the rain of lead. The trench they dug paralleled the east curtain, running in a north-south line between the Scotch and English Gates. From their position a chain length from the wall, the accuracy of the shot was more nuisance than threat. When the Jacobite four-pounders returned fire, the effort was akin to swatting at midges. Their guns would never breach the medieval curtain.

They finished the trench on the fourth day of the siege. Fierce gusts of wintry wind blew thick gray clouds across the sky. The temperature plummeted and snowflakes swirled. The bitter cold intensified the ache in Duncan's knees and back. Sweat dampened his plaid.

"What I would not give for a warm fire and a bed piled thick with furs," Fergus said.

Duncan shivered. "I would fight ye for it, 'tis that cold I am."

"How many did ye bring from the trench this morn?"

"Four."

"'Twas two for me. Frozen stiff like ice on the loch they were. If I am to die in this hostile land, I would rather do so in battle."

Duncan thought of dying, and decided he preferred to do so with Rory at his side when he was old. "We managed to survive the night huddled together. Mayhap if a few lads join with us, we will live to see another day."

Fergus persuaded four others to try their idea. Each man wrapped his plaid around him like a cocoon, and then they squeezed together on the unyielding ground. When those on either end grew cold, they exchanged positions with someone in the middle until each man had slept with one warm body beside him rather than wedged between two. When they woke the next morning, several inches of snow covered their plaids, but all lived.

"A white flag!"

The shout brought Duncan to his feet. Draped over the east curtain was the sign of surrender. Six days they had waited for capitulation. A messenger emerged from the town late in the afternoon. The Duke of Perth crossed the trench.

"Be you the commander?" the messenger asked.

"I am."

"The magistrates beg leave to surrender."

"What of the castle?"

"I know not, your Grace."

"Return to the magistrates. We accept no surrender unless the militia relinquishes its arms and departs the keep. They have until the sun rises on the morrow to decide."

The man slipped inside the gate, and Duncan wondered whether the magistrates would convince the militia to surrender. He applauded the duke's foresight in requiring total submission. The last thing they needed was a standoff similar to the one in Edinburgh. After eight weeks of occupation, they had left the capital without securing the garrison's surrender. Good men had died. Innocent citizens had suffered, their homes needlessly demolished.

~*~

The next day the gate swung open. Eighty men, aged and feeble, marched from the town to the beating of drums. The invalids laid down their muskets near the trench. Behind them came the remnants of two companies of militia. These troops surrendered their arms and horses while their commander saluted the Duke of Perth.

"Is this all your men, *Monsieur?*"

The British officer gave a curt nod. "The rest sneaked over the walls during the night. Cowards the lot of them."

"Do you give your word not to take up arms against His Royal Highness for a year and a day?"

Again, the commander nodded.

"Then you and your men are free to leave."

After giving a stiff nod, the British officer returned to his squadron. The drummers resumed their tattoo, and the militia headed south.

"What of yourselves?" the duke asked one of the invalids.

"By your Grace's leave, the magistrates promised us a month's wages. We did our duty and our time. We want to go home."

"The castle?"

"Is yours, your Grace. We left twenty six-pounders where they stand."

The Duke of Perth nodded. "Ye are free to go, *Monsieur.*"

The invalids hobbled back to the city. Prince Charles joined the duke, and they headed for the gate followed by Perth's regiment. The magistrates bowed low to His Royal Highness. The mayor handed over the keys and conducted the prince within the city walls.

~*~

"We canna proceed without him, Donald," Sandy said, stoking the fire in the quarters assigned to his eldest brother while in Carlisle.

"He is right, brother. Drummond is a likable fellow, but what kens he of fighting?" Archie asked.

Lochiel sighed. "What of yourself, lad? Have ye no opinion on the matter?"

Of course Duncan did, but he considered it best to keep it to himself while he listened to the brothers discuss Lord Murray's resignation.

"I do."

Three pairs of eyes bore into him. The older men waited to hear his thoughts, but he remained silent. This was one of those in-between times when he was uncertain which path to tread. On the one hand, these men had taught and raised him as if they were his father and uncles. On the other, the eldest was his chief. His duty to safeguard the life and limb of the Cameron meant he kept his mouth shut and his eyes and ears alert.

"Ye have acquired Rory's habit of keeping me waiting on your answers, I see," Lochiel said.

Duncan shrugged. "'Tis kept her safe."

"Aye, until ye rile her. Then 'tis a wonder if ye dinna lose an ear," Sandy said. A self-satisfied grin appeared on his face and his eyes twinkled with merriment.

Archie roared with laughter. Although Lochiel chuckled at the joke made at his expense, he rubbed his ear.

Duncan smiled. "Then ye should not provoke my wife if ye canna accept the consequences, Sandy."

"The wildcat has no cause for concern here, lad. 'Tis but a humble priest I be."

"One with a penchant for teasing," Archie said.

Sandy clapped his hand to his chest. "Ye wound me, brother."

"We appreciate your levity, Alexander, but we wander from the issue at hand," Lochiel said. "Duncan, I am waiting on your answer."

Speaking of Rory had opened a flood of memories and a deep longing for her company. With great effort, he shut himself off from the happiness and heartache. He could not keep his mind on the task at hand otherwise.

"'Tis daftness to be sure. Lord Murray is the only man among us who kens how to battle the Sassenach. While His Grace, the Duke of Perth, is an honorable man, he has no head for military matters. I dinna trust the Irish or the French, and I expect they think the same of us. They would sway the prince with whatever means necessary to have him accede to their wishes. If His Royal Highness is after wanting the support of the Highland clans, he must swallow his pride and seek out Murray."

"Well said, Duncan. Donald, why ever did George resign?" Archie asked.

Lochiel sighed. "Ye ken the prince is easily offended?"

Archie nodded.

"He took George's refusal to lead the siege as a personal affront and from then onward sent all messages to Drummond."

"Including the order to oversee the surrender?" the priest asked.

"Aye, Sandy."

"But the magistrates agreed to all the demands," Duncan said. "Why would Murray take exception to the duke if he achieved the objective?"

"'Tis not His Grace to whom George objects," Lochiel said. "'Tis Prince Charles' decision to have a Papist accept the surrender."

"The Stewarts no longer sit on the throne because of their religious beliefs, lad," Sandy said. "The Sassenach threw over His Royal Highness' grandsire because they feared being ruled by another Papist once his son succeeded him. Nocht has changed in the intervening years, but Prince Charles does not grasp this. He wants the Sassenach to support him rather than King George, yet he chose a Papist to negotiate the surrender. Think how the Whigs will use that to sway folk to remain steadfast to the Crown."

Lochiel rose. "'Tis time for the council to convene."

"Will ye put forth the ultimatum?" Archie asked.

"Duncan is right. Our chances of success are slim, but without Murray leading us, they are nil. The other chiefs and I have to make Charles listen to reason. He must do whatever is required to seek George's return."

~*~

While on reconnaissance, Duncan halted atop a snow-covered hill to watch the Jacobite Army depart Carlisle. The Duke of Perth had resigned, citing the ill health that had plagued him since childhood, but the tendering of his resignation was done to placate Murray. Ever loyal to the cause, Drummond now rode at the head of his regiment under Lord George's command.

Duncan peered south, then west, and finally east, wondering how distant the enemy was. He breathed on his hands to warm them. Puffs of frosted air escaped his chapped lips. His gaze returned to the Jacobites below. They moved not in a well-formed column, but spread out in a wide arc. Few adhered to the principles of strict discipline unless they were Lowlanders or French and Irish soldiers. Trained warriors were the exception rather than the rule in this army. Scattered among the farmers, weavers, merchants, shepherds, cobblers, and barbers trudged young lads, ranging in age from ten to fourteen, eager to prove their manhood. They carried scythes, sticks, shovels, or other farm implements with which they waged battle. At the rear, in spite of orders to the contrary, were the camp followers: wives, bairns, old men, and strumpets.

Flickering campfires beckoned to Duncan. The promise of warmth spurred him toward the officers' quarters to deliver his report. A shadow blocked the glow of lantern light illuminating Murray's tent. Duncan stiffened. Why would someone be skulking outside when he could be inside?

Duncan slipped his dirk from its sheath. He watched and listened. Hushed voices came from within the tent, but he was too far to distinguish what they said. The spy was not. From his vantage point Duncan assumed the intruder overheard every word. He crept forward.

A twig snapped under his foot. The man whirled, then butted Duncan in the stomach. He grunted from the impact. Instinct made him grab for the spy. They slammed onto crusted snow and tumbled against the side of the tent. They rolled in the opposite direction before righting themselves. They faced each other with arms extended. The spy feinted to his left, then lunged. Duncan felt a quick sharp tug to his shirt followed by a stinging sensation below his ribs. His opponent raised his dirk to strike again. Duncan ignored the pain and fought to keep the blade from doing further damage.

A shot rumbled through the camp. Rough hands seized the spy. Duncan fell to his knees, clutching his side. Archie knelt beside him.

"What is the meaning of this?" Murray demanded.

"Canna it wait, George? The lad is wounded," Archie said.

"'Tis nocht," Duncan said.

Lochiel touched Duncan's shoulder. "Let my brother be the judge of that. Fergus, bring the prisoner inside."

While Archie cleaned and bandaged his wound, Duncan explained what had happened. Murray, who sat near the fire, approached the prisoner. He brought a lantern close to study the man's face, then whistled. "Do ye ken who this be?"

To a man they shook their heads.

"Allow me to introduce Captain John Weir, late of His Majesty's service. Collecting intelligence for the duke, were ye? What did ye learn from myself and my men?"

Weir gave him a disdainful glance.

"Spying is a serious offense," Murray said. "'Twill go better if ye answer my questions."

"I have nothing to say to cowardly heathens!"

"Heathens and cowards are we? And why do ye think that?"

Weir gave him a fleering look. "I heard what ye did to the women and children of Carlisle."

Surprised by the statement, Duncan exchanged looks with Archie. The doctor shrugged.

"Would ye be explaining yourself?" Murray asked. "I canna recall doing anything at all to them, but mayhap ye will enlighten us."

"Ye bound them hand and foot in chains, and set them before the castle walls so ye could hide behind innocents."

"Now why would we be doing such a thing?"

"To force the militia to capitulate."

"'Tis not us who make war on women and bairns, John Weir, or have ye forgotten the slaughter of Glen Coe? I have no stomach for what ye suggest. The commander himself confessed that his men stole away in the night rather than surrender. The ones slain were my own men."

Weir did not respond. He focused his eyes on the tent flap and sat unmoving.

Murray positioned himself within Weir's line of sight. "I asked what ye learned from your sneaking about."

"You have fewer men than ye claim. Your guns are inferior. You squabble amongst yourselves and lack discipline."

"Yet so far 'tis us who are winning the encounters. How do ye explain that?"

Weir clamped his jaw shut.

"Tell me about your own numbers and where Cumberland is now."

The stoic look on the spy's face vanished. He smiled and withdrew a newspaper from his coat pocket. "I believe this will answer your questions."

Murray scanned the small print. "This reports each regiment under Cumberland's command. It says he has 8,250 foot and 2,200 horse."

"'Tis higher than we thought," Lochiel said.

"Aye. Fergus, escort Weir to His Royal Highness. I will follow anon."

The giant grasped the spy above his elbow and ushered him from the tent.

"What will ye tell the prince, George?" Lochiel asked.

"That we must return home. We canna match these numbers."

"Will he listen?"

"To me? 'Tis doubtful. He will call the council and those who curry his favor will accede to his wishes. He has one goal: to sit on the throne of England. It willna matter to him that the Hanoverians will slaughter us before that day comes."

~*~

Unable to sleep, Duncan roamed the quiet streets of Derby. The welcome he had received earlier almost made the journey worthwhile. Led by Prince Charles, who wore a belted plaid and green bonnet, they had marched six abreast into the town while church bells tolled and beacon bonfires flickered.

He walked down a narrow alley until a stone wall blocked his way. He turned to retrace his steps. Five shadows slithered from the darkness. Duncan eased his hand to the hilt of his sword, waiting for his attackers to make the first move. Were they Whigs? Were they royal foot soldiers? A beam of moonlight revealed a clue to their identity. Their belted plaids told him they were Highlanders. Then why did they bar his path?

The men encircled him. He pivoted, trying to keep all in sight. Who would attack first? Would the first blow come from the front or the back?

"Look who we found."

Duncan stiffened. "Cathal."

"'Tis been over long since last we met."

"Lochiel has forbidden us to fight."

Cathal snorted. "He is not here, and when he learns of this, ye willna be telling him a thing. Grab him."

Two men pinned Duncan's arms. Rather than waste his strength in a futile attempt to gain his release, he waited.

Cathal rubbed his shoulder. "'Tis your fault I canna wield the sword as before. I intend to repay ye for that and every other slight ye have shown me. Once I finish with ye, I head for Achnacarry and that bonny wife of yours. I have a score to settle with her, and will savor my revenge."

Fear crept through Duncan. He could well imagine what torments Cathal planned for Rory. He fought to keep his panic at bay. It would serve no purpose to lose control. To beat Cathal he must keep calm and alert.

"Struggle all ye like, Duncan. 'Twill do no good." Cathal expelled a long breath. "'Twill be a fair fight."

"Fair? Ye dinna ken the meaning of the word. There are five of ye and one of me."

"Ye dinna understand, Duncan. 'Tis myself who is at a disadvantage." He indicated his arm by raising his shoulder. "The lead Lochiel gave me for pilfering that ewe. Ye must have a similar disadvantage."

Another man stepped from the shadows.

Duncan's eyes widened. "Pàdraig!"

"Aye."

"We are friends. Why cast your lot with caterans?"

"I dinna number cowards amongst my friends. Neither do I hold with men who marry the nameless."

"And dinna forget she is a witch, too," Cathal said, egging on Pàdraig.

"Aye, a witch. Who else could sway the Cameron to set a woman above men? Who else could wield a sword like a man? Who else could appear in Edinburgh one minute and Lochaber the next?"

Duncan froze. Pàdraig had seen Rory's *tamhasg*. The image of a scored old woman—bound hand and foot, burning at the stake—flashed in Duncan's mind. He clenched his fists. A primeval curse wended its way up his throat.

"*No!*"

The single word echoed through the empty streets.

Cathal laughed. "So we find your weakness. If these were other times, I would enjoy watching ye watch me take your wife, Duncan. Alas, I canna waste precious time dragging ye back with us."

He snapped his fingers, and Pàdraig slammed his fist into Duncan's stomach. Duncan gasped. Before he could catch his breath, Pàdraig delivered another blow that connected with his chin. His head jerked back. He staggered, but the men holding him kept him upright. He tasted blood on his lip. Pàdraig pummeled him until a sharp whistle pierced the night.

"Now, 'twill be a fair fight," Cathal said. "Release him."

His men pulled back, and Duncan staggered to gain his balance. Someone shoved a weapon at him.

"Take the sword."

Duncan curled his fingers around the hilt. A hum rent the air. Instinct seized control. He pivoted and raised his sword. The clang of steel echoed through the alley. He lunged. Cathal parried. They circled each other.

Duncan needed to divert his concentration to the fight at hand rather than dwell on his body's pain. He felt steadying hands embrace his, but no one was there. Warm breath caressed his neck, and a surge of strength filled him. *Rory.* He fought for her, not himself. She was his heart, and he would sacrifice his life to save hers.

He lashed out with renewed vigor. He feinted to his left, and Cathal stumbled past him. He whirled, then renewed the attack. Their blades became tangled near the hilt. Duncan heard the whoosh of a dirk being unsheathed. He grabbed Cathal's wrist. They wrestled. The dirk's blade pointed first one way, then the other. More than once Duncan felt the sharp tip pierce his shirt. He freed his sword and jumped back. Cathal staggered backward at the sudden release. Duncan gasped for breath, but pressed forward. Sometimes Cathal's sword met his. Other times Cathal used the dirk to hold off the blade.

"What goes on here?"

The unexpected intrusion diverted Cathal's concentration. Duncan took advantage of the momentary lapse. He feinted to the right, then reversed the direction of his slash. Cathal turned into the blade. It sank into his flesh, piercing his heart. His eyes widened. His mouth opened. He dropped to his knees, then fell. Blood oozed from his wound and trickled from his lips. When Duncan knelt beside him, he looked into vacant eyes.

"Are ye all right?" Fergus asked.

Duncan nodded. "The others?"

"Gone."

Duncan went to stand, but his knees buckled. Fergus slipped an arm around him.

"Where are we going?"

"Since I dinna ken if ye need priest or doctor, I am taking ye to both."

Duncan groaned. Fergus' answer meant they headed for Lochiel's quarters. Right now he did not feel up to that confrontation.

~*~

Fergus eased Duncan onto the bed.

"What happened to ye?" Archie asked.

"Cathal," Duncan said.

"From the looks of ye, I say he got the best of ye."

"The beating was given by Pàdraig."

"Red Pàdraig?"

Duncan winced.

"Ye keep strange friends, lad," Archie said.

Fergus shook his head. "Friends dinna pummel each other."

"No, they dinna." Archie said little more while he poked and prodded Duncan. "Ye will be black and blue by morning, lad. Ye have two cracked ribs that need strapping. I doubt ye will be moving much on the morrow. Ye are a good fighter. How could ye let Pàdraig do this?"

"I was not given a choice," Duncan said. "Two of Cathal's men kept me from objecting."

"How many attacked ye?"

"I counted five," Fergus said. "'Twas not a fair fight. From the way the others scattered, 'twas obvious they were up to no good."

"They meant to kill me, and then go after Rory," Duncan added.

The door opened and Lochiel entered. "Brawling against orders?"

Fergus shook his head. "Five men jumped him, Sir Donald."

"Ye saw this, Fergus?"

"Not all of it, but enough."

"Who were they?"

Since Archie was cleaning Duncan's cut lip, Fergus answered. "Cathal and Red Pàdraig. I dinna ken the others. Cathal is dead."

"Dead?" Lochiel asked.

"Aye, 'twas his own fault."

"There is more, Donald," Archie said.

"More?"

"Rory is in danger," Duncan said.

"Mayhap ye best explain from the beginning, lad," Lochiel said.

Duncan did.

Lochiel paced the floor. When he had heard the entire tale, he turned to Fergus. "Take what men ye need and go after them. With Cathal dead, I dinna think they will bother Rory."

After Fergus left, Archie asked, "Do ye think Uncle Ludovic is behind this?"

Lochiel looked at his brother, and then at Duncan. "Is he?"

"I doubt it, Sir Donald. Cathal wanted revenge for Rory besting him and for my part in your shooting him."

"Good. I will visit uncle now."

Archie cleared his throat. "Will he demand retribution from Duncan?"

"He may, but I am satisfied the fault lies with Cathal. I willna brook objections from uncle this time. He must understand 'tis I who am chief. Duncan, your consequence for violating my edict is to get what rest ye can. I will need ye later."

The soreness had already seeped into Duncan's muscles, his joints, and his bones. He groaned at the prospect of stirring from the soft bed, but nodded.

~*~

With each step he took along the Derby street, Duncan moaned. Archie had been right in assessing his aches. Just rising from his bed had been torture. Lochiel walked beside him, and Duncan could swear that from time to time his foster father stifled a chuckle. Another time, Duncan might have challenged him, but Lochiel had seemed preoccupied with weighty matters of late. If he found amusement, albeit perverse, at his expense, then Duncan was willing to suffer.

When they turned onto Exeter Street, Duncan allowed a groan to escape his swollen lips. "Am I to answer to Prince Charles?"

Lochiel blinked. "We have weightier matters to discuss than your brawling in the streets. I want ye to witness what transpires at the Grand Council."

"Whatever for? The bloody mess that was my face will frighten His Royal Highness. Or is that your intent?"

"Not at all, lad, but 'tis an idea." Lochiel grew somber and lowered his voice. "Duncan, ye are like a son to me. John, my eldest, wanted to accompany us, but my brother John was right to convince me that my son should not come. 'Tis ye I depend on to do my bidding. What ye hear within willna sit well with ye, but I felt ye deserved the truth. 'Tis why I ask ye never to speak of this to another."

"Ye are both father and chief to me, Sir Donald. Ye gave me advantages I would not have had otherwise. If I can repay ye by keeping my silence, 'tis a wee thing to ask of me."

"Are ye not beholding to me for introducing ye to Rory?"

Duncan smiled. His lower lip cracked anew, and he licked away the blood. "When ye gave that order, I was not certain which I preferred—death or marriage. Although the path between Rory and myself is not always smooth and has taken a long time to travel, I would not journey elsewhere. She is my heart, and I will always be beholding to ye for having the wisdom to send me to her."

"'Tis glad I am to hear ye say that. Rory is a rare woman, but to me she will always be the wee rebel who dared to defy me. She has curbed the defiance, but it rears its head when 'tis necessary. The two of ye are like the sword and the scabbard—the blade defends while the sheath protects—although I confess that at times I wonder who is which. I promise I will do what I can to return ye to her, alive and safe if God wills it."

Moved by the confession and the promise, Duncan swallowed. He blinked to prevent his eyes from tearing.

Lochiel cleared his throat. "Well, 'tis time to decide our future. Shall we enter?"

A servant conducted them to an oak-paneled drawing room crowded with Highland chiefs, Lord Murray, Lowland gentlemen, the Duke of Perth, and Irish and French officers. Many sat around a polished oval table, while the remainder stood along the walls. Lochiel took the empty seat beside the commander while Duncan, aware of the stares and unspoken questions from those who saw his face, eased himself against the far wall. When Prince Charles entered the chamber, they came to attention.

He acknowledged them with a flick of his wrist, before seating himself at the head of the table. "*Messieurs,* we have accomplished much in the five weeks since we left Edinburgh. In less than a fortnight we shall be in London and the usurper will rule no longer. I will listen to suggestions on how we should best proceed."

For several minutes no one spoke.

Finally, Murray stood. "I am of the opinion, Your Royal Highness, that to proceed will bring disaster upon us. We must return to Scotland."

Charles stared at him dumbfounded. "You would have us retreat?"

"No, 'tis but to regroup."

"We are less than a week's march from London. You cannot be serious."

"I discussed this with the other chiefs, Your Royal Highness," Lochiel said. "We concur with Lord Murray. We are outnumbered. Our enemy's armament is superior. The men are exhausted and the promised support from France has not come. If we withdraw, we can wait for its arrival. By then, we will have enough men and arms to renew the fight."

"I have spoken with the men, Lochiel, and find them eager to wage battle. When we depose the usurper and claim London for my father, they will have their reward. Retreat serves no purpose. Rather it shows weakness to the enemy, and thereby loses all that we have gained. We have met the enemy at Gladsmuir and won. We laid siege to Carlisle and won. We will do so again."

Murmurs of agreement came from the far side of the table. The prince's supporters included the duke, the Lowlanders, and the foreign officers.

"Your cousin, the Duke of Cumberland, commands his father's forces," Murray said. "'Tis but a two-day march that separates us from his troops who flank us to the west. Others head for London and may arrive there before us. I dinna doubt our men could beat any one of these forces even though 'twould cost many lives. If Cumberland converges with General Wade and whoever commands the London forces, however, he will have thirty thousand men to our five. 'Twill be slaughter should we face them. 'Tis folly to think our army invincible and only a fool would believe so!"

Silence fell on the room like the curtain on a stage, heavy and solid. While Duncan agreed with Murray, he would have couched the offensive statement in different terms. To declare the prince a fool was tantamount to throwing down the gauntlet. It tended to evoke anger rather than appease it.

"Your Royal Highness?"

"Lochiel."

"Whether we can win against a greater force is not the important issue."

"Then what is?"

"Yourself."

A frown creased the prince's brow. "Myself? I do not understand."

"Ye unite us. To meet a larger force puts ye at greater risk. If we retire, ye will lead us in a new attack after more men join us. If we press onward, the danger of your capture increases. We canna afford that risk. The Elector would imprison ye within the Tower, a fortress we canna breach, and 'tis doubtful he will allow ye to live."

The prospect of Charles' thin neck being severed on the block by an executioner's ax silenced any comments. If they lost, the prince would not be the only one to meet such an end.

"Your concern touches me, Lochiel," Charles said, "but it is unnecessary. We will persevere. If not, then I would rather die than retreat."

"If I understand my brother and Lochiel," the Marquis of Tullibardine said, "it is the difference in our strength versus that of the British Army that fashes them most." The feisty and frail old man received affirmative nods from his brother George and Sir Donald. "Then, Your Royal Highness, might I suggest we discuss how many London Jacobites will rally to our cause? With their assistance we can take the city with wee concern for your safety."

"Aye, can ye prove they will join with us?" MacDonell of Keppoch asked.

"They sent letters assuring their support," Charles said.

"Show them to us," Murray demanded.

"How dare ye doubt my word!"

Lord George leaned forward in his chair and slammed his fist on the table. "Have ye the letters or not, Your Highness?"

The two eyed each other. The younger man looked away first.

"I thought not," Murray said. "Ye promised us men and arms and gold from the French. Nocht has come. Ye promised support from the Sassenach who have yet to declare themselves. Aye, our men are eager to fight, but I willna sacrifice their lives for your whims. 'Tis time to go home. By spring, we will have gathered men and arms sufficient to meet a stronger force. We will fight them in a place of our choosing instead of theirs."

Lochiel and the other Highland chiefs voiced their agreement, a formidable front for the inexperienced prince to surmount. His eagerness and energy counted for much, but he lacked the wisdom and knowledge men acquired with age. Perhaps the time had come to re-evaluate his goals. The Stewarts already claimed Scotland. If Charles regrouped, he could win over those who remained loyal to King George. Was it not better to settle for a crown that was assured rather than lose it in the vain hope of securing a second?

For the next two hours Duncan endured the prince's harangue. The Highlanders refused to waver, and in the end only two added their votes to those of the Lowlanders, French, and Irish—the Marquis of Tullibardine and MacDonald of Clanranald.

In an icy tone, the prince relented. He pointed a finger at Murray. "You betray us! Since I am given no other choice, I accede to your wishes. Leave!"

The Highlanders bowed and stood.

"One moment, *Messieurs.*"

They turned to the prince.

"This is the last council of war. I no longer require your advice. From this moment onward, I will give the orders and you will obey them."

Duncan shuddered. Clansmen gave allegiance to their chiefs, not the prince. Charles adhered to a belief in divine right. Like his forebears, he was infallible. Highlanders believed the exact opposite. They expected to be consulted in all affairs that concerned them. They did not recklessly follow anyone, not even a king. Charles had learned nothing from history, and because of his arrogance, Duncan feared they would pay for his folly.

~*~

They left Derby before dawn on six December. Duncan thought the shroud of mist both appropriate and ominous. Men keened the loss of their honor. The prince acted like a spoiled child. He lounged in bed until late in the morning. He drank overmuch and cared little about his unkempt appearance. When they passed through villages and towns, angry mobs pelted them with rotten food and stones. Those who had given them shelter before now barred their doors. Snipers shot at them. Farmers beat them. Sleeping clansmen were found with their throats slit.

Fear bred rumor. Rumor bred suspicion. Suspicion bred treachery. Duncan heard the whisperings day and night. Disturbed by them, he sought out his foster father. Murray was with him.

"Ye are busy. I will return another time."

"Not at all, Duncan. Come. George, give him some whisky."

He accepted the *cuach.* Instead of drinking the amber liquid, he stared at it.

"What troubles ye, lad?" Murray asked.

"Have ye heard the rumor?"

Lord George grunted. "I am the Elector's spy."

"Who started it, George?" Lochiel asked.

"I wager 'twas the Irish or the French. They dislike my having command, and would sabotage me if it meant they might curry more favor with the prince."

"I suppose their dislike has nocht to do with your less than tactful ways of responding to their suggestions." Lochiel's eyes twinkled.

Murray snorted. "I have no patience for the likes of them. I despise their interference. They ken neither our men nor our ways. Had we followed their orders, Cope would have decimated us.

"'Tis fine for them to be telling us how to fight, for they risk nocht. If they are captured, they will return to France under a cartel. We, on the other hand, risk all. If we dinna win, the Elector will arrest us and brand us traitors. Duncan, here, will be shot or hanged. Ye and I will be hanged, drawn, and quartered. Our estates will be forfeited and our families ruined."

"What do the men think, Duncan?" Lochiel asked.

"It leaves a bitter taste in their mouths. Some scoff at the rumor. They say Lord Murray is one of us, and he led us to victory at Gladsmuir. Others counter that 'tis he who ordered the retreat. They say he shames us. I heard something else, too."

"What was that?" Murray asked.

"They say ye were reluctant to join the Stewarts."

Murray smiled. "'Tis true. Do ye think less of me?"

Duncan shook his head. "Not at all. Sir Donald himself wanted His Royal Highness to go home."

"Convinced ye to change your mind, too, Donald?"

Lochiel nodded. "He can be most persuasive."

"That he can," Murray said. "I fought for the Stewarts during the 'Fifteen and the 'Nineteen, and lived in exile for ten years because of it. If my brother James had not gone to the Elector on my behalf, I would still live in France with Donald's father and the others attainted for their part in the rebellions. I have no love for or loyalty to the King, but I do to my brother. He risked his title to help me, and I repaid him by turning traitor."

In truth, Duncan realized, all participants in this Rising could be deemed traitors. Whether they sided with the Stewarts or the Hanoverians mattered not, for it was the outcome of the war that would determine who was disloyal to the crown. In the end, it would merely be a question of whether those who supported King Jamie, the *Ard Rìgh* or High King of Scotland, were in the right or whether King George of the House of Hanover was the true ruler of the land.

~*~

Duncan stood on the bank of the River Esk. Forty-two days earlier the crossing had posed no danger. Torrential rains had changed that. Most of his bruises had faded to yellow, but his ribs continued to mend. The racing water would feel like Pàdraig's fists. If he managed the crossing, his bruises would return and it would take longer for his ribs to knit.

The roar of water muffled the thunder of hoofbeats. Prince Charles, accompanied by the cavalry, galloped past. They slowed at the river's edge a short distance above where the foot soldiers would cross. The horses waded into the water and formed into a single line meant to slow the swift current.

Men divided themselves into groups of ten or twelve. Duncan linked arms with the men on either side of him, forging a human chain to aid them in the crossing. He descended into the raging river. The icy water drove the breath from his lungs. Pain shot through his chest. The current pushed him, and he struggled to remain upright. His teeth chattered. His limbs grew numb.

He sidestepped through the water, fighting for every inch of ground. He stumbled. His hands slipped from the man in front of him. Water filled his nose and mouth. His shirt tightened around his throat. He felt himself lifted, and his head reemerged from the water. A firm grip steadied him until he regained his footing. He crawled from the river and collapsed. He no longer felt cold. He no longer felt pain. He just lay there, panting. His eyelids grew heavy. Sleep beckoned.

A bluish white light flashed, and he raised his arm to protect his eyes from the blinding dazzle. A soft hand stroked his upper arm. Its warmth shattered the ice that froze his heart.

"Duncan!"

The voice was somehow familiar, yet he could not shake the drug-like cowl of sleep that warmed him.

"Duncan! Can ye hear me, husband?"

Rory? Was it really her? He peeked out from hooded eyes and saw the light had dimmed. His heart's love knelt beside him. He tried to speak, but no sound issued forth from his lips.

"Shh, Duncan! I ken ye are tired, but ye must listen. 'Tis not time for ye to join Tòmas_and your parents. Ye took a sacred oath binding yourself to me. I have your word ye would return, and I expect ye to be after keeping it."

"M'eudail, is it really ye?" he asked, unable to believe what his eyes saw and what his ears heard.

She brushed her lips against his, breathing warmth into him.

"I promised to come whenever ye needed me. Rise and build a fire. Will ye do that, mo chridhe, *my heart?"*

"Duncan Cameron!" An angry voice yelled his name. Rough hands shook him.

He opened his eyes and stared at his foster father's face.

"Thank God, Duncan! I thought ye lost. Warm yourself by one of the fires. Dinna ever give me such a fright again, do ye hear? I have no desire to tell Rory ye are dead."

Duncan was disappointed not to find her beside him. The dream had seemed so real. He rolled to his side and pushed himself to his feet. While warming himself at the nearest bonfire, a thought struck him. Lochiel thought himself responsible for saving his life, but he was wrong. Rory, his beloved, had saved him! Although not present in body, she was with him wherever he went. She lent him strength when his failed.

~*~

In less than two months Duncan had traveled five hundred eighty-six miles, but still the army did not stop. Rest would not come until they reached the River Clyde. For four days he trudged through knee-deep snow along rutted tracks. The folds of his plaid stiffened with cold. He slept in wet wool and shivered, unable to get warm. His belly rumbled with hunger, but there was no food to feed it. Ice crystals colored his dark beard white.

Glasgow's greeting matched the frigid cold of winter. Its streets were empty. Its doors shut tight. This was a city loyal to King George. They would find no friends here.

Instinct made Duncan put one sore foot in front of the other. He walked a ragged line, kept on track because there were others in front to follow. He did not notice Glasgow Cross, where the High Street, Saltmarket, Trongate, and Gallowgate converged. He did not see the Tolbooth with its seven-story tower. He missed the arches and buttresses of the Gothic cathedral. He knew only that he found himself inside an immense stone church. He collapsed in the nave, curled into a ball, and slept.

"Duncan," a low voice said. "Rouse yourself, lad."

He shoved the hand from him, and turned on his side. The hand shook him until he could no longer ignore its insistence. With a sigh, he pulled himself into a sitting position. He held his head in his hands and asked, "Who are ye?"

"'Tis Sandy."

Duncan rubbed his eyes and peered at the priest. "Is something wrong with Sir Donald?"

"My brother sleeps."

"Then why disturb mine?"

"Archie sent me. A man he tends is asking for ye."

"Is he sick?"

"He is dying."

"Who?"

"Red Pàdraig."

Duncan stared at Sandy. Pàdraig dying? His mind refused to accept it.

"Why should he want to see me? He made it plain he is not my friend."

Sandy placed a hand on his shoulder. "Ye are wrong, Duncan. He is your friend. He just fell in with the wrong lot. Dinna ye recall how easy 'twas to sway Pàdraig to do your bidding when ye were lads?"

Duncan remembered.

"'Twas no different with Cathal. He used that to turn Pàdraig against ye. With Cathal dead, your friend sees the error in what he did. Will ye come?"

He stumbled through the shadowy kirk, then descended a stairway to a lower vaulted chapel where the stench of the unwashed and dying fouled the air. Sandy pointed to a haggard man with matted hair and glazed sunken eyes stretched out on the floor. Pàdraig's flaming red hair resembled the dun coloring of a deer in winter. His face was gaunt, his lips blistered by fever.

"What ails him?" Duncan asked.

"'Tis the sickness," Sandy said. "Archie can do no more for him."

Pàdraig stirred. "Duncan?"

He knelt beside his boyhood friend. "Aye, Pàdraig."

"I am frightened. Will ye stay until—"

"I will."

"I struck a friend and spoke a great lie against his wife. Ye and Rory did nocht but help my family and me, yet I envied ye for what I did not have. I let Cathal sway me, though I kent 'twas wrong. Can ye ever forgive me?"

Duncan's joy at hearing these words was saddened by the knowledge that his friend would soon die.

"Och, Pàdraig, ye are my friend now and always."

"And ye are mine."

Pàdraig coughed. His bones creaked. His chest rattled. Duncan wiped blood from his cracked lips.

"I have no right to ask this, but will ye take care of my wife and son? I willna see them again."

"Morna and Brandubh will want for nocht."

"Thank ye." Pàdraig shut his eyes. He inhaled sharply, then his eyes widened with fear. "Remember me always, Duncan. Dinna let Brandubh forget his father."

A hollow rattle escaped Pàdraig's lips, then he went limp.

With tears streaming down his face, Duncan closed his friend's unseeing eyes and whispered, "I promise."

PART THREE
1746

CHAPTER SEVENTEEN
DESPAIR

Duncan cursed the northwest wind that blew dark clouds across the late afternoon sky. Hail pelted his back. His ribs, newly mended, ached from the mid-January cold. Dark strands of hair hung limp on his shoulders. Damp tattered rags wrapped his hands, but he could not feel the fingers curled around the hilt of his dirk. The saturated pleats of his wool plaid whipped his legs, stinging them bright red. Water squished between the toes of his stockings and the soles of his brogues.

To his left on the sloping moor southwest of Falkirk, where the Stewarts of Appin were positioned, the ground plummeted into a deep ravine. To his right and rear stood two lines of Highlanders from thirteen clans. The tight quarters left him two weapons with which to fight, but rain might have seeped into the powder. Rather than risk his pistol misfiring, he opted to use his dirk.

Below, the soggy marsh at the base of the hill slowed the enemy's advance. Three companies of dragoons rode stiff and straight, heedless of the rain blowing in their faces. Six regiments of foot soldiers formed two lines to their right.

Duncan crouched behind his targe and waited for the signal to charge. When the skirl of the pipes sounded, a musket volley echoed across the moor. Horses tottered and fell; their riders tumbled. The remaining dragoons closed ranks and charged. Duncan whooped and plunged down the hill. The whining whistle of a sword cut the air. He dropped to the ground, rolled under the hooves of the oncoming horse, and plunged his dirk into its belly. The beast screamed. Duncan rolled from under the toppling horse. The dragoon lay pinned beneath his mount, impaled through the chest by his own sword.

Together with seven kinsmen Duncan rushed a platoon led by a trews-clad officer wearing a bonnet that bore moss and three drooping feathers. Although the Munros outnumbered Camerons three to one, all broke and ran except their chief. He parried and lunged, retreated and attacked. He met thrust for thrust, cut for cut. His blows slew two Camerons. When he raised his blade to kill a third, Duncan flung his targe like a plate. The shield snapped the Munro's blade in two. He staggered from the force of the blow. One Cameron drew his pistol and fired. The Munro died clutching the bladeless hilt of his sword.

Duncan gulped air while he scanned the battlefield. The dragoons had turned their mounts and raced back to their lines. At the sight of their own cavalry stampeding toward them, the royal foot scattered. Corpses littered the moor. Duncan's eyes passed over two men—one sprawled on the ground, the other kneeling at his side. A jolt of recognition slammed through him. His heart skipped a beat; his mouth went dry. He ran toward them, dreading what he would find, castigating himself for what he had failed to do. "Archie?"

The physician frowned. "Dinna blame yourself, Duncan. Donald is fine. 'Tis but a twisted ankle. Ye could not have prevented it at all, unless ye have a secret incantation that directs cannonballs to land only where we can see them."

Duncan expelled a deep breath. He had allowed himself to be drawn away from his chief, a clear dereliction of a bodyguard's duty.

"Rest easy, lad. 'Twas my own negligence that put me here. Ye did what ye were ordered to do." Lochiel attempted to rise. He grimaced with pain and ceased the effort.

"I told ye to sit, Donald." Archie shook his head. "I canna tend your foot if ye insist on walking on it."

"How can I help?" Duncan asked.

"Ye can be after sitting on my brother so I can bind his foot."

Duncan applied pressure to Lochiel's shoulders.

"Enough, lad! 'Tis sure I canna be fighting the two of ye. Archie, do what ye must, but do so with all haste. I crave a warm fire, dry clothes, and a soft bed."

"So do we all, brother. 'Tis the worst weather for fighting in, and I am soaked to the skin." Archie ripped the linen bandage down the center, tied a knot, and tucked the ends under the outer layer. "Will ye help lift him?"

Duncan slipped one hand under Lochiel's shoulder while placing the other at his elbow. Archie did the same, and together they helped Lochiel regain his footing. The doctor slipped his arm through a leather handhold of his discarded targe, then slung the shield over his shoulder. With Lochiel between them, they began their descent of the hill.

Two falls off to Duncan's left, a red soldier stepped from behind one of the few trees that dotted the moor. He fired his musket. Archie stumbled. Thrown off balance, the trio toppled like dominoes. Lochiel howled with pain.

"*Chlanna nan con thigibh a so 's gheibh sibh feòil!*"

The shouted war cry came from a dozen Camerons. With Fergus in the lead they pursued the fleeing sniper like hounds after flesh. The hare had no idea what fury he had unleashed with that shot, and Duncan knew the vengeance exacted would cost the soldier dearly.

"Och, no!"

Duncan untangled himself on hearing Lochiel's anguished cry. Archie lay on his back, his hand clutching his chest. Duncan hurried to his side. The physician looked at him with surprised blue eyes. "I am hit."

"Aye." Duncan lifted Archie's bloody hand from the wound. With each rise and fall of his chest, blood spurted from the small hole. "What should I do?"

"Have ye cloth not muddied?"

"The shirt under my plaid. 'Tis wet, but clean."

"Use it to stop the bleeding."

Duncan shed his plaid. After wiping the blade of his dirk on the soggy cloth, he ripped a strip from his shirt. Lochiel, who had dragged himself beside his brother, watched. Duncan doubled and redoubled the cloth before he placed it on the wound.

"Let Donald hold it in place, lad. Ye must lift me to see if the ball passed through my back," Archie said, coughing.

While Lochiel applied pressure to the wound, Duncan eased the physician onto his side. Unable to see through the mud, he ripped Archie's jacket and shirt with his dirk, but saw no break in the skin. He returned the physician to his back.

"'Tis still lodged inside ye."

Archie swore. "Then ye must take me to Falkirk."

Duncan cut a length of wool from his plaid. He applied a second swatch of linen to the wound, then secured it in place with the woolen strip.

"How did he do, Donald?" Archie asked. "Has he the wildcat's skill?"

Duncan was certain his eyes mirrored the relief he saw in Lochiel's. If Archie could joke, then perhaps the wound was less serious than it appeared.

"Mayhap I should have let Rory accompany us," Donald said. "She has a softer touch, in spite of her temper. Her hands are steadier, and she cuts cloth without ragged edges."

His brother chuckled, then grimaced. "Dinna make me laugh, Donald. 'Tis a wee hurtful right now."

Duncan secured the loan of a mount from an officer in Lord Elcho's Life Guards. An Irish picquet volunteered to assist, and they fashioned a litter for Archie that the horse could drag. After getting Lochiel into the saddle, Duncan thanked the Irishman and led the horse down the hill, across the moor, and into Falkirk.

"'Tis good he carried the targe, Lochiel," the physician said after examining Archie. "It deflected the ball, else your brother would be dead. The wound is not serious; Dr. Cameron will recover. I fear, though, the lead must remain lodged where it is. To remove it would most assuredly kill him."

~*~

Duncan peered at the gloomy sky while he waited for Fergus. For four days the gray clouds had obscured the sun, but the battering winds and torrential rains had ceased. Since Lochiel recuperated and did not require his services, Duncan had agreed to deliver prisoners captured at Falkirk Moor to MacGregor of Glen Gyle at Doune Castle.

"How are they?" Fergus asked.

Duncan glanced at the closed door. "Archie swears he willna stay abed past the morrow, and Sir Donald threatens to shoot him if he attempts to rise. 'Tis glad I am to be away. Neither is fit company when they canna be about."

Fergus laughed. "Then I willna look in on them."

The two friends headed for the Tolbooth. A volley of shots rang out from the field behind the kirk wall.

"'Tis done, then," Duncan said. "May the lad rest in peace."

"I heard his father was one of the executioners."

"Lochiel said 'twas so his son died quickly and with wee pain."

231

"Seems a harsh punishment for an accident," Fergus said. "The lad did not mean to shoot Angus Og. He did not even ken the musket was loaded. 'Twas but a trophy he took from a dragoon."

"I ken, but Angus' father demanded retribution, and Clanranald could not refuse the chieftain of Glengarry. 'Twould have meant war between the two clans."

"But Angus forgave MacDonald with his dying breath."

"Glengarry could not accept that his wild and fearless son died without honor, so he heeded the Bible when seeking justice. A man killed his son, so that man must die."

Fergus bowed his head and sighed. "'Tis a terrible waste. Two men, younger than ourselves, are dead."

"I ken, but we can do nocht but pray for their souls."

Duncan placed a comforting hand on Fergus' shoulder. His friend might be a warrior, but he had a tender side that he showed few people. Duncan knew because Rory had told him of an injured robin Fergus had brought to her. He cradled the bird in hands that had the strength to crush a man. He defended himself and those he served, but anguished over those who died needless deaths like Angus and MacDonald had.

Their arrival at the Tolbooth precluded further discussion. The soldiers' coats were turned inside out to label them prisoners. Their hands were bound with rope. Duncan paired up the sixteen prisoners and assigned the six clansmen who would accompany Fergus and himself to positions along the line. Fergus took the lead, while Duncan followed behind the last prisoners.

Once they left Falkirk, they encountered few steadings and even fewer people. Halfway to Doune Castle they stopped at a burn. Duncan broke the surface ice with the pommel of his dirk for those who wished to drink. Near where he squatted, he noticed a boulder worn smooth over many springs by the rush of melting snows. Something about the rock disquieted him. A white hare with brown-tipped ears hopped onto the boulder. It sat on its haunches; its nose quivered.

The coloring stirred a dormant memory of Rory on the bank of a burn. Strands of auburn hair framed a face bleached white with fright. Fear curled up his spine, but it was her words that had unsettled him. *I saw Bean-nighe.*

Duncan stood abruptly and signaled Fergus to continue.

For the remaining nine miles of their trek, Duncan recalled happier memories, but the image of the Fairy Washerwoman kept intruding on his thoughts. She was a harbinger of death, and he had witnessed enough dying to last him the rest of his days. The blood of men killed by his hand stained his plaid. Their faces haunted his sleep. Their screams echoed in his dreams. The single remaining joy in his life was Rory, but he could no longer summon her with the pendant. Death occupied more of his waking thoughts, relegating her to the dim recesses of his memory. She was part of a life he no longer knew, one he doubted he would ever know again. Like Pàdraig, his body would lie in a hastily dug grave far from Lochaber. He would never hear the laughter of his sons or the weeping of his daughters. He would never grow old with the warrior he loved by his side. Wetness stained his cheeks, but darkness concealed his tears.

Framed against the night sky, the silhouette of Doune Castle overlooked the River Teith and the Ardoch Burn. At the sight of the sandstone gate tower, Duncan swiped the back of his hand over his face. He led the prisoners under the pointed arch of the gateway and up the barrel-vaulted passage to an iron yett. A pockmarked man stepped from the guard chamber.

"Who are ye and what do ye want?"

"I am Duncan Cameron with a contingent of prisoners."

The man raised his lantern and peered through the grate. "Cameron is it? 'Tis myself, Robin Og. Dinna ye remember me?"

"Glengyle's cousin?"

"Aye."

"Will ye let us pass?"

"Och, to be sure, but first ye must answer a question. James is in a fine temper, and 'twill mean my head if he learns I did not ask."

"What do ye wish to ken?"

"Under whose orders do ye bring these prisoners to Doune Castle?"

"The Earl of Kilmarnock and Sir Donald Cameron of Lochiel."

Robin Og slid the oak beam into the wall and opened the yett. Once Duncan and the others passed through, he closed the grille and replaced the bar. He squeezed along the wall until he reached the two-leaf door at the inner end of the gate passage. He threw this open and motioned for Duncan and the others to enter.

"Ask at the well where to deliver the prisoners," Robin said. "We are full up, so I dinna ken if there is room left in the kitchen tower."

"Is Gregor here?"

"The guard can direct ye."

"Thank ye, Robin."

The man waved and returned to his post.

Torches lit the walled enclosure. With nightfall the sky had cleared and stars twinkled through four arched windows in the south curtain. Whatever rooms they had intended to illuminate had been lost to history because the residence had never been extended to this side of the royal castle. The smell of burning peat mingled with the aromas of roasting grouse and venison.

Duncan approached a man with a scraggly beard who leaned against the octagonal wellhead. "Robin said ye would ken where these prisoners should go."

The man whistled. A younger kinsman answered the summons.

"Is there room for them in the upper chamber?" the bearded man asked.

The younger one nodded. The guard turned back to Duncan. "The lad will take your prisoners. Ye will find food and drink in the great hall."

Duncan nodded. "I have business with Glengyle."

"He is closeted in a chamber on the floor above the upper hall of the gate tower, but I would not venture there if I were ye."

When the guard seemed disinclined to elaborate, Duncan turned to Fergus. "I will meet ye in the great hall. I must speak with Glengyle before we sup."

His friend nodded and accompanied the others up the stone steps of the kitchen tower. Duncan entered the lord's hall. Irate shouts drifted down the turnpike stairs to the left of the double hearth. He recognized the voice of James Mòr and understood the guard's warning. Duncan took a deep breath before mounting the turret steps.

When he reached the landing, he peered into a six-sided chamber, but saw no one. James' voice echoed in the stairwell from higher in the tower, so Duncan continued to climb. He stepped into a passageway on the floor above the upper hall. The sounds of arguing came from his right and led him to the uppermost chamber in the rounded turret. Abusive epithets flew from James Mòr's mouth as he stormed through the arched doorway. Shoved aside by the glowering MacGregor, Duncan collided with a stone wall. He grunted while his hand clutched his ribs.

"Are ye injured?" Gregor of Glen Gyle asked.

"'Tis an old affliction. 'Tis no sooner mended, than I aggravate it again."

"Will whisky soothe the ache?"

"Aye."

Gregor ushered Duncan into the hexagonal chamber with a barrel-vaulted ceiling. While the older man poured the libation, Duncan noted the sparse furnishings of the room: a bed, two chairs, and a small table. He accepted the *cuach* handed him.

"I apologize for my cousin's rudeness," Gregor said. "As intelligent as James is he can act the raving loon when the temper is upon him."

"Robin and the guard in the courtyard warned me, but I did not heed them."

"Like his father, James is happiest when he is intriguing. 'Tis the idleness that fashes him. He remembers what was done to his mother and their home when he was a lad. He dwells on it until his hatred festers and boils, then he lashes out at friend and foe alike. Most men quickly learn to keep their distance.

"Glencarnaig once thought to question an order my cousin gave. James upset table and chairs, and brandished his sword, heedless of who or what was near him. Then he threw his *sgian* into the table where Glencarnaig sat. The blade skimmed the flesh off the man's thumb. Fearing he would lose life or limb, he hastened from James' presence."

"Lochiel had a similar experience."

"James attacked without my kenning?"

Duncan grinned and shook his head. "'Twas my wife."

"Rory?"

"Aye. She thought me unjustly punished for words she said. Before any could stop her, Lochiel found her *sgian* embedded in his chair an inch from his ear."

Gregor whistled. "What did he do?"

"Nocht. 'Twas a test he set for her. Ever since he and his brothers are fond of reminding me that I wed a Highland wildcat." Duncan felt heaviness settle in his heart. He turned from Gregor and stared at the fire.

"Have ye had word from her since ye left Achnacarry?"

"Sandy brought a letter while we were in Edinburgh."

"Nothing since?"

Duncan shook his head.

"Why dinna ye go to her? Any attack the Sassenach plan willna come for weeks, mayhap months. Surely, Lochiel can spare ye for a wee while."

"I canna go to her." He felt Gregor's eyes on him, but kept his averted.

"Have ye Rory's pendant?"

"Always."

"May I see it?"

Duncan pulled it from his sporran.

Gregor turned the pendant over several times. He polished the stone with the hem of his plaid. "When I last held this, the metal felt warm to the touch. The stone shone with the brilliance of sunlight reflected off snow glazed with ice. No more. 'Tis cold, and the blue is that of a stormy sea, not a sparkling sapphire. Blood and death rob ye of her memory, Duncan. Ye need her love to wash away their bitter taste."

"I canna go to her."

"Why?"

"She carries the weight of a chief's burdens on her shoulders."

"She acts in Lochiel's stead? Then, she is more than a wildcat. I would like to meet your Rory one day."

Duncan walked to a window and rested his hands on either side of the pointed arch.

Gregor rested a hand on his shoulder. "Go to her. Being a MacGregor she possesses the fortitude to overcome adversity. 'Tis in our blood, else we would never have survived the proscription."

"I canna go to her with blood on my hands."

"'Tis war, lad. She willna think less of ye."

Duncan shook his head. "'Tis not me I fash about. 'Tis her. Blood and death haunt me day and night. She will ken this, and I dinna want her to feel the horror and guilt that war inside me."

"Women are stronger than we think, my friend. Without asking what is wrong, she will soothe your heartache. 'Tis the way of women."

"If Rory touches me, she will see what I did. She will feel what I felt. I willna let her suffer as I do."

"Ye are telling me she has the Two Sights?"

"Aye."

"Then I understand why ye refuse to return to her. I am a poor substitute for Rory, but ye are always welcome to share my company. I may lack Lochiel's wisdom, but will listen when ye must speak of what troubles ye."

"'Tis why I came."

Gregor set his *cuach* on the table. "Come, friend. I dinna ken how many came with ye, but 'tis best we seek them out. Strangers are delectable morsels for James when he is riled."

"Can we fetch some venison as well?"

Gregor laughed. "Aye, a man is always at peace when he is fed."

Duncan followed Glengyle down the stairs, across the length of the lord's hall, and through a door. They emerged into a great hall echoing with the din of shouting men. Duncan heard a single loud thud then an awed hush overcame the spectators crowding the dais. Gregor shouldered his way through his clansmen to where the high table should have been. Sprawled on the stone floor lay an unconscious James Mòr. Fergus stood to the side with his hands resting on his thighs. He gulped air.

"Fergus! Fergus!" The cheering men lifted the giant onto their shoulders and paraded about the great hall.

Gregor threw a bucket of water on his senseless cousin. James sputtered and moaned. "What happened?"

"I think ye met your match, cousin," Gregor said, nodding toward Fergus who now stood beside him.

James groaned and rested his head back on the floor. He stared at the hand extended toward him, then at its owner.

"Are ye hurt?" Fergus asked.

"'Twould take more than a giant like yourself to hurt me." James accepted the proffered assistance in regaining his feet. "I would be honored if ye join me at table. 'Tis a rare man who can best James Mòr, son of the great Rob Roy himself."

Duncan handed a *cuach* of whisky to his gaping friend. Fergus tipped the cup and drank the fiery liquid in one gulp. He coughed once, smacked his lips, and held it out for more.

After the meal ended, Duncan noticed Robin and several other MacGregors huddled in a recess under the oriel window. After several minutes, they approached Gregor and spoke to him in low whispers.

He nodded, then stood. "Men!"

The room quieted and all eyes looked to him.

"In honor of our guests, Robin and his friends will dance."

The men pushed the rows of tables against the walls. A piper appeared in the wooden gallery over the screens passage at the western end of the hall. Robin centered himself between the dais and the slatted iron brazier of the hearth marking the center of the great hall, while a companion assumed a similar position on the other side of the room. With great flourish, they laid down their weapons and stood at the tips of the blades. The wooden rafters resonated with a crescendo of martial music.

Robin hopped from toe to toe in step with the stately tempo played by the piper. Twelve swordsmen strode from the vestibule that led from the kitchen. While half encircled the other dancer, the remainder surrounded Robin with their sharp blades pointed at Robin. The piper quickened the tempo. The ring of men circled faster as Robin's feet kept pace with the music. He pointed to a man in the outer circle. Without missing a beat, they switched places while Robin snatched the man's tossed sword from midair.

The dance continued in this manner for some time. Whenever the center man tired, he swapped positions with someone in the ring. The instant of the final exchange, the piping ceased and the center man seized the sword from the floor while the surrounding men closed in until the tips of their swords touched his neck.

The sinister reenactment stirred Duncan's unease. He exited the great hall and stood on the servery stairs overlooking the courtyard. His thoughts returned to Rory and the burn while his fingers burnished the pendant's rim. Moonlight illuminated the wellhead, and seated on the stone was an old woman washing shirts. As if sensing his gaze, she turned to look at him. His eyes widened and his breathing stopped. *Beannighe!*

The night was suddenly filled with muted thunder and shrill cawing. Ravens circled the Fairy Washerwoman. Soon the moor would bleed, and he would fall.

~*~

Duncan stood beside Lochiel watching men carry barrels of gunpowder from the kirk to the open field beyond. Word had come that the Duke of Cumberland and his troops had spent the night at Linlithgow, which was within a day's march of Stirling. Confronted with the inevitable, Prince Charles had abandoned the stalemated siege of the fortress and headed north. The sudden move prohibited the army from securing enough wagons to transport the fifty kegs of reserve gunpowder stored in Saint Ninians, a village two miles south of the royal burgh. Rather than allow it to fall into enemy hands, Lochiel had the task of overseeing its destruction.

"'Tis a waste to destroy what we may need," Duncan said. "Had His Royal Highness heeded your pleas to end the siege, we would have had time to transport the powder."

Lochiel stroked his jaw. "Ye have a firm opinion on the matter."

"I do. We have neither the expertise nor the armament to lay siege to fortified cities, yet Prince Charles insists we do so. Why would Stirling Castle capitulate when it sits atop a crag that our guns canna reach? 'Twas a futile attempt to block Cumberland's advance."

"The prince kens how to wage war on the continent, but not in Scotland where his ideas dinna work."

"Yet he does not learn from his failures. He appoints men to advise him, but he does not heed them. His talk of God giving the Stewarts the right to rule sits ill with me. Canna he understand we follow him because ye do? If the chiefs withdrew their support, the men would cease fighting. Their loyalty lies with the clans, not him."

"Princes tend to practice what they have learned. 'Tis the intrigues of Versailles and Rome that were his lessons, but those willna help here because they are not our ways."

Duncan faced Lochiel. "Have we a chance of winning?"

"Charles kens little of the military aspects of war, though he was taught the skills of soldiering. He sees things in small pieces, rather than on a grander scale. This Rising fulfills a dream that taints his perception as does the advice he heeds from those who dinna ken us. He is too trusting of people, too willing to forgive. 'Tis a luxury the leader of an army canna afford. Neither can he assume his men are invincible."

"Then why follow him?"

Lochiel tilted his head to look at the sky. "'Tis a question I often ask myself. My grandsire was a staunch Jacobite who raised my father and me to believe in the rightness of the Stewarts sitting on the throne of Scotland. I am too old to change what I have lived since I was a wee bairn. The Great Lochiel may be dead, but his influence remains. I would not go against my grandsire then; I canna go against him now."

"Stop!"

The shout drew Duncan's attention toward the kirk where a villager absconded with one of the kegs. The plug had worked itself loose and black powder spilled over his shoulder. The trail led up the stairs and into the kirk. A kinsman aimed his rifle.

"No!"

Duncan's warning came too late. The man fired. Sparks drifted to the ground. Most extinguished themselves on the way down, but one remained lit. It landed on the spilled powder. Duncan heard the sizzle, then watched in horror as the powder ignited. Smoke and flame raced along the black trail.

"Run!"

He grabbed Lochiel by the arm and ran toward the low wall that separated the kirk from the field. He threw his foster father over it, then dived after him, shielding Lochiel with his body.

A jarring series of explosions rocked the village. The church spire shot heavenward like a flaming arrow. Shards of stone, glass, and wood pelted the ground. Black smoke darkened the sky. There was a brief silence, then the outer church walls crashed to the ground.

After the dust settled, Duncan stood. He extended his hand and helped Lochiel to his feet. When he gazed back on the devastation, he saw a massive segment of the kirk spire buried in the ground where they had stood. A hand touched his shoulder. He looked at his foster father. Unspoken thanks passed between them.

~*~

The wind roared in Duncan's ears. Strong gusts battered him from all sides. Freezing rain stung his face. Swirling snow blinded him. Ice crystals clung to his eyebrows and beard. His frozen hands clutched the rope that bound him to the man in front of him. Numbed by the cold, he forced himself to lift one foot, then the other. He plodded through knee-deep drifts until Fergus, who followed, plowed into his back.

His friend caught him before he fell. "Sorry, Duncan."

"At least I can still feel something." He pulled a flask of whisky from his sporran. "Take a sip, Fergus. 'Tis the only warmth we have until we reach Inverness."

"Did ye share yours with the horses?"

"Aye, so drink only a wee dram. 'Tis all I have."

When Fergus returned the flask, Duncan took a sip before returning it to his sporran. He breathed on his hands, but felt no heat. Once he resumed his place in line, he began the arduous task of maneuvering through the late February storm.

~*~

Three days later, they reached the outskirts of Inverness. Men and women with no clan affiliations peered at them from doorways of dirty windowless hovels. Although snow carpeted the littered streets, Duncan still smelled the rotting refuse and contents of emptied chamber pots. Three thousand people inhabited the five hundred sandstone houses of this port city. Most were loyal to King George, but with the withdrawal of the royal army following the rout at Moy Hall, they did not resist the Jacobite occupation.

Coughs and shivers wracking his body, Duncan shuffled into the quarters assigned to Lochiel and his brothers. He stared up the narrow staircase, dreading the climb to the room he shared with Fergus. Each step would intensify the burning agony in his knees. He gritted his teeth and mounted the stairs. By the time he reached the third floor, beads of sweat trickled down his face and neck. In spite of this, he gathered the top of his foul-smelling plaid tighter around his shoulders to ward off the chill permeating his bones. His skin felt as if invisible creatures crawled over him, and he scratched until tiny sores erupted on his arms and legs.

Rory!

Her name stilled the hammering of his heart and eased the tightness in his chest. He fumbled in his sporran until his fingers touched the precious paper he kept secreted there. He clutched her letter to his chest. She staved off the blackness that threatened to consume him. She was his strength. She was his salvation. He must go to her!

Someone rapped on the door, but he ignored it. The knock came again, and when he did not answer, the door creaked open.

"Duncan?"

Focused on thoughts of home, he did not answer Archie.

The doctor seized his arm and swung him around. "Where do ye think ye are going?"

"I must find Rory."

"She is safe at Achnacarry."

"I must find Rory."

"Ye will stay and rest, lad."

Duncan shook his head. He had to find Rory.

"I ken ye want to see your wife, but ye willna get far in your condition. Ye must rest."

"Rory!"

Archie dragged him to the hearth. He held Duncan's jaw and turned his head to face the mirror over the mantel. "Look at yourself. Rory willna recognize ye."

His reflection showed a stranger with limp matted hair, a ragged beard speckled gray, and listless eyes ringed by shadows. If he was a stranger to himself, then how would Rory see him?

Disheartened, Duncan collapsed onto a stool.

"I ken ye want to go home," Archie said, "but your visit with Rory must wait. Ye need rest. If ye dinna heed me, I will render ye senseless and tie ye to the bed myself."

Duncan's will to argue dissipated. Rory would never know him, and he could not bear that hurt. He allowed Archie to lead him to the bed.

"Give me the plaid. 'Tis fit only for burning."

Duncan did as ordered, then crawled under the covers. Archie held the plaid at arm's length by his fingertips. "What do ye hold in your hand, lad?"

"Rory's letter."

Archie pried open his fingers and took the paper from him. He smoothed out the crumpled letter and laid it on the table beside the bed. "'Twill be there when ye wake. After ye sleep, I will bring hot water and soap so ye can wash the filth from ye. I will also find ye clean clothes."

Duncan fell asleep before Archie closed the door.

~*~

It was night. He rode the moors, running from someone or something, he knew not which. All he understood was the need to escape. Lights flickered on his right. He veered toward them, hoping to find shelter. A foul stench filled his nostrils. He gagged. The lights flickered again, but this time he realized they were not torches. Bloated glowing corpses littered the muddy ground. They bobbed in the muck; their unseeing eyes stared up at him. Severed hands reached for him. His horse reared.

Down, down, down he fell. He landed on soft green earth. The sun shone in a blue sky. Birds twittered and insects chirped. The rapid beating of his heart slowed. He breathed in fresh air. A shadow fell across him, and he looked into the sneering face of the enemy. Cathal motioned for him to rise. Pàdraig appeared beside him, smiling. His friend would help. He turned to confront Cathal. A sharp pain pierced his back. He glanced down to see the blade of an ancient great sword protruding from his stomach. Pàdraig had impaled him on his blade. He looked back at his friend, but instead found Rory tethered to Cathal. His evil laugh rang in his ears.

Darkness consumed him. When he opened his eyes, he saw a fire. Five unkempt soldiers stood nearby. A whip cracked against bare skin and a woman cried out. Her outstretched arms were bound at the wrist to two trees. Her dress hung in tatters at her waist. Blood oozed from lashes that crisscrossed her back. The burly sergeant exchanged his whip for a branding iron. He grabbed the woman's auburn hair, then spoke to her. She spat on him. He yanked her head back, and plunged the iron against her cheek. The sweet odor of burning flesh saturated the air. She shrieked, then slipped into unconsciousness.

The soldiers cut the ropes binding her to the tree. They tied her wrists behind her and put a noose around her neck. They tossed the other end of the rope over a sturdy limb and secured it to the tree trunk. The sergeant tossed a bucket of water into the woman's face. She coughed, gasping for breath. When he was certain she was conscious, his men pulled on the rope until her feet no longer touched the ground. She kicked wildly. They snickered at her futile attempts to free herself from the strangling rope. Tired of the spectacle, the sergeant shot her through the heart.

"'*Tis the end of Thistle. Good riddance, I say!*"

The name pierced Duncan's heart like an arrow, lancing it with an agony so intense it blinded him. He screamed the keening wail of the banshee.

CHAPTER EIGHTEEN
VISITORS

Rory paused in the open doorway of a room within Clan Cameron's Inverness quarters. The banter of its three occupants warmed her heart and dispelled her concern.

"Does he fare better, Archie?" Lochiel asked. "If I dinna bring him home safe, Rory will have my head."

"I can be after answering that myself. 'Tis I who must answer to her before ye do." Duncan's hoarse voice did not resonate, but still stirred Rory. She had often yearned to hear him speak during their separation, but his wit and wisdom were lost to her. Now, the gravelly whisper made her heart flutter and her breath come faster.

Archibald propped another pillow behind his patient's head. "He is right, Donald. The wildcat has temper enough for ye both. 'Twill be a rare treat to see ye lashed by her tongue, or mayhap, she will wield the *sgian* again."

They laughed at the joke, still unaware of her presence. She was glad the horrors of war had yet to steal their humor.

She wiped the smile from her face and assumed a staid air. Her finger traced the sharp blade of her *sgian*. "And who will explain why I should postpone doing the deed rather than settle the matter now?"

Their blank expressions made the corners of her mouth twitch. She fought to keep her somber demeanor, but lost. Her grin broke the silence.

"Rory!"

"Sir Donald."

"What do ye do here?"

"Fergus brought your message."

"Message? I sent none. Fergus!"

The giant peered around her. His Adam's apple bobbed. "Aye, Sir Donald?"

"What message did I send Rory?"

Fergus' eyes dropped to the floor. He shuffled from one foot to another. "I did not think ye would object, so I let her think 'twas ye who sent word of Duncan."

"Then who did do the sending?"

"Duncan's friend."

"What friend, Fergus?" Duncan asked.

"The MacGregor with the black mark on his knee."

"Glengyle sent for Rory?"

The giant nodded. "He said ye needed more than Dr. Archie's healing."

The physician cleared his throat.

"Och, no offense meant, sir."

Archie's eyes twinkled. "None taken, Fergus. Did Glengyle tell ye why my healing was insufficient?"

"He said Duncan's heart needed mending, and that required a woman's touch."

Rory felt herself blush. She touched Fergus' sleeve. "Ye must thank this MacGregor for me. He gives a gift more precious than gold."

"Fergus!"

The giant straightened. "Aye, Sir Donald?"

"Ye and I will have words on this later. Fetch Glengyle for me."

Fergus gave a clipped nod, then hurried from the room.

"Go easy on the lad, Donald."

"I will give no punishment, Archie. 'Tis sorry I am I did not think to send for Rory myself." Lochiel turned to her. "Since ye act in my stead, would ye still be after wanting my head or can I be keeping it a wee while longer?"

"Sure, I would not think of depriving myself of your company, Sir Donald. After all, did I not ask ye to hasten home? 'Tis not my desire to remain chief. My husband and I have other pursuits to occupy our days."

Duncan's wink sent a new wave of warmth to her cheeks. Suddenly, she found the room crowded. She had hastened without rest to Inverness, fearing she might not reach Duncan in time. Now that he mended, the days she could spare away from Achnacarry were few. She did not wish to waste this precious gift of time with him in the company of others.

Archie tapped his brother's shoulder. "Donald, did ye not say His Royal Highness was wanting to see us?"

Lochiel gave him a blank look. "I did?"

"Aye, ye did." Archie tilted his head toward Duncan.

Lochiel glanced from Duncan to Rory. His eyes widened with understanding. He cleared his throat. "I must be of an age where my mind forgets."

"'Tis more likely ye did not wish to listen to a long and tedious harangue." Archie pulled a watch from his pocket. "We are late, brother, and will have to listen to one on keeping His Royal Highness waiting. As for ye, Duncan, ye must stay abed for a few more days."

Duncan grunted his displeasure. Rory knew from experience that confinement was not to his liking.

"Ye will see he obeys, wildcat?" Archie asked.

"Ye have my word he willna leave this room."

She bid them farewell and closed the door, but found herself reluctant to face the man she had dreamt of, hungered for, and prayed for. Their relationship resembled the threads of heather used to make rope. Each time they tried to interweave the strands to strengthen the threads, something happened to unravel them. She feared the same was true now, except this parting might well be their last.

"I willna bite, Rory."

His words brought a smile to her lips and eased her dread.

"I ken that."

When she reached his bedside, he caught her hand and pulled her down beside him. A crumbled paper drifted off the table. She retrieved it from the floor and skimmed the first few lines. "'Tis my letter!"

"Aye. When my missing ye became too great, I would read the words ye wrote."

"That explains why 'tis so worn."

He shook his head. "I wanted to come to ye, but the fever took me. Holding your letter was all that kept me from dying. I held it so tight Archie had to pry it from my fingers."

She felt the tears slide down her cheeks. "Och, Duncan!"

He enfolded her in his arms and stroked her hair. "Shh, *m'eudail*. All is well. Ye are here now."

"Aye, I am." She brushed her lips against his, then nestled against his chest. Content and reassured, she relaxed against the familiar embrace of his arms and drifted off to sleep.

~*~

Rory reached for Duncan, but found the space beside her empty. She smiled, amazed that he had stayed abed for ten days, four of them with her. After splashing cold water on her face, she dressed. She brushed and plaited her long tresses, then broke her fast by eating the oatcakes Duncan had left her. While she drank the milk, the door latch clicked.

"Ye have grown a mustache, *m'eudail*," Duncan said.

She reached for a cloth to wipe the white residue from her lip, but he stopped her. "Allow me."

Before she could refuse, he ran his tongue over her upper lip. When he finished, he gave her a roguish smile. "That is to keep ye from telling me I should be abed. I dinna care what Archie says; I am not of resting one minute longer."

"Not for any reason?"

"None I can think of."

"I ken one."

His eyes narrowed.

She knew the instant he understood her meaning. The purple of his eyes grew smoky and he opened his arms. She went to him.

"Ye may be right, but I willna do it for any other." He nudged her chin until her eyes met his. "Can ye say with certainty that ye love me, Rory?"

"Ye have more experience than I, Duncan. How do I ken if what I feel is love? I have kent no man but ye."

"It dinna matter how many or how few ye ken, *m'eudail.* 'Tis what ye feel in your heart. If ye canna say 'tis love, then the time has not yet come for us to lie together. I ken ye care for me, but 'tis your love I want. Ye canna yet trust what is in your heart, and I am sullied by death and blood. 'Tis best to wait until we can cherish and nurture the first sharing of our love."

His lips sought hers. The tender kiss robbed her of her thoughts. She could only feel, and those feelings contradicted each other. She felt frightened, yet safe. Drained, yet alive. Sated, yet unsatisfied. Tremors reverberated through her body. Her legs buckled, but Duncan held tight and lowered them both to the floor.

He leaned his brow against hers. "We dinna dare stay in this room, Rory, else I fear breaking another promise. I willna do that to ye or to us. Not again. Would ye ride with me?"

"Are ye meaning together on Midnight or will we be having separate mounts?"

"I have waited overlong to hold ye in my arms, *m'eudail.* Dinna think I will let ye escape them so easily."

"'Tis a grand day for a ride then."

When they reached the street, Rory noticed a long-limbed man of middle age waiting with Midnight and another horse. A sprig of pine needles and two eagle feathers adorned his blue bonnet. His hand rested on the hairy leg he propped on the step.

"Good day to ye, Gregor Glùn Dhubh. 'Tis honored I am to make your acquaintance."

Glengyle looked at Rory with astonishment. "Duncan said ye had the Two Sights, but I dinna ken 'twas so keen."

She pointed to the birthmark that covered his knee. "'Twas observant eyes that told me who ye be."

He laughed. "'Tis a pleasure to meet Duncan's wildcat. He speaks of ye often."

"Duncan, does everyone ken what the Camerons call me?"

"Only special friends." Her husband mounted Midnight, and Glengyle handed her up to him. Once he sat his horse, Duncan asked, "Where do we ride?"

"Far from this stench," Gregor said, wriggling his nose at the foul odor emanating from the street. "I found an interesting place to the east. Shall I show ye?"

"Aye."

Once they passed the environs of Inverness, Duncan urged Midnight into a gallop. Rory savored the warmth of the sun and the chill of the air on her face. They crossed the River Nairn, then rode another mile until they reached a grove of beech trees where they drew rein at three round chambered cairns, each ringed by standing stones.

While Duncan and Gregor tended to the horses, Rory walked the circumference of the farthest ring of stones that stood like sentinels guarding the graves of the ancients. Although she counted ten, a gap between the stones gave evidence that two more had completed the circle. A kerb of massive boulders supported the loose stone that covered the cairn. Rather than enter the narrow passageway that led to the center of the chamber, Rory skirted the middle cairn and proceeded to the other passage grave. One of the eleven surrounding stones was decorated with small cups and rings. Like its twin, the entrance of this chamber faced southwest.

She returned to the middle cairn. Unlike the other graves, it had no passageway and the nine stones ringing it were taller. Three of them connected to the grave by radiating banks of packed earth.

Muffled footfalls approached. Rory assumed Duncan joined her, but when she turned, she saw Glengyle.

"I must thank ye for your message."

He shrugged. "Duncan is my friend. He would not go to ye, so I arranged for ye to come to him."

Her eyes widened with surprise. "Why would he not come home if Lochiel gave him leave?"

"I dinna think Duncan asked for it. He cares too much to hurt ye."

"How could seeing him hurt me?"

"His soul is blackened by what he has seen and done these last five months. He feared if he touched ye, ye would experience it, too."

"The Two Sights."

"Aye."

Rory's heart ached with her husband's suffering. She knew the realities of war: blood, maiming, and death. Word of the Rising was scant, but she had heard of the battle near Gladsmuir and the retreat from England. Winter had fallen on the Highlands with a vengeance. While she remained within the warmth of Achnacarry, Duncan had endured bitter cold, deep snows, sunless days, and frigid nights. She was glad Gregor had befriended her husband.

"How did ye meet Duncan?"

"Dr. Cameron brought him to me. Since then we have entertained each other with tales of my uncle, Rob Roy, and a certain wildcat who has a penchant for a *sgian*."

She laughed. "So he told ye of Lochiel's ear."

Gregor nodded.

"Ye accepted my husband without wariness? 'Twas not so amongst my kinsmen."

"My cousins were against him, but with Dr. Cameron's endorsement and your husband's wedding a MacGregor, I welcomed Duncan into our fold. Trust dinna come easily for the Gregorach, but I ken a good and honest man when I meet him. 'Tis why I accept him with both head and heart. Is it not time for ye to do the same?"

Should she be offended by Glengyle's words or did he chastise her? No, they merely echoed Nannag's plea and the perpetual warring of her own thoughts.

Her gaze settled on Duncan, who stood outside a small ring of flat stones near the center cairn. He had pledged his love without reserve and wanted the same from her. By waiting until she could do that, he honored her with respect and understanding. Those cherished gifts dissipated whatever anger and guilt MacGregor's words stirred within her.

"What is between Duncan and myself is for us to work through, but I thank ye for your wisdom."

Glengyle eyed her with a look of surprise. "Ye take no offense at my interfering?"

"Those two feathers ye wear in your bonnet signify a chieftain's rank. I, too, wore them once, so I ken 'tis your right and duty to guide MacGregors by wisdom and example."

"But now ye wear three feathers."

"'Tis a temporary honor to be sure. Although Lochiel canna handle all matters pertaining to the Camerons, he remains our chief. Ye spoke words meant in kindness because ye care for a friend."

"Two friends."

"Two?" she asked.

"Aye, Duncan and his Highland wildcat."

She smiled.

"Go to him, Rory. The blackness in his heart has lifted, but he is still troubled. I will wait for ye by the horses."

When she passed between the standing stones, icy coldness brushed her arm. A mournful wind that sounded like a sobbing woman whistled through the stones. The hair on Rory's neck bristled. She hurried to Duncan and wrapped her arms around his waist. His arms folded over hers. She rested her head against his back.

"Is Red Pàdraig dead?"

"How did ye ken?" he asked.

"While we supped on the eve of Beltane, I glanced at Pàdraig. Though I kent where he sat, I could not see him. 'Twas a sign he would die before the year ended."

"Why did ye not tell me?"

"'Tis a terrible burden to ken a friend will die. I did not wish to add to your worries, so I kept the kenning to myself. He was your friend, and I thought 'twould be better if your last days together were happy ones."

Duncan sighed. "'Twas not so. He cast his lot with Cathal. I saw him twice after we left Edinburgh. In Derby, he cracked my ribs. He spoke against ye, and had Cathal lived, they would have proclaimed ye witch."

"Did ye kill Cathal?"

"Ye are my heart, *m'eudail.* I could not let him hurt ye."

"Were ye with Pàdraig at the end?"

"Ye would not have recognized him, Rory. 'Twas fever that felled him, not a glorious death fighting for the Stewarts."

He lapsed into silence. She waited, sensing he had more to say.

"I promised to look after his son and Morna."

"And I will help ye."

He turned in her arms, then pulled her close. "Ye are my strength, Rory."

"And ye are mine, Duncan."

His arm slipped to her waist. She put hers around his, and they returned to Gregor. After mounting the horses, they retraced their route in silence. Once across the river, they came to a bleak treeless glen rimmed by mountains and spotted with steadings. Tufts of moor grass rippled in the wind, parting occasionally to reveal hidden rocks. Brown heather and yellowed bracken covered the grazing fields.

The dizziness came without warning. Rory swayed and dug her fingernails into Duncan's arm. He pulled the reins tight and Midnight came to an abrupt halt. Rory would have sailed over the stallion's head except for her unyielding grip.

"*M'eudail,* what is wrong?"

Unable to speak, she dropped from the saddle. Oblivious to the rough ground and remnants of crusted snow, she stumbled past a heather-thatched cottage and through a break in the turf wall. She sank to her knees before a spring.

The clear water clouded and turned bright red. A cowl of black smoke hovered over a sea of blood. Frightsome screams rent the air.

Tremors coursed through Rory. Her hands flew to her ears to block out the harrowing sounds. She squeezed her eyes shut, but even darkness did not still the grisly images.

Reddish-plumed kestrels and feathery-blue merlins dropped from the blackened sky. Blood dripped from their sharp talons. Straw beneath a trampled eagle wearing a crown of red whortleberries turned crimson. Leaden hail pummeled plumeless goshawks lining a drystone dyke, felling them one by one. Ebon-hued corbies circled a hovel. Light flickered, then burst into flame. The banshee wailed.

A rocking cradle of muscled arms and sinewy legs brought Rory back from the hellish vision. Feathery caresses stilled her quivering limbs. Soft cooing quieted her sobs.

"Tea of Saint John's Wort. 'Twill calm the lass." An unfamiliar voice, frail with age, spoke the words.

Rory opened her eyes. An old woman with a reassuring smile and unseeing eyes held a steaming *cuach* in trembling hands.

"Give it to me, Mother. I will see she drinks it."

While Glengyle held the *cuach* to Rory's lips, she noted the concern etched in his face. When she finished drinking, Duncan pulled her back against his chest. He intertwined their fingers and kissed her hair.

"Ye have nocht to fear, *m'eudail*. I will protect ye."

"'Tis not me I fear for. 'Tis those who will die. 'Tis for yourself."

He expelled a deep breath. "'Twill happen here, then?"

She nodded, tightening her grip.

"I canna fathom what ye are saying, Rory," Gregor said. "Did the Two Sights visit ye?"

Before she could answer, the blind woman asked, "Ye saw the battle, did ye not, lass?"

"How did ye ken?"

"I have not the Two Sights like ye. 'Tis the frightsome moaning I hear. It deafens me."

"Are we to fight the Sassenach here?" Gregor asked.

"Aye, but 'twill be a slaughter, not a fight." When Gregor frowned, Rory reached for his hand. "Dinna fear for ye or your men. Ye willna be here when it happens."

Glengyle straightened. Coldness seeped into his blue eyes. "MacGregors are not cowards."

"I ken that, and ye should not take offense at my words. Cowards dinna survive fire and sword."

He relaxed. "Sorry, lass. I have not met anyone before in whom the Two Sights is so strong. Have ye nocht to say to ease my mind?"

"Ye ken the way of armies better than I. Mayhap ye reconnoiter some distance from here, and willna return in time."

He stroked his chin, then nodded. "'Tis a reasonable surmise. What of Duncan?"

Her lips trembled. She whispered, "'Tis where he falls."

~*~

Rory gave Glengyle a weary smile and bid him goodnight. Duncan guided her toward their lodging in Inverness. Hours after her vision, the violent images continued to haunt her. Sometimes, the hardest part of having the Two Sights was learning to accept the revelations. Experience had taught her she could neither alter the outcome nor forget, especially this time. Her glimpses into the future included Duncan. He might survive his wounds, but evil stalked him. She feared that whatever danger lurked in the shadows would separate them forever.

"I wonder why Fergus paces outside when he could be sitting by the fire," Duncan said.

The giant's hurried steps, hand rubbing, and frequent glances spoke of his agitation. Rory looked past him at the windows of their lodging. Most nights they glowed from candlelight. Tonight they were dark.

"Did ye notice how vacant the house looks?"

Her husband frowned, but before he could answer, Fergus saw them and rushed forward.

"Och! Where have ye been? 'Tis long since they left."

Duncan's frown turned to puzzlement. "Who is gone?"

"Lochiel and the clan. The Keppochs, too."

"Gone where?"

"To Fort William."

"Why there?" Rory asked, forgetting her tiredness.

"They have orders to capture it," Fergus said.

"Whatever for?"

"I can be answering that, *m'eudail*," Duncan said. "'Tis the loch the prince is needing. 'Tis a vital link to the sea."

Fergus nodded. "For his French ships."

"Then he has had word they come?" Duncan asked.

"Lochiel confides more to ye than me. I heard no word of ships."

"Mayhap the prince anticipates their arrival," Rory said.

Duncan grunted. "'Tis more likely he dreams. I canna see why the French king would be after sending help after our retreat."

"Whatever the prince's reasons," Fergus said, "I ken only that Rory is to return to Achnacarry while we join Lochiel."

"We leave at first light, then," Duncan said.

"Sir Donald said at once."

Duncan shook his head. "From Spean Bridge Rory must travel alone. 'Tis dangerous enough in these times for her to be traveling when 'tis light. I willna endanger her more by traversing the Highlands at night. Apart from royal patrols, the darkness conceals caterans from their prey. Dinna fash, Fergus. 'Tis my decision and I will accept whatever punishment Lochiel deems necessary.

"We will travel Wade's road. 'Tis stony, but faster than weaving through braes and bens. Rory will leave us at the gorge and head for Loch Lochy and Achnacarry while we continue to Loch Linnhe. Are we agreed?"

Fergus nodded. They bid each other goodnight and retired to their respective chambers.

Beneath the warm covers, Rory wrapped her arms around Duncan. His soft chest hairs tickled her nose, but she did not smooth them flat. This might well be the last night they lay together. She needed to smell him, to feel him, to hold him.

He drew his finger along her jaw and down her throat. He captured her hand against her heart. "I ken the perils that await me, *m'eudail,* but ye may also face danger. If Cumberland's army defeats us, his father the King will punish the Highlands as never before. He will strike at our weakest point—our women and bairn, our ailing and aged—and he will be ruthless. I would ask a promise of ye."

She lifted her head. The glowing embers of the fire cast half his face in shadow. Lines creased his brow, and she wished she could erase them.

"What would ye ask of me, Duncan?"

"Promise ye will lead the others high on the bens. 'Twill be safer there than at Achnacarry."

"I promise. But what of ye?"

"Dinna fash, *m'eudail.* If I am able, I will find ye, no matter where ye are." His fingers traced her lips while his eyes devoured her.

When they kissed, she felt tears fall on her cheeks and tasted salt on his lips. They clung to one another, giving each other strength while consoling each other's heart.

~*~

"Anne, where are ye? I am come home."

Tam growled at the unfamiliar voice. Rory set aside the ledger, crossed to the door, and peered into the entrance hall. At the foot of the stairs stood an elderly man. When he received no reply to his summons, he turned around. Rory gasped. The stranger bore a striking resemblance to her chief.

"Who is there?" he demanded.

Tam growled again, but Rory silenced him. She released her grip on the concealed *sgian*. "I might be after asking ye the same, since ye entered without declaring yourself. From the look of ye, though, I willna challenge your right to be here, John Cameron of Lochiel."

He squinted at her. "Identify yourself."

"I am Rory, chief of Clan Cameron."

"Chief?" Lord Lochiel sputtered. "'Tis a lie! Never would my son allow a woman to lead. John acts in Donald's stead."

"Your younger son refused to take up arms against the King and removed himself from Fassifern. He resides with his wife's father until the Rising is ended. Ye need not take my word for it. Any clansman will confirm what I say."

"Where is Anne? She will set matters aright."

"Sir Donald sent his wife and bairns to France. He kent ye would keep them safe."

"Dinna take that tone with me, lass. I willna allow ye to admonish me for what I dinna ken. Anne and the lads and lasses will manage without me."

"So they will, Lord Lochiel. 'Tis a great risk ye take coming to Achnacarry."

He grunted. "Why, because I risk life and limb to serve my King?"

"So that is why ye come." Rory made the comment more to herself than to him. Attainted since the 'Fifteen, he was still wanted for treason. She admired his loyalty, but his presence endangered them all. With a nod toward the library, she said, "Warm yourself by the fire. I will bring food and whisky."

"What of your hound?"

She smiled. "He will keep ye company until I return."

When she entered the library, Tam guarded the door and watched their guest. He sat at the desk examining his son's accounts. "Ye continue to make the improvements my son desires."

"Sir Donald left detailed instructions before he departed and gillies carry messages between us. Until he returns, I serve as best as I am able."

"What if he dinna come back?"

"Then I suppose John will assume leadership of the clan. Come and eat."

While he supped, she returned to the figures in the ledger. Once or twice she sensed her visitor watching her.

"Do ye ken the man in the portrait?" he asked.

Rory put away the accounts, then took a seat opposite Lord Lochiel. She scratched Tam's head. "'Tis Ewen Dubh, your father."

"He built this house, ye ken."

"Aye, and killed the last wolf in all of Scotland. 'Tis one of many tales my husband and your sons tell of the Great Lochiel."

His eyes narrowed. "Ye are doubtsome of my father's deeds?"

"'Tis the way of the *seanchaidh*. With each telling of the tale, the legend grows."

"It canna be Cameron blood that runs in your veins, lass, else ye would ken the truth of them."

"I learned long ago 'tis best to be doubtsome, Lord Lochiel, and 'tis being wedded to my husband that gives me the right to claim kinship to the clan."

"Ye are Campbell?"

"Never would I claim kinship to them!"

He drummed his fingers on the arm of his chair. "I wonder why ye loathe such a powerful clan. Both myself and my son wed Campbell women."

"I willna dispute the power they wield, but 'tis too great to my way of thinking. As for your wife and Lady Anne, to me they are Camerons."

"And so they are. Once wed, their allegiance is given to the clan of their husbands. Was it not so with ye?"

"I dinna think I would act in your son's stead if my allegiance remained with the clan of my birth."

"And what clan might that be, lass?"

Her silence did not deter him. He continued to interrogate her.

"Ye willna speak of them, yet ye utter the name Campbell with loathing. Is the wrong they did so great that it canna be forgotten?"

She leaned forward. Through clenched teeth, she asked, "How can I forget seeing them murder my mother? Should I forget how they raped and branded my foster mother or burned our homes and stole our land?"

"Ye are the wee lass who dared defy my son when he gifted ye with the hound. I wondered what happened to ye."

"I became chief of Clan Cameron."

He roared with laughter. "So ye did. Where is my son?"

"At Glen Nevis."

"'Tis not far from Achnacarry. Why dinna he come home?"

"For nigh on two fortnights, he and his men have bombarded Fort William. Will ye be wanting to join him?"

"After a wee rest."

~*~

Lord Lochiel's agility surprised Rory. By evening they emerged from the beech trees that surrounded the home of Alexander Cameron of Glen Nevis. She was about to knock when the door opened and she found herself looking into deep purple eyes.

"What are ye doing here?"

"'Tis a fine way to greet your wife, Duncan Cameron."

He scooped her up in a hug. Upon her sudden release, she knew he had noticed her companion.

"Is Lochiel inside?" she asked. "I brought him a visitor."

Duncan nodded. "I will fetch Archie and Sandy. Welcome home, Sir John."

"Thank ye, Duncan." The elder Cameron shook his hand. "And though it be late, glad tidings on finally getting wed."

Her husband departed and Rory led the way into the house. Lochiel's voice came from a room on her right, so she knocked and entered. The two men in the room rose.

"Rory, has something happened at Achnacarry?" Lochiel asked.

"All goes well there. A visitor asked that I bring him to ye."

"Who is it?"

"'Tis me, Donald," Lord Lochiel said, entering the room.

"Father!"

Rory slipped away, closing the door behind her. She waited outside until Duncan returned with Sir Donald's brothers.

"Wildcat!"

"Good evening to ye, Dr. Archie. How is the wound?"

"Healed. I dinna like carrying the lead, but 'tis preferable to being dead."

"What about me?" Sandy asked, giving her a hug.

"And good evening to ye as well, Father Alex."

"What brings ye here?"

"Ye can be after seeing for yourself. Sir Donald is inside."

After the brothers entered the house, Duncan took her hand. "Come, *m'eudail,* I will walk part of the way with ye."

"How goes the siege?"

"Not well. Our man skilled in bombarding the fort was killed by a shot from the fort's cannon. His replacement kens nocht."

"What will happen if ye canna take the garrison?"

"The Sassenach commander vows he will burn Maryburgh."

"Will the siege end soon?"

"Aye. Lord Murray sent word that Cumberland is in Aberdeen. The weather grows warmer, so the snow willna stay long. Soon he will march west to Inverness."

"And ye will go too." Tears stung her eyes. She was thankful the darkness hid them from him. She did not want him to worry about her. He would need his wits to stay alive.

"Aye, *m'eudail.*" The huskiness in his voice made her look at him. She saw only his shadowed outline—the strong jaw, the crooked nose, the high forehead. She touched his cheek and felt the rough stubble of his beard beneath her fingers.

"Dun—"

He placed two calloused fingers on her lips. "Shh, *m'eudail.* I dinna ken what the future holds for us, but I dinna want either of us to have regrets. Ken that I love ye will all my heart, and will do so forever."

He pulled her against him and kissed her. It was rough and quick, and then he was gone. She stared after him, praying to catch one more glimpse of him. The moonless night did not grant her wish. She brushed a tear from her face and whispered, "Farewell, Duncan. May God protect ye."

~*~

Billowing smoke had drawn Rory to climb the Monadh Gorm, the Blue Mount, at the head of Loch Arkaig. From her perch she watched the blue sky blacken from the burning of Maryburgh. Duncan had departed Glen Nevis three days earlier, but to Rory it seemed a lifetime. She stared at the bens and braes below, but instead saw the moor east of Inverness.

Dark gray clouds blew across the sky. Deafening thunder rolled over writhing heaving heather. Blood bubbled from a spring. Scarlet-coated corbies fed upon the red-stained moor.

A brilliant light exploded, blinding Rory. She screamed, then fainted.

CHAPTER NINETEEN
BLOODIED GROUND

Seated in the woods surrounding Culloden House, Duncan gagged on the bannock. He spit it out in disgust. "'Tis not fodder fit for cattle."

Fergus laughed. "I warned ye 'twas vile."

"What happened to the daily rations we were getting before we left for Fort William?"

"The lads say the quartermaster took ill. His replacement has not brains to find his arse. The carts of food are back in Inverness, and we have not time to fetch them."

Duncan searched the night sky. "'Tis a blessing the clouds conceal the moon. 'Twill make it harder for the enemy to see our approach."

"Aye, but 'tis a curse as well. We willna have light to guide us, and not kenning the trail will hamper us."

"So will empty bellies. 'Tis twelve miles to Cumberland's camp. After scurrying from Glen Nevis, 'twould help if we were fed. A man can only go so long without food."

"We could forage like the others."

"I would like nocht better, Fergus, but we canna leave camp. Too many have gone already. If attacked now, we could not muster men enough to best the enemy. Besides, 'tis our watch on Lochiel."

"Is he with the prince?"

"No. Charles feasts at Kilvarock Castle while we eat bannocks made from oat husks and mill dust."

The injustice nettled. Duncan understood that those of higher rank had more privileges, but now was not the time to flaunt the fact. The prince needed his Highlanders strong and willing to fight. To leave them hungry while he dined in comfort did not sit well.

"Do ye think this surprise attack will work, Duncan?"

"How can it, Fergus? We have too many obstacles to overcome before first light."

"Then why ever are we going through with it?"

"'Tis preferable to fighting on Drummossie Moor. That is an ill chosen place to meet the Sassenach because the flat barren land favors their artillery and dragoons rather than our frenzied charge from high ground."

"Why would the prince be after giving all the advantages to our enemy?"

"Because he willna heed men who ken the Highlands. Since he insists on leading the battle on the morrow, Lord Murray hopes to forestall that confrontation by marching on the enemy encampment this night."

Duncan noticed men passing in front of campfires. He collected his sword and targe. "'Tis time to gather. Remember to leave musket and pistols behind."

"Why choose this night to march on Cumberland?"

"'Tis his birthday. Prince Charles says his cousin will let his men fete him with ale so the royal troops will be fou."

Fergus snorted. "Did the spies not tell us Cumberland maintains strict discipline?"

"Aye."

"Then I dinna think he will tolerate his men getting drunk the eve before battle."

"Aye, but I would rather march than fight on yon moor."

They fell in on either side of Lochiel. When the men had formed into two columns, he signaled to Murray, who led the van. Mackintosh gillies guided them across the moor, shunning the road to avoid anyone guessing their intent. From the sound of rushing water to his right, Duncan knew they followed the River Nairn. When the track narrowed, he was forced to walk behind Lochiel while Fergus took the fore. If they marched single file all the way to Nairn, those in the vanguard would arrive long before those to the rear, and thus waste precious time waiting for all to gather.

Duncan stepped into thick ooze. It took three tries before he freed his foot. In a voice no louder than a whisper, he called to Lochiel.

"Not another word, lad. We must retrace our steps until we find firmer ground. Pass the word."

This delay threatened their chances of reaching Nairn before first light. The longer it took, the more they endangered their chances to escape across the water should the attack turn against them. Retreat meant leaving behind the wounded, but staying signified death or capture.

A ghostly form rose without warning in the dense fog. Unprepared, Duncan stubbed his toe on the stones of the drystone dyke. He bit his bottom lip to stem the oath of curses at another obstacle in their path. If he could not see walled enclosures, then what if those farther back strayed from the indistinguishable track? They could stumble upon a royal scouting party, terminating the Jacobites' one advantage—surprise.

Several hours later, word came down the line to halt. Soon after the man behind Duncan tapped his shoulder. "They say no one is behind us. The rest have disappeared."

Duncan groaned. "Sir Donald, we are separated from the center and rear of the column."

"But that leaves only twelve hundred to subdue eight thousand! Murray must be told at once."

The word continued along the line. Before long an answer came.

"Turn around," Lochiel said. "We canna attack with so few men. Besides, we have four miles more to traverse before reaching the encampment, and already the sky lightens. 'Twould be suicide to continue."

Duncan had known before leaving that the march would end in failure. How could it be otherwise? Rory had seen the battle fought on the windswept moor of Drummossie. He had hoped she erred, but in his heart knew she did not, and on the morrow that meant he would fall.

~*~

Oblivious to the chilled rain that seeped through his plaid, Duncan stumbled into camp at six o'clock on the morning of 16 April 1746. His stomach rumbled. His head ached. He moved by rote. Unable to take another step, he dropped like a stone and was asleep before his head hit the ground.

Someone shook him awake.

He swatted the interloper's hand from his shoulder. "Go away!"

"The enemy is four miles away. Lochiel wants us now!" Fergus said.

With his back to the high wall of the enclosure surrounding Culloden House, Duncan rubbed sleep from hooded eyes. The grayish light that filtered through the dense curtain of mist told him it was closer to midday rather than dawn. He felt drugged despite several hours of sleep.

"Are ye coming?" Fergus asked, offering him a hand.

Duncan grumbled. He shook his limbs to ease their stiffness, but the gesture brought little comfort. His knees and elbows ached. The biting cold dulled his movements. Sleet and snow stung his bare skin. He drew the top of his plaid tight around his shoulders, but the damp wool added no warmth. Disgruntled and miserable, he trudged south through mud, skirting the companies of Life Guards and Horse Guards, then passed through the reserves of French and Lowland troops. Around him, other confused, tired, and hungry men answered the drummers' call to arms. The steady beat rolled like thunder over the moor.

The Highlanders formed the front line at an angle between the stone walls of Culloden Park to the left and Culwhiniac to the right. This meant the MacDonalds, who held the left, had a greater distance to cover than the Athollmen, Camerons, and Stewarts of Appin. The right would engage the enemy first, preventing a united assault.

"The curved wall leaves wee room to maneuver," Duncan heard Lord Murray say as he approached Lochiel. Clad in a belted plaid of green, blue, and red with a matching short coat, the Jacobite commander pointed to the enclosure to the far right of his men, the Atholl Brigade. "'Twill force us into your men."

"'Twill also allow our enemy to outflank us," Lochiel said. "Did ye not discuss tearing it down with His Royal Highness?"

"Aye, Donald, but he willna heed me. 'Tis plain he prefers hearing Irish and French flattery to canny observation. Had I his ear, we would not fight here at all. We would vanish into the bens until we regroup, then choose the time and place to meet our foe." Murray sighed. "'Tis not my decision to make, though. The prince has seen to that. He is not like his father, King Jamie. Charles would rather battle his cousin on improper ground than heed advice from experienced men. Och, well, it matters nocht. 'Tis here he chooses to fight; 'tis here we will die. Pay heed, my friend, that wall will fash us."

Lochiel shook hands with Murray. "We can be after praying God watches over us."

"He is our only hope."

A rousing cheer drew Duncan's attention. "Colonel Anne," who wore a plaid riding habit and sported a white cockade on her bonnet, led the Mackintoshes to their place in the center between Frasers and Clan Chattan. When she saluted her men from her white steed, they huzzahed her.

"*La belle rebelle.*" Lochiel nodded in Lady Mackintosh's direction. Her husband was an officer in the Royal Army, but she, a staunch Jacobite, had raised the clan for Prince Charles. "'Tis what His Royal Highness calls the brave lass. Does the firebrand not remind ye of anyone?"

Duncan smiled. "Aye, Rory."

"I regret not having the opportunity to speak with your wildcat before she left Glen Nevis. Did she see what will unfold here?"

"Aye."

"And was she after telling ye what to expect?"

The question reminded Duncan of the quandary Rory had faced when she foresaw Pàdraig's death. *'Tis a terrible burden to ken a friend or kinsman will die.* He had not grasped the full meaning of her words then, but now he understood.

While he pondered how to answer, he shielded his eyes with his targe and peered eastward through dissipating fog. Fifteen battalions of foot soldiers and three regiments of dragoons deployed along a line parallel to the Highlanders about a furlong away. Their red woolen coats, canvas gaiters, and black tricornes left no doubt regarding their loyalties. Several companies, however, wore different uniforms, belted blue plaids with short red coats. These men were Highlanders—of Clan Campbell—and members of the detested Argyll Militia.

When two enemy battalions moved slightly forward and at right angles to their front line, Duncan realized the Camerons would be caught in the deadly crossfire. Was this why he would fall? And what of Lochiel? Would he too suffer wounds? Duncan wished he had asked, but perhaps Rory was right. Better not to know. This held true for himself as well as Lochiel. If Duncan confessed his wounding, would his chief endanger himself to protect him? Duty precluded Duncan from accepting that risk.

"No." The lie kept him from meeting Lochiel's gaze.

"Ye ken, but willna say. Och, mayhap 'tis best this way. I dinna want to ken who lives or dies beforehand. 'Twill do nocht to assuage my guilt." He clamped his hand over Duncan's shoulder. "Your father would be proud of ye, Duncan. I regret the passing of my friend, but never have I regretted calling ye son."

The words caught Duncan by surprise. He felt his eyes moisten and he swallowed. He opened his mouth to speak, but Lochiel shook his head.

"No words are necessary between us. Today, I ask only that ye be canny so ye can return to your bonny wildcat when this Rising ends. I would rather face King George's wrath than hers if ye dinna." Lochiel cleared his throat. "I must speak with Archie and Sandy."

When Duncan made to follow, the older man shook his head. "'Tis private words I am wanting with my brothers."

On the far side of the moor a gray horse drew rein in front of the thatched cottage where the blind woman had offered Rory comforting words and soothing tea. Although separated by more than a furlong, Duncan recognized the tall porcine figure. At twenty-four, William Augustus, Duke of Cumberland and the second son of King George, was younger than many of the officers he commanded and a veteran of campaigns on the continent, having seen action at Dettingen and Fontenoy.

The sharp snap of a silk banner caused Duncan to glance to his left. MacLachlan of Coruanan carried the Cameron standard that bore Lochiel's arms on a square of green. The banner's red field flapped in the raw northeast wind and its coloring stirred a remembrance of Rory's vision. *Reddish-plumed kestrels and feathery-blue merlins dropped from the blackened sky. Blood dripped from their sharp talons.*

He shivered. He feared death, but dared not let fear rule him else he would die. He shut his eyes and touched the pendant beneath his shirt. The image that came to him was not of Rory, but of a hooded rebel armed with longbow and dirk. Thistle's courage and fortitude mingled with Duncan's. Her warmth drove the cold from him. Her love shielded him.

Flanked by his brothers, Lochiel took his place near his standard bearer. The well-armed gentlemen of the clan formed up on either side. The remaining Camerons arranged themselves behind, making certain that father stood beside son, brother beside brother.

Duncan took his place beside Fergus and behind Lochiel, whose presence amidst his kinsmen would inspire them to stand true and fight no matter the cost. In contrast, their royal leader demonstrated cowardice by keeping to the cavalry's rear. Clad in plaid jacket and trews, buff waistcoat, and blue bonnet with white cockade, Prince Charles stood on a hillock where he would neither see the battle unfold nor arouse gallantry in the men. If he wished to lead, then he should follow the example set by Highland chiefs and assume a position in the front ranks.

A shout preceded cannon fire from guns situated between Clans Mackintosh and Chattan. The left battery fired a second volley. One projectile arced through the air toward the Duke of Cumberland himself. Duncan held his breath. If they scored a direct hit, the fight would end before it began. He prayed the luck of past victories held true, but the shot fell shy of its intended target, killing two soldiers instead. Yet the miss failed to dampen the Highlanders' spirits. Their cheers started low and grew to a crescendo that roared in Duncan's ears. He pulled the bonnet from his head and waved it high in the air.

Thunder boomed. The ground shuddered. Thick swirls of white clouds drifted up from the royal army's sixteen cannon. The stench of rotten eggs assailed Duncan's nostrils. He choked. The enemy three-pounders fired again, and he watched in horror as men fell, their arms and legs ripped away. Like scythes used to harvest grain, the unceasing cannonade cut wide swaths in the Jacobite line.

"Close up! Close up!"

The shouted orders followed each round of devastation. Scores of men died where they stood. A spark of outrage ignited in Duncan. He let his anger burn like a slow fuse until it exploded into a lust for vengeance.

Many of those lost were chiefs and clan officers. Although he knew few except by name, he wanted to avenge their deaths, but no order to advance was given. Why? He clenched his fists and glanced behind him. Others did the same.

A hail of grapeshot rained down from the sky, scattering nails and bolts. Duncan threw his targe up to deflect the barrage and squatted low to the ground, but his height was too great to shield all of him. Small pieces of iron pelted his back, shredding his shirt and burning his skin. He gritted his teeth and scooped up a handful of mud with his free hand. His eyes teared as he tried to apply the cold mire.

"Are ye hit?" Fergus asked.

"Aye."

Fergus angled his targe to Duncan's, then grabbed a fistful of mud and applied it to his back. The cold wetness brought immediate relief.

"Thank ye."

Fergus waved him off. "Ye would do the same for me. I wish I could do more. The mud willna stop the pain for long."

"'Tis enough for now. Fighting will ease the rest."

"What fighting? 'Tis nigh thirty minutes since they started this hell. Does Prince Charles mean for us to die without avenging our comrades? If he dinna give the order soon, he willna have men enough to do battle."

"Ye speak true, Fergus. Even with all my book learning, I canna explain the delay. 'Tis infuriating to crouch like a coward and watch kinsmen fall."

A rousing yell came from their left. A fair-haired man with red whortleberries adorning his bonnet broke rank and raced across the moor.

"Is that not MacGillivray of Dunmaglass?" Fergus asked.

"Aye, and he leads Clan Macintosh into the fray. They wait no longer for orders."

Fergus jumped to his feet and cheered them. The skirl of bagpipes echoed across the moor, and Lord Murray dropped his sword. Athollmen, Camerons, and Stewarts of Appin rushed forward. One moment Duncan had Lochiel in his sight. The next instant he was swallowed by a swarm of Athollmen who came from the right, forced to alter their course by the stone wall Murray had warned about before the battle. Duncan searched for Lochiel, but Highlanders—Stewarts of Appin and MacLarens— plowed into him from the left. The ramming of two sides against the middle created a compact funnel that propelled Duncan toward two regiments of royal infantry.

Red soldiers in the front rank dropped to one knee and fixed bayonets to muskets. The second line fired a volley, then stepped to the side and rear to reload their Land Pattern muskets while the third rank fired. The fourth rank moved into position, followed swiftly by the fifth and sixth.

The unceasing and accurate enfilade of soft lead proved deadly. Hundreds of Athollmen and Camerons died without engaging the enemy.

The jostling and squeezing from both directions knocked the pistol from Duncan's hand. He discarded any notion of retrieving it. The serried Highlanders made it impossible, and their forward momentum had already propelled him past the weapon. Each step also took him farther from his duty. He scanned the mob ahead and spotted a giant. Fergus! No one else was that tall. Perhaps he was still beside their chief. Duncan pushed his way through the *mêlée,* slashing with his sword, stabbing with his dirk, slamming with his targe.

"Give them the bayonet!" a Hanoverian officer shouted.

The kneeling red soldiers regained their feet and swiveled. They ignored those who came straight at them and thrust their bayonets into the Highlanders to their right. Duncan drew a ragged breath, understanding the deadliness of their actions. Highland targes no longer deflected enemy bayonets. Needle-sharp steel cut flesh and bone beneath uplifted arms that wielded swords, stopping those not felled by lead balls.

Duncan saw a flash of metal and shifted his targe to protect the opposite side of his body. The bayonet speared wood. He sidestepped around the dangling shield and plunged his sword into his attacker, piercing the man's heart.

He looked for Fergus and saw Lochiel fall. A shot from a pistol exploded through a Highlander's baldpate, spraying moisture across Duncan's face. He avenged the man's death by slashing the soldier's wrist, cutting him to the bone. By the time Duncan reached Lochiel, Fergus and two others had formed a protective box around their chief. A red wave armed with muskets and bayonets descended on them.

Too many! Retreat! Duncan's silent words echoed what others began to comprehend. Retreat and live. Stay and die. As if one person thought for them all, the Jacobite line broke. Highlanders fled, spurred on by panic and despair.

"Grab hold of Sir Donald!" Duncan said.

Other Camerons heard his order. They gathered around to shield Archie and Sandy from harm while they lifted Lochiel. Bodies littered the ground. There was no clear path for retreat. Musket fire rained down on them from the Culwhiniac enclosure. Campbells of Argyll, positioned behind the protective barrier of turf-covered stone, shot fleeing Highlanders as if hunting capercaillie. Hundreds lay dead or wounded. Unable to run, the Camerons fumbled their way back toward their line.

A bloodied red soldier struggled to his knees. Duncan felt a sharp stab to his thigh. He stumbled and fell.

"Take Sir Donald and go!" Fergus shouted above the din. "I will bring Duncan."

"Go with them, Fergus." Duncan ducked his head as balls of lead whistled around him.

"No! They will manage." Fergus nodded at the bayonet. "'Twill hurt."

"Just pull the bloody thing. We have no time to waste."

Fergus yanked the bayonet from Duncan's thigh. He uttered a stream of Gaelic curses through clenched teeth, struggling to stay conscious. Blood spurted from the wound. Fergus knotted his belt around Duncan's leg to stanch the bleeding. Duncan clutched Fergus' arm and struggled to his feet. His friend slipped an arm around his waist, and they hobbled back the way they had come.

A bloodcurdling yell raised the hair on Duncan's neck. He jerked his head in time to see a flash of steel.

"Fergus!"

The giant raised his arm to ward off the blow. A pistol fired, but too late. The sword severed Fergus' arm above the elbow. He staggered and fell, dragging Duncan down too. A bolt of pain coursed through him. He saw Sandy rushing toward them, then he saw nothing.

~*~

Duncan woke to darkness. The blackness and silence were absolute, so he doubted he lay on the moor where his moans would have mingled with those of other wounded. Wherever he was, he was not alone. Although he heard neither speech nor movement, he sensed the presence of others.

He covered his eyes with his arm. He felt a crusty substance matted to his hair. Was it his blood or Fergus'? Again he saw a flash and heard the horrible thud of steel slicing flesh and bone. He shivered and groaned.

"Duncan?" The whisper came low beside his ear. "Do ye hear me, Duncan?"

"Aye." The single word sounded more like a frog's croak than human speech. His throat felt raw and dry. The other man pressed cold wetness to his lips. "'Tis snow. We have nocht else to drink."

"Archie?"

"Aye, lad."

"Where are we?"

"A crofter's barn."

"'Tis cold."

"We canna light a fire. The smoke would bring the dragoons down on us."

"Sir Donald?"

"He rests over there. His ankles are broken. 'Twas the grapeshot. He will mend, but 'twill be a long time before he walks again."

"Fergus?"

Archie did not answer. Dread filled Duncan. He clutched the physician's shirt. "Where is Fergus?"

"Och, lad. He was dead when Sandy reached him."

Tears welled up in Duncan's eyes. Pain stabbed his thigh and radiated from the wound down his leg, up his torso, and down his arms. A flash of brilliant white blinded him. A low growl grew in his throat until it became a scream. He bit his lip to silence the agony. His hand brushed against the pendant. *Och, Rory!*

A gentle hand stroked his sweaty brow. A soft whisper brushed his ear. "*Rest,* mo chridhe."

The pain left him. He closed his eyes and heeded her words.

~*~

A cold hand clamped his mouth shut. Duncan struggled to free himself, but the tiniest movement brought excruciating pain.

"If ye value your life, *mon ami,* ye will imagine yourself a statue," a man said.

Duncan fell still. The hand covering his mouth belonged to Prince Charles.

"*Bon,* it is good you listen. Do you not hear them?"

Hooves clattered on stone. Duncan stiffened. The approaching horses could mean only one thing. *Dragoons.* Frantic, Duncan glanced around him. Pinholes of light stole through cracks in the thatching, allowing him to distinguish shadows. A dozen men huddled in the small confines of the barn. Several raised their arms, and Duncan heard whispers of steel sliding from sheaths. The prince pressed a dirk into his hand.

"They will give no quarter, *mon ami.* If any of us escape with our lives, it will be me. I am certain the usurper has greater plans than allowing me to die here."

Horses snorted and whinnied. Leather squeaked as dragoons dismounted. One by one, Duncan counted the swish of swords being drawn and the clack of pistols being cocked. Ten. The odds favored his companions, but he wondered if they had strength enough to fight men less tired and hungry.

"Search the croft," someone outside ordered. "If the Pretender is within, seize him. Kill anyone else."

"Women and children?"

"Everyone. All are rebels."

The sinister words made Duncan's blood run cold. The door latch clicked. His hand curled around the hilt of the dirk. Then a new sound came to his ears. Thundering hoofbeats seemed to echo off the walls. The door stopped opening.

"Mount up!" A different Hanoverian gave the command.

"We have orders to search all crofts."

"Your orders are changed. The traitor has been sighted. Mount and follow."

The dragoons sheathed their swords and uncocked their pistols. Duncan imagined them jostling each other in an attempt to mount their steeds and dash after the newcomers. They joked with one another, but he could only distinguish single words: gold, prize, head, traitor, death.

"A narrow escape, *mon ami, oui?*" the prince whispered long after the dragoons rode away.

"Aye, a very narrow escape."

"How is my patient?" Archie laid his hand on Duncan's brow. "'Tis a fever ye have, lad. I think there is time to tend your wound before we steal into the bens where 'tis safe for rebels."

"What of yourself, Archie? Who tends your wounds?"

"Ye mean these?" the physician asked, indicating hastily wrapped linen encircling his right arm. "Dinna fash about me. A ball grazed the flesh. 'Twill heal soon enough. Ye, on the other hand, willna."

He cut the plaid concealing the wound, then placed a rag wet with snow over Duncan's thigh. The cloth cooled his fiery skin.

He eyed the dirk Archie held with wary eyes. "What do ye intend doing with that?"

"I canna see where the bayonet pierced your thigh. The blood soaked through your plaid, and when it dried, the cloth adhered to your skin. I must scrape it free before I can tend to it."

Archie worked the blade between the caked blood and wool. Duncan stuffed the cool cloth from his forehead between his teeth. He balled his fists. His nails pierced his palms, and blood trickled down his hands. Sweat beaded his brow. He felt lightheaded, and rested his head against the cold stone while he endured the slow, meticulous torment.

"Sorry, lad. I dinna have Rory's gentle touch, but 'tis done." Archie examined the wound. He clicked his tongue once or twice before sitting back on his haunches. "'Tis swollen and discolored. I have nocht to treat it with except the snow."

"After caterans wounded me, Rory burned the cut with a heated dirk," Duncan said. "Will ye do the same?"

Archie shook his head. "Cauterizing is the best way to treat a wound of this sort, but we canna risk a hot fire to sear the dirk. All I can do is wrap your leg, and hope infection dinna set in."

Sandy knelt beside his brother. "Is it time?"

"I have just to affix the bandage."

The priest waited until Archie finished, then he made the sign of the cross.

"Is it extreme unction ye are giving me, Sandy?" Duncan asked.

"Not at all, lad. 'Tis asking God's forgiveness I am."

Duncan narrowed his eyes. "Forgiveness for what?"

"We must travel quickly, Duncan," Archie said. "'Twill be less painful for ye this way."

"What way?"

"This way." Sandy pulled back his arm and delivering a solid blow to Duncan's jaw.

For an instant, he stared in disbelief. Then his eyes closed, and his head rolled to the side.

~*~

The odor of charred timbers welcomed Duncan to wakefulness. He rested on a stone floor, but looked upon a starry night sky rather than wooden rafters or thatched roof. Flickering firelight cast a dim glow on the ruins of a grand hall, at the far end of which he discerned the shell of a staircase leading to four rooms, one above the other, which had once opened onto halls in the adjacent tower. He returned his gaze to the grand hall and noticed a raven carved into the stone wall opposite his feet. It was the crest of MacDonald of Glengarry.

Apparently they had traveled south to Loch Oich where they sought refuge in Invergarry Castle, or what remained of the stronghold. The last time Duncan had passed this way, the L-shaped castle had been complete with an oblong tower at one end and a round tower at the other. When had it been put to the torch?

The aroma of boiled salmon reached his nostrils. His stomach grumbled. He could not remember when he had last eaten.

"Ye are awake," Sandy said. "I feared I hit ye too hard."

Duncan rubbed his bruised jaw. "For a priest ye have a mean fist."

Sandy laughed. "I was not always a priest, and with four brothers, I had to defend myself more than once. Besides, Grandsire would not hear of us settling our disputes with mere words. He swore the fist was a most persuasive argument."

"I am thinking he was right."

"Would ye be wanting a wee bite? There is nocht but salmon and oatcakes, but 'tis a feast fit for a prince."

"I dinna care what 'tis as long as 'tis edible."

Sandy helped him into a sitting position, then fed him like a babe. Duncan would have preferred to feed himself, but had neither the strength nor the desire to face Sandy's fist again. Each bite he chewed served as a reminder of the priest's accurate aim.

"How is Sir Donald?"

"Vexed. My brother dinna like depending on others, but he canna walk."

Duncan glanced at Lochiel. Black and gray whiskers adorned his face. Dark shadows gave him the appearance of having hollow eyes. He spoke with the prince.

"What are they discussing?"

"Donald is trying to convince His Royal Highness of the necessity of separating. He must flee Scotland, but canna make haste with ye and my brother."

"Will Charles heed him?"

Sandy shrugged. "'Tis not safe for him here. I doubt loyal Highlanders would surrender him to the Sassenach, but thirty thousand pounds is enough to tempt the most steadfast. Of course, there are many Highlanders who support King George."

"Then why stay?"

"Charles and his men dinna ken the way to Loch nan Uamh where the French ship will anchor."

"I ken someone who can deliver them."

Sandy looked at him. "Do ye ken what ye say, lad? 'Tis a terrible risk for her to be taking."

"Is it less of a risk to face red soldiers with orders to kill innocent women and bairn?"

"I see your point." Sandy called to his brother. "Begging your pardon, Donald, but the lad has a suggestion I think ye should hear."

"You know someone who will take us to our ship?" Charles asked.

"Her name is Rory, and she is my wife," Duncan said.

"Une femme?"

Lochiel's laughter echoed off the stone walls. "No ordinary woman, Your Royal Highness. I would trust the lass with my life. She kens the tracks that lead to the coast. Should ye meet with resistance, she can defend ye with any manner of weapon. 'Tis a true Highland warrior she is."

"Incroyable! There is no one else?"

Lochiel shook his head.

"You give us no alternative, *mon ami.* How do we reach this Rory?"

"Sandy will lead ye to Achnacarry and make certain all is well."

"She will do as I command?"

All the Camerons laughed, but Duncan answered. "Rory is a wildcat, fierce and loyal. 'Tis not to ye she gave her oath. Only Lochiel can command her."

"You are her husband. Why do you not tell her what to do?"

"'Tis not the way between us. I will ask, but if she refuses, I willna be there to persuade her to change her mind."

"Is not her loyalty to the Stewarts enough to convince her?" the prince asked.

Duncan stroked his jaw. "The Stewarts have not always treated her people fairly. She supports neither your father nor King George. Her loyalty is to Sir Donald."

"You will command her to do this, *mon ami?*"

"I will ask this of her," Lochiel said, "but her first duty is to protect the clan. If your presence endangers others, she will do what is best for them first."

Prince Charles raised his hands in defeat. "*Ça va, mon ami.* If I must surrender myself into the hands of *une femme,* then I must trust your judgement."

CHAPTER TWENTY
ESCAPE

Rory watched for a sign—the flare of a fir candle, the scent of burning peat, the sound of muted voices—to betray the intruders, but no light dispelled the darkness. No smoke curled from the chimney. No noise disturbed the quiet. Whoever hid within the stone walls of Donald Cameron of Glenpean's home at the west end of Loch Arkaig did not want to be found.

All her three-hour vigil had yielded was stiff muscles and numb feet. She rose from her crouched position. A tingling sensation spread from her toes to her heel and up her calf. When she put pressure on the leg, the tingle prickled like thistle barbs. She flexed her ankle and bent her knee to restore feeling.

"Give me your foot." The gruffness of the whispered command brooked no refusal. Calloused thumbs and fingers massaged her leg.

"'Twill be another bout with fists if Duncan catches ye," her other companion said. "Or mayhap, 'twill be more interesting to see what Fiona does with ye."

With her hand on Malcolm's shoulder to steady her, Rory felt the low grumble before he voiced it. Previous experience had taught her he had no patience when Jamie's teasing involved his wife. If Rory did not intervene, the badinage would quickly degenerate from argy-bargy to tow-row. Instead of learning who dwelt within the cottage, she would end up with two battered and bruised companions who refused to speak to one another. Too much was at stake to allow them to jeopardize it.

"Whist!" Her scolding quieted both brothers. "'Tis neither the time nor the place for your teasing. We canna risk losing our quarry."

Jamie pursed his lips, then sighed. "Ye are right. Forgive me, brother?"

Malcolm grunted. He turned back toward the cottage. "Be they soldiers?"

"Furtiveness is not their way. 'Tis more apt to be men returning home," Rory said, thinking of the bloodied, maimed, and broken men she had glimpsed during the previous two days.

They stole through the braes and glens, keeping to the woods and avoiding *clachan*. Their plaids were tattered and stained, their faces haggard and unshaven. The few who dared to approach her had a haunted, hunted look in their eyes. They started at the snap of a twig or the warble of a bird. Their news confirmed her vision, but did nothing to allay her fear. Too many had fallen for them to tell her of Duncan's well being. They had fled the confusion with one intent—to escape with their lives.

A single click penetrated Rory's thoughts. She came alert and listened. Leaves rustled in the gentle breeze and waves lapped the shores of the loch, but mingled with these noises she heard a muffled scrape and a strident creak. Someone eased open the door of Glenpean's cottage.

The shadow seemed to float like a phantom. Not until he came within arm's distance of her could Rory discern his measured breaths and quiet footfalls. She motioned for her brothers to slip behind him. When they were in position, she stepped into the shadow's path. Jamie and Malcolm seized his arms and forced him to his knees.

She waited until he ceased struggling and accepted confinement. She kept her voice low so as not to alert any companions who remained closeted in the cottage.

"Identify yourself!"

"Wildcat!"

Rory started at the hissed name. Only a friend would know the name the Cameron brothers had bestowed on her.

"Tell your brothers to release me," the prisoner said.

This time she recognized his voice. She snapped her fingers, then stepped forward to help him stand. "Pray forgive us, Father Alex. I dinna ken 'twas ye who sought refuge at Glenpean's."

"No matter."

She noted his distracted tone and darting glances, then asked, "Looking for soldiers, are ye?"

He swiveled to face her. "Be they near?"

"No, but I expect they will come before long. The governor of Fort William has no fondness for Camerons. He is set on capturing one in particular."

Sandy chuckled. "Poor Donald. Ever a gentle man of peace, he seems to have become over popular."

"They will hang him."

"First, they must catch him." The priest lowered his voice. "I must speak with ye within, Rory."

"What must ye say that ye canna speak here?" she asked, uneasy about entering the darkened cottage without knowing who or what was inside.

"Dinna fash, lass. Ye will find only friends inside."

"As ye wish, Father." She put aside her apprehension of inescapable enclosures. Sandy had never given her cause to distrust him before, and he might have word of Duncan's fate. "Malcolm?"

"Aye, I ken. Guard duty."

She smiled and touched her brother's arm. "'Tis a special talent ye have."

"What of me?" Jamie asked.

"Fetch food and drink without anyone the wiser," Sandy said.

The brothers disappeared into the night. Sandy led Rory into the cottage. When the door clicked shut, a light flared and she found herself staring down the barrels of three cocked pistols.

"Friends, is it, Father Alex?" she asked.

"Put away your weapons."

"Ye were gone but a few moments, *mon ami,*" the tallest man said. "We did not expect your return so soon."

"I did not go to Achnacarry," Sandy said, bowing his head. "Rory watched us."

"Watched us? *C'est impossible!* No one saw us enter."

"They did, but ye did not see them." Rory studied the speaker. She had noted the deference Sandy showed him, almost to the exclusion of the other occupants. The stranger's habit of combining French with English told her he was an educated foreigner of some rank in spite of his rumpled and stained clothes and the torn frills of lace edging his cuffs. An idea of who he was intruded into her thoughts. She hoped she was wrong. She feared she was not.

"Ye have a lesson or two to learn if ye wish to lurk in the Highlands," she said. "Eyes have watched since ye entered Lochaber."

His eyebrows rose. "*Vraiment? C'est incroyable!* I believe Lochiel was correct, *Père* Alexandre. She is different from other *femmes.*"

Sandy nodded. "Your High—"

"Stop!" Rory knew she violated protocol, but current circumstances did not allow time for customary rules of ettiquette.

The priest frowned. "What ails ye, wildcat? I wish only to introduce our guest."

She shook her head. "If ye were wanting to be recognized, ye would not be skulking. I have a fair notion who stands before me."

"You will not bow to your prince?" Charles asked.

"Not at all. When my brother comes with food and drink, ye must leave."

"Rory!" Sandy exclaimed, a look of chagrin on his face. "Ye misspeak yourself, lass. 'Tis not our way to be showing an unwelcome face to guests."

"Dinna lecture me on hospitality, Father Alex. I canna carry out my charge to safeguard the clan with *him* hiding here. He imperils the lives of all."

"Worry not, *Madame.* I will protect your people."

She snorted. "With what army? The men who hide canna defend themselves. How do ye expect them to fight soldiers? I canna stop the retribution we must suffer for the loyalty Lochiel showed ye, but I can lessen it by refusing ye shelter."

"Your words humble me, *Madame.* I would grant your request, but am in need of assistance. Your husband and *mon ami,* Lochiel, assure me no one else can undertake this mission."

Rory stifled a groan. She had no desire to assist in this man's pursuits, but he invoked the two names that would make her listen. While Duncan would never command her to do something, her sworn oath required her to heed the other.

"*Mon ami,* Lochiel, asked me to give you these."

She accepted the twig, ring, and letter from the prince with reluctance. Once she identified them and read the letter there would be no turning back from her duty.

She traced the lobes of the green leaf. "'Tis oak, badge of Clan Cameron."

"First proof that my brother sends us," Sandy said.

She nodded, then examined the second. The ring's crest showed five arrows bound together with gules. She read the Gaelic words aloud. "*Aonaibh ri chéile.* Unite."

"Our motto. Ye ken the seal belongs to Donald and no other?" Sandy asked.

"Aye."

"Then mayhap 'tis time to read his missive."

Rory broke the wax seal. The crackle of unfolding paper resonated in the stillness of the room. She read the scrawled words. *I entrust ye with the life of this man. Since his survival, as well as your own, are in your hands, he will abide by your commands without argument. Take him where the priest sends ye. I ask much, but ye ken well the sacrifices a chief must make. D.C.L.*

A sharp rap startled them. The prince's companions drew their weapons.

Sandy went to the door. "Aye?"

"'Tis Jamie."

Sandy eased open the door, and Jamie slipped inside. He held a bundle and small keg. "'Tis not grand fare, but 'twill satisfy."

"*Merci, monsieur,*" the prince said.

Rory redirected their attention back to the letter. "Lochiel claims ye will heed my commands."

Charles nodded. "I will."

"What of your companions?"

"*Colonel* O'Neil and *Monsieur* O'Sullivan? *Mais oui.* They will also listen."

The Irish officer held himself erect. "No colleen is going to be giving me orders!"

Rory shrugged. "Ye are free to fend for yourself, Colonel O'Neil, but if ye are wanting to keep your head a wee longer, ye will heed me. If not, leave now. I willna risk my life to save yours if ye dinna wish it saved."

O'Neil glowered at her. "I am a soldier with more years of experience than ye have. I will not heed ye."

"As ye wish, Colonel. Then ye will be leaving before first light."

"Not without my prince!"

"'Tis a stalemate then. Without strict adherence to my wishes, I willna be guiding any of ye anywhere." Rory turned to go.

"*Arrêtez! Mon Dieu!* To think I must place my life in a woman's hands after leading five thousand into battle."

"When a rising begins, 'tis a glorious thing," she said. "Men are filled with hope and vigor, but when winning turns to losing, the glory fades. 'Tis no longer a grand adventure. Men die, and one side defeats the other. Ye led five thousand from here to Derby before returning to Scotland. How many of those men still live? How many will survive the Crown's vengeance?

"The Rising is ended. Now, ye must decide what path to follow. Will ye accept my help and flee? Will ye evade the Sassenach alone? Will ye surrender and accept whatever fate the King decrees?"

Rory hoped the ensuing silence meant the men understood the reality of their situation. She gave them time to mull over their options, then asked, "Is it my help ye are wanting, then?"

The prince and his companions nodded.

"Good. The dawn will soon arrive, so dinna set foot outside the cottage. Rest while ye can, for I dinna ken where next ye will sleep. I will come for ye at gloaming."

"*Merci, Madame,* I will not forget what you do. Someday, I will repay your kindness."

"I want nocht from ye, sir. Go home and let us live in peace." Without another word, she eased open the door and slipped outside.

Jamie followed.

Before they got far, Sandy called to her. "I carry another letter. 'Tis from Duncan."

Rory slipped the proffered paper under her belt. She yearned for news, but could not voice her thoughts.

As if sensing her disquiet, Sandy answered the unspoken question. "A Sassenach bayonet pierced his thigh, but when we parted yesterevening, Duncan was mending."

Relief washed over Rory like waves rushing to meet the shore. She expelled a long breath and felt her eyes fill with tears. She wiped them with the heels of her palms. Jamie pulled her close and she rested her head against his shoulder.

"The wound was not mortal, then?" Jamie asked.

Sandy shook his head. "No. I did not mean to upset ye, wildcat, but thought ye would want to ken the truth."

"'Tis not the kenning that fashes, Father," Jamie said. "She and Duncan kent he would fall, but those who passed this way after could not tell how he fared."

The priest's eyes widened with surprise. "How could she ken? Was she not here at Achnacarry?"

Her brother withheld his answer, and so did Rory. Experience had taught her reticence, especially where men of the cloth were concerned. They scoffed at *Dà-Sealladh,* convinced that foreknowledge was the work of the devil. Father Alex was not like other priests, but she did not know if he adhered to those same beliefs.

Before she could decide how best to respond, he answered for her. "Ye have the Two Sights, wildcat?"

"Begging your pardon, Father Alex," Malcolm said, joining them, "but ye are a priest. 'Tis no secret what your kind thinks of *Dà-Sealladh.*"

Sandy nodded. "So I am, but I was a Highlander long before I took my vows. My grandsire had the Two Sights, and he was wont to blaspheme when vexed, but only his enemies thought him the Devil himself. I believe *Dà-Sealladh* is a special gift from God. I dinna ken why or how He decides who receives it, but 'tis His way of warning us of dire deeds to come."

It was a unique view for a priest, but then Sandy followed his own path. Raised an Episcopalian, he had converted to Rory's faith and entered the Jesuit order. His reasoning dispelled her doubts.

"Aye, Father, I have the Two Sights."

"Then ye ken the terrible slaughter."

"I do." She remembered the blood that bathed the images she had seen. A man's face slashed from brow to chin. A pool of red water.

Flickering flames consuming human flesh. Muskets wielded like clubs, and bayonets like dirks. She keened a silent lament, while Jamie's gentle touch stilled the horror.

"Is Duncan with Dr. Archie and Lochiel?" he asked.

"Aye."

"What of Fergus?"

"Och, Rory. He was helping Duncan from the field when a Campbell slew him. He was dead when I reached him."

She squeezed her eyes shut to stem the tears that welled in her eyes. Mourning friends was a luxury she had no time for at the moment.

"And Gregor Glùn Dhubh?"

"The MacGregor who sent for ye when Duncan fell ill?" Sandy asked.

"Aye."

"Safe and well, I assume. Glengyle took his men north to secure that region of the Highlands, so they did not fight at Drummossie Moor."

~*~

When Rory woke, rays of afternoon sunlight spilled through the tall windows of the sleeping room. She rolled onto her back, and heard a crackling sound. She stared at the canopy, trying to identify from whence the noise came. A fire blazed in the hearth, but breaking peat bricks had not made the sound. She pushed herself into a sitting position. The crackle came again. The letter! She pulled it from her belt and smoothed out the wrinkles.

The scrawl of words was jerky and ragged instead of firm and even. She assumed Duncan's suffering was responsible, especially when she noticed several spots where the ink pooled as if he had held pen to paper while waiting for a spasm of pain to subside.

My heart aches, but the fates decree we remain parted a wee longer. Pray forgive me for entangling ye in this affair. The task set for ye is more important now, and the additional burden increases the risk. Pray for us, m'eudail. *Ye are my treasure, my strength. Remember always that I love ye with all my heart.*

Rory brushed a tear from her cheek, then wrapped her arms around herself. She found it a poor substitute for Duncan's tender embrace. It lacked his strength, his warmth, and his comfort. Those were the things she needed.

A beam of sunlight fell on the mantel, illuminating Nannag's love *cuach*. Rory had found the small wrapped parcel upon her return from Inverness and remembered the promise she had given Duncan's grandmother. Time and circumstance contrived to drive all thought of the gift from her mind. She lifted the love *cuach* from the mantel and stroked the velvety petals of the late blooming rose Duncan had sent from Edinburgh. Knowing he had picked it with his own hand lessened the heartache left by his absence. She refolded the letter and set it on the mantel, then placed the *cuach* on top of it.

The front door creaked open. Rory started and glanced over to see who entered without knocking. A giant, silhouetted by a halo of evening sunlight, slumped against the doorway. Twigs, leaves, and thorns protruded at odd angles from his limp stringy hair. He raised his left arm, but the movement caused him pain. A groan escaped his lips, then he toppled to the floor.

The healing side of Rory urged her forward, but the warrior side cautioned restraint. She inched close to his side and prodded him with the toe of her brogue. He moaned, but otherwise remained oblivious to her presence. With one hand on her dirk, she rolled the stranger onto his back. Deep lines of pain etched a bearded face. She reached out to touch his feverish brow.

His eyes flashed open and he grabbed her wrist. "R-o-r-r-y!"

Her eyes darted to his at the gasping of her name. Hazel eyes pierced hers. She felt her lips form his name, but his eyelids flickered shut and his hold lessened before she could speak.

"Malcolm! Jamie! Come quick!"

The thud of running feet echoed through the entrance hall.

Her older brother knelt beside her. "A ghost?"

"He is flesh and blood, but 'tis certain he willna live if I dinna tend the wound."

"Fetch your herbs, lass. Jamie and I will carry him to the gathering room."

Rory snatched her satchel of medicines from the table in her room, grabbed a wooden box from the mantel, and ran downstairs. She had not a moment to spare. Fergus' life was in her hands. She had no idea how he had walked home after the loss of an arm, but he had. If he had the will to survive such an arduous journey, then she prayed she had the knowledge to ease his suffering.

Her brothers had repositioned the table close to the fire before setting Fergus on it. While Malcolm lit candles to give her light, Jamie undressed Fergus and washed the mud and blood from his battered body. Rory set aside her herbs and examined him. Beads of sweat dotted his brow. She wiped them away with a cool wet rag, then rinsed it and placed it on his forehead. The putrid odor of rotting flesh assailed her nostrils. She gently prodded what remained of his swelled arm. The skin crackled. The flesh was cold to the touch and ashen in color. *Gangrene.*

She washed the stump with distilled water made from knotgrass, then rubbed it with the red oil of Saint John's Wort. After packing *Sphagnum* moss around the wound, she prepared a decoction of willow bark. There was little else she could do for Fergus. If the mortification did not kill him, the dead skin would fall off. He would have to adjust to the changes caused by the loss of his limb, but her immediate concern was whether he lived, and who would tend him during her absence.

Muffled voices permeated Rory's thoughts. She shook her head and glanced at Malcolm. "Tend to it."

When he opened the door, the irritated murmuring grew louder. She discerned at least three voices, and recognized two, Prince Charles and Sandy. The former sputtered French.

Malcolm's response was a loud grunt. "Father Alex, I dinna ken what your friend is saying, and I dinna care."

"Rory promised to meet us at gloaming, but she never showed."

"It could not be helped," Malcolm said.

"Soldiers?" the priest asked.

"Fergus."

"Fergus? But he is dead. I saw him fall."

"Rory tends him now."

Sandy hurried past Malcolm and approached the table. He took one look at the prone figure and crossed himself. "Faith, Fergus, can ye ever forgive me? I thought ye dead."

Jamie laid a hand on the priest's shoulder. "He canna hear ye. 'Twould be best if ye prayed for his recovery instead of wasting your breath on begging his pardon."

"He will mend then, wildcat?" Sandy asked.

Rory shrugged. "'Tis in the Lord's hands. I have done what I can."

"He is one of my soldiers, *Père* Alexandre?" the prince asked.

"Aye, and guard to my brother. 'Tis Fergus who helped Duncan from the field."

Charles looked at the unconscious giant, then at Rory. "How will this affect our plans?"

"I must find someone I trust to watch over Fergus," she said. "I dinna dare move him, and canna risk choosing someone who will send word to the governor of Fort William. There is wee chance Fergus will live, but he will die if the soldiers get hold of him."

"I will stay," Sandy said. "Show me what I must do."

"Ye dinna want to go with our guest?"

"Donald bid me bring him to ye, wildcat. What needs doing now is best done by ye and your brothers."

After imparting the necessary instructions, she turned to the prince and his companions. "Ye are ready to leave then?"

"*Oui, nous sommes prêt.*"

She unpinned her brooch and unwound her plaid. She placed the folded wool under Fergus' head. "Shall we go?"

When her charges failed to respond, she glanced at them. They stared, their mouths gaping. She glanced at the floor to hide her smile, knowing her black trews struck them dumb. "Is something wrong?"

Charles cleared his throat. "Ye dress as a man."

"Ye dress as a Highlander, but your speech and mannerisms betray ye. Any who cross our path will ken ye are *gall*. 'Tis safer to travel the summer tracks. 'Tis longer, but we willna meet many folk. We dinna celebrate Beltane for ten days yet, so they abide yet in their winter homes. We will keep to the bens and travel at night. 'Tis faster and easier to climb when dressed as a man. Now, if ye have no other objections, we should leave." *And the sooner ye are gone,* she thought, *the sooner we will be safe.*

With Jamie scouting ahead and Malcolm guarding their rear, she led her charges from Achnacarry. With the trees to mask their progress, she headed west, keeping the southern bank of Loch Arkaig on her right. Twelve miles later they arrived at the head of the loch. She skirted the cottages and turned north, following the River Dessary. After another fourteen miles she started to climb. The summit of Sgor nan Coireachan lay three thousand feet above, but she had no intention of going that high. She needed to isolate her charges from the local population, and the added height would allow her a clear view of the landscape in case she had misjudged the garrison commander. She was certain his patrols would keep to the populated regions where they would find more to fill their pockets and bellies. While she could only guess at what form the retribution would take, she had no doubt the Crown would be swift and merciless in carrying out justice.

The ground rose sharply, and Rory concentrated on the climb. She clawed the earth, pulling herself up with her hands while pushing with her feet. A fine mist began to fall, making the way more treacherous. The scree became slippery and the loose rock cut her hands. She slowed to a crawl, keeping one eye on the prince and the other on the path. Halfway up the summit, she spotted a sheltered corrie. She signaled a stop, and went to investigate. She squeezed through the narrow opening. While she could not make out much in the darkness, she sensed it was large enough to hold all of them.

"'Tis small, but well hidden. We rest here."

Jamie nodded, and led the prince and his companions into the corrie. Malcolm took the first watch, leaving Rory to rest. She chose a spot a short distance from the others, and stretched out on the mossy ground. Wrapped in one of Duncan's plaids, she stared at the few stars visible through the canopy of leaves. She should feel exhausted, but Fergus' abrupt appearance, Duncan's troubling wound, and her perilous task kept her from sleep. If she survived this journey, she would visit Nannag. Duncan's grandmother had the uncanny ability to understand and soothe a person's problems until they were set right. Peace of mind was something Rory craved.

The squish of a boot alerted her to the intruder's presence. She eased her dirk from its leather sheath. She waited until he knelt beside her, then pounced. Her attack sent him sprawling. She scrambled on top of him, and pricked his throat with the sharp point of her blade.

"*C'est moi, Madame!*"

She snorted and rolled from the prince. "Are ye wanting to get yourself killed?"

The words brought back a memory, and she smiled. Duncan had once asked her the same question.

"I assure you my death never entered my mind. I wanted only to speak with you," the prince said, rubbing his throat. "You are smiling."

"Am I? Och, 'tis nocht to concern yourself with. I suggest ye avoid sneaking up on folk. 'Tis a coward who dinna face his foe."

"*Jamais* would I fight a woman, *Madame.*"

"Why? Is it because ye dinna think we can best ye?"

"There are other pursuits for a gentleman and his lady."

"True, but ye will have to find yourself another lady. I am here to see ye safely to your destination. Once I do, I wash my hands of ye."

"I do not impress you?"

"I have no need for court intrigues. 'Twas your grandsire who lost the throne and your father who failed to regain it. 'Twas futile for ye to try again, and because of it 'tis we who will pay for your stubbornness."

"My grandsire was driven from his throne. In his place a German rules. My father and I are the rightful heirs to the crown, and someday we will sit there again."

"Ye might be able to seduce Duncan and Lochiel with eloquent speeches, but the women folk willna heed them. While ye fight, 'tis we who suffer. Our men are either imprisoned or in hiding. When the soldiers come, and they will, 'twill be us they set upon. They will turn us from our homes, then pillage and burn them. If that dinna satisfy them, 'tis us they will rape and our bairns they will slaughter. All because a young, headstrong, and reckless fool could not accept his fate."

"How dare you speak to me like that!"

"I have never been one to hold my tongue. 'Tis a fault my chief oft reminds me of. I canna change who I am to soothe your ruffled feathers. Your grand ideas may come from noble intentions, but ye dinna think them through. There is no shading to how ye see things. They are either black or white, and that keeps ye from understanding how what ye do affects others."

"What gives ye the right to attack me?"

Although she could not see his face, she was certain it was red with anger.

"Many years ago, your great-great-grandsire declared my people outlawed and forbade us from using our name. He sanctioned others to hunt us like animals and murder us without fashing about their freedom. The lessons we learned from the proscription are in our blood. I have lived with death since I was a wee lass. Life is too precious to waste on sweet words and empty dreams, and that is what ye offered Lochiel."

"If you feel this way, then why help me?"

"Because my chief and my husband ask it of me. The hour grows late, and the way ahead is hard. I am wanting to rest, and suggest ye do the same."

~*~

Rory hid behind the jagged ledge that overlooked Loch nan Uamh. She saw no sign of the French ship, but the reflected orb of the full moon danced on the waves. During her vigil she had neither heard nor seen any patrols. They were in MacDonald country and she doubted anyone would betray Prince Charles, but she preferred not to take unnecessary chances.

A stone skipped past her fingertips. She glanced to her side.

"It is ironic, *Madame*," the prince said. "A year has almost passed since I landed on this shore. Then I had such hopes and dreams. Now, they are dashed like those waves crashing on the rocks."

She ignored his pretty words. "Was there someone to take ye to the Isles?"

"Donald MacLeod of Gaultergill," the prince said.

She sent Malcolm to find this MacLeod. The sooner she saw the prince gone, the sooner she could return home.

~*~

Two days later MacLeod arrived with six men carrying a boat. Malcolm and Jamie helped them set the boat upon the water. Since MacLeod needed another to help row and Jamie was an experienced fisherman, he volunteered to accompany them. He took Rory's hands in his and held them tight. "I dinna ken when I will return. Ye will give Sàra and the bairns my love and keep a watchful eye on them?"

"I will."

He nicked her chin with his finger. "Dinna fash about Duncan. He will come when 'tis safe."

"I ken. Keep ye safe." She hugged him.

Jamie shook hands with his brother, then joined MacLeod by the boat. They held it steady while Prince Charles boarded. Rory stood beside Malcolm on the rock-strewn north shore and watched the small vessel depart. The wind whipped her face with strands of her hair and buffeted the boat like a leaf caught in a swirling eddy. High waves sloshed over the vessel's sides. MacLeod, a gnarled seaman of many years, had counseled against sailing, but the prince had ignored his entreaties. For Jamie's sake, Rory prayed they reached their destination. When the blackness swallowed the boat, she and Malcolm turned for home.

CHAPTER TWENTY-ONE
REPRISAL

Rory slammed the door shut, but Fergus remained mute. A tray of food sat untouched on the table. She clutched his chin with one hand while holding a shard from a looking glass to his face.

"'Tis a pitiable wretch ye are, Highlander, sitting on your arse while the rest of us hurry to pack. Ye disgrace both chief and clan. I have no time for ye to wallow in pity. I need a brawny warrior to help protect those we are sworn to defend."

He swung the stump of his right arm toward her. "Ye forget this!"

"Ye think ye are the first to suffer such a wound?"

"Leave me be. I am no good to anyone."

She gritted her teeth, grabbed a handful of oily flaxen hair, and dragged Fergus from his chair to the window. Once, she could not have budged his bulk, but the loss of his limb seemed to affect him as the cutting of hair had weakened Samson.

"Look ye below! Who do ye see?"

Fergus shut his eyes and clamped his mouth shut. She had expected this and pulled tighter on his hair while squeezing his nose. His eyes flew open. He glared.

"If ye want to breathe, answer!"

His defiance was fleeting. He slumped and looked at the man below. "'Tis Neil."

Rory released her hold. "And what is he doing?"

"Giving orders to the lads and lasses."

"What else?"

A gillie approached Neil from the woods. After a brief exchange of words, the runner ran off in a different direction.

"He collects information," Fergus said.

"Has he purpose for what he does?"

"Aye."

"How can he? He is a cripple who canna use his leg."

Fergus' anger flared like flame put to dry thatch. "'Tis his head he needs for doing, not his leg."

Rory softened her tone. "When Lochiel left, Neil hobbled through Maryburgh to glean wee bits of information. The soldiers did not guard their tongues while in his presence because he is a cripple. 'Tis strange how folk think that because one part of a man does not work, all parts of him are unusable. Since Neil did not let his legs hinder him, he saved unsuspecting folk from imprisonment or death. Now, he sees we take all we need into our remote fastnesses."

"Neil kens how to get others to do his bidding. 'Twas always so. I ken nocht but fighting, which I canna do anymore."

"Ye lost one arm, Fergus, not both. Ye can still wield a sword if ye will but relearn the skill."

He shook his head.

"It took stalwart stubbornness to reach home with your wound untended. Had ye wished to die, ye would have lain on the moor until soldiers bayoneted ye as they did the other wounded. I canna believe ye traveled so far to die from pitying yourself. With Jamie gone away with Prince Charles, I need a man who can wield a sword."

"I canna unsheathe a sword, Rory, and willna look the fool dragging one wherever I go."

"In days of yore, men carried sheathed swords on their backs and wielded the great weapon with two hands. Ye are a giant compared to other men and possess the strength of ten. Could ye not wield a great sword with one hand?"

"Of course!" A new brightness lit Fergus' hazel eyes, then faded. "The swords of old are gone."

"Wait ye." Rory stepped into the hall. She hefted the heavy object from where she had propped it against the wall. "I am sworn to protect the clan, but canna do so alone. I need a warrior who can wield the sword, listen with his ears, and see with his eyes. Ye are sworn to protect the clan chief, and if he is absent, then she who acts in his stead. Will ye protect me, Fergus, or will ye hold yourself within these walls until the soldiers hang ye?"

His gaze drifted back to Neil. She held her breath, wondering if her final insult had pricked his pride. Death by hanging was the ultimate degradation for a warrior. Had she stirred Fergus' anger enough to make him fight, and if so, had he energy left to fight for her?

"Your belief in me is great, Rory," he said, shaking his head. "If ye think cripples can help, then I will do your bidding."

"Then I bestow on ye what belonged to Allan, the sixteenth chief to lead the Camerons. Though outlawed for protecting clan and lands from powerful enemies, he coupled might with cunning to win pardon and peace. He would want a true warrior to wield his *claidheamh mór*." Rory offered Fergus the two-edged great sword. "I have work to attend to, so eat. When ye are washed and dressed, join me below."

~*~

Rory stood before the hearth, gazing up at the vacant library wall. Each day of the Rising, she had felt Ewen Dubh's penetrating gaze while she worked. Now, the portrait was gone, secreted away. Upon Sandy's recommendation, she had sent the more valuable papers and items to John of Fassifern for safekeeping.

"Did ye hear me, wildcat?" the priest asked.

She sighed and faced Sandy. "I heard. The whispers of the clans gathering to rise again spread like fire."

"Ye dinna sound pleased."

"Pleased, is it? With word that they will gather at Murlaggan and the garrison less than half a day's march from us? And if the rumors be true, how do ye expect me to feed them when we have not enough for our own? Every time the patrols strike, they reive cattle and burn stores."

"Jesus served five thousand with but two fish and five loaves, lass."

"Then I suggest ye pray for Him to grant us another miracle, Father Alex. If the clans ken the prince hides on the Isles, they will gather. I just dinna ken if there are enough left to raise the standard. Three hundred Camerons forfeited their lives at Drummossie Moor, and from what Fergus says, 'tis likely another two thousand Highlanders died there, too."

An incoherent babble filtered through the oaken door. Rory frowned, wondering what demanded her attention this time. She excused herself, and rubbing her forehead, stepped into the entrance hall.

Malcolm carried a scantily clad woman. Her hair had been roughly shorn close to her scalp and blood caked her limbs. A small lad of two or three years clung to Fergus' hand, while Neil herded three older lads.

A maidservant entered from the rear of the house. Her eyes fell to the woman in Malcolm's arms. She dropped her bundled linens, brought her hands up to ashen cheeks, and shrieked. "'Tis Mrs. Archie! 'Tis Mrs. Archie!"

Rory slapped the maidservant. The woman fell silent.

"Sorry, Rose," Rory said, "but the wee lads need us to be strong. Would ye help Neil and Fergus with them?"

The maidservant nodded. "Shall I feed them?"

"'Tis a grand idea. Some hot porridge, I think." Rory started to turn her attention to Mrs. Archie and Malcolm, then thought better of it. "Rose, may I borrow your *bréid?*"

The perplexed look on the older woman's face disappeared when Rory nodded toward Jean Cameron. Rose handed over the kertch. "Come, lads. Your mother is in good hands now."

After the boys left, Malcolm spoke. "I dinna mind holding Dr. Cameron's wife, but she is heavy. Shall I take her upstairs?"

"Aye. I must fetch my herbs." When Sandy started to follow, Rory caught his arm. "No, Father. 'Twould be best if ye visit with your nephews."

"But—"

"If my observations are true, Jean willna be wanting to see ye or any other man when she awakens."

"Think ye she was ravaged?"

"Aye, and from the looks of it more than once."

Sandy's fingers curled into tight fists. "Tell me what bloody bastards did this! I will avenge my brother's shame!"

"No! Ye are a man of God, not an avenging angel. Jean needs the peace ye find serving the Lord more than your anger."

Rory kept her other suspicion to herself, knowing if she gave voice to it, she would rile Sandy further. When he was calmer, she would tell him his youngest nephew was dead. Jean and Archie had five sons, but only four had arrived with their mother. Since the youngest was but a mere babe, Rory guessed the soldiers had either slain him or he died from cold and lack of nourishment.

Inside the room where Malcolm had placed Jean Cameron, Rory poured water into a bowl and washed the doctor's wife. Blackish blue marks covered her battered arms, thighs, breasts, and face. Rory rubbed oil made from Saint John's Wort over the bruises, then dressed Jean in a chemise left behind by Lady Anne. Rory tossed the water out the window, then poured another pitcher-full into the bowl. She washed what remained of Jean's hair with soapwort, then rinsed it with clean water.

"Ye have a gentle hand," Jean said. "'Tis many a year since someone has taken care of me."

Rory noted the woman spoke without inflection. She laid her hand over Jean's. "'Twas a nasty blow to your jaw, so 'twill hurt to chew. Would ye try some broth?"

Archie's wife gave a slight nod, which pleased Rory. Her face must have betrayed her relief at this slight evidence that Jean would not sink into the lethargy that had once claimed Fergus, for she spoke. "'Twill take time, but I will mend. I am peaceable, but can fight when 'tis necessary. I willna let the beasts who did this win. I still have a husband and sons to care for and love."

Rory wiped the tears that trickled down Jean's cheek. Someone rapped on the door.

"Come," she said.

Upon Malcolm's entry, Jean turned her gaze to the ceiling where Scriptures written in Latin adorned the plaster wash covering the timbers.

Malcolm studied the floor. Rory knew this was because cruel handling of their women angered men, but also embarrassed them. The attack was a daily reminder of their failure to protect those they held most dear. Malcolm handed over the broth, then departed.

Jean sipped small spoonfuls of the hot liquid.

When she finished, Rory poured heather ale into a small *cuach.* "Duncan's grandmother is a great believer in heather ale. She says it cures all ills. 'Tis also good for fortifying a body when they must speak of what they dinna wish to remember. I would not ask this of ye, but as chief I canna keep silent if I am to protect those under my care."

Jean regarded Rory for some time before her gaze returned to the ceiling. Perhaps the Holy Scriptures gave her solace and strength to relive the ordeal. Through quivering lips, she spoke. "Two days ago soldiers routed us from our beds, stole what they pleased—silver, jewels, weapons—then torched house, crops, and food stores. The lack of coin displeased the sergeant. He spoke at length of how wig makers pay dearly for human hair, then while he clinked gold from one hand to the other, his men hacked off our hair with their dirks.

"He penned our bairns into an old byre Archie meant to rebuild but never seemed to find the time to do. With lips curled in a sneer, the sergeant said the only sure way to stop Highlanders from rising again was to slay those who bred them. Being a fair man, though, he was willing to compromise. With a torch held to the byre's dry timbers, he offered us a choice: submit or watch our wee ones burn.

"One lass, not wed a year and just kirked, fled with her son hidden under her plaid. The soldiers cornered her as hounds do a fox, taunting her with bayonets while the sergeant snatched the babe by the leg and slammed him against the chimney stone. When the shrieking mother attacked the sergeant, his men stabbed her over and over again.

"When there was nocht left to amuse him, the sergeant rent my shift in two and threw me to the ground. After forcing himself on me, he laughed while his men used me. I must have swooned, for when I woke, the day was near done. We had not strength to bury the dead, so we gathered our bairns and walked here."

Rory felt anger roil like churning liquid in a hot cauldron. Jean's tale brought back memories of the attack on Mairi and her mother. Tears slid down her cheeks and dripped onto her palms. The salty drops stung. Blood from skin pierced by the fingernails of her clenched fists trickled down her palms to her wrists.

"'Twas so cold," Jean said, her voice low. "We had nocht to light a fire and only rags to clothe us. They left us no food, and I had no milk for my son. He died in my arms." Jean covered her face with her hands and sobbed.

Rory gathered the woman in her arms and rocked. When Jean quieted, Rory eased her back onto the pillows. "Drink this. 'Twill ease the pain and help ye sleep."

Rory lacked healing herbs to soothe Jean's heartache. The tea was but a balm for bruises and aches. Nothing but time would dull the memories.

~*~

"Ye ken what to do?" Rory asked, standing outside Achnacarry.

Neil rolled his eyes and heaved a sigh. He leaned on one crutch while lifting the other. "I have oft wondered if this would make a good switch, especially for women who plague men. What think ye, lads?"

Malcolm choked and turned away, but not before Rory saw the barest hint of a grin on his stoic face.

Fergus rubbed his bristly whiskers. "'Tis stout enough, but 'twould be of no use to ye after. She would fight like the wildcat she is, and if that did not snap the wood in two, her hard head would. Mayhap steel would be the better lash."

Neil roared with laughter. Rory crossed her arms and tapped her foot. She enjoyed hearing their laughter in these sorrowful times, even if it was at her expense.

"Ye made your point," she said. "I have two last requests before we take our leave."

Neil tucked the crutch under his arm, then eyed her suspiciously. "What would ye have me do now?"

"Have this package delivered to Nannag. Ye ken the corrie where she abides?"

He nodded.

"The gillie who brings it should ken to keep his mouth shut. If he fears capture, then he is to secret it away."

"'Twill be as ye say. And the other request?"

"I leave Midnight and Tam in your care. The soldiers must not find them."

"I remember a place we oft hid cattle when we returned from reiving. No one will find him unless ye wish it."

"Then we take our leave of ye. Remember, no one is to linger here. After what the red soldiers did to Mrs. Archie and the others, ye ken they will give no quarter."

He nodded again. Rory retrieved her longbow from Malcolm and slung it over her shoulder. Giving no warning of her intent, she kissed Neil's stubbly cheek.

He jerked his head back and stared. "What do ye think ye are doing?"

She winked, waved to Jean and her sons, then left with Malcolm and Fergus. For the next two weeks, she intended to survey Cameron lands to determine if the clan did her bidding and took refuge. She would also discover where and how many patrols occupied Lochaber.

Fergus suggested a circuitous route that took them to pockets settled by Camerons, as well as septs that gave Lochiel their allegiance: MacSorlies, MacMillans, Macphees, MacLachlans, MacMartins, Macgillonies, MacMasters, and Cummings. At each deserted *clachan,* Rory was struck by a sense of foreboding. She was not certain if the eerie silence that greeted them or the unnatural stillness that seemed to follow them from one village to the next caused her unease. On rare occasions they met pairs of men who watched for intruders or checked on the progress of planted crops. None reported contact with soldiers, but rumors circulated of sightings near MacOnie land. The dour faces of the men and suspicious gazes of the women sent chills down Rory's spine whenever she thought of her brief sojourns amongst them since Brandubh's birth.

"Do we press on or shall we rest?" Malcolm asked.

They should keep moving, but she was exhausted from the pace they kept. She also lacked the fortitude required to tangle with Douglas MacOnie, who being unwell at the start of the Rising had not joined Lochiel.

"We continue on the morrow," she said. "Ken ye a safe place to pass the night, Fergus?"

He did a slow survey of the mountainous terrain, pivoting until he faced a crag rising fifty feet above them. "Aye, Raven's Rock."

From what Rory could see the sheer rock face provided no foothold to reach the precipice.

"Have ye wings for us to reach it?" Malcolm asked with a sneer.

"No, but I ken the path. 'Tis reached from a cave hidden by bracken. Few ken of it, and once on top we can light a fire inside where none will see it. From the crag itself, we can spy on others without being seen."

Rory waved her hand. "Lead the way, Fergus."

Atop the precipice, she realized it encompassed a greater area than she had thought and was surrounded by a rampart of stones erected to resemble a natural formation. With the wall in front and the cave behind, the enclosure formed a ring and in its center rose a standing stone with five stylized figures cut into it. Three depicted animals—a raven soaring over intertwined wolves—while the other two were a comb and a spear. Rory felt certain the figures had relevance, but could only guess their meaning. The raven, a harbinger of death, implied the wolves' demise. The comb was a woman's tool, and the spear, a man's. Their close proximity to the wolves suggested the beasts represented male and female.

"What is this place?" she asked.

Fergus shrugged. "I dinna ken. I discovered Raven's Rock when I wandered into the cave as a wee lad."

After feasting on ptarmigan snared by Malcolm, Fergus offered to take the first watch. While Malcolm opted to keep him company, Rory wrapped her plaid around her and drifted off to sleep.

~*~

Rays of sparkling sunlight danced on the rippling water of a stream. A blackbird's fluty warble joined with the robin's mellifluous trill to serenade. Tortoiseshell butterflies darted from thistle to nettle. Red squirrels scampered down fissured trunks of ancient pines. Bushy-tailed pine martens leapt from stone to stone across the stream.

To the west appeared a flicker of red and a wisp of black. The contrasting colors inched toward the stream. Birds halted their songs. Insects ceased their chirps. Pine martens and squirrels became statues. Crackling filled the silent void, growing ever louder as the red flamed and the black billowed. The winged creatures took flight while legged ones scurried away.

The acrid smoke lingered in the heated air. The stream sizzled with soot and ash. From above, a shaft of light illuminated a raven blacker than night, circling higher and higher. Just as it reached the light an arc of bluish gray struck the raven. It plummeted into the water. The ululant baying of a hound and the piercing shriek of the banshee echoed through the dead forest.

Rory woke with a start. She struggled from the plaid that had become tangled around her during the dream.

"What is it, lass?" Malcolm asked.

"No time to explain. We leave now."

Fergus groaned and rubbed his eyes. "'Tis sleep I am needing. Why canna we wait for the dawn?"

"There is no time to waste. It may already be too late!" She gathered her weapons and hastened down the sloping path into the cave, ignoring the frantic calls of her brother and friend. The dream had left her with a sense of urgency that would not dissipate. She felt her way through the unfamiliar passageway, relying on her keen sense of direction to reach the glen below. Curses and shouts trailed her, but she welcomed the growled utterances, assured that Malcolm and Fergus followed.

They headed east until they reached the base of Sgurr Thuilm, at which point they turned south, paralleling the border between Cameron land and that of Clanranald. They followed the water of Dubh Lighe halfway to a glen that bore the same name. At a small cairn, they turned west along the tributary that led to the MacOnie *clachan*.

Silence—oppressive and profound—stopped Rory. It enveloped the land as a shroud wrapped around a corpse. No leaves rustled. No insects hummed. No birds warbled. No animals chattered. No children shrieked with laughter. Malcolm and Fergus cast wary glances in every direction. A shiver of dread chilled Rory. Unwilling to go farther, but having no other choice, she crept forward. Her companions followed, their swords drawn.

Had the dour-faced, suspicious inhabitants of the *clachan* greeted her, she would have rejoiced. Instead, she bowed her head and made the sign of the cross. Wisps of smoke curled from the charred remnants of once-thatched hovels. The stench of rotting carcasses mingled with the odor from bloated corpses. Black corbies, perched on singed timbers and blackened stones, ruffled their feathers. Rory squatted near a wooden-framed animal hide still adorned with rowan branches. These simple people had feared the unknown and the unexplained, but neither had slaughtered them. Rather their countrymen, royal Lowlander and Highlander alike, had done this foul deed in the name of the King and by order of his son, the Duke of Cumberland. Another name came to mind—one more appropriate to the carnage before her—*Butcher.*

In one swoop their lives had been extinguished. Never more would young Gerald collect oatcakes as a Beltane offering to the birds and beasts. The women would no longer gather to wash clothes at the stream. The old woman would accuse no one else of witchery. Timid Morna would never again cradle her raven-haired son or sing him to sleep with gentle lullabies.

"Over here!" Malcolm's shout halted Rory's tears.

He knelt beside a man who clung to life. His legs were broken in several places. Stab wounds pierced his body. Blisters festered on his pockmarked face. Rory choked back bile.

"Douglas?"

Morna's father turned lidless eyes on her. "The lass with a royal hound." He croaked the words.

She would rather have heard his snarl.

"Saved once. Save again." His labored words perplexed her.

She had not the power to save him. His wounds were fatal. That he still breathed was a miracle.

"Saved once. Save again."

His plea ripped her heart. Tears poured down her cheeks. A warm hand patted her shoulder.

"Ye canna save him, Rory," Fergus said.

"I ken."

"Noooo!" The strangled word from Douglas' parched throat echoed in the stillness.

She stared at him, not comprehending.

"'Tis not himself he wants saved, lass. Is there another ye helped before?" Malcolm asked.

A ray of hope warmed the coldness in Rory's heart.

"Morna and Brandubh." She stared at Douglas. "Are they the ones who need saving?"

"Stream." The single word escaped his lips with his dying breath. He had survived long enough to deliver his message, then surrendered himself into God's keeping.

Rory pondered the single clue. The stream ran the length of the glen. Where to start the search? The wash! Perhaps that was the place to start. She grabbed her bow and ran for the water.

Women, young and old, had fallen where they worked. The old woman who had accused her of witchery lay sprawled on the stones, clutching a piece of cloth. The torn skirt of another covered the face of one cruelly used by savage brutes. When Rory straightened her clothes, she recognized Meg, the red-haired lass with freckles who had fetched her medicines during the crying last summer.

"No!" Rory fell to her knees, sobbing.

"*Dia!*" Fergus' whispered cry to God sounded like a shout. Malcolm made the sign of the cross, and knelt beside Rory.

"'Tis not fair! She was innocent!"

He pulled her into his arms. "There is nocht fair in this life, lass. Ye ken that better than most."

"Why did I not come here first, Malcolm? I felt something was not right. I could have prevented this."

"No!" Fergus' vehement denial made Rory look at him. "Ye warned the clan of danger. MacOnie lived by the old ways. He ever thought himself wiser than a woman, and 'twas pride that kept him from heeding the runner's warning. Ye canna blame yourself for his daftness. These deaths are on his head, not yours."

"Mayhap 'tis why he wanted to save his daughter," Malcolm said, nodding toward Meg's body.

Rory shook her head. "She is not Morna."

The two men exchanged looks, and then Malcolm lifted Rory's chin. "Ye are chief, sister. 'Tis a great responsibility and at times a chief has no pleasure in doing what must be done. Only ye kent Morna. Only ye can find her."

Rory swallowed and brushed away her tears. Her brother helped her to her feet. She walked among the dead, whispering a prayer for their departed souls. She found her friend's crumpled body near a tree.

"'Tis her?" Malcolm asked.

She nodded, biting her lips to stem more tears.

"Did ye hear something?" Fergus asked.

"Soldiers?"

Fergus shook his head in answer to Malcolm's question. "A soft cry, like that of a kitten."

They held their breath and listened. The whimpering, low and mournful, was barely audible.

"It comes from her," Fergus said, pointing to Morna's body.

"But she is dead," Malcolm said.

Rory's eyes grew wide. "Quick, turn her over."

The men frowned, but obeyed.

The whimpering came again, louder than before. Rory carefully slit the plaid Morna wore, then sheathed her dirk and pulled apart the wool. Hidden within lay Brandubh. She cradled him in her arms. The raven-haired lad wailed, filling his lungs with air.

"'Tis a miracle!" Fergus and Malcolm exclaimed.

Rory did not hear them. Her eyes were drawn to the blood-soaked stone on the far bank of the stream. There sat Bean-nighe, washing linen shirts and singing a dirge. A raven took flight behind her. The higher it flew, the dimmer it grew until the sunlight absorbed its darkness.

Rory understood. When she had seen the Fairy Washerwoman before, Bean-nighe had foretold the deaths of the MacOnies, not those who followed Prince Charles. The soaring raven on the standing stone had triggered the dream that warned of danger to Brandubh. Had Rory ignored the vision, the babe she held would be dead.

"Aye," she said, "'tis a miracle!"

~*~

Seated before the hearth, Nannag tapped her foot against the rocker of the hooded cradle that her husband had carved for their son, Duncan's father. Lulled by the gentle sway, Brandubh slept with one fist curled at his mouth. The peaceful scene stirred Rory's heart, quieting the horrors of previous days.

Duncan's grandmother set aside her sewing and patted the empty space beside her. "What troubles ye, Granddaughter?"

"He willna ever ken his parents."

Nannag clucked. "And was it so with yourself?"

Rory frowned. "I kent my parents."

"Duncan said ye lost your mother when ye were a wee lass. Ye canna have many memories of her."

"But I do. She scolded when I disobeyed, but hugged when I brought her flowers. When I was sick, she put honey on my porridge. She combed my hair before bed every night, and told fantastic tales of fairies and dragons, of monsters and selkies."

"How do ye remember this?"

"Father told me."

Nannag smiled. "Then ye ken your mother because your father wished it. Dinna ye think ye and Duncan will speak to Brandubh of his parents?"

"Aye, we will."

"And his sorrow will dim with a house full of brothers and sisters."

Brandubh cooed in his sleep. Rory leaned over to rub his back. In less than a sennight he had stolen her heart. She loved him as she would a child of her own.

She sighed. "Those he may never have."

"Och, Rory! Ye must believe Duncan will come home, else he will die."

"Of course he will come home!" She clasped his grandmother's hand to reassure her. "Ye mistake my meaning."

"Ye are strong and healthy, Granddaughter. Ye will bear Duncan bonny sons and daughters."

Rory stirred the peat ash in the hearth with the iron tongs Duncan had given her when he had first brought her here. Tears burned her eyes. "Not until I can say I love him."

"So that is the way of it. Why ever would ye think ye dinna love my grandson?"

"'Tis what I want, but I canna tell him the words. Without the words, we willna…"

"Ye must only speak the words, Granddaughter."

"He will ken the lie for what 'tis."

"'Tis not a lie. Ye do love Duncan."

"How can ye ken that when I dinna ken it myself?"

Nannag sat back, amazement showing on her face. With a shake of her head, she retrieved from a kist a package wrapped in plaid and placed it in Rory's hands. "Sit yourself on the *clach an t'seabhdail* and ponder what is in your heart. Folk often wed for reasons other than love what with fathers having the say, but there are times when love comes after vows are said. Ken ye no husband and wife who love each other?"

Rory gave a hesitant nod.

"Then think on the why of it. When ye have your answer, open this. Then ye will ken the truth of what is in your heart."

Duncan's grandmother pushed Rory toward the door. She doubted pondering the older woman's words would render an answer, but she needed to calm her warring spirit. Perhaps thoughts of Duncan would wash away the death and rapine that seemed to absorb more of her waking hours each day.

Streaks of golden sunrays cast the long shadows of eventide. A gentle breeze rustled the leaves, dispelling the day's heat. Cool moss cushioned the stone's hard surface. Rory leaned her head against the cottage and cleared her mind of all thoughts except those of her husband.

Mo chridhe. My heart. Two simple words. Why could she not tell Duncan what he longed to hear? She swallowed the tears that filled her eyes. She yearned to feel as he did. Why could she not do so?

Ken ye no husband and wife who love each other?

Aye, Iain MacGregor. Even before her uncle left for the sea, he preferred to flirt with the lasses. None caught his fancy, and he often boasted of retaining freedom others lost on their wedding day. His travels frequently took him to France, and after becoming master of his own ship, he conducted his business with one particular merchant. One day the man fell ill, and having no sons, he sent his daughter in his place. Bold and brazen like Iain, Bernadette argued and cajoled until he acceded to her prices. Her ability to best him so intrigued Iain that, whenever he put into port, he insisted she arrange the trade rather than her father. Pleased with the profit his daughter brought him, the merchant agreed to the Scotsman's strange request.

With each encounter, Bernadette's haggling improved until Iain made little profit. Unable to distract her with pretty words, he chose another tact. On his next visit, he strode into her father's shop with his arms loaded with riches. Bernadette named a price, but he refused. The negotiations grew heated, and when she could not budge him, she cursed his stubbornness and turned from him. He spun her around and kissed her. When her father questioned her on the profit she had made for him, she informed him there was none. She had accepted Iain's terms without haggling. Astounded, her father demanded she tell him why. *He finally kissed me, Papa.*

Iain and Bernadette married with her father's blessing, but she refused to be a proper sailor's wife and wait for him ashore. She sailed with him, and any superstitious crewman who objected was given leave to find another berth. Spending every day together in a confined space inevitably led to fierce argy-bargies between Iain and Bernadette, but their love flourished and their happiness enveloped all who sailed with them.

Whether they followed or defied tradition, each thought of the other first. They valued one another's opinions without resenting the intrusion. They trusted one another. They cherished each other. They laughed. They teased. They argued, but always tempered their ire with tenderness and affection. They claimed friendship soothed the storms that pounded their marriage. Rather than speak in anger, they separated until the gale ebbed and they could solve the problem without hurting each other.

If these traits signified love, Rory wondered if they existed between Duncan and her. From the first, he had not wished to compromise her. Their friendship had begun while she nursed his wounds, but was strengthened the day of the horse races. She cherished memories of precious gifts exchanged and an evocative dance gamboled. He kept her secrets close to his heart, and heeded her warnings rather than ridiculing and dismissing them.

Though a fierce warrior, Duncan was a tender man. He tickled her ear with his warm breath and stirred tingles when he stroked her. He cradled her in his plaid, offering comfort, warmth, and safety. He wiped away her tears and calmed the terror left by her visions. Twice, without thought to his well being, he saved her life. He wed without her love, then wooed her with devotion. He declared before others that she was his equal.

Tears spilled from Rory's eyes. Without him she was not whole. She ached to feel his calloused fingers on her lips, her flesh. She yearned to see his crooked nose and brush acorn curls from his brow. She wanted to smell him, to feel him, to hold him.

Her hand fell on the plaid Nannag had given her. Its hues of purple and blue matched the hue of Duncan's eyes and hers. Wrapped within the wool were the folded garments that belonged to Thistle. Cradled within their folds was the love *cuach* that still held the velvety petals of Duncan's rose sent in answer to her letter. What had she written to make him believe its words kept him alive? She closed her eyes and tried to remember.

Love.

She blinked!

Yes, she had written "love, Rory." Gregor Glùn Dhubh had said she must accept Duncan with both head and heart. Nannag had told her she loved Duncan. While her head hesitated, her heart had settled.

"Och, Duncan! Hurry home, *mo chridhe*. My heart."

~*~

"Ye must go, Granddaughter?" Nannag asked, sitting down on the wanderer's stone.

Rory laid a reassuring hand on the old woman's shoulder. "I willna be gone long."

"What of the danger?"

"Fergus goes with me. Malcolm stays to watch over ye and Brandubh. Grandmother, I would stay if I could, but am bound by duty. I must confer with Father Alex and see that all heeded my orders. No one is safe, but at least the shielings and caves provide more protection than staying below."

"What did ye call me, Rory?"

"Grandmother. Dinna ye wish me to call ye as Duncan does?"

Nannag clutched her heart. "'Tis been my fondest wish since we first met. Whatever changed your mind?"

"I love him."

With a wink and a smile, Rory hurried to meet Fergus. They kept to the woods, keeping close watch on the journey south. The corrie had offered a peaceful respite, but its safe haven was an illusion. Soldiers patrolled in ever increasing numbers. While some were Sassenach, most hailed from the Lowlands, and Rory had come to realize that these men were to be more feared than the others. They employed the Duke of Cumberland's edict of no quarter given with ruthless rancor.

"Ye are humming."

She glanced at Fergus. "What?"

"I said ye are humming."

"I am?"

"Aye, Rory."

"Sorry."

"There is no need to apologize unless the enemy hears ye."

He fell silent, and she continued to edge her way through the thick grove of trees. Her eyes searched for any sign of danger. A streak of gray flashed through the pines ahead, and then Tam emerged from the thicket. The hound insinuated itself betwixt Fergus and herself.

"Have ye a reason for humming?" he asked.

Rory smiled. "The best in the world."

"And that would be?"

"I love Duncan!"

Fergus laughed. "'Tis not news to me. I dinna think 'twill be news to Duncan either."

Tam rushed up the hill ahead of them. The rocky boulders made climbing difficult for Fergus, so Rory gave a helping hand when necessary. Emerald green grass, knee-high in length, waved in the breeze.

Tam growled. Rory walked toward the hound, while he began backing toward her. His snarl turned to a whine.

"What does he ken?" Fergus asked.

She shrugged. "I have never seen him act like this before."

Fergus shielded his eyes and scanned the treetops. "There!"

Thick black smoke darkened the blue sky. Without thinking, she broke into a run. "Achnacarry!"

"Rory, wait!"

Just before she reached the crest that overlooked the house, Fergus slammed into her. As they tumbled, he grabbed her waist and twisted so she landed on top. While taking deep breaths, she thanked God for Fergus' quick thinking. Had he fallen on her, he would have crushed her. She started to rise, but he held fast.

"Have ye taken leave of your senses?" he asked. "What if the fire was set?"

Her only thought had been of Father Alex. Fergus' question made her realize how much she endangered them. She rolled to her right and crept forward. Below, soldiers swarmed over the grounds, trampling the beech saplings Lochiel had planted and wreaking havoc with his prized fruit garden. Plundered silver, weapons, and other items of value were heaped in a cart. The wind fanned the red-hot flames until all that remained of Achnacarry were the stone gables.

"Give him the lash!" The order, shouted over the fire's roar, came from an officer sitting a white horse.

The crack of a whip echoed so loudly that Rory thought it came from behind. She started to look back, then froze on spotting white against the brown trunk and green leaves of a sycamore. Father Alex stood with his arms bound to a branch above his head. His shirt hung in tatters at his waist. A streak of red crossed his bare back.

"N—"

Rory clamped her hand over Fergus' mouth, stifling his cry. She leaned close and whispered in his ear. "There is nocht we can do. If ye go to his aid, ye will be giving them a new weapon to wield against him. The lashing willna loosen his tongue to betray Lochiel, but making him watch the torture and slaying of ye may. Would ye have his brother's blood on his hands?"

She did not waver under Fergus' piercing glare. He hid neither his anger nor his loathing, and she accepted them with reluctant understanding. She would be the first to go to Sandy's aid, if she thought the effort had any chance of success. They were but two, however, and no match for the soldiers.

"I would gladly give my life for Father Alex's, but am responsible for all Camerons, and dare not risk them to save but one."

Fergus squeezed his eyes shut and gave a curt nod. He took himself away from the horror below. Rory cringed with each crack of the whip.

Her body and mind screamed for vengeance, but she gritted her teeth and forced herself to watch in penance for sacrificing a friend. On the seventh lash, Sandy vented his pain. Amidst his screams, he begged God to forgive his attackers.

~*~

Rory awoke in darkness. A gentle breeze blew, and she smelled charred wood. The brutality she had witnessed came back to her, and she brushed unbidden tears from her cheeks with the back of her hands.

"Is he dead?" Fergus' whispered words sounded loud in the dark.

"No," she said, "but 'twould have been a kindness had they killed him."

"How can ye say that? As long as he lives, there is hope we can rescue him."

"I heard them say he is bound for the prison ship anchored in Loch Linnhe. He will lie in the black hold where rats and vermin thrive. If they dinna tend his wounds, he will sicken and die. 'Tis not an honorable death, not even for a priest."

CHAPTER TWENTY-TWO
SACRIFICE

Rory stared into the dense mist that clung to the hilltops surrounding the cottage. A chill smirr of rain dampened everything. The rare cooling in mid-August made her think of icy winds, snow-choked passes, and frozen ponds. This *Samhein,* which would be in about two months time, would not find folk driving the cattle down to winter pastures. They would bide the winter in summer shielings or caves rather than risk the perils wrought by soldiers.

"'Tis a serious face sister wears, is it not?" Malcolm asked.

Taken unaware, Rory kicked the milk pail, but righted it before spilling more than a few drams in the hollowed out center of a stone. She put a hand to her chest and felt the rapid beating of her heart.

"'Tis lucky ye are, Malcolm MacGregor," she said, raising her fist, "not to be facing Nannag's wrath for spilling the share for the *gruagach.* Herself would never give ye peace had it splattered the ground rather than filled the brownie's stone."

"Since they got their wee offering, they will keep watch over the cow."

Surprised anew by the unexpected voice, Rory flung herself into Jamie's open arms. He hugged her close.

"Think she is happy to see me returned, brother?"

"Aye," Malcolm said, "but I think I will take what is left of the milk to Nannag else there will be nocht to feed the babe."

"Babe?" Jamie asked. "What babe?"

"My son," Rory said.

It was Jamie's turn to show surprise. He held her at arm's length. "Your son? I was not gone that long."

"Four months! I expected ye before now."

He shrugged. "I would love to tell of my travels and hear how ye came to have a son, but 'tis over long since I saw my family. Surely, ye understand my heart longs to see Sàra and our bairns."

"Go and take our brother with ye. 'Tis time he visited his own family. Fergus and I will visit on the morrow."

~*~

"Aunt Rory!" A freckle-faced lad of seven plowed through Camerons and MacGregors alike.

Rory braced herself for her nephew's impact. When he flung his arms around her legs, she tousled his reddish curls. "'Tis good to see ye too, Conn. Ye look more like your father each time I see ye."

He beamed at the compliment, as she knew he would. He worshipped Malcolm whom he strove to imitate, much to his mother's chagrin. His father enjoyed wrestling, and in an effort to follow in his footsteps, Connor often challenged other boys to matches. Unfortunately, most were older and stronger, and Fiona was left to patch up their handiwork.

"Ye are just in time to hear Uncle Jamie tell of Prince Charles wearing a dress!" Conn pulled Rory by the hand toward the loch.

"A dress, is it?" she said. "Why ever would he be doing that?"

"Ye will have to listen to the whole of it," Jamie said, "before ye get an answer." He sat on a stone surrounded by his son and daughter, nephews and nieces, and neighboring lads and lasses.

Connor pushed his way through gathered parents eager to hear Jamie's tale, until he reached his uncle's feet. Fergus remained on the fringe, his eyes alert for danger.

"Ye must forgive my sister," Jamie said, apologizing to his audience. "Rory is like a wee one when there is a story to be told. She prefers sitting on the teller's lap, but since my own daughter has that privilege, she must content herself with my feet."

Peals of laughter rang through the crowd. The merry sound was a boon to Rory's heart. Too long a time had passed since Jamie had teased her, and it brought back memories of happier times. The joyousness lightened the sadness in her heart.

"We ken ye love to hear yourself talk, Jamie, but the bairns are soon to their beds," his wife said.

A collective chorus of youthful groans greeted Sàra's comment.

"So, husband, if ye want to be getting on with your tale, 'twill be most appreciated."

Jamie winked. "Since the day we wed, love, ever have I granted your wishes."

Several loud smirks issued forth from the women. Sàra shook her head, and smiled.

"Now, what was that story ye were wanting to hear?" Jamie scratched his head. His daughter whispered in his ear. "The prince in a dress, is it? Are ye certain, precious?"

A head of tawny curls bobbed. Jamie tweaked her nose and began his tale. "When I left Aunt Rory and Uncle Malcolm on the stony shores of Loch nan Uamh, there were thirteen of us, an unlucky number to be sure. Though 'twas two nights after the fullness of the moon, ye could not see farther than the length of your arm. Soon after we put to sea, the winds began to howl. Thunder crashed and lightning flashed. Such rain fell that I could not see the man in front of me. The poor boat was tossed hither and yon, and we prayed for deliverance. By God's grace we survived, and for two months sailed from isle to isle.

"Throughout our journey, soldiers searched for His Royal Highness, but no Scot aided them. While on South Uist, we met Neil MacEachain, a schoolmaster. He led us over the moor to visit someone who could help us reach the Isle of Skye.

"Flora MacDonald welcomed us with a *cuach* of cream. A sensible lass, she declined to help us. After all, her stepfather was captain of the militia and 'twas dangerous to aid any rebel. Prince Charles held her lovely hand, and told her he kent she was a loyal subject who would never betray the Stewart cause. ''Twill be a grand adventure,' he said, 'and ye will be remembered as the angel who defied a king to save her prince.' What could Mistress Flora do but agree to help? She promised to sail with us to Skye where her mother would hide us, but until all was ready we must fend for ourselves.

"When she sent word, we kent where to meet, but getting there was no wee matter. While I hid in the rocks with the prince, Neil searched for a boat. We expected him to return before the day ended, but he never came. The next morning I was setting off to find him when he scurried over the brae. Soldiers had arrested him. He would still be in gaol had Mistress Flora's stepfather, the captain, not arrived that morning and sent him on his way.

"Fearing 'twas no longer safe to abide on Uist, we hastened to the boat. The rowers took us to another isle, but since 'twas dark when we waded ashore, we waited for the dawn before continuing our trek. What a woeful sight greeted us! The isle we sought was not where we stood. We were on a wee one across the water and nocht lived on this place. Neil offered to swim over for another boat, but thought it best to wait until the tide ebbed. 'Twas a wise decision indeed because when the water ran back to the sea, a sand bridge between the two isles remained.

"We waded around sea lochans and trudged through peat bogs to reach the meeting place. All the while the wind lashed us with rain. 'Twas midnight before we arrived, and to our horror, we found not

Mistress Flora but soldiers at the bothy. We hastened away to another where the good wife fed us and gave us a place to rest.

"She woke us before dawn when the soldiers came to fetch their milk. We waited in the rain, getting soaked to our skin. After the storm, the midges came. The wee beasties swarmed around us, and for three hours we endured their biting. I dinna ken how Mistress Flora found us, but she came that night when 'twas decided we would travel as her companions. Since I kent our tongue and the prince did not, I became her servant. The prince played her maid, Betty Burke. Mistress Flora told him to shed his clothes, excepting his breeches. Then she dressed him in petticoats over which she pulled a calico gown. She covered his red hair with a cap, then handed him stockings and shoes.

"'Hand me my pistol,' he said to myself, but Mistress Flora stayed my hand. 'What use have ye for such a weapon?' she asked. 'To defend myself,' he said. She shook her head. 'No pistols in your petticoats! If ye are searched, 'twill give ye away.' 'If I am searched, Mistress,' he said, 'I will be discovered anyway.' She allowed that was true, but would not allow him the pistol.

"When all was ready, she took us to the boat. The water was calm and no wind stirred. While we rowed, the prince entertained us with song. Suddenly, rain and wind came from the west. With waves washing over the boat, we abandoned the oars to bail the water. Without steering or compass, the wind blew us where it would.

"When the mist of early morning faded, we offered thanks to God for seeing us safely to the Isle of Skye. Once ashore, Mistress Flora decided she should travel on alone, while we waited for word 'twas safe to come. What we did not ken was that soldiers had also come to the isle, and at that moment their commander was having tea with Mistress Flora's mother. Och, but that is a tale for another evening."

"More! More!" the children shouted.

Jamie shook his head. "Off to bed with ye!"

"'Tis not fair!" Connor said under his breath.

Rory leaned close to whisper. "I would not be saying those words too loud, Conn, else 'tis a lesson your father will be teaching ye."

Connor's hand went to his backside. He scrunched up his face. "Life is not fair, and I had best learn it now."

She smiled. "He has taught the lesson before?"

"Aye."

"More than once, I am thinking."

Her nephew nodded.

"Off with ye, then."

Connor scurried away. Halfway to the cottage, he whirled around and raced back to her. He wrapped his arms around her neck and whispered, "Thank ye, Aunt Rory," then off he went to bed.

She waited until the circle dwindled to herself, Jamie, Malcolm, and Fergus. She leaned back on her hands. "'Tis time for the real telling, Jamie."

"I dinna think ye want to hear it."

The simple sentence confirmed her suspicions. "He has come back."

"Who?" Malcolm asked. "Cease your riddles, and speak plain!"

"I think Rory refers to the prince," Fergus said.

Jamie nodded.

"Where is he?" she asked.

"In the Dark Mile near Achnacarry."

"Why does he return?"

"He waits for Dr. Archie."

"How long?"

"Within a sennight."

~*~

A thin wisp of smoke curled skyward from a hole in the cottage's thatched roof. Rory scowled. "Fools the lot!"

Fergus scolded her. "He is the prince, Rory! Ye should not be speaking of him like that."

Malcolm grunted. "'Tis certain ye dinna ken my sister well at all."

"Aye," Jamie said. "She is not one to hold her tongue."

"Whist!" A distant sound had reached her ears. She put a finger to her lips. "Listen!"

At first there was silence, then the clatter came again. Although muffled by the thick undergrowth, the sound drew closer. She knew what made the din—the clanging together of light swords, kits, and canteens.

"Red soldiers!"

"Aye, Fergus," she said. "There is no time to waste. They canna find the prince."

"We must hurry if we dinna want to risk capture," Jamie said.

Rory shook her head. Already, she could hear the soldiers' voices but not their words. "Ye three must take the prince and his companions to Tòrr a' Mhuilt."

"And what will ye be doing?" Malcolm asked, suspicion furrowing his brow.

"Diverting the soldiers."

Fergus gasped. "Dinna ye ken what they will do to ye?"

She knew, but her first responsibility was to the clan. If the prince were discovered on Cameron land, it would portend a worsening of the reprisals.

"We have no other choice. While one leads him to the new hiding place, the other two must protect his rear. If I fail, they will follow ye."

"I canna go, Rory. I am bound to defend ye."

"Aye, Fergus, but ye also gave your bond to heed any order given by your chief. If ye attempt the diversion, the soldiers will ken your motives. While there is danger in what I intend, there is no other way to see the prince to safety."

"But—"

Malcolm laid a hand on Fergus' arm. "She is right, though I dinna like it any better than yourself. The sooner we see to our task, the less we endanger Rory."

Fergus stared at her. She sensed his indecision, but he followed her brothers down the hill. He looked back once, then hastened to catch up with them.

Rory headed in the opposite direction. She found the soldiers near the charred ruins of Achnacarry. She hid her weapons in the hollow of an oak. The Crown had ordered all Highlanders to disarm, and if the soldiers found her otherwise, they would arrest her. Once chained, she would never escape.

She counted ten men, one of whom—a sergeant, perhaps—appeared to be in command. A scar lanced his face from his left cheek through both lips to his right jaw, giving his features a permanent snarl. He had the stocky build associated with a sailor, and his shovel-like hand curled around a musket. The buff-colored facings of his red woolen coat were worn and stained. Mud speckled his gaiters.

Neither he nor his companions possessed the army's spit and polish, so Rory assumed they were Vestry men, Lowland caterans forced to enlist after the Rising began. They lacked discipline and were often flogged for their misconduct. The cruel lash of the cat-o'-nine-tails could turn the punished into a sadistic soldier bent on making others suffer similar pain.

The sergeant barked an order for his men to reassemble. Rory dared not delay any longer. She whispered a short prayer, then asked for Duncan's forgiveness. She slipped through the trees to get ahead of them. When the first man rounded the bend, she crossed the track in front of him.

"Halt!" he shouted.

There was no turning from her course now that they had seen her. She darted into the woods, drawing them from the path that led to the prince's hovel. Her pursuers crashed through the undergrowth. She heard a musket's report, and a ball whistled past her ear. She tripped over the gnarled root of an ancient pine. Her first instinct was to fling out her arms to break the fall, but instead, she landed on her side and rolled, tangling the plaid around her legs. By the time she regained her footing, bayonets ringed her.

The pounding of her heart filled her ears. She gasped for breath. The soldiers jeered and taunted, prodding her with their muskets. She felt like a cornered doe hunted by hounds. With a lecherous gleam lighting his beady eyes, the sergeant ran his tongue over thick lips. Fear uncurled its sleeping tendrils in the pit of her stomach. She stifled the scream that crept into her throat, and took a step back. A sharp stab stopped her retreat.

The sergent laughed, a guttural squawk laced with menace. "A lucky day, lads. Another whore to share."

"Fairer than the last!" one soldier said.

"More meat, too!" another added.

The lewd comments drew collective laughter from the men. The sergeant wrenched Rory's arm behind her and swung her around to face the circle of men. He grabbed a fistful of hair, twisting it until flickering lights danced before her eyes. She struggled, but he twisted her arm higher. She cried out and grew still, afraid he would break the bone if she continued to fight.

He put his lips against her ear. Stale whisky and rotten fish smells assailed her. "A bit of fun first? Savor the wares before we buy?"

A chorus of "ayes" greeted the suggestion. The men set aside their muskets, then closed in on her. The sergeant released her into their clutches. They smacked their lips. Two hands grabbed her from behind, while the man facing her squeezed her breasts. His tongue hung from his mouth. His eyes glazed with feverish anticipation. The man holding her shoved her into the hands of another. They passed her around—pawing, prodding, fondling—until her sleeve ripped. Someone raised the trophy high. His companions cheered, and someone pushed her into him. He crushed his lips to hers, and his slimy tongue invaded her mouth.

Someone tugged the belt encircling her waist. The leather tightened, driving the breath from her lungs. Another tug and the belt fell. They tore the fold of her plaid from her shoulder, then passed her round the circle, unwinding the wool. A hand shoved the hem of her shift up her leg. Rough fingers pushed between her thighs. She reared back and kneed the beast. He doubled over, howling his pain.

"Seize her!" the sergeant ordered.

Step by deliberate step, he advanced. She shrank from the venomous hatred in his eyes. The ragged scar pulsed with anger. He smashed downward across her face with the back of his hand. The blow knocked her free of his men's grasp. She fell to the ground, dazed. Blood trickled from her lip. Her right eye began to swell shut.

He kicked her. Tears stung her eyes. She curled into a ball. He shouted. Men pinned her arms above her head. Stones jabbed her back. Pine needles pricked her flesh. The sergeant flung aside his coat, then kneed apart her legs while fumbling with his breeches.

"That is enough!" The cocking of a pistol punctuated the command. "Step away from her!"

The soldiers backed away, their steps slow and measured. The sergeant scrambled to his feet.

The man aimed his pistol at the undressed sergeant. "Ye are out of uniform!"

"We was just having some fun. No harm done, sir."

"I warned ye of the consequences if this happened again. Arrest him, Corporal!"

The corporeal remained still.

"Now, or ye will also be flogged!"

The corporal disarmed the sergeant.

"Take him to the garrison, and be quick about it!" the man with the pistol commanded.

Unable to focus her eyes, Rory listened to their hasty departure. She did not know who had stopped the assault, but knew her guardian angel must be an officer, for Highlanders would have slain the soldiers. The creak of leather warned that he dismounted. The rustling of cloth reached her ears. He meant to finish what his men had started in spite of the commands he had given. A sound, halfway between a moan and a whimper, escaped her lips.

She listened to his approaching footsteps with dread. When they halted, she waited, but he came no closer. She peered at him with her good eye. He stood with his back to her, holding out a white cloth. She reached for it, but searing pain stopped her. She sucked in air, but that too hurt. With tears slipping from her eyes, she clenched her teeth until the spasm faded. "I canna reach it."

He whirled. "Ye speak English!"

He handed her the material. It was a shirt, and she realized he wore none. She clutched the linen to her, and wept.

He muttered a curse. "Shall I help ye?"

She nodded, and he took the shirt. Somehow, he clothed her without causing much pain. He gently held her chin to examine her battered face. He drew a sharp breath. "Mistress Rory!"

How could a soldier know her name?

"'Tis I, Captain Scott. John Scott. Dinna ye remember tending my wounds before seeing me to Fort William?"

A year had passed since then, yet he had not forgotten her kindness.

"I remember," she said, her teeth clattering.

"Ye need whisky."

The tiredness crept over her without warning. She let her eye close while he rummaged through his haversack. She heard a whoosh, but each painful breath, each vexatious movement clouded her thinking. When the sound's meaning registered she jerked up her head. Two men rushed from the trees. One drew forth a great sword from behind his head. He swung, intending to cleave the captain's head from his shoulders.

"Noooo!" she screamed.

Fergus attempted to halt his swing, but the momentum propelled him forward. Scott ducked and rolled, thudding into two feet. Malcolm's blade pressed Scott's throat.

"No!" Rory tried to stand, but pain blinded her. Fergus eased her back to the ground. She dug her fingernails into his arm. "Stop Malcolm!"

"Lass, let him do what needs doing."

"He is a friend!"

"Friends dinna attack friends."

"He stopped the soldiers!"

"Malcolm, hold!" Fergus said.

"Why?"

"She claims him friend."

Malcolm snorted. "He is a soldier!"

"Aye, but she says he stopped the beasts."

Malcolm sheathed his sword and offered his hand. Scott, rubbing his throat, looked at it dubiously.

Malcolm stiffened. "If ye helped my sister, then I thank ye for it."

Scott accepted the proffered hand. When he regained his feet, he said, "I was about to give Mistress Rory whisky. May I proceed?"

Malcolm nodded.

The captain handed her the flask, but when she attempted to drink, her hands shook. Amber liquid trickled down her chin.

Fergus took the whisky from her. "Open your mouth, lass."

The whisky burned, but its warm potency numbed the chill seeping through her limbs. She sagged against Fergus.

"What payment seek ye?" Malcolm asked.

Scott tensed. "Nocht! I would rescue any woman from those *men*."

Malcolm regarded him for a long moment, then gave a slight nod. "'Tis the rare man ye are, Captain Scott."

"Those I command are drawn from the dregs of society. Mistress Rory once showed me kindness, and did not deserve such cruel use. The sergeant will be punished, but 'twill only make him more determined to avenge himself. 'Twould be best if she hastens away."

"Dinna fash. Once ye are gone, we will disappear."

Scott mounted his horse. Rory watched him ride away, then Malcolm hefted her in his arms.

"Where do we take her?" Fergus asked.

"Home."

~*~

The pounding cascade rained on Rory's battered skin. She stood unmoving, letting the water wash away the vileness. An occasional flinch was all she permitted herself to acknowledge tender skin, sore muscles, and bruised ribs. When those sensations dulled, she scrubbed until her skin matched the pink-flecked granite in Duncan's secret glen.

When she emerged from the linn, the soft hues of gloaming illuminated the silvery birches and red pines. After patting herself dry, she sat on a velvety moss cushion and applied oil to the welts and abrasions she could see. She slipped Duncan's old shirt over her head. The saffron linen fell to her knees. She wrapped herself in a plaid of blue and purple.

A jackdaw's shrill 'keeya' echoed through the glen. She tensed, even though she knew Fergus, Jamie, or Malcolm gave the call to warn that someone entered the corrie without invitation. Reluctantly, she left her sanctuary.

A gray-haired man with stooped shoulders sat beside the wanderer's stone playing with Brandubh and his chunks of wood. On occasion, the man twisted his face into silly or grotesque shapes, making her son squeal with laughter.

"Good evening to ye, Dr. Archie."

"And to yourself, Rory."

Brandubh stretched his arms toward her. She tried to lift him, but grimaced with pain.

Archie guided her onto the *clach an t'seabhdail*. "Sit yourself down, wildcat. The lad is able to crawl onto your lap."

Her son threw himself against her knees and grabbed hold of her plaid. He struggled to lift his pudgy legs onto the stone. Archie helped with a gentle push to his rear. Brandubh tumbled into her lap. She tousled his unruly black curls while Archie examined the swelling around her eye and the healing split of her upper lip.

"I thought ye kent better than to endanger yourself," he said.

"Would ye have me fail in my duty to your brother and my husband?" she asked. "'Twas they who bid me protect the prince."

"He is forever in your debt. Ye have but to ask."

Her anger flared. "I want nocht from him!"

"Rory!"

Brandubh's lower lip trembled. He began to bawl, and Rory rubbed his back to soothe him.

Nannag appeared in the doorway. "Upset the wee lad, have ye? Shame on ye both for airing words best left unspoken while a wee one is about. Give the babe to me, Granddaughter."

Archie stared at the scuff marks on his shoes. Rory expelled a measured breath.

Nannag cooed while rocking from side to side. "Bran, look what I have for ye."

He contemplated the small bannock, then sniffed and reached for it.

"'Tis been a long day, so Brandubh and myself will say goodnight. There is heather ale by the hearth."

"Rest well, Nannag."

"And yourself, Archie. Granddaughter, wake me if ye need me."

"He is a fine lad, wildcat," Archie said.

"Aye, he is."

"Nannag spoke of the day ye found him, Rory. Is that what riled your temper?"

"'Tis but a wee part of it. I have no liking for the Stewarts, and 'tis a terrible burden that rests on my shoulders because one could not relinquish a dream."

"But dreams nourish us, lass."

"One should ken the difference between a dream that can be realized and one that canna."

"Are ye saying Prince Charles could not win? How do ye explain our victories?"

"Those dinna matter, since he lost the most crucial one. Defeat never concerns just the warriors. Those left behind suffer worse than those slain in battle. If the carnage of the MacOnies is not proof of that, ye have but to look to your own family."

Archie's shoulders sagged. He bowed his head. "That sorrow forever scars my heart. Though I ken 'twas your duty, wildcat, I am grateful for the solace ye gave my wife and sons."

"I did not tend them because 'twas my duty."

He waved his hand. "I ken that, and meant no offense. Ye have a good heart toward anyone in distress, but never accept payment for your kindnesses, even when 'tis the prince who offers. He would grant whatever wish ye make of him."

"Empty promises are what he offers, Dr. Archie. When we parted at Loch nan Uamh, he made the same offer ye bring now. I told him then I wanted him gone from Scotland. He could not grant that simple request, so how do ye expect him to manage the one most dear to my heart?"

"Only my brother can grant that request, but mayhap the prince could persuade him."

"And who would persuade Duncan? I canna ask for what would offend his honor."

"He can be stubborn."

"Aye, he can. Would ye care to partake of Nannag's ale?"

"I am parched what with our talking and the trek to the corrie. I never understood why Tòmas insisted on staying so far from others, but in the present circumstances, I am thankful for his wisdom. The remoteness offers a safe place to rest from the weary burden that weighs on ye."

"Aye, but if the patrols dinna end soon, the day will come when soldiers happen on the corrie."

"Then let us drink that that day dinna come for many months."

She accepted the arm he offered her. In the gathering room, he handed her a *cuach.* "To sanctuary."

"Sanctuary." She lifted the drinking cup to touch his and winced.

"Would ye have me look at the rib, wildcat?"

"'Twill mend in time."

"Is it broken?"

"Bruised, I think."

"Then ye should let me look at it. Your husband's bruising has given me practice to tend yours."

She allowed herself a small smile. "I thank ye for the offer, Dr. Archie, but ye did not come to tend my ills."

"No, I came to thank ye for aiding my family and to bring this." He extracted a small packet from his pocket.

"Did Duncan send it?"

Archie nodded.

"How fares he? Has the wound mended?"

"'Tis healed right enough, but…"

Rory's eyes narrowed. The muscles in her stomach tightened. "But what?"

Archie shrugged. "There is nocht I can pinpoint exactly. Circumstances did not allow me to tend the wound as I would have liked, but I did what I could to see it healed. The leg is scarred, and Duncan favors it when he walks."

"Then what fashes ye?"

"His eyes. They dinna twinkle when he smiles or brighten when he laughs. If I did not ken of their purple hue, I would think his eyes were black like Donald's."

The news unsettled Rory. She had only an inkling of what Duncan had witnessed and experienced, but believed his will to survive strong. Had despair replaced hope? She prayed otherwise, refusing to believe he had entered her life only to die. *Please Lord, dinna abandon he who is my heart,* mo chridhe. *Let him draw strength from your guiding hands and my tender love.*

Open what I sent.

Duncan's words filled her head. Rory blinked, wondering how she heard him speak when he was not present. The unspoken answer drew her gaze to the parcel she held. The tingling at the nape of her neck filled her with a vague disquiet. She unwrapped the soiled plaid. Her hand covered her mouth to stifle a gasp.

"What is it, wildcat?"

"'Tis what I gave Duncan before he left."

The pendant twirled on its delicate chain, catching the firelight and reflecting it off the blue sapphire. Eerie spectral lights danced on the cottage walls. The flickering radiance compelled her to caress the pendant's intricate design. The metal warmed to her touch. She sealed it between her palms, then centered her thoughts on Duncan.

Gray eddies spiraled around her, alternately suffocating and billowing as if they possessed life. The mist acted like a blindfold, concealing all that surrounded her. It had neither taste nor smell, but magnified sound. Her mind sorted through the varied clatter. She identified the clang of swords, the boom of muskets, the thud of boots, the brattle of manacles, and the shuffle of feet. Sounds of fighting. Sounds of defeat.

Splotches of color seeped through the mist—red and white, buff and black—until the hues took form. Red soldiers encircled five men clad in tattered plaids. Iron bands bound their hands behind them. Heavy rope coiled from one neck to another like the lead put on horses. Matted curls crowned the last prisoner's beaded brow. Blood dripped from his crooked nose. A darkening bruise stressed the scar creasing his chin. He peered through eyes of the dead, empty and sightless.

The smell of burning flesh snapped Rory from the vision. Someone plunged her hands into a bucket of water, cooling the searing pain.

"Rory, do ye hear me?"

She stared at the ripples, then blinked. Dr. Archie watched her, his brow furrowed with concern. She licked her lips, then swallowed and nodded. He removed her hands from the water and examined them, casting furtive glances at her while he did so. The right was undamaged, but burnt flesh scarred her left palm.

Nannag, wearing a shawl over a white shift, appeared beside Dr. Archie. Wisps of gray hair fluttered from the thick braid draped over her shoulder. "I thought I heard Rory scream."

"Ye did. She was holding this." Archie retrieved the discarded pendant, which Nannag took from him.

"I have not seen this before. Where did it come from?"

"Duncan asked me to give it to her."

"Granddaughter?"

Rory heard their words. She even understood them, but when she tried to answer, the vision kept her silent.

"Look at me, Granddaughter!"

She lifted her eyes to Nannag.

"Duncan loves ye with all his heart. He has oft told me ye are his strength. Dinna fail him now. Is he in trouble?"

Rory nodded.

"Then how can we help him?"

"There is nocht ye can do."

"I willna let my grandson die without a fight!"

"There is only one who can save him."

"Then we will send a gillie to find him."

Rory grasped Nannag's hands, ignoring the stab of pain in her own hand. "Ye willna understand, but trust me."

Nannag's purple eyes scrutinized her, then she nodded.

Rory turned to Archie. "Where do ye take the prince?"

He frowned. "To my brother."

"Ye must also take me and those I choose."

"Why?"

"Your brother is the only man who can tell us where to find Duncan."

"When do ye wish to leave?"

"This night else he willna survive."

"I will meet ye on the north shore of River Arkaig before the sun lightens the sky."

"Agreed." Once Archie left, Rory turned to Nannag. "Fergus and my brothers go with me. Ye must take Brandubh and leave the corrie. 'Tis no longer safe to abide here."

"Ye are certain?"

"Aye."

"Where shall we go?"

"To William. Tell him to gather all from the *clachan*."

"To what purpose?"

"Ye must go north to my kin."

"Ye would have us leave Lochaber?"

"Ye and the others are dear to me. I would have ye safe while I am about my business. Once Duncan is free, we will join ye."

With pursed lips, Nannag looked around the small orderly room. "I have lived here many years, most of them alone with only the nearness of my husband's and son's graves for company. When Duncan brought ye here, I thought to spend my last days with my new family gathered around me. Now, ye say 'tis not to be."

"I, too, wanted to raise my bairns here, but 'tis a dream that canna be. I love Duncan, and if he dies before I tell him, he willna ever ken peace. I canna subject Brandubh to the perils of my trek, but willna abandon him or yourself kenning danger threatens. Mayhap the day will come when we may return, but for now ye must leave. Will ye do what I ask?"

Nannag touched her cheek and nodded.

~*~

Rory glanced across the river at the charred ruins of Achnacarry. Tam's cold nose nudged her palm. She ruffled the hound's wiry gray coat.

"Go with Neil."

The dog barked once, as if it understood the command.

"Ye will see that Tam and Midnight reach the *clachan* before they leave?" she asked.

Neil nodded. "Aye."

"Ye are in charge then. When I see Lochiel, I will ask him to give ye his blessing. No matter the outcome, I willna return here."

"Dinna fash about us, Rory. 'Tis Duncan who needs ye more. We will manage." Neil's eyes strayed to the ground, then lifted toward the starry sky. "Before ye go…"

"Have I forgotten something?"

"No!" His retort was brusque. "Sorry."

"If ye have words to say, they are best spoken quickly. I dare not linger."

"I thank ye for kenning I have worth when others brushed me aside. 'Tis many a year since I trusted one of your persuasion."

Her lips quivered with the barest of smiles. "Ye are a true friend, Neil. It gladdens my heart that I could help persuade ye there are more good women than bad. I wish ye a long and happy life once this trouble ends."

"And I ye."

"Ready, wildcat?" Archie asked, coming to stand with her.

"I was just bidding farewell to Neil."

The physician extended his hand. "My brother trusts ye, so I dinna think he will disagree with the lass' choice. If ye need help, ye ken where our brother John is."

"I do."

"Then we best be going, wildcat."

She started to turn, but Neil's final words made her pause.

"Dinna think 'twas only yourself who did the restoring, Rory Cameron. There is another who works harder at it."

"Give Rose my best," she said with a smile.

"And here I thought we had kept the secret." He shook his head and waved. "Godspeed, lass."

Rory ran to catch up to her companions. Fergus, Malcolm, and Jamie formed an arc around her. Their protective stance reassured her. Ahead walked Prince Charles and his companions. Archie guided them eastward, skirting the southern tip of Loch Lochy. Rather than follow the road, they forged a path that paralleled the River Spean. At Highbridge, Fergus and Jamie slipped into the darkness to search for soldiers.

The tumbling water in the gorge below drowned the sounds of the night. Rory regarded the bridge built a decade earlier by General Wade. This was where the first blood of the Rising had been spilt.

Jamie emerged from the darkness. "'Tis safe to proceed. Dinna lag, though. Tirnadis House smolders, so the soldiers willna have left over long ago, and we canna find their trail."

The man who had led the attack on Captain Scott and his men had lived at Tirnadis. How many more houses would be put to the flame before the Crown was satisfied? With a shake of her head, Rory hurried across the bridge.

When dawn was almost upon them, she sent Fergus to find a spot from which he would see any who approached from the road. They would shelter in the blackened ruins of Keppoch House, another monument to the reprisals.

She took the first watch, remembering the night she and Duncan had spent in the ancestral home of the MacDonells of Keppoch. He carried a message to their chief, and after reading the missive, Alexander had offered them food and shelter.

She climbed over toppled stones and charred timbers until she stood in the great hall where Alexander's *seanchaidh* had recounted the horrible murders of the twelfth chief, also named Alexander, and his young brother, Ranald. When their father died, an uncle managed the clan's affairs until Alexander reached the age of majority. Among the guests at the banquet to honor their new chief were six men who belonged to a sept who preferred the uncle retain leadership of the clan. They quarreled with Alexander and Ranald, and in the ensuing commotion, slew the two brothers.

Iain Lom, bard to the Keppochs, did not believe the tale of accidental death told by the six men. He swore they had murdered his young chief. When the neighboring chief, MacDonell of Glengarry, refused to avenge the killings, Iain secured a commission of fire and sword and a force of fifty from MacDonald of Sleat on the Isle of Skye. After Iain slew the six men and their father, he cut off their heads, then washed them in a well on the shore of Loch Oich. He delivered the severed heads to Glengarry to show justice had been done.

The MacDonells of Keppoch razed the castle stone by stone until nothing remained to remind them of the terrible deed committed within its walls. Less than a century later, the second castle was put to the torch, not by the clan, but by the Crown. Like his namesake, Alexander of Keppoch was dead, slain on the bloody field of Drummossie Moor.

~*~

Crouched behind a rock, Rory scanned the southeastern slope. The dusky hues of a late August sunset crowned Ben Alder's flat crest. Thickets of holly and moss carpeted the steep craggy mountain, but she found the posted sentries.

"How many?" Archie squatted beside her.

"Seven."

He frowned.

"How many should there be?" she asked.

"Between those posted by Donald and those of Cluny's men, there were twelve."

Cluny—Ewen MacPherson—was chief of his clan, and knew this wild terrain. With Lochiel in hiding with him, men of both clans would stand guard. To whom did the missing five give their allegiance and why did they not watch for intruders?

As if reading her thoughts, Archie said, "We willna find answers staying here. His Highness grows restless, and ye must seek out my brother. Shall we go?"

She followed the prince and his companions, preferring the security of her own guards. When the challenge came, Fergus stepped in front of her while Jamie and Malcolm shielded her from the sides.

"'Tis far enough!" the sentry commanded.

"*Creagh Dubh,*" Archie said.

The sentry emerged from his hiding place. "Identify yourself."

"Archibald Cameron, brother of Lochiel."

"Your companions?"

"I canna say, but all are loyal Jacobites."

"No names, no entrance."

Rory thought she knew a name that would gain them entry. "Thistle."

The sentry did not respond, but neither did he and his companions attack.

In the ensuing silence, Prince Charles asked, "Who is this Thistle?"

"A smuggler with a price on his head," she said. "The reward is not so grand as the £30,000 for yourself, but 'tis no wee amount."

"This smuggler, he is not among us. Why use his name?"

"Lochiel will ken the why of it."

One of the Highlanders motioned for them to follow. He led them through a grove of holly to a turfed-roof, cave-like dwelling where six men played cards. Their joviality irked Rory. While they amused themselves in their secret hideaway, innocent people suffered because these men had dared to take up arms against the king.

"Well, Lochiel, where is the smuggler?" a plump old man asked, stepping from the cave. "I see your brother, a woman, three Highlanders, and—" He dropped to one knee. "Your Royal Highness!"

"Rise, *mon ami,* I do not stand on formality here. It is likely to get me shot."

"He is right, Cluny," Lochiel said, hobbling forward on crutches. "I am glad to see ye survived your travels."

"*Moi aussi, mon ami.* Do I not look like a Highlander?" Prince Charles did a slow pirouette. He had long ago discarded more elegant attire for a frayed flock coat, tattered belted plaid, and filthy shirt. His wig was gone, revealing red locks that matched his unkempt red beard.

"Ye do, and a fine one at that," Cluny said.

Rory ignored the inane prattle, and scanned the growing crowd. Duncan's absence triggered her disquiet. Fearing time had run out, she pushed past the prince until she faced her chief. "Where is Duncan?"

Silence fell like a thunderclap. One by one the men slunk away until only her contingent of guards remained.

"Rory did all ye asked and more, Sir Donald. Dinna ye owe her an answer?" Fergus asked, stepping forward.

Lochiel's eyes widened with surprise. "Ye are alive!"

Fergus nodded.

"Have ye switched allegiance to Rory then?"

"Since I did not ken where ye hid, my duty was clear. I guard she who acts in your stead. Where is her husband and my friend?"

"Come, wildcat, we must talk."

Rory shook her head. "The time for speaking is ended, Lochiel. Where is Duncan?"

"He is a prisoner of the Crown."

CHAPTER TWENTY-THREE
THISTLE

The words slammed into Rory. She swayed from the impact of their punch. She clung to the hand that steadied her, fighting her way through images of fetid darkness, dank dampness, and gnawing rats. No! Duncan would not suffer Father Alex's tragic fate. He would know freedom, even if she must sacrifice hers in the process.

Her anger flickered and ignited, but she refused to succumb to heedless fury. Restraint tempered the seething fires that urged her to act. Thistle's canniness assumed control, and the smuggler's mask descended even though she did not wear the black wool.

Before she could formulate a plan, she required information from Lochiel.

"When was he taken?"

"Yesterevening before the sun set."

"Was he alone?"

Lochiel hobbled to a nearby stone and sat. "There were four with him."

She saw the presence of extra prisoners as both asset and hindrance. With more to guard, the soldiers would divide themselves, making it easier to overcome them. If any Highlanders were wounded, however, they would slow her down when speed was of the essence.

"How were they taken?" she asked.

"Word reached us that soldiers approached. I canna go far on these." He interrupted the massaging of an ankle to lift his crutches. "We waited for Archie and His Highness. Duncan and the others circled round to attack the soldiers from behind. Five Highlanders against twenty are good odds, but swords do wee harm against muskets."

"Did ye not send others to their rescue?"

"I could not risk revealing where we hid. That would have thwarted Duncan's plan. Had MacPhersons and Camerons swarmed down on them, word would get back to Fort William. With the prince expected, we could not afford more soldiers searching the area."

"But Duncan is like a son to ye!"

"Aye, and I love him dearly, but we must all make sacrifices, Rory. He swore to protect me and kent the danger in doing so. I suffer his loss, and will bear that guilt along with seeing our people suffer for what I wrought."

"Dinna be speaking to me of sacrifices, Lochiel! I thought death and persecution would end after I wed, but instead I have witnessed barbarism more terrible than when Campbells attacked my people. I did nocht then, and I did nocht when soldiers burned Achnacarry and imprisoned your brother. No more! I willna forfeit Duncan's life on a cause lost before it began."

"And if I forbid ye?"

"I am finished heeding your wishes. I came to ask ye to release me from my pledge to act in your stead. Whether ye grant it or not dinna matter. I fight for my husband with or without your blessing."

"Ye love him."

"With all my heart."

Lochiel stroked his chin. His gaze went to Malcolm and Jamie. "And do ye support Rory is this matter?"

"It can be no other way," they said.

"What of yourself, Fergus? Ye swore allegiance to me. If I grant Rory's request, ye are bound by your word to return to my side."

"I ken my duty."

"But ye would rather go with them?"

"I thought myself half a man, but Rory showed me the wrongness of such thinking. By her side, I have witnessed slaughter more fearsome than what we faced on Drummossie Moor. Are we never to live in peace again? Must our blood forever soak this country? The love Duncan and Rory share offers us hope when despair weighs heavy on us. If I dinna help reunite them, 'twould be like plunging a dirk into my heart."

"Ye warned me not so long ago, wildcat, that ye are a rebel," Lochiel said. "'Twould seem ye inspire others to emulate your example. Since I followed my convictions, I canna deny ye the same. The fealty ye owe me is lifted, and may God protect ye in what ye are about to do."

"I would ask another favor of ye."

Lochiel's dark eyes twinkled. "Your boons sound more like demands, wildcat."

Rory allowed a small smile to play on her lips. "'Tis what happens when a woman gains power."

He laughed. "What would ye ask of me?"

"Release Duncan from his oath."

Lochiel hesitated, then nodded. "'Tis done. I canna remain in Scotland, and I doubt ye or Duncan would be happy in France. Go swiftly on your way, Rory Cameron. Save my foster son before they imprison him within Carlisle Castle!"

~*~

After exchanging her female attire for Thistle's black trews and shirt, Rory paced the narrow clearing in front of the dilapidated cottage. She chewed her lower lip, agitated and annoyed at the delay.

"Where are they? What keeps them? Dinna they ken that with each night's passing Duncan grows closer to death?"

Jamie swung her around to face him. "Stop torturing yourself! 'Tis daft to search without kenning which way the soldiers went. We are but four, and the distance is too great to risk choosing wrong. All would be lost if we went north thinking they took the military road through Killiecrankie and Dunkeld to Perth, when all the while they went south to where the drove roads meet at Tyndrum before heading for Stirling."

Her brother's cautious words drove the bluster from her. He pulled her against his chest and stroked her hair. "'Tis hard to be separated from the one ye love, but dinna let the ache in your heart overwhelm ye. Duncan needs the courage of his warrior wife and the canniness of a wanted smuggler."

She resumed her pacing. "I ken, Jamie, but the waiting wears on me. I need to be doing, to be planning, but canna do either without the kenning."

A stone skittered to a stop at Rory's booted feet. She stared at the grayness, then lifted her eyes. Fergus skidded down the hillock, dragging his sword behind him to slow his descent. When he reached the bottom, he swallowed great gulps of air.

"Did they go north?" she asked.

He shook his head. "No one...saw soldiers...escorting prisoners.... They say...'twould be daft...to drive...Camerons and MacPhersons like cattle through Dalwhinnie.... 'Tis a gathering place...for Highlanders...where they have long held fast...against greater forces."

"They headed south, then," Jamie said.

"Aye, by way of King's House." Malcolm joined the trio. "They travel through Glen Coe to Tyndrum where the military road will be taking them to Crianlarich where they'll turn east through Glen Dochart and then south to Callander and Stirling."

Rory felt a glimmer of hope. "They play into our hands."

Her brother nodded.

A puzzled frown wrinkled Fergus' forehead. "How?"

"They must pass through MacGregor country."

"And how will that be helping us?"

Rory smiled. "Did Duncan never tell ye he wed a MacGregor chieftain?"

Fergus' hazel eyes bulged.

She laid a gentle hand on his hairy forearm. "Dinna fear, I will protect ye from thieving outlaws."

Her brothers chortled with laughter. She collected her bow and quiver of arrows. "Have ye the cloth, Jamie?"

"Aye."

She handed the black fabric to Fergus.

He stuck a finger through one of two holes. "A mask, is it? Whyever would I be needing this?"

"I would make another confession, but ye must swear on the dirk to never reveal what I tell ye."

His eyes narrowed. "Does Duncan have this kenning?"

"Aye."

"Then ye best be telling it. We dare not delay any longer."

She pointed to the mask. "I canna disguise that ye lack an arm, but 'tis not such a rarity these days. Your face, though, distinguishes ye from every other man minus a limb. Ye are already deemed traitor, so a wee more outlawing willna matter."

"Outlawing? Never yourself, Rory Cameron. I ken Duncan well, and he would not hold with it."

"The outlawing I do depends on who ye ask. The poor and hungry praise God, while the Sassenach put a price on my head."

He stared at the mask he held. His gaze drifted to her, and for the first time, he seemed to see her black clothes and weapon. "Thistle?"

"Aye, and I would be honored if ye join my wee band of smugglers. The work we are about is not our usual, but 'tis thwarting the Sassenach just the same."

He squared his shoulders, then bowed. "'Tis an honor to serve, my lady."

"A touching scene," Malcolm said, "but we must hasten. Kenning Rory, we willna be taking the easy way."

The soldiers had a two-day start. To reach MacGregor country before they arrived at Callander, she led them south to Glen Lyon, passing the western end of Loch Rannoch and the edges of Rannoch Moor. She could ill afford to unearth memories best left buried with the stumps of ancient pines in the black peatland of lochans, boulders, and tussocks. Her thoughts must remain with the living.

After skirting Ben Lawers, they stole like shadows through the moonlight to avoid the militia garrisoned at Finlarig Castle. When they reached Glen Ogle, Jamie stopped at a steading to ask for water. While conversing with the wife, he learned no escort of prisoners had passed. Rory offered a silent prayer of thanks. From there, they headed in a southwesterly direction until they reached the Braes of Balquhidder, where they slipped inside a gray stone church.

"This is God's house. Put aside your weapons," a black-frocked minister said without turning from his prayers at the altar. He kept his head bowed for a time, then stood.

Rory kept to the shadows, preferring to let her companions interact with their host. She would have avoided the kirk, but needed help in contacting someone. With Rob Roy MacGregor entombed in the churchyard, she felt certain the minister would know where to find the man she sought.

"Rebels seeking sanctuary, are ye?"

Fergus answered. "I am declared rebel, but not my friends. We seek someone."

The minister raised his bushy white eyebrows. "And has this person a name?"

"Glengyle."

"Also a rebel. What do ye want of him?"

"A friend needs him."

"Attainted men are not so willing to be found these days. If I can deliver your message, and I make no guarantee of that, how will he ken ye mean him no harm?"

Rory knew only she could answer the question. She drew on her mask, and stepped from the darkness. "Do ye ken who I am?"

"One of God's guardian angels."

"Then ye ken I mean Glengyle no harm."

"The matter is urgent?"

"Aye."

"Then I will take my leave. I have wee to offer, but ye will find food and whisky beneath the altar." The aged minister left.

Rory did not fully trust him, so she retained her mask. Fergus and Malcolm took the first watch while she and Jamie slept.

She felt a sharp jab to her foot, then toppled from the pew. When she rolled onto her back, smoldering blue eyes regarded her.

"Being roused from my bed is never to my liking. How is it to yours?" the man asked, shoving a lock of silver-tinged flaxen hair behind his ear.

"Not to mine either." She glanced at the three men who held dirks to her friends' throats. "I kent the day would come when someone surprised us. I just did not think 'twould be MacGregor against MacGregor."

"Ye claim kinship with the nameless?"

"I do, as do those two." She pointed to Malcolm and Jamie. "The other is of Clan Cameron."

"Bring the light closer to his face," Glengyle ordered. "Ye are Duncan Cameron's friend, the one who bested my cousin James."

"I am. 'Tis because of Duncan that I come."

"Ye enlist the help of a smuggler, then seek me out?"

"No, Gregor Glùn Dhubh. 'Tis myself who sought ye," Rory said.

"Your voice is familiar." The chieftain pulled her to her feet, then unmasked her. After initial surprise, he burst into laughter. "Duncan claimed ye warrior and rebel, but I thought 'twas half jest. I thought never to see shadows haunt your eyes as they did that day in the old woman's cottage on Drummossie Moor, but I do. What ye saw then has come true? Duncan fell on the slaughtering field?"

"He did," Fergus said, "but he did not die."

Glengyle glanced at him, then returned his gaze to her. "Where is Duncan, lass?"

"He is on his way to Carlisle to be judged traitor. The soldiers take him there by way of Callander."

"Ranald."

"Aye, cousin?"

"Send runners to visit the steadings along the road to Callander and Dunblane. I want word of where the soldiers are. Sound the call to rise among the Gregorach. All who are able should meet at Loch Lubnaig."

"And the reason?"

"To help one of our own."

Ranald hurried from the kirk.

"Come, friends," Gregor said. "''Tis time we were away from here."

~*~

From her stone perch Rory surveyed the glen. A tumbling river of rapids and falls confined the drove road to a width no greater than two cattle standing abreast of one another. The soldiers would have to adjust their line to the limits dictated by the narrow space. When ambushed, they would have few alternatives: stand and fight, take their chances in the river, or lay down their arms and relinquish their prisoners.

"Ready?" Glengyle asked.

"Aye. How long before they enter the glen?"

"Not long. Ye best don your mask. Remember, remain hidden until the Gregorach surround them. It willna do for Thistle to be hurt before we rescue Duncan." He laid his hand on hers. "Dinna fash, lass. We willna fail ye."

"I ken."

"Tack-tack, tack-tack. Tack-tack, tack-tack." The harsh alarm of a warbler echoed through the grove of oak and fir.

Gregor scrambled from the rock and disappeared into the trees. He and the fifty who had answered his call moved like wraiths through the woods, invisible to the eye, imperceptible to the ear. He dispersed fifteen men along each side of the pass with orders to spread themselves. Fergus and nine others waited to prevent retreat, while half that number hid behind a straw-laden cart that blocked the track ahead. The remaining MacGregors, all masked, hid below her.

The vanguard of red soldiers, six in number, walked two abreast. Next came a sergeant and corporal. Behind them shuffled the prisoners, each guarded on either side by a pair of soldiers. Stripped of their plaids, the Highlanders wore soiled, threadbare shirts. The rain-soddened cloth clung to wasted skin. The rope nooses around their necks yoked them like beasts of burden. The rear of the line consisted of four additional red soldiers.

Those in the lead entered a place ideal for ambush, but rather than survey the terrain, they hunched forward against the rain. Being in MacGregor country should have increased their alertness. That it did not demonstrated the Crown's belief of having vanquished the Highlands and crushed the people's spirits. Their cockiness would be their demise.

When the last soldiers cleared the entrance to the pass, the MacGregors guarding against retreat crept into position. The warbler's alarm sounded a second time. The red soldiers halted at the disabled cart. Thistle nocked her bow and stood.

"Move the damn thing and be quick about it!" the sergeant commanded.

The soldiers scurried to obey, but not before a black arrow pierced its wood. The sergeant whirled, and Rory recognized an old nemesis—Geordie Campbell.

"Thistle!"

"How fare ye, Sergeant? 'Tis a wee while since last we met. Do ye not yet owe the MacGregors for ransacking their homes?"

"Kill him!" The sergeant's bellowed order brought the MacGregors below her to their feet. They aimed their muskets at him.

"Dinna heed Geordie's order," Thistle said to the soldiers. "'Twould be most untidy. My men are excellent marksmen."

Campbell's face reddened until its hue matched the scarlet of his uniform.

"And Geordie, if ye are thinking of some other plan to get the upper hand, I suggest ye look around."

Not only he, but also his men, turned their heads to the left, then the right. With the trees shading their faces, more MacGregors showed themselves.

"Dinna forget to look behind."

Geordie spun around. A hooded figure rose from the straw, while four companions stepped from behind the cart. The soldiers tossed aside their weapons.

"What do ye want, Thistle?" Campbell said through clenched teeth.

"Och, Geordie, I thought ye had more brains than to ask so obvious a question. 'Tis your prisoners we are wanting."

"No! They are traitors. I intend to see the hangman stretch their scrawny necks."

"I tried to warn ye."

Thistle released a second arrow. She had sent the first in warning. This one served the same purpose, but with personal emphasis. It pierced Geordie's tricorn and wig, sending both sailing from his head. His hand flew to his baldpate.

Thistle nocked another arrow in her black longbow. "'Tis my final warning. Next time ye willna be so lucky. Now, release the prisoners!"

The scrawny corporal stooped to unlock the iron chains shackling the Highlanders' ankles. A private cut the ropes binding their wrists, while another removed their nooses.

"To the rear with ye, Highlanders. Someone will guide ye to safety." Thistle waited until they rounded the bend before returning her attention to Geordie. "If ye and your men would lay facedown with your feet crossed and your arms stretched wide, we can be after finishing our business."

Campbell glared but obeyed. His men followed suit.

Malcolm led his hooded companions down to the road. They gathered the chains and tossed them into the river. Working in pairs, they stuffed rags into the soldiers' mouths, then bound their wrists. After lashing their crossed ankles together, they bent the soldiers' knees and trussed ankles to wrists. To further delay escape, the masked Highlanders fashioned nooses around the soldiers' necks and tied these to their ankles.

"'Tis been a pleasure doing business with ye, Geordie," Thistle said. "I hope the governor of Fort William is not too hard on ye. Until we meet again, I leave ye with a fond remembrance of our encounter. Mayhap someone will see it and come to release ye."

Jamie affixed a short length of cloth to her arrow and touched fire to it. She sighted on the cart and let loose the arrow. The straw burst into flames.

"On second thought mayhap no one will come. After all the torching ye and yours have done, 'twill be a wonder if folk think 'tis anything but another steading put to the flame. Good day to ye, Geordie Campbell."

As she ascended the hill, Rory ignored his muffled shouts. He deserved whatever humiliation she served him and more for the indignities and pain he had inflicted on her husband and the others.

Glengyle met her at the top of the hill. His blue eyes twinkled with satisfied amusement. "'Twas a grand sight, lass, and not one soldier was hurt except for his pride."

She removed her mask. "Kenning what I do of men, wounding their pride makes them more bitter than injuring their flesh. They will exact revenge for this day's work."

"Never fear, lass. No MacGregor will suffer for what we wrought. We protect our own."

"I am grateful for all ye have done, but I must hasten to Duncan."

"And I to my Mary. God be with ye and your love."

"And with ye and yours, Gregor Glùn Dhubh."

~*~

Rory wound her way along the rock-strewn path, climbing one of the lofty mountains that flanked Loch Katrine. A moonbeam shone its silver light on two boulders standing perpendicular to each other. She scampered over the last rock and squeezed between the monoliths, emerging on the far side at the entrance to a cave. "Duncan?"

"Over here, Rory," Fergus said.

She followed his voice without watching where she walked. Her foot caught on something stretched across the cave floor. A cry escaped her lips as she fell, but hairy arms caught her. Her cushion grunted.

"Rory," Fergus said, standing over her, "he is not Duncan."

Embarrassed by her clumsiness, she rolled off the rescued man who had broken her fall. "I thank ye for saving me from a hard fall. Are ye hurt?"

"By a wee wisp of a lass? Not at all."

"Rory." Fergus' quiet tone compelled her to look at him. He handed the torch to the other man, and put his hand on her shoulder. "Ye best prepare yourself, lass."

She sucked in her breath, fearing she knew which prisoner was Duncan. "Dinna be telling me I am too late."

"He yet lives. 'Tis his appearance."

"Aye," the other man said. "When the soldiers wanted to have their sport with us, he riled them with his words. I dinna ken what he said, but they slammed him with the butts of their muskets. The sergeant seemed to ken him, and delighted in torturing him before we bedded down each night."

Rory squeezed her eyes shut and balled her hands into tight fists. Her whole being screamed for revenge, but she blinked away the hot tears that stung her eyes and followed Fergus. He led her to a man curled like an infant on the floor.

She dropped to her knees, then caressed his bruised and swollen face. She smoothed matted curls from his shuttered eyes and kissed his feverish forehead. "Duncan? Can ye hear me?"

In a raspy murmur, he asked, "Rory?"

"Hush, *mo chridhe.* Close your eyes and sleep. I willna leave."

"Rory?" Jamie knelt beside her. "Tell us what ye need."

"Water. Clean linen. Herb Robert. Lady's mantle. Thick porridge."

"Fergus, cook the porridge for her. Malcolm, fetch the water. I will gather the plants, but ye must describe them so I ken what to look for," Jamie said.

She sniffed. "Herb Robert has leaves like the fern. They are deep green tinged with a fiery red. When ye crush them between your fingers, they give off a pungent odor. The stem is hairy and ye will find it growing in moist woods. 'Tis also the leaves of the lady's mantle ye are wanting, but they are lighter in color and have seven to nine toothed lobes that will remind ye of stars. Look for it close to the ground, but make certain no dew clings to the leaves."

Jamie hurried from the cave.

Malcolm returned with the water. "Tell me what to do for the others."

"Wash their burns and cuts," Rory said. "Pretend they are Fiona, and treat them with gentleness."

He snorted. "Lads, do ye hear what she is saying? I am to be treating fine warriors like women. Are ye wanting me to do that?"

"No, indeed!" The one who had broken her fall drew near. "Ye wear the black of Thistle. Ye are the one who saved us?"

She nodded.

"I am Alasdair MacPherson and this is my brother, Manus. Lachlan and Colin are friends of Duncan. We are indebted to him and ye. If there is anything we can do, ye have only to say the word."

"Thank ye, Alasdair. For now, let my brother tend ye, then rest."

Rory washed the purplish-black bruises covering Duncan's face, then bathed the red rope burns encircling his wrists and the bloody gashes marking his ankles. The manacles, too small for his thick legs, had cut deep into his flesh.

"Are these the right leaves?" Jamie asked.

She held the plants close to the firelight. "Aye. Crush the herb Robert, then add water and let it boil in the fire. Pour boiling water over the lady's mantle and let it steep."

"Mistress Rory?"

She looked into the pale face of a young man, no older than she, whose hazel eyes belonged to those of a much older man.

"Is it poultices ye are wanting from the plants and porridge?" he asked.

"Colin, is it?"

He nodded.

"'Tis," she said.

"Shall I make them for ye? I helped Dr. Archie tend the wounded after Gladsmuir. He showed me what to do."

"Thank ye, Colin. The herb Robert should heal the bruises. The lady's mantle is for the cuts, but before ye apply those poultices, wash Duncan's ankles with the steeped water."

He smeared porridge on a bandage, added hot leaves, then put the poultice on one of her husband's many wounds. When Colin began to bathe the ankles, Duncan moaned and grew restless. Rory combed through the tangled mass of brown curls with her fingers. He quieted and Colin resumed his work.

Fergus positioned himself behind her, and slipped his arm around her waist. She stiffened.

"Ye need to rest, Rory. Ye willna do Duncan any good if ye sicken. While ye cradle him in your arms, ye can use me for a pillow. I am softer than leaning against the cold stone."

She allowed him to draw her against his chest. She kissed Duncan's brow, then closed her eyes. The sonorous rhythm of raspy breathing and soft snores quieted her unease. She drifted off to sleep.

A low moan woke her. Duncan twitched, shifting restlessly in his slumber. His face glistened in the firelight. She touched his forehead. Beads of fiery sweat dampened her palm.

"What is it?" Jamie asked.

"Fever."

She started to rise, but he arrested the movement with a calloused hand. "What can I fetch?"

"Do ye ken the plant your mother calls 'bird's foot?'"

"The one whose leaves occur in threes and has white blossoms?"

She nodded.

"I will fetch it anon."

While she waited, she blotted Duncan's brow, face, and neck with cold water. After Jamie returned and the tea was ready, she coaxed a few drops down her husband's throat. There was little else to do except wait and pray.

~*~

By dawn of their third day in the cave, Duncan still burned with fever. Rory yearned for the chest of vials filled with the roots, bark, leaves, and flowers she had gathered, but she had given it to Nannag. The remedies available now were few and scarce.

Malcolm squatted beside her. "We canna delay any longer. 'Tis too dangerous to stay."

"I willna leave Duncan."

"The Cameron and MacPherson lads are wanting to return to their families, so they canna help carry him. Fergus is unable, and while Jamie and myself are strong men, Duncan is too brawny for us to support all the way home."

"I willna leave him, Malcolm. I will die before we are separated again."

He put a reassuring hand over hers. "I have protected ye since ye were a wee lass, Rory. I willna abandon ye now."

"Then how do ye suggest we solve our dilemma?"

He smiled. "Come with me."

She hesitated.

"We go only to the rocks that hide the cave."

The daylight blinded her, and she shielded her eyes until they adjusted to the bright grayness. Her mouth opened, but words escaped her. Four garrons grazed on the grassy slope.

"From where did they come?"

"A gift from Glengyle. Fergus told him of Duncan. He said 'twas for she who learned to listen with her heart."

Rory smiled through tear-clouded eyes. It seemed a lifetime ago that Gregor Glùn Dhubh had spoken those words. In reality only six months had passed.

She hastened to gather her things. Lachlan and Manus carried Duncan to the mountain ponies. Malcolm mounted, then took Duncan in front of him.

Alasdair lifted her onto a dun-colored mare. "Farewell, Rory. We are indebted to ye."

"I wish ye a safe journey home," she said, adding a silent prayer that once they arrived, they found their loved ones safe and well. She waved farewell.

They rode north, traveling by night, resting by day. They opted for weed-festooned tracks through lands held by Campbells, Robertsons, Menzies, Camerons, MacDonells, and Frasers rather than follow well-traveled roads. They sheltered in heavy woods, burned-out steadings, ancient burial mounds, and obscure caves that offered seclusion from prying eyes and enemy patrols. The journey was long and hazardous.

Duncan drifted in and out of consciousness. His fever climbed, then fell, but never broke. By the time they reached the Great Glen, they had traveled for three days, but only covered half the distance to the *clachan.*

Duncan's condition worsened, spurring them to ride harder and faster through lands belonging to MacDonells, Chisolms, and Mackenzies. Six days after leaving Loch Katrine they rode into the MacGregor *clachan.*

Malcolm shouted to men reaping a field. "Follow me!"

They dropped their scythes and ran after him.

Rory reined her garron to a halt in front of Nannag and Mairi.

"Where is my grandson?" Nannag asked.

"They take him to the burn. I ken nocht else to break his fever. Where are my medicines, Grandmother?"

"Inside. Will Duncan live?"

Nannag voiced Rory's greatest fear. She squeezed the old woman's hand. "Pray 'tis not too late."

A gasp escaped Nannag's trembling lips. Mairi put a comforting arm around her, and led her away. Rory hastened inside to prepare for Duncan's return.

"What can I do, Rory?" Fergus asked.

She turned from searching the vials. Her friend stooped in the doorway, a lost look on his face. He had been unable to help much during the journey, and she knew it weighed heavily on him.

"When the men bring Duncan, ye can pat him dry. Though he burns with fever, he will be cold from his dunking. Cover him with the wool, then see if ye can find animal skins to lay atop the plaid."

While Fergus tended to her husband, she placed chips of willow bark in boiling water, then set the decoction aside to steep. For it to be most beneficial, she must wait half a day before administering the liquid. By the time she finished, Fergus had returned with the tanned hides. The long ride and constant strain suddenly hit her. She collapsed on the stool beside the bed.

"Ye should rest, Rory. I will be outside if needed."

She shed her filthy clothes, then splashed water on her face and neck. After checking on Duncan, she wrapped herself in a plaid in front of the fire. She fell into a deep sleep.

Tiny fingers tickling her bare toes woke Rory. She peeked through hooded eyelids, and smiled. She stretched her legs, maneuvering them until she caught the culprit between her feet. Brandubh squealed in surprise, then bumped against her until she released him. He crawled onto her stomach and grabbed her hair.

"Och, Rory, I did not mean for him to wake ye." A girl with ebony hair bound with pink ribbon stood in the doorway.

"'Tis all right, Anna. Brandubh is just what I needed."

"He got away while I was listening to what happened."

"So ye have met Fergus."

The blush on Anna's cheeks matched the hue of her ribbon. "He is a giant of a man."

"He is, but he is as gentle as a wee lamb. Have ye fed him yet?"

"No."

"Then would ye take him and Brandubh to Angus' and see that they both eat? I must tend to Duncan, and 'twould be a great favor to me if I need not worry about them."

The girl almost tripped over her feet to carry out Rory's wishes. Once the three were gone, Rory rummaged in the chest for an old shift to wear. She loosened her hair and brushed the tangled knots from it. Duncan lay unconscious on the bed. She touched his forehead. He was still hot, but less feverish than earlier.

She rinsed down a bannock with heather ale while she waited for the decoction of willow bark to boil. When ready, she strained the bark and then divided the liquid by pouring some into a *cuach* and the rest into a bowl. She washed Duncan's face with a rag dipped in the willow decoction. The herb Robert had begun to heal his bruises, turning them from purple to yellowish-black. Thankfully, none of the blows had broken any bones. She pulled back the skins and plaid, and bathed the rest of his battered body. Scabs had formed over the abrasions, and the burns on his wrists had healed. She rubbed the red oil of Saint John's Wort on his ankles, then bandaged them. While kneeling beside the bed, she forced willow tea into him. Then she resumed her vigil.

~*~

Angus entered the sleeping room with Brandubh slung over his shoulder like a sack of grain. Rory's son chirked with delight when he saw her. She set aside her sewing to place him on the bed. He played with her ball of wool.

"Where is the shadow?" Angus asked.

"Who?"

"The giant."

"Och, Fergus, ye mean. I dinna ken. Anna fetched him, saying her father needed his brawn."

"That one is a flirt."

"Aye, she is."

"How is Duncan today?"

"His fever broke last night."

"'Twas a long time for a fever. Do ye think 'twill addle him?"

"I—"

A hand closed over hers, startling her into silence. Too large to be Brandubh's, she lifted her gaze from the hand to her husband's face.

Duncan gazed back with a questioning look. His words sounded more like a frog's croak than a man's voice. "Will ye please tell me who this is, Rory?"

She held a *cuach* to his lips, allowing him a few sips of water. She glanced at Brandubh, who tugged on Duncan's beard. She lifted the boy from his chest with a smile. "'Tis our son."

Duncan frowned. "Our son? I dinna remember bedding ye."

She felt her face warm. "'Tis Brandubh."

"Pàdraig's son?"

"Aye."

"And where is his mother?"

"She is dead. All the MacOnies are dead."

A heavy silence settled over the room.

Angus cleared his throat. "'Tis glad I am ye are better, lad. Ye gave us quite a fright."

"Angus? What are ye doing here?"

"And where else would I be? 'Tis the MacGregor *clachan* ye be in."

Duncan tried to rise. Rory rushed to stop him, but it was the man who entered the room who halted her husband.

"Where do ye think ye are going? Lie down or I will sit on ye."

"Fergus?"

A wide grin spread across the giant's face. "Aye."

"But ye are dead!"

"So I have heard, and would be if Rory had not tended me as she does yourself."

"Step aside. I want to see for myself that my grandson is well." Nannag shoved Fergus from her path. She rushed to the bed, and clutched Duncan's hand to her chest. Tears trickled down her wrinkled cheeks. "I was sore afraid ye would not come home to me."

"When have I broken a promise to ye, Grandmother?"

She sniffed. "Never."

Rory put her hand on Nannag's shoulder. "Duncan needs to rest."

The older woman released his hand, and tucked the plaid under his chin. She kissed his brow, then turned to Angus and Fergus. "Ye heard my granddaughter. Out with ye!"

Rory watched them go, then turned back to Duncan. "Shall I sit with ye, *mo chridhe?*"

He nodded. She brushed a lock of hair from his forehead and held his hand. He looked at her until his eyelids grew heavy. When she kissed him, she whispered, "I love ye, Duncan Cameron."

CHAPTER TWENTY-FOUR
GIFTS

The macabre pitch of an anguished wail startled Rory awake. She heard a faint whoosh, then something slammed into her back, driving air from her lungs while propelling her toward the rough stones of the cottage wall. She threw up her hands to shield her face. Shards of pain exploded in her head, her arms, her back, her chest.

Salty tears prickled scratches and scrapes. Her breath came in rasping gasps. Her forearm stung. Her back throbbed. She struggled to sit, then winced when her shoulder brushed the wall. With her left hand cradling her right elbow, she searched for answers.

Nothing seemed out of place. The furniture remained where it always was. Only she and Duncan occupied the room, and he slept beside her on the heather mattress. The woeful cry came again. She cringed, waiting for a second blow. It did not come. Instead reality smashed into her, shattering her world into tiny slivers.

Tears streamed anew down her cheeks. She stared at the man beside her. *Why, Duncan? Why did ye hit me?*

His keening grew agitated. He thrashed, twisting the bedclothes around his body like a winding sheet. He flailed his arms. The bed creaked in protest, adding its screech to his lament. Then silence, eerie and oppressive, engulfed the room.

He mumbled. Rory strained to decipher his raving, then wished she had not. His words painted a gruesome nightmare that she knew was no dream.

"Balls tearing heads from limbs…rain stabs…blood drips…fiery nails burn…canna escape…. *Mo righ's mo dhuchaich!* For king and country!"

Duncan's ear-shattering Highland yell made Rory tremble with fear. She saw the rush of wild men sweeping over the moor. She heard the loud clash of sword on targe, the sickening thud of steel cleaving flesh and bone. Heads split wide from brow to chin. Twitching torsos. Spurting blood.

"The heather heaves and writhes...climb bens of arms and legs.... Och, the crying and moaning. Blood and bile. Bile and blood. Maggots crawling. Corbies hovering. No mercy! No quarter! Death to Highlanders. Fire! Burning! Roasted while they yet live. Make it stop! Please, make it stop!"

Duncan keened again. Mindless of her pain, Rory crawled to him. She cradled his head and shoulders against her breast. She assuaged his furrowed brow with a kiss. "Hush, *mo chridhe.* Hush. 'Tis ended. Ye are home."

She rocked him like a babe, soothing away the torment that haunted his sleep.

~*~

Rory stooped by the hearth to place another peat brick on the fire.

"My grandson is gone. Mairi tends Brandubh. Ye, Granddaughter, will be explaining the yelling and keening I heard last night." Nannag's jaw was set in grim determination. Her hands rested on her hips and her foot tapped the hard earth. "Granddaughter?"

She touched Rory's back. Stabbing pain radiated from the tender spot between her shoulders. The hearth blurred, and she reached to steady herself.

Duncan's grandmother gasped, staring at the jagged scratch that ran the length of Rory's forearm. A violet welt specked with red swelled just below her elbow. Nannag pulled a bench from under the table and made Rory sit.

"Where else are ye hurt?"

"My back between my shoulders."

"Loosen your clothes and let me see."

Nannag eased the chemise from Rory's shoulders, drawing a sharp breath after she did so. She touched the sore spot. Rory winced.

"Did my grandson beat ye?"

"No."

"Dinna lie to me, Granddaughter. Ye did not get this bruise from bumping into a wall."

"'Tis how I hurt my arm, not my back."

"Then I ask again, did Duncan do this to ye?"

Rory blinked away the tears threatening to spill again. Duncan had not deliberately hit her. He reacted to ghoulish moments relived while he slept, but understanding brought little comfort. What had happened last night could happen again. She had no remedies to erase the horrors. The only way to prevent further injury would be to distance herself from him, a tack she refused to follow. He had sheltered her in his arms when she was troubled. How could she do anything less?

"Aye, but he dinna ken it."

"How could he not?" Nannag asked, plainly not believing her.

"'Twas done while he slept. Och, Grandmother, terrible dreams torment him. I canna believe the horrors he saw."

"He spoke of them?"

"While he slept."

Nannag busied herself with preparing a poultice for the bruise. She ladled porridge from the cauldron hanging over the fire, stirred herb Robert into the bowl, and then dabbed the mixture on the bruise. The door opened. From her sudden cessation of the application, Rory knew Duncan had entered. She felt his eyes bore into her exposed back.

"Who did this?" His simple words dripped with venom as blood from a sword. "Grandmother?"

"'Tis not my place, though if 'twas up to me, I would lash your hide with the belt ye wear. Shall I finish, Rory?"

"No."

Nannag set the bowl on the table and left the cottage.

"Duncan, will ye put the dressing over the poultice?"

Rory heard him walk to the table. When he drew near, she felt the warmth of his hand hover over her back. She thought he would touch the bruise, but instead he applied the bandage.

"Ye must bind it to me. Wrap the linen strip from back to front to back until ye reach the end of the cloth."

He coughed. She glanced over her shoulder. Their eyes met, and he dropped his gaze. He took up the bandage and held one end against the dressing. When he reached around her front, his thumb nudged her breast. He jerked away his hand. The cloth fell. After he retrieved it, he held it out to her. She drew the bandage across her chest then returned it to him. In this manner, they wrapped her. He knotted the ends together, then tucked them under the wrapping and turned from her while she retied her chemise.

He held himself rigid, his hands in tight fists at his sides. She knew, then, that he guessed the truth. A new ache filled her heart, and she touched him. He pulled away. The rejection felt as if a honed dagger stabbed her heart.

"Duncan?"

"I want the truth of it, Rory," he said through clenched teeth. "I did that to ye?"

"While ye slept. 'Twas an accident. Ye did not mean to strike me."

She yearned for him to take her in his arms, but he crossed to the door. Without turning to face her, he said, "I never meant to hurt ye."

The soft click of the latch echoed in the silence. Vast emptiness and great loneliness flooded Rory's heart. Her nose tickled. Her chest tightened. Her eyes moistened. She covered her mouth to hold back the sobs.

~*~

Rory shredded the last fir root into strips. She spread the splinters across a barred griddle, then hung it on a hook inside the chimney. The peat smoke would dry the wood, creating fir candles used to dispel the darkness of long winter nights. With her chores done, she stepped outside and came face-to-face with a scowling Angus.

"Jamie says ye willna attend the *céilidh* this night. Ye may not be chief, but our people expect ye there and ye have no right to deprive them of your presence or your sharing."

She rubbed her forehead with soiled fingers while she listened to the unexpected scolding. Smudges probably adorned her brow now.

"My answer remains steadfast, Angus."

A movement near the stable drew her attention. Intent on the lean man, who spoke with Andrew, she no longer heeded her foster father's words. The blacksmith pointed in her direction. The man walked with the uneven gait of someone long akin to the deck of a rolling ship. Without a second thought, she flung herself into his open arms.

"Uncle Iain!"

His joyful hug sent a spasm of pain across her back. She clamped shut her lips to silence a gasp. When she regained her feet, she hoped her smile betrayed no hurt.

"I see ye dinna miss me at all, lass." Iain laughed. His sorrel hair had grayed since their last meeting and his weathered face showed more creases, but his azure eyes radiated warmth and love.

"I canna believe 'tis really yourself. Ye vowed never to set foot on Scottish soil, and yet, here ye stand. What made ye break the oath ye swore when I was but a wee babe?"

He bowed low with great flourish. "Yourself."

Her eyes widened, then narrowed. "Me? For three years ye helped smuggle goods, but never before did ye come ashore. Not even when asked."

"'Twas not ye doing the asking, lass. Thistle's cause is a good one, but he is still an outlaw. How would it look to law-abiding merchants if they kent I associated with such a scoundrel?" His lips twitched, and she knew he teased her.

"I take your point, Uncle, but ye should consider it from Thistle's point of view."

"Which is?"

"What would folk think if they kent he mixed company with yourself, a man more righteous than Saint Michael himself?"

"Ye blaspheme, lass. I willna discuss the matter further."

She laughed. "How did ye ken I am returned?"

"I met Lochiel while visiting Paris."

"And on a whim ye decided to visit?"

"Ye ken me too well, niece. I have a proposition for ye and your husband."

"Duncan is not here at the moment, and I must tend to a wee problem."

"Ye mean Thistle does the tending."

She shook her head. "No, 'tis myself who is needed. I would speak with ye, but there is some urgency to the matter."

"Ye swear 'tis your affairs ye attend to and not Thistle's?"

"I swear. Why dinna ye want Thistle to be about?"

"I canna say. Since coming ashore, I have felt a coldness creeping at my shoulder."

"I thought 'tis myself who has the Two Sights."

He waved his hands. "I dinna have it, and ye are welcome to it."

"Are ye come for talk or have ye cargo to unload?"

"Both, but the cargo will wait another night. Go on with your business." He handed her two bundles. "'Tis a wee late, I ken, but 'tis in honor of your wedding."

Rory kissed his cheek. "We will meet on the morrow."

~*~

The rumble of white water tumbling over the tiered crag into an amber linn masked Rory's footfalls. Duncan, who perched on a moss-covered stone, rubbed his thigh. Captivated by the swirl of yellow, orange, and red leaves caught in an eddy of wind on a carpet of purple heather, he did not know of her presence until she knelt.

"'Tis the wind of the fairies," she whispered, swatting away his hand.

"I can do it myself. I dinna want your sympathy."

"I give none." She kneaded the leg that pained him. "Do ye truly believe I pity ye?"

"No."

They lapsed into silence. She worked the knotted muscles beneath the scarred flesh until the strain faded from his face.

"I am not made of glass, Duncan."

"Flesh and bones shatter when struck hard enough."

"Aye, and when torn and broken, they mend. Your nose is crooked, but ye breathe. Your leg is scarred, but ye walk. 'Tis no different for me. The bruises will fade and the scratches will scab. Neither hinder me."

"But I raised my hand against *ye!*" He uttered the words in anguish and anger.

"Misadventures are not new to me, Duncan. Since we first met, I have been shot, stabbed, and beaten. Other hands delivered those wounds, not yourself. If I can survive them, dinna ye think I will survive an accidental bruising?"

"'Tis an unfair way of looking at it. Before ye married, 'twas your family who protected ye. When we wed, that duty passed to me. How do ye think I feel kenning I failed? Not by neglecting my duty, but by striking ye with the very hands sworn to shield ye."

She had no ready answer to that logic. He had not struck her, but rather the evil riddling his heart and mind had injured her. He was unready to accept this truth because he had caused her pain, and therefore deserved to be punished. Rather than salt the festering wound, she set aside the topic and offered him a parcel.

"A wee gift from Uncle Iain. He arrived as I left to find ye. A belated wedding present he said."

Her husband accepted the gift, but waited for her to break the string and open hers. She stared dumbfounded at folds of blue and white fabric. Nestled within were soap and comb. He extracted a small object from his parcel. After opening the blunted metal protruding from its oyster shell casing, he brushed his thumb against the honed steel.

"Iain seems to think I should shave." Duncan stroked his white-flecked bearded chin. "What think ye?"

"It makes ye looked distinguished."

"Distinguished?" He stooped by the pool to peer at his reflection. "How old does distinguished make me? Sixty? Seventy? Ninety?"

He mulled that over, then nodded. "Aye, ninety."

She giggled. "I willna be saying quite that ancient, but 'tis more than your score and eight years. I prefer a man closer in age to my own. Do ye think ye can part with such a long beard after all this time?"

He turned his head to the right, then the left. When he looked back at her, he wore an impish grin. "If ye wish it gone, then 'tis yourself who must shave it, Rory."

"Me?"

"Would ye have me cut myself?"

"If ye trust me to throw a *sgian* beside your ear, I guess I can hold the blade steady enough to shave ye."

She sliced off a fistful of beard and laid it aside. When she finished trimming, she extended her hands to pull him to his feet. For an instant they stood a finger-length apart. She wished he would take her in his arms, but instead offered him the soap Iain had given her.

"'Tis women's soap, but 'tis all I have."

Duncan sniffed it, then shrugged. After wetting his face, he lathered it with the soap and returned to his perch. She tilted his chin to scrape the straight-edged razor the length of his throat. When she finished his left cheek, she switched to the other side to shave the rest of his beard.

"How did I do?"

He rubbed a hand over his jaw. "Mayhap I will have ye shave me more often. 'Tis smoother than when I do it."

His compliment helped dissipate the tension between them.

"Shall I trim your hair?"

At his quick nod, she fanned the thick acorn brown strands across his back. She used his dirk to slice off several inches. When finished, she patted his shoulder.

"I have no looking glass, but the linn reflects my handiwork."

While he squatted beside the pool, she sneaked behind him. When he turned, she laid her hands on his chest. His muscles tensed beneath the shirt. With some trepidation, but committed to her path, she pulled the top of his plaid from his belt and tossed it over his shoulder. She freed his shirt and slipped her hands beneath the cloth. Her fingers skimmed the soft curls covering his chest. He drew back, but she locked her hands behind his back to prevent his escape. He tightened his arm muscles and broke free. She tried to renew the embrace, but he lifted her from him.

"No!"

She squared her shoulders. "If ye canna bear my touch, then 'tis yourself who must touch me."

"Och, Rory, I dinna fear your touch! 'Tis myself I fear. I canna control the dreams and I would rather cut off my hand than use it against ye." He spun around to face the linn.

She clenched her fists to hips to keep from reaching for him. "Duncan, ye watched friends die horrible deaths while ye lived. Their slaughter stirred your anger until ye lusted for the enemy's blood. Though ye abhor killing, ye struck down those who slew kith and kin. After a time ye despised yourself for the bloodlust, yet honor and loyalty allowed no peace. When ye learned of the suffering inflicted on us who ye swore to protect, shame sickened ye and guilt consumed."

She waded into the water to cup his face. "Do ye recall the telling of Malcolm soothing my fright when the terrible dreams of my mother's slaying visited me? I wanted to forget, but could not. 'Tis the same for ye. Only time can distance ye from the horror that plagues ye, and I canna say how long 'twill take. Sixteen years passed before I felt true peace, but 'twas not time that brought it. 'Twas your love. 'Tis what I offer ye now. Will ye accept what I freely give, *mo chridhe?*"

A single tear fell from Duncan's eye. He enveloped her hands within his and bent his brow to hers. "If 'tis truly freely given."

"How can I prove that ye are my heart?" She brushed the wetness from his cheek with her thumb.

His eyes pleaded to make him believe, but doubt clouded the amethyst orbs. Thrice she had declared her love, so three proofs were needed to convince him she meant the words.

She untied the pouch that hung at her waist. "Give me your hand."

Into his palm she placed two rings. "The circle is eternal, without end. Gold is the sun's light that shines on us. Silver represents healing. We mix my herbs with your gentleness to renew our bodies, hearts, and heads. The interlacing of these two metals shows we cleave to each other. When ye canna be at my side, the amethyst in my ring protects me. Whenever I look upon it, I ken ye watch over me. Sapphire adorns yours. 'Tis the symbol of clarity. When ye gaze at its blueness, ye will always ken the truth of my love."

"Rory—"

Her finger pressed to his lips quieted him. "Before long, we will see the passing of the second year since ye pledged me your love. 'Tis my turn to finish the pledging that I began twelve months ago. The letter I wrote declared what my heart kent, so it represents the first year of being wed. These rings symbolize the second. Like the circles, our love is unending. And as the gems are bound to the metals, so are we bound to each other."

She retrieved a small roll of purple and blue plaid from her basket, then offered it to Duncan. "When dying the wool, I thought of nocht except ye and the kisses we shared in your secret glen. My heart tried to tell me the truth then, but I was not listening. Look inside."

He unrolled the plaid to reveal the love *cuach.*

"I canna say when I fell in love with ye, Duncan. It might have been the day ye held me while I told of the Campbells' attack. Mayhap it happened when ye kissed me in the linn. Or perchance 'twas the day I received a single red rose from my warrior husband." She upended the cup, spilling its fragile contents into his palms. "These are the petals from that rose. I return this most precious gift with a request. Hold it close to your heart, for 'tis my pledge of love for the third year of our marriage. When the year passes, and if ye still love me, give them back so I can keep them close to my heart."

He cradled the petals for a long time before returning them to the safety of the *cuach.* "Do ye trust me, *m'eudail?*"

"Aye, Duncan."

"Then give me my dirk."

She retrieved the weapon from the stone. He held her left hand and lightly drew the blade across her palm. A thin line of blood formed. He offered her the dirk and his hand. When his palm showed a similar red streak, he clasped his hand to hers and bound them together with the soft purple and blue wool.

"Rory, *is tu m'annsachd.* My blood flows from my heart where my love for ye lives. That which is my life and my strength I give to ye."

Tears threatened to spill as she listened to the ancient declaration of love. She swallowed, then answered him. "Thou are my best beloved, Duncan. As your blood is mine, so is mine yours. With this mingling we are no longer two, but one."

He slipped the amethyst ring onto her third finger. She eased the sapphire one over his knuckle. Together they spoke the final words of the blood oath. "Like the metals woven together and the plaid that secures our hands, we are bound together for this life and beyond."

Duncan drew her face close to his with his right hand and kissed her. "I love ye, *m'eudail,* with all my heart."

He untied their wrists and turned her around. He undid her braid then combed her hair with his fingers. Her scalp tingled and goose flesh covered her arms and legs. He nudged aside her hair to kiss her neck. She gasped at the silky caress of his breath on her skin. He circled her, trailing his fingers the length of her arm. Hot and cold shivers raced through her body. He unclasped her brooch and loosened her belt, then unwound the plaid and tossed it aside.

He gathered her in his arms, then waded through the cool water to the center of the linn. His tongue swept across her lips, tickling her. After a moment's hesitation, she parted them. He deepened the kiss, and she felt consumed by a blossoming of heat deep inside her. She groaned.

When she opened her eyes, a mischievous gleam lit his. His smile reminded her of a wee lad up to some devilment. Suspecting his intent, she opened her mouth to take a deep breath, which was the moment he chose to dump her. When she surfaced, he stood naked under the cascading waterfall. He dove into the pool, then rose from the water beside her. Rivulets of water poured off him as he loosened the lacings of her chemise. With infinite slowness, he pushed the fabric off her shoulders. She quivered under the scalding touch of his rough hands.

She no longer distinguished the pounding of her heart from his. Her fingers trailed up and down his back. Uttering a moan, he lifted her. She slid down his length, wrapping her legs around him as she did so. The lapping water stoked the fiery pulses that rippled through her as they became one.

~*~

Soft pelting sprinkles fell from a sky blanketed by gray-blue clouds. A raindrop skidded down Duncan's face. Rory traced its path from his forehead along his nose to his mouth. His lips captured her finger. The slippery feel of his tongue sliding across her flesh stirred new memories. Her body arched against his. He released her finger and hungrily sought her lips. When he ended the kiss, she could not stop an escaping whimper.

He chuckled at her protest. "'Tis raining, *m'eudail.*"

"I willna melt. Will ye?"

"Not at all, but if our pleasuring is to last, 'twould be easier done twining ourselves on a soft bed rather than standing in the linn."

The erotic image sent a warm flush through her. She turned to hide the blush. Enwreathed in his arms with his chest pressed to her back, they spooned. She enfolded her fingers around his forearms.

"Look high on the brae across the clough," he whispered in her ear.

Sunlight illuminated the dark afternoon sky. Droplets of rain shimmered like diamonds on the antlers of a red stag. Radiant hues of violet, blue, green, yellow, orange, and red arced behind the majestic beast.

"Make a wish, *m'eudail.* 'Tis lucky to see a rainbow."

Rory closed her eyes.

"For what did ye wish?"

"'Tis between Himself and me. If He grants the wish, ye will ken soon enough."

"I will allow ye this one secret, wife, but no other. Shall we search for a spot to lie before the moon and stars cast their light upon the shadows of the glen?"

"We dinna have to look. Our bed awaits behind the lower falls."

"Ye would drown us?"

"Gather our belongings and I will show ye."

He scooped up new clothes and discarded ones, retrieved the basket, and followed her around the linn. She climbed over boulders dampened by the spray of cascading water, then dropped to her knees to crawl along a rock shelf behind the waterfall and through a hole into a hollowed out chamber where golden light flickered like a beacon guiding a ship safely into the harbor.

"Ye planned this tryst!" Duncan said, eyeing the flaming torches and pallet of fresh heather.

"Not planned. Hoped, *mo chridhe.*"

"Do others ken of this cave?"

"'Tis my secret. I often came here as a wee lass when I needed to hide where no one would find me."

"Especially after defying your father?"

Rory laughed. "I never denied being a rebel. Ye kent my faults when we wed."

He tapped the tip of her nose with his finger. "I did, but ye must remember ye are my rebel. No one else can claim ye!"

"And if another does?"

"He will wake one day to find himself minus his head."

Duncan led her to their marriage bed. He spread out his plaid and sat, pulling her onto his lap. He traced the scarred flesh of her left palm with his finger. The feathery touch tickled, but Rory did not pull away her hand.

"'Tis an odd burn. The markings are familiar yet strange. How came ye by them?"

She retrieved the pendant from the basket.

He held the tarnished metal beside her hand and turned it until the pattern mirrored the scar. "This burned ye? How?"

"I held it between my hands after Dr. Archie gave it to me. I heard the din of fighting, then saw fettered Highlanders imprisoned by soldiers."

"How did ye ken I was one?"

She touched his nose, then his chin. "I recognized your oft broken nose and this wee scar."

"I might have escaped. How could ye ken they meant to hang me?"

"Your eyes. When I looked on them, I saw the eyes of the dead."

He brushed away the tears sliding down her cheek. "Look into them now and tell me what ye see."

They sparkled like cut amethyst, changing in radiance from grape gentian to violet nightshade to crimson purple heather.

"Love?"

"Aye, love for ye and no other. I dinna pretend to understand the powers held within the pendant. I ken only that it brought ye to me. 'Twas yourself that saved me from a freezing death after I crossed the River Esk, and when I saw Thistle on the brae, 'twas like witnessing Saint Michael come to slay the dragon. I never thanked ye properly for saving my life."

He laid her on the blanket, then fanned her auburn tresses over her shoulders. He skimmed her breasts and stomach with a soft lock of her hair. She squirmed under the teasing. She raised her hand to caress his face, but he captured it and placed it behind his neck. He drew her other hand there, then rolled onto his back, pulling her on top of him. His hands rubbed the small of her back, while her fingers twisted the curls of dark chest hair. She twined her legs with his like the metals in their wedding bands.

"I canna promise the dreams willna come again," he whispered.

"Dinna think to scare me away with threats. No matter what the future holds for us, we will face it together."

"I love ye, Rory Cameron."

He took hold of her waist and lifted her to her knees. He entered her as if sheathing his sword. In harmony with the crackling fire and tumbling water, he swept her over the falls to a sanctuary she had never visited.

CHAPTER TWENTY-FIVE
UNITY

The melodious trill of a pipit and the quivering jingle of a dunnock woke Rory. She watched her husband sleep. Fresh stubble dotted his chin, but she preferred it to the bristly beard. The worry lines had disappeared from his brow. A peaceful smile creased his lips.

She brushed his tousled hair from his eyelids. "Good morning, *mo chridhe.*"

He grumbled. She tickled his nose and lips with her hair. He waved his hand in front of his face and rolled onto his side. When she dusted him with her long tresses, he grabbed her arms and dragged her over his hip. She cradled his face in her hands and kissed him.

"We must return, Duncan."

He fell onto his back and sighed. "'Tis a powerful magic we weave. I dislike ending it."

She snuggled close. "Who says 'tis ended? 'Tis only smoored while we tend to other matters. When we are able, 'twill be there to kindle anew."

"Our love is a wondrous gift. I am glad I dinna take ye until ye freely gave yourself." He rubbed his knuckle against her cheek. "Since I canna keep my hands from ye, I suggest ye take yourself to the linn to bathe alone. If I join ye, 'tis certain our son willna be seeing us before the sun sets."

While Rory washed, she sensed Duncan watching her, but he kept himself hidden. After toweling off, she pulled the new chemise over her head and smoothed the wrinkles from its long sleeves. She fastened the buttons of her dark blue skirt, then donned its matching waistcoat. She flattened the collar of her shift, tied an apron around her waist, and slipped on her brogues.

"I am wed to the bonniest woman in all of Scotland!"

She smiled, turned, and drew a sharp breath. Her husband stood rolling his sleeves up to his elbows. Wisps of brown hair curled around the neck of the half-open shirtfront. The reddish purple waistcoat, trimmed in black and silver, hung open to reveal black breeches that clung to his brawny thighs. High leather boots accentuated his height. A ribbon, matching the color of his waistcoat, gathered the hair from his clean-shaven face.

"Is something wrong?" He glanced down to ascertain if he had done up all his buttons.

Rory smiled. "How could anything be wrong when I am looking at a man more handsome than the King of France? I like eyeing your bare legs when ye wear the plaid, but since the Disarming Act forbids me that pleasure, I think I will enjoy undressing ye more."

"As ye did the day of the horse races?"

"I never!"

"Ye did. I kent exactly what your eyes were doing when ye looked upon my strengthy thighs."

"Mayhap ye speak true, but the tight cut of your breeches entices my imagination more, especially when seeing ye from the rear."

Duncan clicked his tongue. "'Tis quite brazen ye are, wife."

"No more than yourself, husband."

He laughed and led her to the log that bridged the clough. On the other side of the deep ravine, he put his arm around her shoulder. She slipped her arm around his waist and they strolled down the mountain. When they arrived at the cottage, he set down the basket and drew her back from the door. He cupped her face and gave her one last lingering kiss. She sighed, wondering when they would next share a private moment together.

Inside, Nannag and Fergus sat by the hearth watching Anna feed Brandubh. Rory wondered which wore more porridge—her son or his shirt.

"Have ye any for us? I seem to have forgotten to eat with other pleasures to occupy me," Duncan said, winking at her.

Rory felt her cheeks grow warm. Thankfully, Brandubh recognized his father's voice and began to fuss, turning his head to avoid another spoonful. Anna threw up her hands in defeat. She wiped his face and hands, then handed him to Rory. While she held their son, Duncan encircled her waist. Anna drizzled honey over two bowls of porridge and set them on the table.

Duncan ushered Rory to the bench, then bowed low to Anna. "I thank ye, mistress, for your kindness."

The ebony-haired girl giggled, then curtseyed. "Ye are welcome, kind sir."

When he finished breaking his fast, Duncan asked, "Where are Angus and Iain?"

"Waiting at the stable with Andrew," Fergus said. "Iain said he had business he was wanting to discuss with ye."

"'Tis most likely the proposition he mentioned," Rory said.

"Then Fergus and I will leave ye to your work." Duncan kissed her and his grandmother, tousled his son's hair, then left with Fergus.

"I promised to visit Mairi this morning," Nannag said. "Shall I take Brandubh with me, Granddaughter?"

"If ye dinna think he will trouble ye and Mairi over much."

"He will be no trouble at all. We spoil him something fierce."

The instant the door closed, Anna spoke. "'Tis not fair!"

Rory sighed at the half-accusatorial, half-petulant declaration. From Anna's serious countenance, Rory guessed the discussion would be a weighty one.

"What is not fair?"

"Ye already have Duncan, but canna settle for just him. Ye want Fergus, too."

So Anna, who was forever flirting, had set her heart on Fergus. He had given Rory no indication of having affections for the girl, but she had accompanied him on several visits to the cottage.

"I love my husband, Anna, and would never shame or dishonor him. Fergus is my friend, nocht else."

"When ye are present, he sees no one but yourself. He walks with ye. He converses with ye."

Jealousy oozed from each statement. If Rory could not persuade Anna she had the wrong impression, she might well turn her tongue to vindictive gossip. Rory had no desire to tackle another crisis. She wanted peace.

"Has Fergus told ye of his duties before coming here?"

"He guarded Lochiel! 'Twas a grand honor."

"Has he spoken of his wound?"

Anna's large eyes grew moist. "No."

To break a confidence was a rarity for Rory, but if Anna had more serious intentions toward Fergus, she needed to understand that pity was the one thing he would not tolerate, particularly from a wife.

"Fergus was like a wee lad lost on the moor after the wounding. He was a warrior trained to wield a sword and defend others, but lacking one arm, he thought himself useless."

Anna snorted. "Ye speak false. I saw him brandish his sword."

"'Twas not so at first, but he came home whilst soldiers harried the Camerons. I persuaded him he could wield the sword if he but altered the how of it. Later, when a patrol approached Prince Charles' hiding place, Fergus and my brothers led him to safety whilst I diverted the soldiers."

Anna's eyes widened. "What happened?"

"They beat me. 'Twas Fergus who rescued me."

Rory rearranged the truth to suit her purpose, but Anna need not know that. Her eyes glowed with pride and a bright smile lit her face.

"He saved your life!"

"He did. He also helped rescue Duncan. Fergus is my friend, Anna. My heart belongs to my husband and no other. Since Fergus allows ye to walk with him, I doubt he only has eyes for me. Mayhap, he is uncertain of your feelings. He willna tolerate pity."

"I dinna pity him!"

"Good."

"'Tis just that…" Anna fell silent. A scarlet flush crept up her neck and spread to her cheeks.

"I willna stand between ye and Fergus, Anna, but he has a gentle heart and is easily hurt by a woman who would set him aside whenever another man pleases her more."

"I willna set him aside! Fergus is not like the lads. He is older, stronger, wiser."

"But?"

"Ye are older than myself, but ye must remember yearning for a man to encircle ye with his arms and cleave ye to him."

Rory bit her lower lip to keep from smiling. Although she was only seven years older than Anna, the girl made her feel ancient.

"No matter how old a woman is, she wants her man to hold and protect her. Losing one arm willna keep Fergus from cradling the woman he loves. He wants a home where his wife tends and loves him. He dreams of the day when he holds a wee babe for the first time. He will have all these things, and will find ways to compensate for what he lacks. His wife will also adapt, and together they will find ways to pleasure each other."

The frown lines around Anna's eyes eased and she seemed to weigh Rory's words carefully.

"Have ye spoken to your parents of your feelings for Fergus?"

"My father is not opposed. He says only an older man has the experience to handle me. Mother agrees. Since Fergus is more settled, he willna stray from home."

"Do ye disagree?"

"No. The lads of the *clachan* are good lads, but they lack Fergus' maturity. They want to frolic or kiss all the lasses. He wants to settle with one and raise a family. They prefer keeping company with themselves and searching for adventure. He wishes to spend time with his wife and shield her and their bairns from danger."

"Ye are more observant than ye lead others to believe, Anna."

The girl shrugged. "'Tis living with nine brothers who love to tease that makes me so. May I speak of a fear I dare not tell my mother?"

"If 'twill ease your fashing."

Anna turned to stare out the window. "I am wee compared to Fergus. He is a giant. If we wed, I fear he will tear me apart when we lie together the first time."

The confession took Rory by surprise. During her tenure as chieftain, she had listened to many express fears and hopes, but this was the first time anyone had sought her advice on the private affairs between a husband and a wife.

To reassure Anna, she chose her words with care. "I ken nocht about men and size. Should Fergus ask to wed ye, dinna hide your fears from him, else they may be realized. Mayhap if he kens what fashes ye before the bedding, he will find a way to ease the pain of the first taking and make your time together one of great joy."

"Ye make it sound so easy."

"'Tis an illusion, Anna. Nocht in life is easy, but if 'twas, it would not be worth having. If Fergus and ye are suited to one another, ye both must work together. If ye are honest with each other, ye will be good friends. 'Tis a strong foundation upon which ye can build if ye are meant to marry as well."

"Does Fergus like me, Rory?"

"We have not spoken of it. Why dinna ye ask him?"

"And how can I do that with my brothers and father watching over me? They give me no peace unless I am chaperoned by someone they trust, like yourself."

"They dinna want ye hurt because they love ye."

Anna smirked. "They choose a strange way to show it."

"If they did not love ye, they would not tease ye."

"I suppose. Thank ye for speaking with me. Mother would never allow me to say such things to her, and I needed to ken the answers."

"Ye are always welcome to come to me, Anna. Now, ye had best be about your chores or your father will be next to visit me."

~*~

A trio of black-clad figures climbed the sea cliff. The first to achieve the summit pulled off the black wool that covered his face. "How do ye stand the wearing of it? 'Tis enough to suffocate a man."

Rory laughed and removed her mask. She scratched her scalp, tousling her long auburn tresses. "What think ye, Fergus? Do ye agree?"

"Dinna be asking me, for I willna take sides. If I agree with Duncan, I will likely find myself missing an ear for riling ye. If I side with yourself, 'tis your husband who will challenge me."

"Spoken like a true friend," Duncan said, clasping forearms with Fergus.

"Aye." Rory placed hers atop theirs.

"What a touching scene!"

They whirled at the unexpected intrusion, instinctively reaching for dirk or sword. A man—dressed in a soiled plaid of blue, black, and green, and a tattered shortcoat of scarlet—stepped from behind a granite boulder. While he kept one eye trained on them, he drew the tip of his *sgian* under his fingernails.

"Geordie Campbell!"

"Aye, Mistress MacGregor," he said, sparing Duncan a glance. "Or mayhap I should say Mistress Cameron."

He sheathed his weapon and approached. Before she could reckon his intent, he snatched the black mask from her. He waved it high, a triumphant sneer spreading across his malevolent face. "Or have I the pleasure of addressing Thistle?"

Still clutching his prize, he backhanded her. She stumbled backward into Duncan, who steadied her then put her behind him. His hand gripped his weapon, but she clutched his arm.

"Be angry, *mo chridhe,* but dinna let anger rule ye. He plays with us. Bide a wee. He will betray his true intent."

Duncan sheathed his sword. He advanced on Geordie Campbell with fisted hand. "'Tis a coward who strikes a woman. Honor demands punishment."

Geordie shook his head while waving a finger as if he addressed a recalcitrant boy. "Ye willna strike me, Cameron."

"And why not? If not for the blow ye struck my wife, then I owe ye for the beatings on the march to Carlisle."

Geordie spit. "A rebel cur deserved no less. If not for Thistle's interference, ye would have hanged for your deeds. As for the smuggler, I have hunted her for three years seeking redress for this!" His finger traced the puckered scar that marred his face. His hooded eyes glistened with hatred and his lip curled in a snarl. "And now she owes for the welts that stripe my back and my mustering from the Watch. Before this day ends, she will pay for disgracing me!"

"Not before she delivers what is owed me."

Rory recognized the minacious voice. She pivoted until she faced her true enemy—Ludovic of Torcastle. Lochiel's uncle retained a Highland warrior's agility, strength, and cunning although twice Duncan's age. What he lacked were the grace, charm, and compassion of his nephew.

A growl escaped Duncan's throat. "My wife owes no debt!"

"'Tis not true, lad. 'Twas my man whose sharp blade drew first blood. And by my nephew's words, 'twas Cathal who rightly won. Your bonnie bride bled, and so must pay the price. 'Tis herself who will come to my bed this night."

"Ye must slay me before she will lie with ye!" Duncan vowed.

"And me!"

Ludovic's gaze flickered over Fergus. "A cripple? 'Twill be like snapping this twig."

The crack reverberated in the silence. Torcastle returned his attention to Duncan. A wicked grin spread across his bearded face. "'Twas ye who deprived me of Cathal, and I would demand payment in kind, but canna. Sentimental Donald is over fond of ye, and since I go to France after collecting the wager, I dare not anger my nephew. To slit your throat would be to slit my own. Since I have a liking for this neck, old though it be, I must decline your tempting offer. 'Tis another who will forfeit her life if Rory fails to welcome me."

He snapped his fingers and Geordie disappeared behind the boulder. He reemerged dragging a young woman with ebony hair.

"Noooo!" Fergus' strangled yell echoed through the woods.

Campbell pressed a dirk's sharp tip to Anna's throat. The sight of trickling blood brought Fergus to an abrupt halt. The giant gritted his teeth and held himself rigid.

Anna's whimpering strangled Rory like a noose tightening around her throat. Terror-filled eyes gutted her like a knife and the blood cleaved her like the blade of an executioner's ax. In her head, she screamed; outwardly, she betrayed no emotion. Anna's life depended on her remaining levelheaded. Ludovic of Torcastle had constructed his trap with singular and malicious care. To best him she must be cannier.

"The girl has nocht to do with what is between us," she said. "Release her."

Ludovic shook his head. "She is but a means to an end, but serves a purpose still."

"Ye war against innocents?" Rory asked. "'Tis what I expect from a cursed Sassenach. A true Highlander would not dishonor himself with such trickery. It demonstrates to all his cowardice."

Schooled in the old traditions, Torcastle could not allow the slur—made worse by a woman's utterance—to go unpunished. He sent Rory reeling into Duncan, who managed to keep them both upright. Once steady, her husband made to shove her behind him, but she dug her fingernails into the taut muscles of his upper arm until he drew his gaze from Ludovic to her.

She lifted her scarred hand and traced the pendant's marking forever burned into her skin. His eyes followed her finger, and she thought the warning she wished to speak. *'Tis but another bruise that will fade in time. I am whole. Dinna show anger, mo chridhe, 'tis but another weapon he will use against us. Consider Anna. I would win her freedom. Have I your trust?*

Palm touching palm, he twined his fingers with hers. She heard his answer even though his lips did not move.

Forever, m'eudail.

He released her, and she faced Ludovic. "Ye would have me honor the bargain we made?"

A lecherous gleam brightened the older man's eyes. He expelled a long breath, venting some of his anger. "'Tis why I came."

She issued her condition, wincing at the hurt she gave Fergus. "Then release Anna into the cripple's keeping. He is no threat to ye, nor is she."

Torcastle shook his head. "The lass insures ye pay what is owed."

"What lies between us concerns honor. Would ye forsake what a Highlander esteems most? By keeping her, ye negate the wager. Free her, for 'tis the only way I will come to your bed."

Torcastle studied her. Did she speak true or did she play him false? He knew of her, but was of an age where women held their tongues and kept his house. He expected them to spread their legs and birth his seed. They did not think. They were not canny. These were the traits on which Rory gambled. When his eyes glazed and his tongue licked, she knew lust had won over brains. His eyes stripped away her shirt and chemise, her trews and boots. Unbidden sensations of prodding hands, torn clothes, and taunting jeers slammed into her. His lechery violated her as had the soldiers. A chill, deep within her bones, crept through her.

"Let her go, Campbell," Ludovic said, his voice low with lust.

"Ye said she was mine!"

"Feel her. She is but scrawny. 'Tis a grand reward for delivering Thistle. With gold in your pocket, ye willna lack for lasses to bed."

Campbell's free hand squeezed Anna's breast. He snorted, and pushed her away. Sobbing, she stumbled to Fergus, who gathered her to him.

"Take her and go!" Torcastle said.

Fergus stood his ground.

"Go," Duncan said.

"I canna leave ye and Rory."

"Aye, ye can. 'Tis what must be done. See Anna safely home. Dinna fash about us."

Fergus hesitated. Rory knew he warred with himself, uncertain which path to follow. Time was precious, and Ludovic could change his mind before they made their escape.

She made the choice for him. "The gift of a clan's father is most precious, Fergus. Take heed and hasten ye!"

His eyes narrowed, then understanding dawned. A thin smile formed on his lips. After a whisper to Anna, he stooped and she climbed onto his back. Once she cleaved to him, he hoisted his great sword and tossed it. Duncan passed his to Rory and stepped forward to catch the blade once owned by a Cameron chief. When Rory looked for Fergus, he and Anna had disappeared.

"A sly one, ye are," Duncan whispered, positioning his back against hers.

"A fine show of trickery, but 'tis for nocht." Ludovic aimed a cocked pistol at them. "The time has come for ye to deliver on your promise."

Rory smiled. "I gave no promise. 'Twas but a scratch Cathal delivered, and his shame disavowed any right ye have to claim the wager. Your nephew declared me victor, and as chief his word is law."

"Then ye die."

"'Tis what ye planned from the start. Not by your hand, for ye command others to soil theirs. Geordie, here, is not so smart as to ken I am Thistle. Ye sold him the kenning for your own gain. 'Tis for nocht, though. Kill me, for 'twill earn ye no more than ye had before."

Duncan added his own slight. "'Tis ever the way of the Sassenach to threaten with pistols. Ye both have forgotten who ye are, who your forbears were. Highlanders meet Highlanders on equal footing because we esteem honor above all else."

Geordie tossed aside his weapon and drew his sword. "It matters nocht whether I use ball or steel, Cameron. Your life is ended, and once dead, 'twill be your wife who warms my bed before the hangman gets her."

Rory ignored the taunt. Geordie was quick to anger and lacked Torcastle's cunning. "What of ye, Ludovic? Do ye dishonor your father's memory, or do ye have the mettle of Ewen Dubh? He shunned your brother for sleeping on a pillow. What would he think of a son who favors the pistol, when himself slew the enemy with his teeth?"

Torcastle's face reddened, and his knuckles whitened. For a moment, Rory imagined she saw him exhale the fiery breath of a dragon. He shoved the pistol into his belt, and unsheathed his sword. "'Tis long past time ye learned your place. When ye are disarmed, look for no mercy."

His sword slashed the air, but she deflected the blow with her weapon. The clang of steel echoed through the fissured pines. Since she needed to protect Duncan's back, she dared not stray far from him.

Ludovic recognized the disadvantage and feinted, drawing her parry. He swung her blade beneath hers, and lunged. The point sliced through the loose fabric of her shirt. She swung her sword like a hammer, knocking away his blade. He grunted and retreated a few steps. He paced, keeping a wary eye on her.

A strangled scream drew her attention. In that instant, Ludovic charged. She tried to turn, but tripped over a stone. The jolt of the fall knocked the sword from her hand. Ludovic trapped her between his legs. He marked her with the tip of his blade, wrapping both hands around the hilt and raising his arms high. He made to stab her through the heart. She squeezed her eyes shut.

The cold breath of steel touched Rory. A jarring clang rent the air, then silence. A soft thud sounded near her. She peeked through half-closed eyes. Ludovic's sword lay beside her.

"'Tis your call," Duncan said.

She dared to look. He lifted Torcastle's sagging chin with the point of the great sword. Ludovic swallowed then gave a hoarse reply. "'Tis ended."

"Aye, forever." Duncan lowered his blade.

"What will ye do?" Ludovic asked.

"I would run ye through, but for who ye are."

"Ye will let him live?" Rory asked.

Duncan pulled her to her feet. "He dinna deserve it, but aye. Ludovic, ye will take yourself from this place, else Lochiel will learn of your treachery."

Torcastle turned to go.

"And Ludovic."

"Aye?"

"This is for Rory."

Her husband's fist slammed into the older man's face, knocking him flat on his back. Duncan dropped his sword to run his hands the length of her arms, reassuring himself that she was unhurt. Once satisfied, he tilted her chin until their eyes met. "'Tis the last time ye will offer to warm another man's bed. Ye rip out my heart with such words, though I ken 'tis but a rouse. No more, do ye hear? I willna share ye with another."

"Aye, I hear."

He raised an eyebrow at her brazen tone. "Rory!"

She caressed his cheek with her fingers. "I heed your words, *mo chridhe,* but dinna expect me to obey your other commands. I pledged ye my love, not my obedience."

He ran his finger down her nose, and smiled. "If ye did, I would not ken ye were my wife."

"'Tis twice ye saved my life," she said, catching his hand and holding it to her heart.

"Aye, but I am still owing for another."

"And how would ye think to repay me?"

He skimmed his fingers down her back, then nibbled her ear. "I am certain we can come to terms that satisfy us both."

"*'S rioghal mo dhream!*"

"*Aonaibh ri chéile!*"

The Gregorach rallying cry, answered by that of the Camerons, startled Rory and Duncan apart. A host of MacGregors and Camerons surrounded them. Their solidarity warmed Rory's heart.

"'Tis one less Campbell to prey on MacGregors," Malcolm said, sneering at Geordie's corpse. He nodded toward Torcastle. "What of him?"

"Not so lucky. He yet lives, though he dinna ken it," Fergus said. He turned a pouting face to Rory. "Ye left none for us."

"Dinna my husband tell ye not to fash?"

The giant grinned. "He did. I was forgetting what a dangerous pair ye are when smuggler and warrior join forces."

"Anna?" she asked.

"Flustered, but safe."

"Then 'twas worth the risk." Duncan took Rory's sword and tossed it to Malcolm. He handed his to Fergus.

Without warning, Rory found herself hefted off her feet and cradled in Duncan's arms. She thought to protest, but the men shouted their approval. Warmed by their acceptance and united front, she smiled. "Come, 'tis time to go home."

~*~

"Did ye have words with Anna?" Fergus asked.

Duncan gave her a quizzical look, and Rory knew he had heard their friend's question.

"I did."

"She claims she fancies me."

"Dinna ye believe her?"

"I want to, but the men say she is a tease."

"I willna lie, Fergus. Anna has flirted with most of the lads here." Rory let her gaze sweep the crowded stable where they gathered. "I dinna think she trifles now."

"She has serious feelings for me then?"

"'Tis herself ye must ask, but I think ye ken the answer. 'Twas ye Anna trusted to protect her from Campbell and Torcastle. From your reaction at seeing her held captive, I think ye share a similar affection."

He nodded.

"Then ye should be discussing this with her. Ye have kent her but a short time. Mayhap in visiting with each other, ye will find what ye seek."

"Her father invited me to sit with him this night."

"Go then. Ye willna find your answers here."

Fergus crossed to where Anna and her family sat. Hugh welcomed Fergus, then offered him a place between himself and his daughter.

Duncan nudged Rory. "Arranging marriages now, *m'eudail?*"

"Never, *mo chridhe.* Since I objected to my father's arrangements, I willna subject others—particularly friends—to the same."

"Do ye still object to wedding me?"

"No, but if I did not love ye, I would not stay with ye."

Angus raised his hands for silence. "Iain heard of Scotland's woes from Lochiel. 'Tis plain the Crown intends to obliterate the threat of another rising. Soldiers plunder the land and spill our blood. Parliament forbids us arms. They mean for us to become like themselves, to forget all we claim for our own—our language, our laws, our music, our clothes. Iain proposes an idea I think ye would do well to consider."

Iain exchanged places with Angus. "When I first heard the tales Lochiel told, I could not believe the horrors of which he spoke. To punish all for what a few wrought speaks ill of the King who rules. The Gregorach have long suffered persecution, but never have I feared for loved ones as I do now. 'Tis why I came to see Rory and her husband. After speaking with Duncan, though, I could not give to one what I would deny another. Therefore, what I proposed to them, I tender to all.

"I have acquired extensive holdings in the colonies, but being much of the year at sea, the land lies fallow. If ye are willing to work hard and share what profits ye garner, I will give ye land to own in your own right."

Her uncle's generous offer stunned Rory. No one had ever owned the land. They leased it, sharing the fruits of their labor with their chiefs. Iain also offered them escape from punishment for supporting a Stewart prince or claiming allegiance to a proscribed clan. She and Duncan could evade imprisonment and death. Her rescuing of rebels had increased the price on her head, and too many were privy to Thistle's identity. Faced with the prospect of starvation this winter, someone might betray her. She would hang, and so would Duncan: she for the smuggling and being MacGregor, he for joining the rebellion and killing Geordie Campbell. By accepting Iain's offer, they all could start life anew in a land where no one knew them.

Yet, she had lived in Scotland her entire life. Dare she leave the land that was so much a part of her? If those she loved chose to stay, could she forsake them knowing they would never meet again? And what of Duncan? How did he feel? She thought she knew, but before she asked him, there were other questions that needed asking, not just for herself, but for any considering Iain's offer.

"Winter fast approaches, Uncle. If we accept, when would we leave?"

"Ye ken two ships anchor off the coast already. Three more will arrive by week's end. If we set sail within a fortnight, ye will reach your new home before *Nollaig*."

"Willna it be winter there?" Anna's father asked. "Without crops to feed us, how will we survive?"

Others echoed his concern.

"Hugh is correct. The winter will be well upon the land, but 'tis less harsh than Highland winters. My ships carry food and supplies enough to see ye through until spring. There is also seed for planting."

"And where do ye expect us to shelter?" Malcolm asked.

"Two stables and a stone house occupy the land. They are sturdily built, but may require minor repairs. Wood for burning and stone for building are plentiful."

"To which colony are ye after taking us?"

Iain grinned. "'Tis a proper place indeed, Fergus, for ye who fought for the Stewarts. Maryland honors Henrietta Maria, the wife of the first Charles."

A collective groan echoed through the rafters.

"What say ye, Rory?" Jamie asked. "Will ye and Duncan accept Iain's offer?"

"Aye, what answer give ye?" someone else seconded.

Duncan took her hand in his. A febrile eagerness shone in his eyes and on his face. "Do we go to this place called Maryland or do we bide here?"

"My home is wherever ye are, Duncan. If ye wish to seek adventure in this new place, then I go with ye."

"We go with Iain!" he shouted.

Everyone began to speak at once, discussing and arguing over whether to follow them or stay.

Duncan ignored the din and swept her into his arms. "From this day forward, *m'eudail,* we will decide matters together."

"If I were ye, I would reconsider those words," Iain said, sitting beside Duncan. "If ye forsake what is a man's due and give your wife more power, ye will rue this day. Women need and want a firm hand controlling them. Ye dinna want to be feeling Rory's claws when she turns on ye."

If not for the twinkle in her uncle's eyes, she would have let him feel the sharpness of those claws. She knew well his thoughts on women, and his wife would never have wed him if he believed the words he spoke.

"Thank ye for the advice, Iain, but I already sampled both my wife's temper and her love," Duncan said. "We dinna always agree, but willna make decisions without consulting each other. 'Tis why there will be less arguing and more loving between us."

Iain sighed. "Ye two remind me of Bernadette and myself."

"Did she accompany ye on this voyage?" Rory asked.

"Ye ken your aunt better than to ask such a question. She waits aboard *Caledonian*. We thought it best for me to survey the situation before bringing her ashore. When she heard of your marriage, she did nocht but plague me about visiting to inspect your young man. I dinna ken what she will be like once she learns of Brandubh. 'Tis our one sorrow that the Lord dinna see fit to bless us with bairns of our own."

"Watch your aunt with eagle eyes, lass," Angus said. "She will be after spoiling Brandubh."

Iain nodded. "I fear Angus speaks the truth. She will have no time for me once she sets eyes on the wee lad."

"And I suppose ye have no such designs on our son, do ye, Uncle?" Rory asked.

Iain grinned. "Ye ken me too well, lass. Much too well."

~*~

With the yearly rent sent to the Mackenzie, Rory helped the women pack blankets, wool, food supplies, medicines, and cooking utensils. The men carted looms, tools, kists, benches, weapons, and churns down to the shore where sailors rowed them out to the ships to be stowed. Duncan oversaw the loading of animals, including Tam and Midnight. On the morrow, everyone—including those who had stayed behind once before—would set sail for their new home.

Rory placed the last of her medicines into a basket then swept her gaze over the sleeping room. Except for the mantel, the room was bare. She took down the tinker's box. Beside the heart-shaped pendant lay the matching brooch worn by her mother on her wedding day. To these Rory added the love *cuach* containing rose petals; the pearl brooch Duncan had given her before leaving for Glenfinnan; the ancient pendant that linked them during their long separation; and his and Tòmas' *sgian*. She meant to keep these precious heirlooms to give to the children she would bear Duncan, and in turn, they would give them to their children.

She nestled the tinker's box in the basket. Around it she placed a black mask, a brick of peat, a chunk of pink-flecked granite, a thistle blossom, sprigs of oak and pine, and heather. These provided a link to the past for the generations to come. In this manner she hoped to pass on her love for the land where she and Duncan had been born, grown, met, and loved. They would also bind their children and their children's children to the history of their two clans and the circumstances that had made her and her husband who they were.

"What are ye thinking, *m'eudail?*" Duncan asked, examining the contents of the basket. "I seem to have wed a wise woman with a romantic heart. Is it hard to leave, Rory?"

She smiled. "I shall miss the Highlands, but ken there is nocht left for us here. Our new home may be far from these rugged and bonny bens, but a wee bit of Scotland will survive in each of us."

"Aye, Rory, that 'twill. Is it not time to be joining Angus?"

"'Tis. If ye fetch Brandubh, we can be going."

He lifted their sleeping son from the bed and offered her his arm. "Ken ye why your foster father wants to see us?"

"I do, but he asked me to let himself explain."

"Has he ill news to tell?"

"No."

She opened Angus' door and stepped aside to let Duncan enter first. She noted his look of surprise when he found the men of the *clachan* gathered. He bent close to her ear. "I dinna ken what ye are up to, wildcat, but ye dinna fool me at all. Ye meant for us to arrive late."

"We are not late, *mo chridhe.* We came when we were wanted."

"Duncan, give Brandubh to Bernadette to mind, then bring yourself and your wife here," Angus said.

Iain collected their son and carried him back to the corner where his petite wife sat.

"And dinna be giving him any more presents," Angus said, "else there willna be room on board for the rest of us."

Laughter filled the cramped space. Bernadette giggled and held up the newest toy for all to see. Even Angus cracked a smile, but quickly regained his dour expression.

"Duncan, we summoned ye and Rory to put before ye a proposition. We gathered first to settle the details because we did not want ye to have a say in the matter."

A scowl appeared on her husband's brow. Rory laid a settling hand on his arm.

"Och, dinna be looking at me that way, lad. We dinna mean to offend. If ye canna abide by what we resolved, feel free to object."

"Not that we will heed ye," Jamie said with a flash of teeth.

A few chuckles acknowledged his jest, but his father glared at him. Angus cleared his throat, then resumed speaking. "Since ye wed Rory, several others and I share the responsibilities of a chieftain, but we are too old to fash about clan affairs. Now that we journey to a strange land, 'tis a younger chieftain we are needing. Someone who is strong and wise, and kens the ways of others and will help us adjust. Being of two clans, though, turns a simple decision into a more difficult one. 'Twas Malcolm who suggested a resolution to our dilemma, but 'tis Fergus who presents it."

The giant wound his way through the crowd. He nodded to Angus, then faced Duncan and Rory. "During the past fortnight, we argued in secret over who would make the best chieftain. The MacGregors have their favorite, the Camerons theirs. We are all agreed Malcolm's is the best solution. Since we are of two clans, we must have two chieftains. Ye, Duncan, will speak for the Camerons, while Rory speaks for the MacGregors."

Fergus' revelation took Rory by surprise. Angus had told her only that they wanted Duncan to be chieftain. She looked to her husband.

"Did ye ken of this, wife?"

"Half of it."

"Which half?"

"That they had chosen ye."

"Ye have governed both clans, so I defer to ye in deciding whether we accept."

While her gaze drifted over their kinsmen, she weighed the trust Duncan placed in her with that bestowed by their family and friends.

"Ye honor us with your offer, but we canna accept. We ken what happens when two clans disagree. If I represent MacGregors and Duncan stands for Camerons, ye are asking us to take sides. He is my husband, and although born of the Gregorach, I am bound by our vows to honor all that he is. I willna stand against the man I love."

Duncan squeezed her hand. "Neither will I stand against she who is my heart. Malcolm, your suggestion is a good one, but I would amend it slightly. What if the chieftainship was not of two separate clans, but a united one? 'Tis for ye to decide which ye would rather—harmony or strife. We will wait outside for your answer."

"There is no need to go, lad," Angus said. "Does any MacGregor object to Duncan's suggestion?"

Receiving only silence, he nodded to Fergus who asked, "Does any Cameron object?"

No one disputed the revision.

"Then we are of one mind. Whether Cameron or MacGregor we choose harmony. In so doing will ye, Duncan, and ye, Rory, accept the chieftainship? Will ye watch over us as a father and mother tend their bairns?"

She looked to her husband. He winked and gave a slight nod. She answered for them. "We do."

Angus unfolded the cloth that lay upon the table. He affixed two feathers from a golden eagle to one bonnet, then placed it atop Duncan's head. Fergus added two chocolate-brown feathers to a second bonnet that he set on Rory's. While the men toasted them, Duncan swept her into his arms and kissed her.

Angus coughed. "'Twould seem ye have a new way to proclaim decisions. 'Tis more common to affix seals to paper."

Rory smiled. "'Tis more enjoyable to seal it with a kiss, Father."

~*~

"Rory Cameron, I will be having words with ye!" Duncan barged into the small cabin.

She groaned. "Go away and let me die in peace."

"Is it the sickness again?" He knelt beside the berth and felt her forehead. "Ye have no fever. I am thinking what ye need is fresh air."

Rory preferred to stay abed, but could not dissuade Duncan. She dragged herself to her feet and allowed him to bundle his cape around her. He tossed a blanket over his shoulder, then slipped one arm around her shoulders and the other beneath her knees. Before she could protest, he lifted her off her feet. She wound her arms around his neck and rested her head on his shoulder. Once topside, he made his way to a sheltered section of the forecastle where he draped the blanket over her legs then cradled her in his arms.

"Is this not better than the dank darkness where we sleep?"

"Aye, Duncan."

"When I went below, *m'eudail,* I said I wanted words with ye. How could ye not tell me? Why did I have to hear it from Fergus?"

"Hear what?"

"Of the soldiers raping ye!"

She stiffened. If he said he had the tale from Fergus, then she believed him. She had sworn Fergus and Malcolm to secrecy, however, and knew neither would knowingly betray her. So how had Duncan learned of it?

"What exactly did Fergus tell ye?"

"I told him nocht."

Rory jerked her head up to look at Fergus. His eyes pleaded with her to believe him.

"'Tis all right. I ken ye would not speak without reason. Duncan will be telling me how he learned of this."

With his head lowered, Fergus retreated along the quarterdeck. Rory waited until he was out of sight before she confronted Duncan. "Ye owe him an apology."

"I ken, but not until after ye explain yourself."

"First, ye will tell me the truth of how ye found out."

"Anna asked him how he saved your life."

"And did he speak of rape?"

"No, 'twas what I inferred."

"Well, ye inferred wrong and hurt our friend in the doing. The soldiers did not rape me."

"Then why did ye not tell me?"

"Ye were in no condition to hear of the attack. Had I told ye how they beat, kicked, and fondled me, and tore my clothes, ye would hurt more. I could not do that to ye. I love ye."

He squeezed her hand. "And I love ye, *m'eudail*. I just dinna understand how ye would give yourself to them, but not me."

"I gave them nothing, husband! They were after taking what they wanted." She laid her hand against his cheek. "I never meant for them to catch me. I only wanted to draw them away so Fergus and my brothers could lead the prince to safety. When I tripped, the soldiers pounced. I had no weapons, and there were too many to fight."

"But Fergus and Malcolm saved ye?"

"Not exactly."

"'Tis what Anna said."

"'Tis what I told her when we spoke of Fergus. He came, but another had already stopped the soldiers."

"Who?"

"Their captain."

Duncan smirked. "Ye want me to believe a red officer stopped his men from having their sport?"

"He was repaying the kindness I had shown him. Do ye remember the day ye took me to Neil's place?"

"When we brought him the wounded captain of the Royal Scots?"

Rory nodded. "'Twas Captain Scott who saved me. He covered my nakedness with the shirt he wore and gave me whisky."

"'Twas he whom Fergus and Malcolm found with ye?"

"Aye."

Duncan drew his arms tight around her, and kissed her forehead. "I ken ye risked your life to save Prince Charles because of Lochiel and me. I could not protect ye then, but would like to help now. Is there nocht I can do to rid ye of this sickness? I canna bear your suffering."

"'Tis yourself who caused the sickness, but 'twill soon pass. As for suffering, this is nocht compared to what I will face before next Michaelmas."

He paled. "I caused ye to be sick?"

"Aye, but the pleasuring ye gave more than compensates for the ailing."

She felt him tense and draw in his breath. She waited, watching to see how long he would go before exhaling. Before the ship dipped and rose again on the waves, he let out a prolonged breath.

"Are ye saying we are going to have a son, *m'eudail?*"

"Or a daughter, *mo chridhe.*" She took his hand and placed it on her stomach. "'Tis too early, but before long ye will feel the babe kick."

He looked at her with awe. "Can I touch ye?"

"I hope ye never stop, Duncan."

Rory felt the quickening of her pulse. How had she ever dared to consider leaving him? Duncan confessed to her his fears, shared his dreams, offered his strengths, revealed his weaknesses, and bestowed his desires. He accepted her in spite of her rebelliousness, her penchant for doing the unexpected, and her ability to portend the future. He gave her his heart to cherish and nurture, yet waited until she found the courage to listen to and follow her heart.

In the privacy of their small cabin, he undressed her. He never once took his eyes off her while he removed his garments. She drew him down beside her on the bed and he enfolded her in his sheltering embrace.

EPILOGUE
BEGINNINGS

"Hold me, *mo chridhe*."

Duncan swiped his forehead with the back of his arm. He would like nothing better than to cradle his wife, but dust clung to his chest and arms from the backbreaking exertion of splitting stones under a hot summer sun. "Och, Rory, if the filth willna deter ye, I am certain my stench will."

She stamped her foot. "Mud can cover ye from head to toe. Ye can have the fetid odor of rotting fish. I willna heed a no from ye!"

To forestall another endless and pointless argy-bargy, he acquiesced. Shaded by an apple tree, he pulled her into his arms and kissed her. Heavy with child, she looked more beautiful than the first time he saw her, yet dark smudges shadowed her eyes. She slept little and worked hard. He worried, but to voice his concern inevitably drew her wrath. Nannag's assurances that Rory's irritability was natural and temporary provided little comfort. He had learned to tread carefully and retreat quickly whenever he sensed a storm brewing.

"I love ye, *m'eudail*." He turned her to face away from him and encircled her with his arms. She clung to his bronzed forearms and propped her chin atop her fingers. He nuzzled his cheek against her ear.

"And I ye, *mo chridhe*." She lapsed into silence.

Her reticence after a vision had taught him when she worried. Although the Two Sights in her had quieted since leaving Scotland, he sensed her need to speak. "Rory, I willna ever tire of holding ye in my arms, but 'tis not why ye came. Tell me what fashes ye."

"'Twill be a grand house, Duncan."

He smiled at the obvious ploy to deter him. "The roof willna have thatch and I added two extra rooms, but otherwise 'twill be like the one in Lochaber. Now, wildcat, ye have not said what ye came to say."

"Have I no secrets left me?"

"None."

She sighed. "I dinna wish to hurt ye with my words."

"Dinna ye feel my brawny arms? 'Tis certain I am not made of glass. Shall I tell ye why ye sought me out, Rory?"

"I thought I had *Dà-Sealladh.*"

"I never claimed to have the Two Sights. 'Tis loving ye and kenning what ye dinna say when we speak that tells me how ye feel. I am after thinking ye prefer that I not attend the crying."

"Do ye mind?"

"I would rather be with ye, but 'tis our first babe and ye fear 'twill frighten me. I may be a warrior, but where ye are concerned, my fierceness abandons me at the thought of what terrible suffering I will cause ye during the birth of our son."

"Or daughter!"

He grinned. "Or daughter."

"The miracle that comes from our joining is one of love and wonder, but I canna keep my thoughts from Brandubh's crying."

Duncan felt the blood drain from his face. He remembered Morna's screams and Rory's worry. "'Twill be the same for ye?"

She patted his arm. "No, but it frightens me a wee bit."

"Ye will have Nannag and Mairi with ye. Since ye ask it of me, *m'eudail,* I will keep myself from the crying. Mayhap if the Lord blesses us with more bairn, ye will allow me to share the wee miracle with ye later?"

She nodded.

To turn her thoughts to other matters, he asked, "Have ye chosen a name for the *clachan?* I am fond of your foster father, but Angus plagues me for an answer."

"'Tis because I told him to leave off asking me," she said, laughing.

A sharp gasp strangled the laughter. She dug her fingernails into him, squeezing until her knuckles turned white. When she doubled forward, he tightened his grip to keep her from falling.

His voice trembled with fear when he spoke her name. "Rory?"

She did not answer, but the pressure on his arms lessened. He wiped beads of glistening sweat from her face with his thumb.

He kissed her trembling lips, then hugged her tight. "I am here, *m'eudail.* I will protect ye."

She grabbed his wrist. "Och, Duncan, I did not mean to lance ye!"

He glanced at the half-moon indentations left by her nails. Blood oozed from several. When he saw tears trickle down her cheek, he cupped her face. "'Tis nocht, Rory. They dinna hurt and they will mend."

Unable to distinguish the words she mumbled against his neck, he set her from him. "What did ye say?"

"Ye canna stop the pain, but I ken ye shield me with your heart." She dried the last of her tears with her fingers. "Take me home, Duncan. 'Tis time."

He strode through the open door of the house they shared with his grandmother and her foster parents. After he laid Rory on their bed, Mairi tugged on his elbow and shooed him toward the door.

"Am I permitted to kiss my wife before I leave?"

The woman pursed her lips, but nodded.

He clasped Rory's hand between his, kissing her fingers while he gazed into moist pools of blue sapphire. He brushed strands of loose hair from her forehead. "I love ye, *m'eudail.* If ye need me, I will come."

"Kenning ye are near strengthens me, *mo chridhe.* I feel ye cradling my heart close to yours."

"Always, *m'eudail.*"

Mairi pushed him toward the door. When he reached the portal, he looked back at his wife. A smile formed on her lips and he saw a twinkle in her eyes. The teasing sparkle reassured him.

"Return to your work, husband," she said. "'Twill ease your fashing and keep my thoughts on the birth of our daughter."

He grinned. "Or son!"

"Aye, *mo chridhe,* or son."

~*~

"Duncan!"

"Aye, Jamie?" he asked, anxious for news. He had waited outside the house for a time, but soon wearied of pacing. His hands fidgeted for something to occupy them. Ignoring Angus' astonished and irate shout at defying custom, he had returned to work. When the darkness descended, he built a bonfire and continued to erect the gathering room wall. The strenuous labor and the need to pay careful attention to the task at hand helped focus his mind away from thoughts of Rory.

"How can ye work when my sister struggles to birth your son?"

"'Tis better than drinking myself into oblivion as ye did during Sàra's crying."

Jamie shrugged. "'Twas Malcolm's doing, not mine. He tired of listening to my prattle."

"I am doing what your sister told me to do. Now, have ye news or did ye come to see if I left Rory to muddle through on her own?"

"Temper, temper, brother."

"Jamie!"

His brother-in-law raised his hands in mock surrender. "Rory asks for ye."

Fear nudged Duncan. "Is she well?"

"Aye, but tired."

"Have I a son or daughter?"

"I dinna ken."

Duncan ran. When he reached the house, Malcolm, Fergus, and Angus barred his entry.

"Let me pass."

Angus shook his head. "I thought ye were to tell him to wash."

Jamie, huffing for breath, said, "He…did not…give me…a chance."

"Let me pass!" Duncan's growled words had no effect on the three men who resembled standing stones.

Fergus and Angus moved aside only to allow Nannag to pass between them. She poked her finger at Duncan's chest. "Ye willna be visiting your wife, Grandson, until ye wash. Ye will find soap and water and clean clothes around back."

He started to object, but she cut him off with a wave of her hand. "My granddaughter foresaw your refusal. I said I could handle ye, but she insisted I give ye this."

Duncan unfolded the paper and held it close to the candle.

Ye are my strength and my heart, mo chridhe. *Since ye did not want to soil me with your filth, I ken ye willna want to dirty our babe. I pray I did not distract ye over much. Ye were after asking if I chose a name—Thistle.*

He chuckled. Angus scowled while Fergus and Malcolm gave him puzzled looks, but he ignored them and went to wash. Upon his return, he held out his hands for Nannag's inspection. When he passed her scrutiny, she waved the barrier aside and allowed him entry into the house. As he passed Angus, he said, "Rory says she has chosen a name."

"Have ye a son or a daughter?"

"I dinna ken. What I meant was she chose the name for the *clachan.* 'Tis Thistle."

Angus chortled. "My daughter is canny."

"Aye, she is."

Inside, Duncan watched Rory sleep. A smile played on her lips. The tautness of irritability in her face and the shadowy lines of worry around her eyes had dissipated. Although reluctant to disturb her, he ached to feel her soft skin against his calloused fingertips. He crawled onto the bed beside her.

She opened her eyes. "What think ye of my choice?"

"Thistle is perfect, my canny wildcat, but have we not more serious matters to discuss? I willna be kept in the dark any longer, wife."

"Then close your eyes and dinna peek."

"Rory!"

She intertwined her fingers with his. "'Tis a wee thing I ask, Duncan."

He looked askance at her. Her face glowed with a childlike eagerness that flooded him with love anew. He kissed her, then complied with her request. Two sets of footsteps approached the bed. He curbed the urge to peek.

"Grandson," Nannag said, "fold your arms so the fingertips of one hand touch the elbow of the other. Now, tilt one arm a wee bit higher than the other."

His grandmother put a tiny fragile bundle into the cradle of his arms. He started to open his eyes, but she clapped her hand over his face.

"Dinna be peeking," she said, "until ye hear the door close."

He sighed. The two sets of footsteps retreated. He heard the soft click of the door being shut, but found he could not open his eyes until Rory nudged him.

"Ye have a healthy son, *mo chridhe.*"

He marveled at the infant who stared up at him with smoky blue eyes. When Duncan brought his finger close to his son's rosy pink face, the baby grabbed his finger. His hand dwarfed that of his son's. "If ye have no objections, *m'eudail,* I would call him Michael."

"Why Michael?" Rory asked.

"'Twas Michaelmas when passion first flamed between us."

"Did I wed a tenderhearted warrior?"

"What other kind is there?" He tried to sound indignant.

"Ye canna fool me, husband! The twinkle in your eyes and the quiver of your lips betray ye. Michael is a grand name for our son, but your daughter is needing a name."

He turned to his wife. His eyes widened and his jaw dropped. Awe and disbelief flooded him as he gazed upon the dark-haired bundle his wife cradled at her breast. This baby clenched its fists tight and flailed its arms. Unable to grasp the truth of the crying, Duncan looked back and forth between the tiny bundles. He wet his lips, swallowed, and took a deep breath.

"Twins?"

"Aye, *mo chridhe,* just like yourself and Tòmas. Have ye a name for your daughter?"

"Cailean."

"'Tis a lad's name."

"And what is Rory?"

She laughed. "So 'tis. Why Cailean?"

"Our daughter represents our victory over the trials we faced to love each other. Kenning her mother, she will be both brazen and daring as a young pup, and gentle and compassionate as a dove."

A single teardrop slid down Rory's cheek. Duncan freed his finger from his son's grasp and dried the wetness. "Do ye think, *m'eudail,* we will face a wee more adventure than we thought?"

"If Michael and Cailean follow in our footsteps, husband, 'tis a certainty."

Duncan winked at her. "Then 'tis glad I am we gave each other plenty of practice so we can rescue our bairn whenever they are in need."

Rory nodded.

He leaned over and kissed her. "Ye have given me many gifts, *m'eudail,* but none so grand as our son and daughter. Ye are my heart, Rory Cameron."

"And ye are mine, *mo chridhe,* for now and forever."

~THE END~

POSTSCRIPT

The battle fought on Drummossie Moor is better known as Culloden. The National Trust for Scotland maintains the battlefield, which includes Old Leanach Cottage—the blind woman's home where Duncan carried Rory—and the Well of the Dead, a spring turned red by the blood of dying Highlanders including Alexander MacGillivray, the Macintosh commander who led the charge against the royal army. The 'Forty-five was the last civil war fought on British soil, but it was not a war that pitted Scots against English. Highlanders and Lowlanders fought on both sides, and during the reprisals that followed Culloden, much of the brutality was carried out by Scots against their own countrymen.

When the two armies met on 16 April 1746, the Jacobite army numbered five thousand men. They faced a force almost twice that size. The Duke of Cumberland lost fifty men whereas 1,200 to 2,000 rebels perished. Afterward royal soldiers bayoneted the wounded and killed innocent bystanders who either came to watch the battle or who lived nearby. Three thousand, four hundred seventy-one men, women, and children were imprisoned. English courts convicted and executed one hundred twenty for treason, four of whom were Camerons. Of the 936 transported to the colonies, less than half survived the journey. The Crown released 1,287 and banished 222 others, while the remaining prisoners either escaped or died.

One of those who died in the hold of the prison ship, HMS *Furnace,* anchored on the River Thames, was Father Alexander Cameron. The third son of John Cameron of Lochiel, Sandy was both priest and soldier during the 'Forty-five.

His younger brother, Archibald, escaped to France with Prince Charles. Although attainted for his role in the rebellion, Dr. Archie returned twice to Scotland. Betrayed by a spy, he was hanged, drawn, and quartered on 7 June 1753. He was the last participant of the 'Forty-five to be punished.

Sir Donald Cameron of Lochiel, the nineteenth clan chief, also fled to France with Prince Charles, but died on 26 October 1748, of an inflammation of the brain. As for his children, John succeeded his father as chief at the age of sixteen; fourteen years later he died without ever having married. James, a captain in the Royal Regiment of Scots, had died three years before John, so the youngest brother, Charles, became chief in 1762. Isobel and Henriet both married, while Janet became a Carmelite nun.

The Cameron lands, forfeited to the Crown after the Rising, were restored to the family in 1784. Lochiel's grandson began rebuilding Achnacarry in the early 1800's, but it was not completed until 1837. The stone gables of the original house are all that survived the fire set by the Duke of Cumberland's men. The beech trees Lochiel planted before the prince's arrival still grow on the property.

The Rising of 1745 was the high point in Prince Charles' life. He had one child, a daughter, born to his mistress in 1753. He wed Louise, Princess of Stolberg-Gedern, in 1772, but the marriage was not a happy one. He died sixteen years later from alcohol abuse, frequent epileptic fits, and a stroke. His cousin, Prince William Augustus, the Duke of Cumberland, was hailed a hero after Culloden, but the battle earned him the nickname "the Butcher." Two decades later, he died from the effects of a stroke and asthma.

Lord George Murray survived Culloden without a scratch. After hiding for a time in the Highlands, he fled to Holland. His older brother, the Marquis of Tullibardine, died before his scheduled execution. James Drummond, the Duke of Perth, died at sea on his way to France. Ten days after parting company with the prince, Flora MacDonald was arrested. Released from the Tower of London the following July, she later married and moved to North Carolina. After the American Revolution, she and her family returned to the Isle of Skye where she died in 1790.

After the Rising, James Mòr MacGregor convinced his younger brother, Robin Og, to marry into wealth. To this end, Robin abducted an eighteen-year-old Edinburgh widow. Whether the kidnapping occurred with or without her consent, she died soon after, and both James and Robin were arrested and convicted for abduction and rape. James' daughter helped him escape by switching clothes with him. He died in France. Robin was hanged in Edinburgh in 1754. MacGregors escorted his body back to Balquhidder to be buried beside his father, Rob Roy.

Gregor MacGregor of Glen Gyle became chieftain of his clan at the age of eleven. At eighteen he married Mary Hamilton of Bardowie. Their daughter, Jean, wed Ranald MacGregor, the oldest of Rob Roy's sons to take part in the 'Forty-five. Gregor held the rank of colonel, but his participation in the uprising failed to tarnish his reputation. One of the prisoners he oversaw while Governor of Doune Castle was John Witherspoon, a future signer of the Declaration of Independence. Glengyle died in 1777.

Even though the MacGregors did not participate in the final battle of the 'Forty-five, they were hunted down, imprisoned, and executed. They were not included in the 1747 amnesty given to participants of the rebellion. Another twenty-seven years passed before they were legally permitted to use the name MacGregor.

While I made every effort to remain true to history in telling Rory's and Duncan's story, I did invoke literary license in a few instances that I hope the reader will understand and forgive. (1) Rory is a man's name, but her father wished to protect her as much as possible and raised her in the warrior arts, a male pursuit. Therefore, he also chose a name of strength that also represented her reddish-brown hair. Angus is a Pictish name, which MacGregors rarely used for first names. (2) The early proscription against the MacGregors was vindictive and horrid. The incidents Rory described to Duncan did occur, but were more common in an earlier century. The use of hounds to hunt MacGregors occurred in the late sixteenth and early seventeenth centuries, but at least one branch of Clan Campbell used them for this purpose. When the proscription was reimposed in 1689, it took a more legal form. (3) At times I use Scots, a Lowland dialect, to give the reader a sense of Scotland even though Highlanders in the eighteenth century spoke Gaelic rather than Scots. (4) Although firearms replaced the longbow, MacGregors were forbidden to use any weapons. Rory chose the longbow as a symbol and because it allowed her to place herself at a safe distance from the enemy while remaining a lethal threat. (5) The *arisaid* that Rory wore for the handfasting was more typical dress for Highland women. Although they did not wear belted plaids, I used those words to make for easier reading and described the women's outfits as reaching their ankles. (6) Persecution of witches in the Highlands was rare and witch-prickers were outlawed in the seventeenth century. Highlanders did believe in white and black witchcraft, though, and to provide the aura of superstition that abounded in the Highlands, I chose to incorporate witchery and witch-pricking into the story. (7) Today, the confrontation between Sir John Cope's forces and those of Prince Charles is known as the Battle of Prestonpans. Since the Jacobites referred to this battle as Gladsmuir, I did the same. (8) Jamie MacGregor was not the Highlander who accompanied the prince. The man who actually did that was a MacDonald. (9) Although commonly thought of as a trial marriage, handfasting did not last a year and a day at which time the couple either formally renewed their vows or declared the union ended. The inaccuracy stems from a misinterpretation by scholars. The medieval ceremony was a formal declaration before witnesses that two people intended to marry sometime in the future. If the syntax of the vows changed from future tense to present, then the couple was married rather than betrothed. Once a couple consummated their relations during the betrothal, they were no longer engaged but married. The time period of a year and a day stems from a legal requirement before one spouse could inherit property from the other spouse. The first literary use of the time restriction came from Sir Walter Scott. The incorporation of a trial marriage may simply be a literary device used by authors.

I hope you enjoyed reading Rory's and Duncan's story. For those who would like to explore the places in Scotland where they lived or enjoy pictures from the 2001 International Gathering of Clan Cameron at Achnacarry, visit me at my web site, Thistles & Pirates (http://www.cindyvallar.com). I, also, enjoy hearing from readers. If you are so inclined or wish to receive my newsletter, please write me at cindy@cindyvallar.com

Slàinte,

Cindy

About the author of THE SCOTTISH THISTLE

Born and raised in Pennsylvania Dutch Country, Cindy Vallar spent her formative years reading books and writing poetry. While in college, she saw a movie based on the life of Jean Laffite, a gentleman pirate who helped Andrew Jackson win the Battle of New Orleans in 1815. Intrigued by the mysterious, she started researching and writing a novel about Laffite. Graduation, career, and marriage put that manuscript on a shelf where it remained until she started working as the school librarian for seriously emotionally challenged teenagers. She returned to writing to relieve the stress inherent in working in special education facilities. During a boring staff meeting, she started writing about a caped figure who crossed the Scottish Highlands during a fiercesome storm. After ten years and numerous revisions, that kernel of an idea blossomed into her first published novel, *The Scottish Thistle*. She is currently working to complete that pirate novel started many years ago while researching another novel based in the Dust Bowl of western Kansas during the Great Depression.

During her senior year at college, a friend of Cindy's mother introduced her to a young man who had attended the same high school Cindy had seven years before she had. Not only did they live on the same street as children, but he delivered her parents' newspapers, his mother taught Cindy's Sunday school class, and she went to school with his youngest brother. Tom and Cindy married a year later and celebrated their twentieth wedding anniversary by making a major life change when they moved from Maryland to Kansas.

Having retired from library work, Cindy pursues her dream of being an author. Her passion for doing research and a desire to make history more interesting inspires her to write historical novels intertwined with love stories. She's the Contributing Editor of Pirates and Privateers, a maritime history column, at Suite101.com. She reviews books for *Historical Novels Review*, *Ivy Quill Reviews*, *Appraisal*, and *The Book Report*. In April 2002, NovelBooks, Inc. will publish *The Scottish Thistle*, her first novel. Cindy is also an editor and copyeditor for Wings Press, Ltd.

Her mother fondly refers to Cindy and her three younger sisters as her "Little Women." Cindy holds a Bachelor of Arts Degree from Towson University and a Master's Degree in Library Science from the University of Maryland. She is a member of EPIC, The Historical Novel Society, Dalriada, and the Kansas Authors Club. She loves to read. Her favorite authors include Stuart Woods, Clive Cussler, Leon Uris, Nigel Tranter, and LaVyrle Spencer. When she's not reading or writing, you're most likely to find her watching professional bull riding, listening to country or Celtic music, collecting Teddy bears, or visiting Scotland.

You can write to Cindy at: cindy@cindyvallar.com

You can visit Cindy at her website, Thistles & Pirates: http://www.cindyvallar.com

NBI

Treat yourself to some good reading from

NovelBooks, Inc.

Finders Keepers by Linnea Sinclair   SF Romance
When Captain Trilby Elliot rescues a downed pilot, all she wants is a reward. She doesn't want to fall in love. And she definitely doesn't want to die.

Lions of Judah by Elaine Hopper   Romantic Suspense
Who can a dead woman trust?

The Gunn of Killearnan by Dorice Nelson   Scottish Historical
Treachery, lies and love...

The Chance You Take by Linda Bleser   Contemporary
Sometimes taking a chance on love is the biggest gamble of all.

Wild Temptation by Ruth D. Kerce   Historical
When a mysterious stranger comes to town, Skylar Davenport must discover if he's really a hot-blooded rancher, or a cold blooded killer...her life depends on it.

Fate by Robert Arthur Smith   Paranormal/Suspense
Compelled by the spirit of a murdered woman, Toronto writer Judy Armstrong tries to save a boy's life.

Winter's Orphans by Elaine Corvidae   Fantasy
Will she save them...or enslave them?

Trouble or Nothing by Joanie MacNeil   Contemporary
He was her kid brother's best friend. And now he's back in her life...more man than ever.

Desert Dreams by Gracie McKeever Paranormal
Old World Evil vs. New Age Passion...Can their love survive?

The Anonymous Amanuensis by Judith Glad Regency
Regency England is a man's world, until one woman writes her own rules...

No More Secrets, No More Lies by Marie Roy Contemporary
Secrets, lies, and consequences. What consequences does Sydney Morgan pay when all secrets are exposed?

The Blood That Binds by Rie Sheridan Fantasy
In Ancient Days, when elves were king...the legends tell of wondrous things...

The Dragon's Horn by Glynnis Kincaid Fantasy
Three Dragons. Three Immortals. One Choice. But what will they choose? Will they rescue their loved ones, or fight to redeem the world?

Escape the Past by K. G. McAbee Fantasy
Can they escape their pasts and find a future in each other's arms?

The Binding by PhyllisAnn Welsh Fantasy
He's an Elf Lord trying to save his people. She's a fantasy writer trying to save her sanity. Chosen by the gods to rescue an entire race, they first have to save each other.

Dream Knight by Alexis Kaye Lynn Medieval
Do you believe in the power of dreams?

Allude to Murder by Emma Kennedy Suspense
Balkan smuggling conspiracy entangles two Americans

Mating Season by Liz Hunter Contemporary
One lucky sailboat captain + His fetching first mate + Hurricane Season=Mating Season!

The Last Light by Ana Salazar Regency
Small and pale, Grace Radbyrne is a timid vicar's widow, burdened by a seemingly impossible dream. Damian Ward, Duke of Carisbrooke, is a bitter man, damaged by betrayal. Failing to locate her missing brother alone, Grace agrees to become Damian's mistress in exchange for his assistance...a devil's bargain only love can break.